"I see no reason for feminine companionship!" the marquis roared.

"Nor do I need company for dinner!"

Marke leapt to her feet and balled her hands into fists. Of all the overbearing, insufferable, arrogant... She would not, *must not* for the sake of her promise to Dr. Barrows, allow him to dismiss her from the house. "Lord Perfect!" she commanded. "Do not order me from your presence in such a tyrannical manner. I shall not be dictated to by you in this instance."

Claymore spun his chair with remarkable dexterity to face the defiant young woman. "And just when have I ordered you anywhere, Miss...er, Miss..."

"Penwell. My name is Miss Margaret Penwell!"

"Miss Penwell, I think you had best give pause to consider that it is within the walls of *my* house that you are refusing to heed *my* wishes!"

Dear Reader,

Taylor Ryan's first book, *Love's Wild Wager*, was part of our annual March Madness promotion featuring four talented new authors. In *Beauty and the Beast*, the author tells the story of a remarkable young woman who teases, goads and physically inspires an injured young nobleman into regaining his health, and his will to live, following a devastating fire. Don't miss this wonderful book.

We are also delighted this month to welcome back award-winning author Dallas Schulze and her long-awaited Western, *Short Straw Bride*, the heartwarming tale of a couple who marry for practical reasons, only to fall head over heels in love.

Reader's Choice Award winner Laurie Grant also returns with *My Lady Midnight*, the intriguing medieval novel about a Norman widow who becomes a political pawn when she is forced to become a governess in the home of the baron she believes responsible for the death of her best friend. And Miranda Jarrett's new Sparhawk book, *Gift of the Heart*, is a touching story set in the wilds of the New York frontier where a woman, abandoned by her no-good husband, discovers happiness in the arms of a fugitive haunted by his past.

Whatever your taste in reading, we hope Harlequin Historicals will keep you coming back for more. Please keep a lookout for all four titles, available wherever books are sold.

Sincerely,

Tracy Farrell
Senior Editor

Please address questions and book requests to:
Harlequin Reader Service
U.S.: 3010 Walden Ave., P.O. Box 1325, Buffalo, NY 14269
Canadian: P.O. Box 609, Fort Erie, Ont. L2A 5X3

Taylor Ryan

BEAUTY and the BEAST

Harlequin Books

TORONTO • NEW YORK • LONDON
AMSTERDAM • PARIS • SYDNEY • HAMBURG
STOCKHOLM • ATHENS • TOKYO • MILAN
MADRID • WARSAW • BUDAPEST • AUCKLAND

ISBN 0-373-28942-1

BEAUTY AND THE BEAST

Books by Taylor Ryan

Harlequin Historicals

Love's Wild Wager #262
Birdie #312
Beauty and the Beast #342

TAYLOR RYAN

A passion for solitary mountain trails, a love of restless, cloudy skies and a propensity for long daydreams on rainy afternoons led her to abandon a penthouse condo and hectic corporate life for romance in the golden hills of Northern California. Perched high in the vineyards, far above the mists, she feeds her soul with liberal portions of shimmering lakes, towering redwood trees and nature's wildlife.

This book is dedicated to that perfect predawn moment
when, thigh tucked between mine, fingers tangled in my
hair, sleep-warmed breath on the nape of my neck,
I encounter pure contentment.
And because every woman, at least once in her life,
should experience such a man as
George James Silva III

Chapter One

Sitting in the ancient coach, swaying nauseatingly side to side over rutted roads on bad springs, Marke Penwell surveyed the elderly Irish maid sent to chaperon her from the docks of Bantry to St. Catherine's Court. Actually an archaic practice, when one scrutinized it. Just who had chaperoned the maid on the first leg of the trip? She smiled at the woman and asked, "And how shall I find my mother? I trust she is well?"

The maid gave a good-natured smile, showing gaps where teeth had given up the ghost and departed her mouth, before answering, "Oh, she be right as rain, miss. As fine in this life as 'twill be in the one what follows."

Marke lifted an eyebrow in wonder. Whatever that statement signified was beyond her. Personally she thought rain was fine. Rain was wonderful. Rain was marvelous. But then there were those who thought rain was the worst thing to befall a person, regardless of the fact that it induced the flowers to grow and cleared the soot from the air. But, alas, it also dampened feathers on bonnets and wilted the curls beneath as her sisters would repeatedly lament. So how was she to take this statement in answer to her mother's health? Marke pondered this a moment and swallowed the rest of her eager questions. It would appear a spot of patience was required at present. She must simply wait until she arrived at St. Catherine's Court to ascertain her mother's true condition for herself.

As diversion for her impatience, Marke avidly surveyed the mist-laden countryside. "Ireland," she breathed, in the way a man calls the name of the woman he loves.

The maid glanced up puzzled. "Beggin' yer pardon, miss?"

"Ireland," Marke repeated, gesturing out the window to the green hills and valleys of the country of her birth.

The maid stared for a moment, then grimaced as if deciding the girl was as daft as the old lady. Of course, it was Ireland. Any fool could see that.

Marke did not see the expression, for she had eyes only for the vastness of the landscape. She could see, hear and smell adventure as if it were a physical thing and she was avid for it. She had left England's gentle shores and its strictures, its formality, its rules of formal behavior, with little regret. She welcomed the unanimous decision of her older siblings that she, as the youngest and the one with the least prospect of an acceptable marriage in the near future, should be shipped off to Ireland to tend their ailing mother. And, besides the appalling truth of her prospects, as the only Penwell child born in Ireland, she was also the only one to feel any kinship with the country.

Despite the jolting of the coach, the maid tried unsuccessfully to stifle a wide yawn and blinked sleepy eyes until finally her chin bounced upon her chest in slumber. Marke wanted to shake her into wakefulness. Excitement coursed through her being. She wanted to leap about and shout for the maid to look at the hills emerging from the mist. Just look at the vibrance of the green. But then Marke Penwell was one not much for sleep. Even on Mother England's soil, she did not slumber for too long. It had always been her belief, considering the short number of years one was allowed, it was a terrible waste of life to be unconscious for even that small part of it.

Interestingly enough, if queried of her beliefs, Marke would have readily admitted to the hope that the human spirit lived forever, but if allowed freedom to expound, she would have added that she felt very certain it did not. Although to voice such a statement would have brought argument and censure down upon her head, for the Penwell family professed piety in all things. Therefore, she quietly believed what she wished, and what she believed was that once the last breath was drawn, one's role in the play was quite simply complete, but the play went on and on. And it was because of this belief that she tended to live each day to its fullest. She consciously made time to sample every taste, smell every scent and see every sight. She turned away from nothing, for people, things and events were never truly beautiful or ugly, good or horrid—they simply *were*.

As the coach approached the gatekeeper's house, the gatekeeper rushed out to swing the gate wide with a cheerful smile. Marke could only gape in awe at his full scarlet livery. He resembled an animated playing card, most appropriate for St. James's palace perhaps, but jarringly out of place against the green of the rural countryside. Marke was filled with apprehension and eagerness. Did her mother truly maintain a life-style as grand as all this?

Marke's teeth worried her lower lip, suddenly feeling like a pauper in her hand-me-downs. She self-consciously smoothed the wool of the hooded traveling cloak, which truly was the most unbecoming shade of puce. Unbecoming for her own coloring, that is, but not for its original owner, blond, vivacious, beautiful sister Sarah, who had tired of this cloak in as appallingly rapid order as she did her gowns. Therefore, as routine, with many hours still left in the wearing of it, the garment had passed down the line of Penwell daughters until coming to rest in the wardrobe of the youngest. But even with the richness of the wool, there was just enough visible wear along the hem to mark it as used. And it was this, Marke feared, that gave the impression she was perhaps a lady's maid sporting a generous gift of her mistress's castoff.

But then Marke straightened her shoulders, mentally reprimanding herself for missish nonsense. She *was* a pauper, even if she *was* a daughter of the house. She didn't have a feather to fly by, wore hand-me-down gowns from her sisters, and begged any pin money for books and personals from her brother. But she would never want to complain. There were others who had it far worse. Failing the establishment of a respectable marriage, she need never fear being tossed into the streets. There would forever be a place for her at one or another of her siblings' tables. A dismaying thought that, for she could not picture herself content, as Mercy apparently was, acting as maiden aunt and governess to Sybil's four rowdy youngsters.

While it was not like Marke to fret about such things until the necessity arose, it was with no small spark of realization that she knew her circumstances would forever be altered by this trip home to St. Catherine's Court. Regardless of that exciting fact, at eighteen years of age and not all together difficult to look at, she should have been making her debut in society this year, instead of being sent from the country in the manner a wayward child is sent to bed. Although logic dictated, if one of the Penwell children must be dispatched to care for their banished mother, it should be the baby of the family. It had been a strong and tediously repetitious argument by Sarah, one which had been vehemently echoed by Kathleen and Charity that, as the elder sisters, it was most important they remain in London society. Notwithstanding their unyielding dislike of Ireland and all aspects of country life, an extended absence was understandably not conducive to their collective purpose at present. A purpose that was, namely, enchanting some unsuspecting noble with warmer-than-average pockets into stepping up to the mark with an offer. And, as bluntly stated by the impertinent Sarah, it was distressing enough to share the limelight of the season with two equally blond, blue-eyed, although not quite so equally beautiful sisters without adding a third to the fray, no matter how significantly unfortunate her coloring might be.

That unkind remark, speaking of such blatant vanity on Sarah's part, had elevated Marke's chin to stubbornness, and she had steadfastly refused to budge from London. It was because of such uncharacteristic obstinacy by Marke that Mary, as self-appointed surrogate mother of the family, had suffered dreadful pangs of guilt over the whole thing and prompted Thomas to sweeten the directive to their baby sister. Thus pushed and prodded, a reluctant Thomas had finally proposed the settlement of the Ireland estate upon her as a permanent residence, but only if Marke would devote her life to their mother's care. It had flashed across Marke's mind to take insult that she must be bribed to care for her very own mother. But, while she did not wish to appear mercenary, she supposed the offer of a home and income for life could only be considered just payment for possibly passing up a husband and children of her own. Regardless of Sarah's patronizing praise for the Irish male, it seemed foolish to Marke to expect an agreeable number of suitors to skulk about the bushes at St. Catherine's Court, ardently seeking a red-haired, freckle-faced wife.

Besides, Marke consoled herself, it was only proper that she should have St. Catherine's Court, for of all the Penwell children, only she spoke fondly of the summers spent in Ireland. And, reluctant though he might be, Thomas, as heir, still retained the London town house, and King's Gate outside Sussex, *and* control of Penwell Shipping Company. He was not slighting himself in the least by being generous with her. Although it might have been unreasonably cruel of him to declare, with Mary and Sybil already settled, and Josephine promised, the rest of the girls must fend for themselves. To be sure, a great deal of shrill wailing and condemning comments arose over this. An outcry that Thomas had quickly stifled with an authoritative announcement that any of the others could step into Marke's place and accept the proposition offered, if they so wished. The room had gone vastly quiet at that.

Marke pulled a wry face at the thought of her brother. Old, paunchy and as set in his ways as a man of sixty, Thomas was only nine and twenty, but already burdened by the responsibilities of an ever-growing family. And to Marke's mind, he could avow hatred of the tyrant that had been their father all he wanted, but he was every inch a duplicate of the late Captain Horace P. Penwell. Although, with some generosity, she supposed one should take into account the fact that not only had Thomas inherited the holdings of the Penwell Shipping Company, he had also inherited the vast responsibilities of their father, which included an eccentric mother and eight younger sisters, six of whom were of an age to clamor for husbands. That, combined with the unfortunate fact that he had buckled himself to one as condemning and complaining as Jessell, quite possibly defined the surly unpleasantness of Thomas Penwell's personality.

Upon topping the last rise, just past the stone remains of the sheep herders' cabin that marked the northern boundary of Penwell land, Marke thrust her head and most of her shoulders out the coach window in her eagerness to capture her first sight of St. Catherine's Court. The wind snatched the hood from her head. Although she would arrive tossed and tumbled, she made no move to replace it but rather let the wind have its way with the unfashionably short, red curls. An impish grin curved her generous mouth for the recollected wails of horror that had echoed down the halls when her sisters had seen her hair. To Marke, it had been an act of practicability to arm herself with a pair of shears and lop off a good ten inches of useless length. Cutting the front very short, she had created a profusion of soft curls about her face, leaving the back only long enough to form a curly knot at the crown of her head. Unfashionable it may be, but it made her eyes look enormous and, she hoped, accented her high cheekbones to advantage, despite their deplorable frosting of freckles. The others could wail and reprimand to their heart's content, but not one of *them* had hair the color of water leaking from rusty metal pipes. And not one of *them* had to contend with unruly, riotous curls that were a painful nuisance to comb out each and every morning of their lives.

St. Catherine's Court burst into view. It was everything you could have asked of an imposing English estate planted defiantly in a country that wished its English descendants to bloody hell. The house, rising four solid stories from expansive green lawns, was back-dropped by the lushness of the misty mountains. The rich, yellow stone, muted by multi-green creeper with leaves just beginning to turn autumn crimson and gold, gleamed warmly in the early afternoon sunlight. Marke's heart rose into her throat with emotion and tears sprang to her eyes.

"There she is! St. Catherine's Court! Oh, it's like a painting. It only needs a girl in a red dress to make the picture come alive," she exclaimed.

"Pardon, miss?" the maid asked, waking with a yawn.

Marke dropped back into the coach seat to swipe at her tears. The maid was looking at her as if she were daft to be showing tears over a house, but she resolved to let that look of disbelief wash off her as water from a duck's back. This was her home, and this was the country of her birth, dear to her even with the English blood that flowed through her veins, and if she felt deep emotion, then she would express it, and that was that.

Chapter Two

The coach had no more than grated to a shuddering halt on the gravel of the driveway, when Marke threw open the door and leapt to the ground, well before the startled groom could descend his lofty perch to pull down the steps. She fairly flew up the front steps and shoved through the front door, startling the butler to near speechlessness. Or perhaps it was the way she threw her arms around his scrawny shoulders in a hearty hug or the hurried kiss she dropped upon his withered cheek that provoked the affliction.

"Oh, Mr. Biddle! It's just ever so good to be home! Where's my mother?"

"Ah—ah—" The old man huffed and puffed, finally forcing out, "Upstairs. So-south wing sitting room, miss."

"Thank you, Mr. Biddle," she called over a shoulder as she dashed up the graceful curve of the mahogany staircase, taking the steps two at a time with a noisy clatter.

Although Marke had been gone a full five years, the sight and smell of the house was overwhelmingly familiar to her. Nothing ever changed at St. Catherine's Court. It just got older, darker and dustier. She raced through the rose hall and down the south wing hallway, her undignified haste noted by portraits of glaring ancestors from beneath a thick layer of dust and neglect, to burst unceremoniously into the dimly lit family sitting room. At the far end of the chamber, her mother sat before a pitifully small fire, miserly laid in an impressive marble hearth. She was, as always, surrounded by innumerable dogs. Every childhood memory

Marke had of her mother included dogs—just as memories of her father meant long absences, the way men fade in and out of life and dreams like shadows and ghosts.

Mrs. Mary Ashley Penwell, referred to as Mrs. P by the captain, and therefore by her children and servants alike, was as strikingly blond as most of her daughters. Her hair, surprisingly untouched by the silver of age, set off a smooth, pale face with snapping china blue eyes that flickered on and off. She was just as Marke remembered, and a flood of emotion washed over her.

"Mrs. P? It's me—Marke."

"Well, so you have come," Mrs. P called, waving a hand in the air. "A jolly hurrah for you, but all that town bronze will not help you here. Nor any airs you may choose to put on. We're in the country, not society. Tenants, that's what we have. Muddy boots, sheep and wool and dung, and—and good dogs."

"Yes, Mrs. P, I remember it well," Marke said, holding her tongue over the elaborate scarlet livery on the gatekeeper. She hurried the length of the room to drop a kiss on her mother's cheek. Perching casually upon the edge of a tattered, stained divan, dislodging a pile of spaniel pups in the process, she studied her mother closely. She appeared most hale and hearty, with no visible trace of the wasting illness she'd been led to suspect. "And you, Mrs. P, are you well?"

Mrs. P seemed to have become distracted by the dogs and ignored the question. "Roman, come here this instant, you naughty boy. Pepper, I will not countenance impudence. Cleo, behave, behave yourself. I am warning you, Cleo. Simon? Simon—of course, I am well, Marke, though it must not be said that I do not try." She fluttered her hands about. "I try, I try. Do I not try, my darlings?"

The fur-backed, waggly-tailed group looked up in unison at her words. Marke smiled at the picture. As long as Marke could remember, Mrs. P had been surrounded by dogs. On her lap, at her feet, on the furniture. Dogs at the back door and dogs in the stables, lolling and napping, rolling and playing, breeding and whelping—spaniels

mainly, but setters, terriers, poodles and retrievers, too.
Regarding them now, Marke was somewhat taken aback.
Had there always been so many, now some thirty in all?
Roman pawed the floor. Simon, or was it Pepper, piddled
on the slate in front of the hearth. And the puppies pooped
behind the divan and next to the Windsor chair and over by
the fireplace and under the window. One had a flea and tick
problem. There were others with curious complications, as
Mrs. P went on to explain in great detail. Dity would not
eat. Rover had a disgusting sore on his back. Bit tried to run
away all the time. Marke was beginning to understand why.

Her mother had apparently attired herself especially for
the return of her youngest daughter. The taffeta bodice was
pearled blue, and the abundant skirts silvery gray. There
was an overdrape of fish-scale net and it was simply the
most beautiful ball gown Marke had ever seen, except that
it was highly inappropriate, very soiled and smelled strongly
of dog. The petticoats drooped a trifle, and there was a rip
in the hem, stains here and there. Holes under the arms. A
burn spot on the sleeve. Marke was beginning to suspect
strongly that everything was not as right as rain. A sense of
foreboding crept up her spine to shiver down her arms as
gooseflesh.

"Thomas and the girls..." Marke ventured, gently
shoving away a spaniel pawing at her puce cape in search of
heaven knows what.

"Oh, yes," Mrs. P interrupted. "My children." She fas-
tened her eyes on Marke again, went out of focus, came
back in. "Delightful children, each and every one of them.
Let's see, there is—yes, one boy I believe, and all the rest
are beautiful little girls. It's the girls that will be your
charges."

Marke could only gulp with a terrible sinking in her
stomach. Did her mother mistakenly assume she was a
governess or a nursery maid interviewing for a position?
Apparently so. Shifting her gaze to her fingers idly
scratching the head of a grinning dog the size of a small
pony, she blinked at the tears that wanted to fill her eyes.

St. Catherine's Court from the weeds, spiders and mice. I think we should commence with Mrs. P's rooms, and move from there to the most frequently used family rooms. Also, a fire should be lit in this room, and kept lit until the damp is chased away from these books. Station a night watchman if you fear an unattended fire."

"Yes, Miss Penwell. I shall attend to it immediately."

"Thank you, Mrs. Lithgow," Marke said with a genuine smile of gratitude. The housekeeper was making it very easy for her to take over the helm. "At what time does Mrs. P dine? And where?"

"Ah, well—" Mrs. Lithgow bit her lip in disquiet and dropped her eyes uncertainly from Marke's.

"Mrs. Lithgow, I spoke briefly with my mother upon my arrival, and readily discerned that she is somewhat confused. I would allow you to speak frankly with me on this subject."

"Thank you, miss," Mrs. Lithgow answered with apparent relief. "It's just that Mrs. P keeps no regular hours for meals, or bedtime, or—well, anything. She merely comes and goes as she sees fit. She, ah . . ." Again she hesitated.

"Please continue," Marke prompted her.

"Well, she tends to serve herself, and the, er, the dogs—" she shrugged as if apologizing for allowing such deplorable conduct "—from the kitchen's stores late at night."

"I see," Marke murmured. Her heart sank into the pit of her stomach and lay there like a stone. "How long has she been like this?"

"Staff was aware of her, er, distractions when the captain was lost and your brother requested that Mr. Biddle and I accompany her here to St. Catherine's Court. And, well, they have only worsened over the last few years, until she is greatly isolated from reality. It is most distressing, miss."

"Has a physician been consulted?"

"Yes, Dr. Barrows comes regularly—once a month or more."

"And was my brother notified of this situation?"

The housekeeper raised her chin and stated rigidly, "Yes, miss. Repeatedly and in great detail by me personally, as well as Dr. Barrows."

Marke turned her back to hide the emotions that must be displayed plainly upon her face. She wanted to disbelieve Thomas would allow an ill mother to remain in this remote location with no one but indifferent staff to care for her, but then, hadn't he just sent her to Ireland? Although without a word of preparation. The blackguard!

She spun back to Mrs. Lithgow with a brightly optimistic smile. "Well, Mrs. Lithgow, I am here now. And we shall do our best to rectify the situation, shan't we?"

"Of course, Miss Penwell," Mrs. Lithgow returned her smile. "And, somehow, if I may say so, I believe things are going to take a turn for the better. If you will excuse me, I shall see to your rooms as you have requested."

"Thank you," Marke said. "And I would like dinner in the family dining room at seven—with my mother. Please send someone to help her wash and dress. Do we have someone that she trusts?"

"I shall attend her myself, Miss Penwell."

"I appreciate that, Mrs. Lithgow, and I promise, it shall only be for a short while. If you would send for the physician on the morrow, I shall request his recommendation for a nurse, and she shall be added to the household immediately."

"Thank you, miss," the housekeeper said, then turned once more before slipping through the door. "And welcome home, miss."

Marke answered with a weak smile and a nod. Turning to stare out the window over the vast lawns, eyes tracing the tall laurel hedge showing gaps and straggly growth, she watched the early autumn shadows lengthening to claim St. Catherine's Court in dusk. Yes, a whole lifetime of work.

Chapter Three

Marke paused her pacing before the library hearth and
stared moodily into the flames. She was waiting for Dr.
John Barrows of Bantry to rejoin her after his examina-
tion of Mrs. P. Though she would hope for encouraging
news, she did not expect it. This was the physician's second trip to St. Catherine's Court in the past month, and
despite his earlier suggestions, there was no marked improvement in her mother's awareness of present-day activities.

She sauntered to the window, staring past her reflection
into the fading light beyond. She wished it was as simple as
writing a letter to Thomas demanding he do something, but
she had, in fact, dashed off two rather stern letters her first
week here, neither of which had generated so much as a
sneeze from London. No, she must come to grips with the
fact that the responsibility of their mother rested squarely
upon her own shoulders. She gave a deep sigh with the
heaviness of the responsibility and the loneliness of it. Not
so amazingly, she was missing her family. She thought of
Sybil's little boys, so sweet, so full of mischief, growing up
without their favorite aunt to applaud their most outrageous pranks. How she treasured the moments when a
simple gesture, or a slant of an eye, the tilt of an eyebrow,
showed the young men they would become. Thomas's
children were sweet enough, but one did not get to know
them as well as Sybil's, for Jessell had them firmly controlled by a dragon of a governess and one saw them only

on their best behavior. That's something she herself had
sworn never to do with her own children. She planned to be
very involved with her children. Marke sighed deeply. If
there were ever to be children for her. Did Mary, having
proved barren, feel this emptiness? Or did she derive
enough satisfaction from mothering her younger siblings?
Was this, St. Catherine's Court and her mother, to be
enough for her? At first, she had more than enough to oc-
cupy her mind and energies, but now time sat heavily on her
hands. She felt so pent up, so restless. There wasn't even a
decent mount in the stable to allow for escape from the
confines of the house to roam the hills. A tear slipped over
her lashes and traced down her cheek.

"Miss Penwell?"

"Oh, Dr. Barrows!" Marke gasped, startled from her
reverie. She quickly swiped fingers across her cheeks to
eradicate the self-pity before turning a smile toward the
physician.

To Marke, who believed men of medicine should be men
of great knowledge, and therefore possessing years of a
suitable number to have acquired that great knowledge,
John Barrows looked woefully like a boy. He was slender,
hardly more than her own height, and possessed hair more
white than yellow, lying flat against his forehead like a limp
shock of wheat. His complexion was quite pale and, despite having been raised and educated as befitted the
youngest son of an English baronet, he stood attired as a
country physician should be, in serviceable, hearty woolens.

"I must compliment you, Miss Penwell. I am truly
amazed."

Marke brightened the smile she flashed him. "And just
what have I done to instill such amazement, oh, learned
man of medicine?"

John laughed easily at her tease and came farther into the
room. Marke moved to wave him toward the inviting fire,
realizing she was being far too familiar with a gentleman of
such short acquaintance, but loneliness did that to a person. And she freely admitted to a great deal of loneliness.

She could not afford the weeks, months and years normally applied to the building of a friendship, and retain her sanity at the same time.

"Ah, I can see by the tear trails on your cheeks, that you were thinking of illness, despair and dying, were you not?" John asked, abruptly changing the direction of their conversation.

"Absolutely not!"

"Oh, come now," he admonished. "I think of it often, myself. At least, whenever I have a free moment."

Marke laughed at his glib admission. "With your greatuncle preparing his retirement, I seriously doubt you have many spare moments, although it distresses me to think that even your leisure is plagued with illness and dying."

Again he changed directions, openly eyeing the smart gown of raspberry silk with appreciation. "You are quite comely for a governess, you know."

"Governess?" Marke puzzled, then brightened. "Oh, I see—so, Mrs. P has divulged the truth of my station at St. Catherine's Court? How bothersome."

"Perhaps, but I heartily uphold the comely part," he countered.

"You are quite impudent for a physician."

John leaned against the mantel and affected a pose he hoped would be considered debonair, and flattering enough to draw attention from his deplorable lack of height. "Oh, I must cry unfair. Pray do not tell me it is your opinion that physicians are not to be allowed the expression of emotions and desires as other men are?"

"As I perceive it, anyone can express whatever they desire, and do so whenever and wherever they please. As for being comely, I am actually quite plain, though it matters little—" she shrugged her shoulders slightly "—for nobody ever sees me here, and year by year I shall only become plainer."

John drew back his head in mock dismay, and tilted white, nearly invisible, eyebrows toward his hairline. "My goodness, you *are* feeling sorry for yourself."

Having no desire to venture into her homesickness for fear of disgracing herself with tears that seemed too irritatingly close to the surface, Marke waved his comment aside with a laugh. "Have over with it, and tell me what it is that inspires you to associate such an agreeable word as *amazing* with me."

John gallantly gave into her desire to change the subject. "The amazement I was expressing is for the complete, and radical, changes you have wrought in this place! And over such a short span of time, I must add."

"Oh, that."

"Oh, *that?* False modesty now, Miss Penwell? You must know it is nothing short of a miracle. You forget I have been a frequent caller to this house in the past."

"Trust me, Dr. Barrows, there is nothing that cannot be accomplished with a virtual army of workers willing to follow sensible directions."

John readily nodded his agreement to that truth, but he was not willing to let her brush aside the compliment as easily as that. "You must give yourself more credit than that. Where you found shambles, Miss Penwell, now stands a warm, inviting home. It shows in every room, and on every servant's contented face."

Marke glanced around the library with pleasure. Brass fittings gleamed from ardent rubbing, and the mahogany bookshelves glowed with red warmth in the candlelight. The ruby and gold pattern in the carpet, released from its dirt and grime, was again discernible, and new drapes of claret velvet graced the tall windows. She had effectively banished the masculine feel of the room by replacing the exiled leather wing chairs, all stiff and cracked with age, with overstuffed upholstery in floral prints. The stale hunt scenes on the walls had given way to soft artwork more reflective of her own personality. The library was now a place of warmth and invitation.

"Yes, it is inviting, isn't it? And I *am* quite proud of it," she declared, flashing a radiant smile that snagged at John's breath. "There! You have effectively drawn an admission of conceited satisfaction from me in a most efficient manner. So, may I now offer you a libation before dinner, Doctor?"

"Yes, you may. A touch of spirits before dinner would suit just fine."

Glancing at Mr. Biddle, Marke saw he was already one step ahead of her, coming forward with a tray bearing a glass of amber liquid that must have been the physician's usual when visiting Mrs. P. Seating herself before the fireplace, she gracefully spread her skirts over the chair, thus granting the young physician license to seat himself as well. She held her questions until Mr. Biddle had served the libation and withdrawn from the room. "Now, please tell me of my mother, Dr. Barrows. Do you see any improvement at all?"

John's face took on a professional demeanor, all prank and flirtation aside, and he shook his head solemnly. "As much as I would like to offer you hope, Miss Penwell, I know you would only accept total honesty from me. Your mother will never improve. We do not know why it is so, but in these cases, the patient will only continue to regress. For want of a better explanation, I can tell you it is as if the mental aging process has reversed itself. You can expect your mother to become more and more dependent. More childlike in her thinking process. And, like a young child, she will require more and more care, more attention so that she does not do injury to herself. I am truly very sorry."

Marke dropped her eyes to her hands clenched tightly in her lap. So much for lamenting the loss of children of her own, she thought. Already resigned to the news, she raised her head to smile at the concerned young man. "I have spent a great deal of time with her these past weeks, and occasionally there was a spark that gave rise to hope, but they were so fleeting that I suspected it was as you say. But I thank you for your frankness."

"I would not insult you by giving you less."

"For the most part she seems quite content, but she is capable of throwing the most dreadful tantrums. I usually give in to her, as I feel it must be dreadful for her to feel herself slipping away," Marke said.

John leaned forward to pat her hand in the most comforting manner. "I must tell you, of all the illnesses of the mind, this seems the kindest, for she truly does not know that she is regressing. I fear it's harder on those who love them than the ones afflicted. But I am here to reassure and support you in every way I can. You need only call on me to receive it."

Marke studied the young man in front of her with open gratitude for his empathy. Even with his pale coloring, he really was very attractive. She shifted the conversation away from her mother, for to dwell on her deteriorating health would only draw her further down in the doldrums. "I am so pleased you have decided to join me for dinner, Dr. Barrows. I will admit to a spot of loneliness sometimes, and have looked forward to your visits," she admitted. "Tell me all the news of the county. I am woefully isolated here, and I feel you, with your many rounds, surely have your fingers on the pulse of the populace, so to speak, and are privy to all the gossip."

"That I am and, although I shall be defamed for doing so, I shall share it all with you—but only up to the point that I might be accused of breaking doctor-patient confidences," he promised, eagerly leaning farther toward her though lacking the courage to retain his hold on her hand. "Anything to return your delightful smile upon me."

"Splendid!" she declared, clapping her hands in anticipation. Flattered by the open admiration of the only eligible gentleman she had met, she felt herself blush and hoped it was becoming rather than distracting, for it was a deplorable spawn of her coloring . . . as were the freckles.

Mr. Biddle, with the announcement of dinner, interrupted the confidences before they could commence, much to John's disappointment. Marke gracefully rose to place her hand neatly into the crook of his arm. He smelled faintly, and pleasantly, of winter wind, pipe tobacco and whiskey—and nothing at all like dog.

Marke's first dinner party was laid out in the main dining hall for celebration of company. The table, very heavy mahogany, displayed, remarkably well, the delicate bone china and ornate sterling service, unearthed from the attic not two days before. A slight breeze from the window set the great cut-glass chandelier tinkling like so many tiny bells and cast a glow from wavering candles across the polished wainscot and frescoed ceiling. Tempting smells beckoned from the sideboard. Fowl with prune sauce, whole fish in pastry, green-pea soup, jams and pickles, potato pudding, and rich seed cake had been planned. She suddenly felt very grown-up indeed, being handed to her seat by her handsome escort, and proud to be mistress of all this.

Mrs. P sat regally at the foot of the table, with John on her left and Marke on her right. The head of the table was purposefully left vacant, as her mother would repeatedly insist the captain was only away on a lengthy voyage but might return at any moment, and this minor point had finally been conceded to her stubborn mother. Surveying her now, attired in her best green gown, properly pressed and presented, Marke was quite proud of her striking good looks. She could be a lady of a decade less than her actual years.

"I think we should have a toast," Mrs. P announced, lifting her glass high over her head. "A toast to our new governess."

"A toast then," John declared, raising his glass high.

The doctor winked at Marke's stricken look so merrily that she smiled back and raised her glass in answer. Absurd as Mrs. P's comments were, it pleased her to see her mother content and expressing merriment, even though the party seemed to take on an attitude of playacting. Her grown-up feeling was transformed into that of a little girl playing in her mother's clothes as she sipped her wine. John tilted his glass toward her slightly and sipped his wine.

Mrs. P spilled her wine down the front of her best green dress and onto the floor. "Oh, dear. Georgie, Georgie, come here." She ineffectually dabbed at her bodice with her napkin. "Doggies, come lap up the wine."

Marke slowly set her glass on the table, fearing a scene when the dogs did not answer her mother's summons. Having banned them from the dining room, and all but a favored few from the house proper, she had quickly set about conquering dogdom. Now she released the breath she had been holding when her mother seemed more distressed over the stain on her bodice than Georgie's failure to appear. Mrs. Moran, an experienced nurse retained specifically to care for her mother, stepped quickly forward to replace the napkin on her charge's lap with undue fuss.

"Thank you, Mrs. Moran," Marke said, closing her eyes for a moment. So much for her wonderful dinner and the enjoyment of company. Although she tried for patience, annoyance at her mother flooded her, then the guilt she felt over the annoyance brought a paleness to her cheeks.

John, accurately reading her rapidly changing expressions, caught her eyes when they opened and smiled companionably at her. "Miss Penwell, it is truly of no consequence, you know," he announced casually. "There's no one of importance here to notice? And, for that matter, even if they were, would it be such a terrible thing?"

Marke thought for a second, sorting it out in her head, then grinned with dawning relief at him. "Of course not!" she declared. "You are absolutely correct. It does not matter in the least, does it? The only thing it signifies is that she is safe and content."

"Exactly!"

"Then I shall make a pact with you, as long as Mrs. P is happy, I shall be happy, too. Does that please you, Doctor?"

"Yes, for quite frankly, I am far more concerned about you than I am your mother. Mrs. P is happy enough with her life and as absorbed with her dogs as ever, which gives her great pleasure. But you are far too comely to be shut away as if this were a sick house under quarantine. And to that point—" he clapped a palm against his forehead "—well, beyond me! I have just had a thought so profound that it nearly knocked me from my chair."

"Oh, surely you exaggerate! I did not notice any visible sign of such a revelation," Marke chided, lifting a teasing eyebrow at him in pretend astonishment.

"You are wonderfully quick, Miss Penwell," John remarked, willing to persist with his compliments all night if it assured her smile remained upon him in such an agreeable manner. "I do so enjoy that. Very stimulating, you know." He shook his finger at her "But I shall not be deterred from my purpose by your wit and your stunning smile. I would ask a favor of you, a favor of the most pressing matter."

"Considering your wonderful diligence with Mrs. P, and your kindness to me, I will grant you any favor you wish. You need only ask, you see."

John blushed a bright red, giving no doubt to the direction of his thoughts. He cleared his throat quickly and persevered through his embarrassment. "Miss Penwell, you had best hear me out before you agree so readily. It might be more than even a dauntless lady such as yourself would be willing to assail."

"Now, you have piqued my curiosity beyond all bounds."

"Ah, but curiosity killed the cat, you know."

"But, good doctor, surely you are aware that satisfaction brought him back," Marke countered. "So on with it!"

"As you wish," John capitulated, with a show of reluctant defeat. "Then tell me, are you familiar with the Marquis of Boothe-Ashmore?"

"My family spent every summer at St. Catherine's Court during my youth, and though we did not aspire to entertain the nobles of Innisfree, they were certainly of such magnitude that we heard of them now and again. But that was a time ago."

John nodded as if that made a good deal of sense. "The Marquis of Boothe-Ashmore has only recently returned to take up residence at Innisfree, and has called upon my services. It's actually a most tragic story, and I am quite concerned for him. I feel if I cannot instigate something rather miraculous in the near future, he will be lost. And you are the most miraculous thing I know."

"Well, I thank you very much for the compliment, but I fear I am lost as to your direction with it. Is the marquis ill?"

"No... and yes, actually quite ill—in more ways than one. You see, just this time last year, nearing the end of the season, their London residence was ravished by fire. The entire family—the marquis, his wife and young daughter—perished in that fire. The surviving son, Lord Perfect, was injured, quite severely actually, in his attempt to instigate rescue."

"Oh, that is terrible! I did not know!" exclaimed Marke, horrified at the picture the physician's words conjured in her head. Being of a large family, her heart was moved by the horror the man must be feeling at losing all of his in one brutal blow. "So tragic! Was he badly burned?"

"Oh, no, nothing like that," John assured her. "A support beam of goodly size and weight crashed, pinning him down and causing an injury to his lower back. But he has since fully recovered, with no impairment to his strength or his limbs. That is to say, if he would just deem to make use of them, but there is the rub. He absolutely refuses to entertain even the slightest acknowledgment of recovery, and seems determined to will his own death through self-neglect and lethargy."

Marke's forehead furrowed. Ever optimistic in her outlook, such a thing was inconceivable to her. "His grief must be terrible, indeed, to wish to die. But he did the best he could have to save them, even at risk for his own life. Surely he's understanding of that. I accept the need to grieve such a terrible, terrible loss, but life does continue in its relentless cycle for those who are living."

"Precisely, but..." John agreed, pointing his finger toward her with meaning. "But he needs someone of refreshing insight and spirit to make him see that."

"But what is it you would have me do? I have no acquaintance of the man, nor the family," Marke asked, shrugging her shoulders in confusion. "If you say his injury has healed—"

"Yes," John interrupted. "But you see he is most severely depressed in spirit." He leaned forward earnestly and looked deeply into Marke's eyes as if wishing to touch her tender soul as apparently the situation did his own. "I am a good doctor, Miss Penwell. A very good doctor. But I have not been able to reach him with my logic. His grief goes far past mere rationalism. And I truly fear, unless he can be made to come to grips with his pain and gain some value for the life he feels he has through some great injustice of fate, he shall only continue to decline until there is nothing but an empty shell of a man remaining. And that would be a shame. Lord Perfect is an admirable man, and it would be a great waste to see him succeed, through sheer will, in following his family to their graves."

Marke slipped slender fingers about the stem of her wineglass to stare into the ruby depths. The physician's words brought forth the most piteous mental picture of a grand and gallant marquis wasting away in mourning for his tragically lost family. "How sad," she murmured, then declared with feeling, "I *will* do it. I *will* help you." Before he could answer, she went on, her words rushing, tumbling, hurrying out, as if the floodgate of her emotions were suddenly lifted and her passionate spirit released. "We'll bring the marquis back to life. We'll show him that to live, and to live fully, is the only possible way. What shall my part be? What would you have me do?"

John eased back in his chair, grinning sheepishly as if somewhat embarrassed at his display of emotion, and perhaps a little startled at the enthusiasm he had aroused in Marke. "Er, I haven't thought that far ahead yet," he admitted. "As you witnessed, the idea came to me quite suddenly, after seeing how well you are coping with Mrs. P, and observing the advances you have made reversing the decay of St. Catherine's Court." He grew pensive. "It is only the thought that perhaps you might also reverse the decay that is devouring Lord Perfect's very soul."

Chapter Four

Although the hour was well before noon, the sky was still feathered with diverse grays and violets. The shadows seemed long for such an early hour, and quite dull, without much sign of the countless vibrant greens one so expects in Ireland. Marke whipped up the shaggy pony and rounded the corner into Bantry. As she drove through the village, the town dogs ran alongside the pony cart, darting dangerously close to the wheels. There was a new dog from property to property, each one picking up the barking of the previous one like relay runners on a mission of importance. Marke was heartily sick of dogs.

Leaving Bantry and rounding the headlands, she followed the doctor's directions. She supposed he had been as explicit as permitted in Ireland, but it all seemed somewhat vague to her. Perhaps she should have brought a more knowledgeable companion than the young groom now grasping the cart framework with white knuckles. She wanted to reassure him that the pony, as old as the cart he pulled, could not gain the reckless speed required to overturn them in the ditch, but decided to let him acquire his trust of her excellent driving in his own way.

What had Dr. Barrows said? Bantry, two miles of bog, another village—Hillscroft—three miles of bog, a church, five miles of bog, Teddy O'Flannigan's bar, Beckett's shop, two miles of bog, a church, three miles of bog, and take the right fork when she reached the Dunmanus Bay. Moving at an amazingly steady gait for such an aged pony, all this was accomplished with an ease that surprised her. Drawing in the pony at the fork in the road to allow him his wind, she left the trap to walk out to the cliffs. Dunmanus Bay was far below her and sparkling brilliantly despite the lack of sun. She breathed deeply of the salt-tinged air. It felt wonderful to be out and about in the world. The doctor had been right, she must do this more often in the future. It did no good to lock herself behind doors at St. Catherine's Court. Turning back to the ragged cart and ancient pony, she resolved at that very moment to purchase a suitable mount for herself. Perhaps even two or three, plus a tilbury and a splendid pony of considerably fewer years than her own eighteen to pull it. After all, she was not a person without resources. St. Catherine's Court boasted a thriving wool enterprise, and wasn't she its mistress? No, she would never again pay a call at Innisfree, or anywhere else for that matter, driving a servant's cart. Assuming, of course, upon leaving her calling card in the tray at Innisfree, she was invited to call a second time.

Climbing back in, she whipped up the pony and the cart bounded forward. The lane now ran along the edge of the island, and in places seemed about to disappear altogether. The young groom beside her drew in his breath sharply and looked as if he would faint away. Out of consideration for him, or so she told herself, she slowed the pony to a shuffling walk. The coastline here was as uneven as an irregular heartbeat, and Marke could only guess at the distance to the blue sea below her. Two or three hundred feet possibly. That was something Dr. Barrows had neglected to tell her. She edged the pony nearer to the wall, marveling at the nerve of any coachman who would attempt this six-mile stretch of trek with a coach and four of any size.

The lane was strewn with stones and rocks, covered with sheep dung in the places where the old sheep trails crossed the road, and quite suddenly descended steeply toward a little bay, only to rise again on the other side. The sea roared into the little bay here, and had eaten deeply beneath the rocks. She passed the small cemetery for unbap-

tized children that was a landmark on her mental map. A
single grave was all that was still to be seen, bordered with
pieces of quartz, as all the other bones had been carried
away by the sea. The pony cart pulled carefully upon an old
bridge in surprisingly decent shape, sporting a new rail and
unweathered replacement planks along its length. Then
Innisfree burst into view.

"Good Lord almighty!" Marke exclaimed.

Set overhanging the cliff, Innisfree was a great pile of
gray stones, majestic and mysterious. It rose up from the
rocks like a king's castle displaying forbidding walls, gables and turrets, twists and turns, and most assuredly dark,
dank dungeons within. Scarlet and black-striped pennants
flapped in the wind. Still somewhat shrouded in a mist that
Marke thought might never burn away from this remote
place, it was as if perpetual darkness hung over Lord Perfect's home. Every shade of gray between black and white
had found its own little place on the stone walls, and even
the sky overhead was covered with a plumage of innumerable grays. Not a streak of blue above, not a scrap of Irish
green below. What a deplorable place for one to retire to
heal from grief and depression. She shuddered.

"Oh, miss," wailed the boy beside her. "Dinna ye be
thinking to change yer mind about going up there?" He
even went so far as to grasp her arm with clutching fingers.

"Of course, we are going up there," she admonished
bravely. "Buck up now! Just think of the tale you'll have
to tell the others at supper tonight."

That thought seem to strengthen the lad and he conceded to release his painful grip upon her arm. Marke, for
all her reassurance to the lad, was filled with a sense of
foreboding as she crossed the bridge and drove through the
arch into the mews. The stones of the gables, washed free
of mortar, were neither quarried stones nor tiles, but small
boulders, just as if the mountain had rolled them down to
fall in this uniform way, and a family of nobles had strolled
over from England to take up residence in much the same
way the pesky starlings nested under the eaves of Thom-

as's house. But then, passing beneath the towering gables, her sense of dread lifted. Neatly trimmed grass bordered the driveway, and though moss had crept over much of the stone walls, it had been shaped and trained into decorative patterns quite pleasing to the eye.

A smartly turned out groom rushed to take the pony's head, and her own lad, not to be outdone by anyone, sufficiently recovered himself to leap to her aid as she departed the cart. Marke nervously smoothed her black wool driving coat and straightened her bonnet. Then squaring her shoulders and taking a deep breath for confidence, she proceeded determinedly to the front entrance. The massive metal-studded doors swung open even before she could raise the heavy lion's-head knocker and, surprisingly enough, without the anticipated squeak of protesting hinges imitating the sound of tortured souls. She was admitted into a remarkably inviting interior by a majordomo as old and as formidable as one would expect to find in charge of a residence with dungeons. The man's eyes flickered beneath awesomely shaggy, white eyebrows to express momentary astonishment at the sight of a fresh, freckled-faced young woman upon his lordship's doorstep.

Marke slipped a card from her reticule to present confidently to the elderly majordomo. "Would you please inform the Marquis of Boothe-Ashmore that Miss Margaret Penwell of St. Catherine's Court has come to call?"

Quickly recovering himself, the man bowed deeply and accepted the card between forefinger and thumb as if it were a dangerous thing to have about one's person. "If you will please allow me to hand you into the drawing room where there is a warming fire, Miss Penwell, I shall inform the marquis of your arrival."

"Thank you," Marke murmured, following the stooped man through the cavernous entry hall and into a drawing room of invitingly warm hues of golds, cinnamons and teals. It was a gracious room for all its awesome size, betraying a definite woman's touch in its history, even to a Windsor chair just the right size for a child, covered in faded roses with a wee flounce around the bottom. She crossed the room very tentatively, as though her old black chamois shoes might damage the exquisite carpet. Although she had not been relieved of her outdoor things, Marke carefully removed her black crepe bonnet and leather driving gloves to smooth her hair. As Dr. Barrows had given her every indication that Lord Perfect was not keeping days at-home in which to receive local callers, the majordomo's unspoken assumption that the marquis would not receive her and she would be departing forthwith was most probably correct.

"What is this? The presence of another woman of literacy and breeding in this godforsaken place?"

Startled, Marke spun to confront the abrupt appearance of a lady. A lady of middle years by the gray at her temples, but if so, that age was belied by the bounce in her step. As she advanced with both hands outstretched, Marke could make no determination of her station, but her attire was faultless and her manner definitely above friendly. Of average height, with unbent shoulders and the willowy figure of a young girl, she boasted smiling eyes of a brilliant blue. Marke, for want of any way to decline gracefully, gave both of her hands to the lady as if she were greeting a friend of long standing.

"I see by your rather startled expression that the good Dr. Barrows did not tell you as much about me as he did me of you. Men! Aren't they just the most distressing creatures?" the lady demanded. Without relinquishing her grasp on Marke's hands, she drew her over by the divan closest to the fire. "Let's yield the care of your outdoor things to Heaven and settle in to cose. Tea is on its way."

Marke swiveled eyes to the majordomo. Heaven? She swallowed a giggle and dropped her eyes to her fingers on the buttons of her driving coat. At the sound of his name the old man shuffled forward obligingly to relieve her of her things. Marke, eyeing the woman's smart merino gown, was pleased that she had worn her best calling dress. Touching the rigid mandarin collar of the black velvet bodice and smoothing the sapphire blue skirt, she knew she

looked nice, although the gown had suited Kathleen El-
len's rounder figure far better than her own willowy frame.

"Come, sit here." The lady patted the cushion beside her
on the floral divan. "You must forgive Lord Perfect for
hiding in his room, but surely that is what you expected after Dr. Barrows's confidences. Oh, no, don't look embarrassed. John—Dr. Barrows, that is—has explained his
thoughts concerning you in great detail and I approve most
heartily."

"I, ah, yes—" Marke muttered, then decided, as the lady
herself indicated, straightforwardness was definitely called
for in this instance. "I am so sorry, but—just who are you?
Dr. Barrows, as you said, did not mention you to me at
all."

"Oh, here is Heaven with tea."

The arrival of the heavy sterling tea service and the accomplishment of filling two thin, useless cups with the
weak, tepid stuff, and the placement of hot cranberry and
orange tea cakes, liberally stuffed with English walnuts, on
equally delicate tea plates, took an interminable time to
Marke, as she was brimming with curiosity. But, thank-
fully, the unusually candid lady was willing to jump right
back into the conversation without the delay of social
prattle of meaningless things.

"I, my dear, am Mrs. Elisa Sittlemeyer. Better known to
one and all as Sitter," she explained with a wide wink at her
young guest. "And as we are to embark upon a project of
such intimate deviousness, I shall immediately place you at
the very top of my list of friends, and grant you privilege to
call me thus also."

"Thank you, er, Sitter. My name is—"

"Of course, Marke! John has told me all. I am so sorry
to hear of your mother. Such things are most unfortunate,
and can be trying at times, are they not? But I do so ad-
mire you for leaving what must have been your first season
in London to devote yourself to her care. But, while it is
most praiseworthy of you, you must not give up your life
for her, you know. Remember that you are but a young
thing and try to act like it occasionally."

"Yes, I sh-shall try to r-remember that," Marke stuttered. She could only stare at this woman who would refer to her mother's affliction as unfortunate and trying, *and* offer such familiarity on short acquaintance. Obviously the good doctor was, indeed, the town crier. She must also remember *that* in the future and guard her confidences. Then, as she could not help herself, she returned Sitter's open, warm smile. This whole affair was so deliciously absurd and marvelously diverting.

"That's better," Sitter remarked, patting her hand softly. "I feel we shall be the closest of friends, as well we should, since we are to plot against Claymore in such a devious manner."

"Claymore?" Marke asked, carefully placing her empty teacup on the tray. She looked longingly at the pot, but she resigned herself to the observance of good manners, which forbade her requesting a refill, but necessitated she wait patiently until her empty cup was noticed and more tea offered.

"Yes, my dear. Lord Claymore William Perfect, the Marquis of Boothe-Ashmore. Surely you are familiar with the family?"

"No, I am afraid our father did not believe in his children moving about society before their twentieth year, and in fact, kept the family in the country for most of the year. It's only been since his passing, five years ago, that the Penwells have descended upon London in force. My eldest sister, Mary, is Lady Alfred Bixby—" she paused but the lady gave no indication of any acquaintance "—and she is chaperoning three of our sisters this season, and as they move quite prominently in society, I am most certain they are familiar with the marquis's family."

"Ah, well, it was a tragic thing. Lord Edward Perfect, his lady wife, Elizabeth, and their small daughter, Libby—" her eyes darted briefly to the child's chair "—were all taken quite suddenly by fire at their town house. While I was not acquainted with Lady Perfect on a social level, I knew both father and son."

Marke was saddened to see tears fill the lady's eyes before she paused to look down with emotion at her teacup. Moved by the pain in the woman's voice, she reached to touch her hand in empathy. While she wasn't certain she understood Mrs. Sittlemeyer's attachment to the family, she was willing to offer as much comfort as allowed, for that was her nature. Although, having no idea of the marquis's age, she was not above speculation. Could this charming, outgoing woman be Lord Perfect's mistress? Her eyes strayed to the child's chair again. Surely there could not have been such a great deal of age difference between Lord Perfect and his sister, could there? Having spent a large amount of time in various libraries, and adroit at secreting forbidden books in the attic, she was not unaware of the practice of fashionably impure ladies of the demimonde being engaged to introduce adolescent gentlemen to the realities of life's pleasures. Considered by some, if she was to analyze correctly what she read, as a critical form of education, far more important even than a course of study at Cambridge. The possibility of that being the case, she carefully withdrew her hand.

Sitter dabbed gently at her eyes. "And, well, with things as they were, I simply could not allow Claymore, so hurt inside and out, to disappear into the wilds of this place alone, now could I? And therefore, my dear, I packed up and here I am." She spread her hands wide, offering a watery smile.

Again Marke returned the smile. While she supposed, if her assumptions were correct, she should not be sitting here in such companionship with a lady of questionable virtue, she must admit to being quite taken with the openness in which the lady seemed to revel. It matched her own disdain for innuendo and paraphrasing, which did nothing but stifle most conversations. It was with genuine caring that she said, "I am so glad that a man with the troubles of the Marquis of Boothe-Ashmore, has one such as you to stand by him, Mrs. Sittlemeyer. Although, I am still uncertain just what Dr. Barrows proposes I do in this situation. I am merely a shipmaster's daughter—"

Sitter waved away her protest and interrupted her. "Do not tease yourself about that. When John first came to me announcing he had a proposition for me, I told him quite up front, 'John, first of all I am too old for propositions'—" she giggled like a young girl "—whereupon he turned the most delicious shade of red and rather bluntly told me to stop my sparring." Marke could not halt a giggle, for the thought of young Dr. Barrows suggesting an indecent proposal to anyone, much less to a lady such as the forthright Mrs. Sittlemeyer, was very comical, indeed. "But I will say, when he expressed his concerns for Claymore's mental state, they merely mirrored my own. I fear the dear boy has simply given up on life."

At the mention of the marquis, Marke's face became sober. "I am not aware of the extent of your knowledge of me, although it appears Dr. Barrows was very generous, but of course, I shall do whatever I can to aid in the marquis's recovery," she offered. "If you will only tell me in what way I might act to his benefit."

Sitter watched Marke in a speculative way, tapping a forefinger upon her pouting lips before confiding. "John did, in fact, tell me a great deal of you, and of your mother. Oh, I can see that troubles you, but it mustn't. He is a dear, kind soul and was merely expressing much the same concern for you as for Claymore. And, as I've said, it's not healthy to grieve so deeply over things that one can never change." She reached to pat Marke's hand. "I feel the good doctor's scheme is a sound one. You are certainly pretty enough for the task, and bright as a new copper penny."

Marke stirred uncomfortably. "Bright," she could understand, but just what did "pretty" have to do with this plan that was being hatched? "I still do not understand."

Sitter rushed on to reassure her. "It's just that Claymore must somehow be made to view life as something other than worthless. I expect he harbors a heavy load of guilt that he is alive, while those closest to him are not. I will warn you though, he is surly much of the time, and acts like a small boy in that he stubbornly refuses to be engaged in conversation, and will not listen to any reasonable arguments—" she gave a deep sigh and flipped her hand helplessly in the air "—when one can extricate him from his bedchamber, that is."

"Oh my, he does sound most difficult," Marke said. Though she searched her brain, she could not see what she could do that this vivacious lady of an obviously long relationship could not. "But if he is set upon hiding in his rooms," she said, and shrugged her shoulders helplessly with a wry grin, "well, I can't very well accost an unmarried gentleman in his bedchamber, now can I!"

Sitter bubbled over with laughter. "Oh, my dear. John did say you were the most wonderfully forthright, inventive person he'd ever come across. I am certain, given the opportunity of being at Innisfree, you will make a way to draw him out."

The sound of squeaky wheels on marble, accompanied by an obviously irritated voice, interrupted Sitter. "Bloody damn, man! Are you trying to take my leg off on the door frame? Where the hell are you taking me, Henry?" The angry words floated around the corner a second before the appearance of a young footman in somber livery propelling an invalid chair in front of him.

Of older years than herself, but far younger than Sitter, the gentleman was wonderfully handsome for all his paleness. She supposed he was *dressed*, for, above his light brown pantaloons, he wore a loose, soft shirt open at the neck. Over this, he had carelessly thrown a gentlemen's morning robe of green velvet, delicately embroidered in vibrant tints. His hair was a deep brown—the hue, and with the shine, of well-rubbed walnut—and every bit as curly as her own. His eyes might have been an interesting shade of ruddy brown if they hadn't been so overshadowed by a frown drawing his eyebrows down. But even with the scowl and the thinness of his face, she would grant he was absolutely, utterly, breathtakingly gorgeous.

Sitter leapt to her feet and, choosing to ignore the scowl, rushed to place a soft peck on his cheek. An affectionate gesture he obviously sought to avoid by pointedly turning his head away from her. "Oh, Claymore, do come see. We have company!"

"So I observe, Sitter," he barked. "I am not blind, as well as lame."

"My dear, may I introduce Lord Perfect, the Marquis of Boothe-Ashmore? And do not let his terrible manners put you off," Sitter advised Marke with tilted eyebrows of significant meaning. "Lord Perfect, this is Miss Margaret Penwell. Of St. Catherine's Court, on the other side of Bantry." She moved behind the invalid chair to push it nearer the divan, only overriding his reluctance with a sharp slap of her hand on his to loosen the thwarting grip on the wheel staying its progress forward. The marquis whipped his hand from the wheel as if dealt a crippling blow and directed a deep frown of censure over his shoulder.

Marke was strongly reminded of her nephews, aged one to five years, and swallowed a grin. She started to rise, then considered his seated position and quarrelsome attitude, and thought it best not to tower over his head. "I am most pleased to make your acquaintance, my lord," she said sweetly.

When the marquis would do no more than sit with his arms akimbo, making no attempt to be polite other than to incline his head slightly in Marke's direction without granting her so much as a glance, Sitter came forward to settle herself before the tea service. She addressed the marquis at a level of familiarity fully intended to set the small gathering on familylike terms. "Tea, Claymore? This, I fear, has grown quite cold, but Marke and I were just going to ring for fresh—"

"No, I do *not* wish tea," the marquis said through gritted teeth. "I was on my way to the library when this fool—" he turned, with a stern, disparaging frown, to indicate the quiet young man standing at rigid attention beside the door "—apparently became disorientated and made a wrong turn. He *would* bring me in here."

Marke glanced at the young footman's face, impassive now although she was sure he could expect a rounding setdown once the marquis made his escape from Sitter. She did not envy the young man's position, nor Sitter's as she made yet another attempt to smooth the way, seemingly prepared to ignore any amount of rudeness he chose to put forth. As she was prompting herself to do the same, Marke swallowed a large lump of irritation and smiled agreeably into thin air.

"Claymore, please do not speak so of Henry," Sitter reprimanded gently. "Even if it was misguided, well, your joining us is only to our delight. Isn't that so, Marke?"

"Oh, Sitter, please!" the marquis interjected sharply in a manner that expressed patience tried beyond belief.

The marquis glared pointedly at Marke with such a damning expression that she sat back a fraction. It would have been blatantly obvious to a blind and deaf person, that the man desired to quit this social gathering and its inane chitchat above all else, she mused, but having been reared with a loud, blustering father, she was not one to intimidate easily. Now, faced with such arrogance and ill manners, she suspected he was trying to goad her to stammers, *and* a hurried exit, with his disagreeable behavior. Why, she was even sure she detected a hint of mocking scorn in his brown eyes. Well, handsome and dashing though he may be, she would not stammer and blush in his presence. Nor would she be cowed into fleeing in a flurry of skirts. Perhaps it was merely grief and the masochistic desire to be simply left alone with it that prompted his ill manners, but the possibility that he just might be using that as an excuse to indulge in tantrums caused her fighting spirit to reassert itself.

"Of course, that is so, Sitter. It would have been a regrettable shame to miss making your acquaintance, Lord Perfect," she simpered, smiling sweetly with pretty company manners at the marquis, "simply because a footman had, at some earlier time in his life, developed an excellent sense of orientation."

The marquis's head satisfactorily snapped around at her remark, and he seemed to see Marke clearly for the first time. She merely smiled at him with what she hoped was not a simpering please-look-at-me-as-a-future-wife expression she so often perceived upon her sisters' faces. Well, perhaps only Sarah, Kathleen and Charity. The others, having already secured a husband, or having decided one was not necessary to their existence, always managed perfectly normal, pleasant expressions in the company of such a gorgeous noble as this one. She must try to remember just how that was done.

Sitter, watching Claymore's face closely with some concern, cleared her throat uneasily and intervened as if fearing the marquis would be unkind to her young guest. "Claymore, I have invited Marke to stay for dinner, what with feminine companionship being so scarce at Innisfree. I thought, or hoped rather, that your coachman could see her safely home afterward, as she came by pony cart. Perhaps that can be sent on ahead with her groom...." Her voice drifted off in uncertainty.

To Marke's chagrin, the marquis ignored Sitter and glowered pointedly at Marke as if the whole invitation had been her idea and hers alone. He then spun his chair and sent it speeding toward the door with a practiced flip of his hand. "I see no reason for feminine companionship, Sitter!" he barked. "Nor do I need company for dinner!"

Marke leapt to her feet and balled her hands into fists. Of all the overbearing, insufferable, arrogant—she would not, *must not* for the sake of her promise to Dr. Barrows, allow him to dismiss her from the house. "Lord Perfect!" she commanded. "Do not order me from your presence in such a tyrannical manner. I shall not be dictated by you in this instance. Perhaps *you* do not require feminine companionship, but pray consider for a moment that the suggestion for such might not have been intended for *you* in the first place."

Claymore again spun his chair with remarkable dexterity, to face the defiant young woman. "And just when have I ordered you anywhere, Miss...er, Miss..."

Marke bridled at the imperious note in his voice. "Penwell! My *name* is Miss Margaret Penwell!"

"Miss Penwell, I do think you had best give pause to consider that it is within the walls of *my* house that you are refusing to heed *my* wishes," he declared, wheeling the chair closer to her in what might have seemed a threatening gesture had he been on his feet.

Marke refused to back away from him. She lifted her chin higher and replied haughtily. "Rudeness is rudeness wherever."

The marquis stared up at her, craning his neck to do so, but Marke felt to retake her seat would be viewed as backing down before the glower on his face. She did, however, soften her voice somewhat, merely to defuse the situation, you understand.

"I would hope, my lord, that you would give a thought to Mrs. Sittlemeyer, for after all she is your guest even if she is of long acquaintance. Innisfree is remote, as remote as St. Catherine's Court is for me, and the days do grow long without occasional amusement. It is for me, as well as for herself, that she has so graciously issued an invitation for dinner."

Properly chastised, Claymore cast guilty eyes at Sitter. Then as if suddenly tired, he sighed deeply and dragged his hand through his hair, greatly disarraying the dark curls. "Oh, God, Sitter, forgive my thoughtlessness. Of course, invite whomever you please to dine. Miss Penwell, I ask for your forgiveness, as well."

Marke conceded to incline her head slightly as way of answer. The marquis then excused himself politely and motioned for Henry to remove him from the room. No sooner had his chair cleared the doorway than Marke flopped down onto the sofa. "Good Lord a'mercy!" she gasped, while expelling a great breath she hadn't been aware she was holding.

Sitter too let out a deep breath. "Oh, my." She fanned herself with her hand, while pressing the other to her chest. "I was so afraid—I mean to say—oh, Marke, I am astonished! In the span of five minutes, you quite removed his attention from himself and—and, why, he even apologized for his temper! My dear Miss Margaret Penwell, John Barrows was certainly correct in his assessment of you. You are indeed most definitely resourceful. I rest comfortably

48   *Beauty and the Beast*

certain that you shall have Claymore back to his old wonderful self in no time.''

Marke sat upright and flipped her curls out of her face. Resourceful? Perhaps, but she felt quite whipped in the process. She was painfully aware that she did not share Sitter's high regard for the marquis. In fact, she would maintain Sitter was blinded by her affections to the actuality of Lord Claymore Perfect's true personality. He was an arrogant, overbearing, domineering, totally infuriating tyrant, but she had made a promise to Dr. Barrows, and there was a genuine affection budding for the forthright lady beside her, and that was enough to bind her to the task ahead. But Lordy, Lordy, just what had she gotten herself into?

Chapter Five

Marke dropped her carefully packed personals case in the hall for Mr. Biddle to place alongside her trunk in the carriage, then rushed in search of her mother. As usual she found Mrs. P on her knees in the temporary kennel that had been constructed in the red and crimson drawing room. The elegant drawing room, centered between ballroom and conservatory, typically accommodated sedentary guests desiring escape from music and dancing for conversation and games of whist during a grand ball. But for now it served as housing for the ever-present puppies until a proper kennel could be planned.

"Mrs. P? May I speak with you a moment?" Marke asked.

"Of course, Marke," Mrs. P agreed, then squinted at her through eyes age had rendered a trifle farsighted. "Is this about my girls? Are the scamps giving you trouble? You do have permission to send them to bed without supper, you know."

Unlatching the haphazard kennel gate as her mother regained her feet, Marke shoved the puppies back with her foot before they could tumble through the opening onto the newly scrubbed floor. "Your daughters are admirable women, Mrs. P, and should never be mistreated by anyone."

"Bed without supper never hurt a naughty child," her mother persisted, seating herself on the regal gold settee. "No supper for bad little boys and girls alike. Sugar and candy for good little girls. Bread and jam for boys and dogs. They are such good dogs, Marke. I'm sorry that you do not like them and feel you must give them away."

"You still have plenty of dogs about you, Mrs. P," Marke said with a calculating glance at the ever-increasing pack lolling about the converted drawing room. Kneeling beside the settee, she leaned forward to capture her mother's restless hands in her own. "Mrs. P, do you know who I am?"

"Of course I know who you are. You're the new governess, you silly thing."

"No, Mama," Marke replied with a smile and a quiet voice. "I am Margaret Catherine, your youngest daughter."

Mrs. P squinted her eyes, seemingly searching her memory for clues. "Yes, of course. Supposed to be a son, you see, but surprised us all and arrived without—" She leaned forward to tap her forehead against Marke's and whispered, "A man thingie!"

"Mama!" Marke exclaimed with a giggle.

"But you are a good governess. And you deserve sweets!" Mrs. P dragged her hands from Marke's and clapped them loudly. "Sweets! We want sweets!" The dogs began to yap and jump around the settee on their hind legs as if singing "sweets, we want sweets!"

Marke quickly clasped her mother's face between her hands and planted a hasty kiss on the soft cheek in a farewell that was acknowledged with a sweet smile. Marke knew Mrs. P wouldn't take note of her absence, and certainly would suffer no loneliness with all her canine company. Marke grinned wryly at the lolling, capering dogs. She would most probably return in a fortnight to find the whole kit and caboodle of them roaming the house, begging for eviction.

Climbing nimbly into the carriage, Marke glanced over the darkening sky. She was departing later than she had planned, but could still make the trip in good time to dress for dinner. It did not take long for the fresh air, the crisp greens of Ireland and the optimism of youth to clear her head and turn her mind to the purpose ahead.

Having been twice more to Innisfree under the guise of dinner guest, Marke had yet to experience the marquis's delightful company after that disastrous first call. He remained firmly hidden from view whenever she was there, although whether for that specific reason or not, she had no idea. It had been Sitter's inspiration for her to return for an extended stay. With a constant presence about the place, surely something would come to mind as to how they could further their aim.

Heaven met her at the front door with a relieved Sitter hard on his heels, declaring herself fearful that Marke had changed her mind. With no time for dalliance, she was hustled upstairs to change for dinner. Even short of time, she paused to gape at the bedchamber that was truly fit for Queen Adelaide herself. With thick carpets and plush upholstery, the room wrapped around her with warm welcome. A print of cabbage roses, in gold, ruby and soft pink, covered counterpane, bed curtains, portiere and chaise. All the wood was red hued, either mahogany or cherry, and well rubbed with scented beeswax. This errand of mercy was certainly proving to be one of overstated comfort, she thought.

A knock on her door brought in her case, and a young maid offering to unpack it for her. "'Tis Kittie I am, miss, and sent here to see to yer things. I can be doing the dressing of yer hair, too," the girl said, blushing furiously and edging toward the trunk as if unsure of her welcome. "If that be pleasing ye, that is."

"Of course, Kittie," Marke said with a smile to put the girl at ease. "That would be most appreciated, but we must hurry for I'm afraid I've arrived quite late."

There was a clock somewhere in the hall and by the time it struck seven, Marke was bathed, dressed and had her hair tidied, or at least arranged as tidily as unruly hair can be. She had selected her second best evening gown for this dinner. Not that Sitter hadn't seen it before, but at least it would be new to the marquis, *if* he decided to grace them

with his appearance. Smoothing her hand lovingly over the
gold net frock, she admired the way the deeper hued satin
slip altered tones with her movement. Originally sewn for
the much older Sybil but deemed unsuitably immodest by
her clergyman husband, the gown had passed down the line
of sisters to Marke. Not that Jessell had ever allowed her to
wear it. Perhaps the décolletage was extremely daring for
one of her age and unmarried state, but a country holiday
at Innisfree was not to be considered the same as the rigid
haute-ton of English society with its many strictures and
rules. Besides, wasn't she her own mistress? Answerable to
no one but her own sense of propriety? Marke turned this
way and that in front of the pier glass before deciding it well
suited her coloring and, even by her own assessment, her
creamy shoulders and full bosom were rather fine and deserved to be displayed.

A quick knock on the door brought Sitter's head peeking in, followed by the rest of her body attired dramatically in black and ablaze with diamonds. "Oh my, you do
look very fetching tonight. A most becoming color for you,
dear."

"My Lord, Sitter! Are all of those real?" Marke exclaimed before she could swallow her words. Sitter, clad in
a most elegant boat-necked taffeta, was very much over-
adorned for this remote place. Marke estimated every dia-
mond in the world must have been draped about the lady's
slender neck and wrists. She created an imposing yet
blinding sight.

Sitter merely chuckled at Marke's youthful forthright-
ness, and gave her arm an affectionate squeeze. "Oh yes,
dear, quite real. Now if you are ready, let's see if we can
beard the bear in his den, shall we?"

Marke flushed with the rudeness of her outburst but still
could only wonder just what this kind lady's station could
be in this household. If her suspicions were to be confirmed, just who could her generous benefactor be? Then,
as it had nothing to do with her mission at Innisfree, she
tossed it from her mind and inquired brightly, "So you
truly believe the marquis shall join us this evening?"

Sitter sighed deeply. "He has said so, and I can only hope he will keep his word. I did reprimand him most sharply for his continued absence."

Marke bit her tongue to keep from adding a list of other deplorable traits besides mere absence that needed reprimanding, like ill temper and arrogance and bossiness and rudeness.

If the drawing room, the family dining room and her bedchamber had suitably impressed Marke, the formal dining hall rendered her speechless. She gaped at the size of the marble hearth, the towering tapestries on all four walls, and the gigantic gold and crystal chandelier blazing from the frescoed ceiling. Though the mahogany table was fully capable of seating thirty or more, there were only three place settings along the upper half. The head of the table, pointedly missing its chair, gave indication that the marquis was indeed joining them for dinner. Marke ran her tongue over dry lips and, if asked, would have admitted to more than a little nervousness at the prospect.

Fully expecting to find the marquis already in attendance, Sitter seemed flustered, and more than a little resentful, at his absence. She had just thrown her hands into the air in resignation and suggested they withdraw to the drawing room to await his pleasure, when the squeaking complaint of the invalid chair could be heard in the hallway. Sitter dashed to the door, her eyes bright, obviously eager to greet him. Marke wondered again, uncomfortably, if the relationship between the two could be more intimate than Sitter would have her believe. But, even as straightforward as Sitter appeared, it was just not the thing one could simply ask. The same unfortunate Henry pushed the chair through the door, propelling it rapidly toward the table.

"Claymore, it is so good of you to join us," Sitter exclaimed, reaching to grasp his hand. Claymore turned to dismiss Henry in decidedly hostile tones before rounding on Sitter, as everything and everyone seemed to displease him in some way. He roared so loudly that Marke jumped and,

had she been the type of female to scream, would have
emitted just such a sound.

"Damn it all to hell! Why must I be forced to drag myself down the stairs for a dinner with company that I have
no use for? And you—" he rounded on hapless Henry
again "—have quite battered me to pieces. I doubt I can eat
a bite, not that it will be palatable in the first place." Henry
bowed slightly and backed from the room with such remarkable indifference to the marquis's laments that Marke
was astonished.

"Oh now, Claymore," Sitter began, clasping her hands
in front of her in distress at his anger. "Please do behave."
Claymore turned his glare at Sitter hovering over the chair.
"Oh, for God's sake, Sitter! Sit down! I do not require you
to remind me that I am a cripple. I quite recognize my
lameness without you forever towering over my head in that
way."

Marke quickly moved to the table and hastily placed
herself in her chair without a word for fear the marquis's
anger might be redirected toward her. This situation was
going to be most uncomfortable if he could not be per-
suaded to adjust his attitude, she thought, and continued
to think the same thought in a variety of ways, throughout
the first three removes. She doubted that there could possibly be a meal more properly prepared, nor one that sat so
heavily in her stomach with each bite she placed in her
mouth. It was as if she ingested tension with each swallow.

Sitter kept up an admirable though nervous prattle, re-
galing her two silent dinner partners with various *on-dits*
from London. Some were so absurd that Marke could only
imagine that she must be inventing them as she went along,
merely to fill the dreadful silence. Marke used the time and
the inattention of the marquis to study him in glances from
beneath lowered lashes. His illness, other than weakening
his legs, seemed not to have ravaged his body at all. His
shoulders were remarkably wide, and his neck strong above
his white cravat. His hands were slender, finely made and
sensual as they toyed with his sterling. He certainly did not

look like the sort of man who would treat one as sweet as Sitter the way he did.

Marke felt at such a loss to aid the lady, whose voice was rising toward shrill with her desperate efforts. Just as she had almost despaired of any way to turn the soliloquy into a conversation, Sitter addressed her directly. "I understand that you are an artist, Marke. Does your talent extend to portraits, perhaps?"

Marke choked in her surprise and required a refilling of her water goblet and several moments to right herself before she could speak. A blush of embarrassment flushed her cheeks as the marquis gave a deep sigh of forbearance for untutored company. Finally she recovered herself enough to stammer, "I—I have attempted to do p-portraits, but I fear I have found the, er, human ear most difficult to capture. I'm afraid I confine my limited talents to still life. Things with well-defined lines and surfaces that don't move about."

"I believe you have packed your pencils and paints, so you must display your skills for us while you are here," Sitter prompted, smiling and nodding encouragement for her to expand on the topic.

Marke drew a deep breath and smiled back. She had committed herself to this task, unpleasant as it seemed, and so she supposed it best to jump right in with both feet. Besides, she simply would not allow this man to reduce her to missish stammers and blushes thus proving his every assessment of her correct. "Certainly, Sitter. If that will amuse you, then unquestionably I shall oblige, but you must allow that I am the least talented one in my family."

"Oh, and how can that be considered so?" Sitter asked with seemingly great interest and head-bobbing encouragement.

The marquis merely grunted and stared over Marke's head at, well, whatever was behind her. She barely resisted the urge to twist in her chair and follow his gaze, for surely it must be something of great interest for such a large amount of rudeness on his part while she was speaking. Then, her resolve strengthened by his rancor, she point-

edly ignored him and turned her dazzling smile upon Sitter
again.

"My sister Mercy writes poetry. Her words are absolutely lyrical, and she is capable of drawing emotions pre-
viously unknown from one's soul. And then, of course,
Mary Elizabeth is a most accomplished pianist. She has
been featured at more than one musical evening. Sarah
plays the cello, and one could not help but say that Josephine creates masterpieces with her baking."

"Such a variety of talents," Sitter mused. "And all in
one family. Don't you agree, Claymore?"

Claymore shifted his eyes from the object of interest behind Marke's head to Sitter's face, giving her a look as if to
say *please spare me your social prattle, for I am in no mood*
before expelling a sigh of sheer exasperation. Picking up his
fork, he pushed the steamed fowl about his plate one, two,
three times, then violently flung the sterling down upon the
china with a loud clatter, eliciting a small shriek from Sitter and bringing three of the five footmen leaping to attention.

"A man cannot be expected to garner strength on this
pallid, tasteless fare! I need sustenance, by damn!" he
swore loudly.

Sitter's hand flew to her throat in distress. "Really,
Claymore, your language is deplorable! It's regressing further into the taproom every day! I will not allow you to
speak that way in the presence of company. And you, of all
people, should certainly understand that the diet John has
regimented is for your own good."

Marke glanced from her own plate to his. She had so
thoroughly enjoyed the rich turtle soup that she had not
noticed the marquis might not have had the same. But now
she would see that her plate of roasted pork tenderloin,
with pears and prunes, and spiced apple loaf was far su-
perior to his fare of pale steamed fowl and vegetables boiled
to limp submission. She jumped when the marquis turned
to her abruptly, fixing her with a forbidding stare.

"And your opinion, Miss, er, Penwell? Do you also think
it suits a man's recovery to starve him to skin and bones?"

"Ah, well—actually no, I do not. I would think a rich beef broth would strengthen the body more than—" she peered uncertainly at his plate "—well, whatever that is. But, of course I would not presume to counter the doctor's orders. I am sure he must—"

Claymore threw his hands in the air as if all were against him and bellowed, each time louder than the last. "Bull! Bull! And *bull!* Then I'll damn well not eat at all!"

"Claymore!" Sitter squeaked, so appalled at his continued use of strong language in company, especially the company of such a young miss, that she became quite flushed and fanned herself vigorously with her dinner napkin. The marquis, even with his indignant outrage, was pouting like a little boy, his brows pulled down into a straight line and his lower lip pushed out in childish defiance. They both were so outrageously serious in their separate dramas that Marke quite forgot polite company manners and burst out laughing, drawing startled stares from both directions. Sitter's eyes grew quite round in disbelief, and the marquis glowered at her in a most uncivilized manner.

"So, Miss Penwell, you find the fact that they are intent upon starving me to my death vastly amusing," he growled in a manner positively threatening.

"What so greatly amuses me, my lord, is to see you acting as if every aspect of your life is entirely in someone else's hands," she countered, her characteristic frankness restored by her laugh.

"And I assume *you*, in all your vast wisdom, have a different view of things?" he demanded sarcastically. The curl of his lip gave vent to his thoughts on her wisdom.

As the marquis so obviously expected her to shrink before his wrath and slither down in her chair to disappear beneath the table, Marke instinctually straightened. She refused to be intimidated by an oppressor or hold her silence any longer. It was time someone put him in his place, and since Sitter seemed incapable of doing so with any degree of efficiency, then apparently she must see to it herself.

"Yes, actually I do. It's just that from where I am seated, I have full view of the sideboard there—" she waved her hand toward the ornate sideboard behind Sitter "—whereupon rests a saddle of roasted pork of a size to feed a family of ten for a week. I do not comprehend why, if you are feeling so deprived, that you do not order the attention of a footman, and once you have that attention, simply demand he carve a sizable slice and serve you. And if my opinion is further solicited, I should recommend chancing that one right there—" she indicated one young man quite smaller than the rest "—for he looks to be of a size to quail before childish ranting and raving."

"Humph!" Claymore grunted again. He glared defiantly at her, then turned to glare at the roasted pork taking up a full half of the sideboard, and finally at the nervous young footman swiveling his eyes from the marquis to his fellow footmen as if judging the support he could expect should the marquis leap at him with the fires of hell bursting from his nostrils.

Marke fought the urge to grin at the marquis. She could almost see the wheels of reason turning in his head. Lifting her crystal wineglass to study its delicate etching of grape cluster motif in the silence at the table, she finally prompted, "Go ahead, Lord Perfect. There is no one to stop you. And, as you are in plain sight of the footman, I do not think he will become disorientated between the sideboard and the table. But, just in case, I assure you I shall keep a diligent watch, and stand ready to instigate vigorous hand signals should he look the slightest bit confused as to your direction."

Claymore brought his speculative gaze back upon Marke. The chit, he thought. All nutmeg brown and golden, and sporting an unruly mouth if he'd ever seen one. But the worst part of it, she spoke with a great deal of logic...damn her.

Sitter seemed to be holding her breath, pressing her napkin tightly against her mouth, swiveling eyes from one to the other. Judging by her horrified expression, she obviously expected Lord Perfect to heap the worst abuse imaginable upon poor Marke's head. Marke did not vary her gaze but returned the marquis's stare evenly. When she saw his brown eyes soften, the corners crinkling into a tiny starburst of lines, and his mouth spread into a grin that brought out the most charming dimple in his right cheek, she giggled delightfully.

"Well, I do suppose John has his reasons for what he does, disagreeable though they may seem," Claymore finally admitted, then the grin slipped into oblivion and he resumed eating his pallid fare with more resignation than enthusiasm.

Sitter allowed her breath to escape in tiny little slips and carefully restored her napkin to her lap, as if afraid to disturb the air of tentative peace in the company.

Marke took up her utensils and resumed her meal, also, maintaining her silence as she felt she had created quite enough stir for one meal. She was sorry if she had upset Sitter, and she must remember to apologize to the young footman for placing him in such peril, but it was just too much to bear, watching the marquis indulge in infantile temper in the presence of all. A little public chastising should teach him humility and, who could tell, might be beneficial to his health, as well. Most assuredly, it had aided Marke's and Sitter's digestion to turn the black expression that normally marred his good looks into one of congeniality and warmth, even for so brief a time.

Chapter Six

"It's a woolen day," Marke admonished herself as she pulled a shawl-necked sweater of cream-hued merino over her head. That was an expression she remembered her mother saying every morning of her life from the appearance of autumn's first yellow leaf to the first brave show of spring's crocus in the garden. This morning reminded her of the familiar expression as she glanced out the window, watching the mist lift to a day promising to be cool and clear. As much as she loved summer's freshness, she welcomed its retreat. Autumn came as eagerly to Ireland as Marke's desire to be out in it. Gathering her pencil box and sketching tablet, and slinging her utility bag over her shoulder, she dashed out of her room and skipped down the stairs with a clatter of good humor. Heaven stood at the bottom, having apparently been watching for her descent.

"Ahem, good morning, miss. His lordship is in the library."

"Oh, thank you, Heaven. Is he wishing to see me?"

"Not that I am aware, miss."

Marke's brow creased for a moment in confusion, then cleared as the truth dawned on her. Obviously the majordomo was giving her the marquis's direction of his own accord. Or possibly of Sitter's accord. She gave him a wide smile and a wink. "Oh, I see. Plotting against our master now, are we?" she teased.

The elderly man would only bow his already bent body forward stiffly and murmur, "If that is how you wish it stated, miss."

"Is he alone, or has Mrs. Sittlemeyer descended stairs already?"

"He is alone, miss."

Marke worried her bottom lip between her teeth. It was extremely presumptuous of her to barge in on the man without having been issued an invitation, but then, wasn't that why she was here? To be presumptuous and irritating enough to overwhelm the man with the joys of being alive? Not such a difficult thing for her, if one believed her sisters' slander over the years. Ever optimistic and oppressively joyful, they called her. She hoisted the bag higher on her shoulder and swung off in the direction of the library in a long stride that was ideal for tramping about the woods. Noisily rounding the door frame, she slid to a halt. The marquis was seated before the fire with a shawl tucked over his legs, looking the perfect part of a pensive invalid.

Disrupted from his reading, Claymore glanced up to see Marke staring about her in apparent awe, as if she were too much a hoyden to be allowed access to the library at home. A flicker of irritation brought his eyebrows down in a disagreeable frown. He had no wish to be disturbed this morning, or anytime in fact, by the meaningless chatter of a giddy, untutored schoolgirl with an unruly mouth.

Marke met his cold eyes, shivered slightly, then flashed a delightful grin as if having no doubts in the world of her welcome. "Good gracious, never have I seen so many books in one place!"

Claymore glanced around him, attempting to see the room through her eyes. The bookshelves ran to the ceiling on all four walls, filled with multicolored leather book spines, offering knowledge on just about every subject imaginable. He supposed it would be an imposing sight to one not inured to such as he was. "Yes, there does appear to be quite a lot of them, doesn't there? And does such extravagant abundance seem ridiculous to you, Miss Penwell?"

"Good Lord, not in the least," she retorted, as if that were a silly question to be asked. "It simply makes me want to start in one corner and read, and read, and read. Persevering until I have discovered the author's purpose for writing each and every one of them. Cover to cover, so to speak."

"That might take a great deal of one's life, don't you think?" he said with an inward sigh. He hadn't meant to encourage more pointless chatter from the girl. He smoothed the page of his book in a gesture that he hoped was a transparent indication of his wish to continue his reading undisturbed.

The gesture was not lost on Marke. It made her uncomfortable to appear blatantly obtuse, but his desire to see her gone was so disagreeably obvious she found herself taking no small degree of pleasure in thwarting him. She merely hoisted her bag higher on her shoulder and moved to lean against the chair opposite Claymore. "Yes, I suppose it might. And that would seem a shame, don't you think?" she challenged. "To focus so stridently upon one objective, and one objective alone, in a world of bountiful delights of such variety to discover?"

Silence filled the room. Finally deciding she was going to insist upon an answer to what he had hoped was a rhetorical question, Claymore replied flatly, "Then I take it, Miss Penwell, that you are not an advocate of setting goals and remaining nose to the grindstone until that goal is obtained?"

"Goals, and the wherewithal to see them through, are fine things I suppose, as long as one does not neglect to raise one's head once in a while to ascertain the goal is still worthwhile," she countered. Crossing to the window, she noted with gratitude that it gathered the north light. If she must be trapped indoors on such a glorious day, at least finding agreeable light was a slight compensation. Without preamble, she dumped her artist accoutrements in a pile on the window seat of goat leather, calling to him over her shoulder, "I do hope you do not mind my joining you this morning, Lord Perfect."

Claymore lifted an eyebrow in her direction as she settled comfortably against the window and opened her pencil case without benefit of his answer. "It appears it signifies little whether I mind or not, but it seems as if you had planned a day out-of-doors," he drawled caustically, his eyes sweeping over her plaid woolen skirt and walking boots with significant meaning.

Marke chose to ignore his sarcasm and smiled sweetly. "Only an original idea that is easily changed. I thought, this morning, I would work on a still life I am presenting to my sister as a Christmas gift." Gathering her sketchbook, she carried it across the room to exhibit her drawing of summer squash, pumpkins and three varieties of mushrooms. "As a man of letters, and the owner of such a vast collection of books, perhaps you would venture an opinion of my talent. Is it a presentable Christmas offering?" she queried. She saw no need to inform him that every member of her family had amassed collections of her still life drawings already—each and every one dutifully framed and hung upon the wall with apparent pride for all to see.

Claymore studied the excellent line of delicate pencilings and glowing warm colors for a moment with some surprise. It really was quite charming. He glanced up at her expectant face and teased her dryly. "I am no critic, but it would seem you have a marked fascination with fungi, Miss Penwell. Particularly the many varieties of, er, mushrooms are they?"

"Well, Lord Perfect, I do not consider them to be vegetable outcasts, if that is what you mean. And I assure you that I have not deliberately focused on things others do not care about." She sniffed at his comment and deftly removed her pad from his hand. "I happen to view mushrooms as beautiful and shall make no apologies for them. The paintings are not meant for scientific study, but little portraits. In my watercolors and drawings, mushrooms are individuals with real character. There is a power behind them that has nothing to do with science."

"Sorcery now, Miss Penwell?"

"Of course not. It's just as each day brings pleasant episodes, so does each collecting trip. And as time rolls on they become bright spots which the memory loves to refer to. You see, when the cold, dark days of winter arrive and I am housebound near the fire, I turn to my sketchbook. Each page delights me with a record of pleasant recollections. Oh, of some little woodland glen where I've walked, some private nook I discover where wildflowers bloomed in stunning abundance. That sort of thing."

"I see," Claymore muttered, his interest waning. He shifted the heavy tome on his lap and smoothed the page with a fine hand, seeking to pick up the thread of his reading. "As for the Christmas present, I think it would entirely depend upon your true feelings for that particular sister."

Marke blinked in surprise. Whatever was he implying? That she must hate Josephine to give her one of her terrible drawings? Oh, of all the loftiness! "I happen to like my sister immensely," she retorted, turning her back on his disregard and returning to the window seat. Settling herself, she leaned against the wall and drew her knees up for a makeshift easel. The marquis was a man who deserved to be snubbed, she fumed. Tilting her pad to catch the strong north light, she drew forth a sharpened pencil, determined to do just that.

As the silence lengthened in the room, broken only by the snap of the fire, Claymore glanced up at Marke, resumed reading, then glanced up again. She looked such a young thing, sitting in the window seat with her knees drawn up, playing with her pencils. He paused to study her, surprised to find that she really was fetching with the strong light falling on her disarrayed curls. There was certainly something about her that must be appreciated. Her cheeks were richly colored with good health and sunshine. She was rather boyish, but it was a dainty boyishness that in no way marred her femininity. There was about her a disconcerting combination of innocence and frankness which, together with the charm of her gender, was certain to fix the attention of any mere male with an eye for the ladies. And if her behavior at Innisfree was any indication, once turned loose on society, Miss Penwell was bound to be one that both gentlemen and ladies instinctively discussed with different degrees of interest.

Claymore grimaced at his thoughts. He could not lay blame for her presence at Innisfree upon her own shoulders, now could he? Sitter must be taken to task for that! He felt a twinge of guilt for having hurt her feelings. It would not have altered his life one bit to have paid compliment instead of sarcasm to her pencilings, for in truth, the work was quite good. With a short snort of irritation at the unwelcome feeling, he closed his book, trapping a finger as bookmark. He really was becoming a bore, he thought, to be rude to children. Resolutely he set about amending his behavior, although from politeness rather than interest. "And which sister is this? From your conversation of last night, I gather there are Penwells aplenty?"

Marke looked up in surprise. Now this was a good sign, wasn't it? A display of healthy curiosity? Sitter had described him as morose and sullen. And while he did not appear more agreeable this morning than the other occasions she'd had to study him, she would take a willingness to engage in conversation as an encouragement. A positive sign, if you will. She gave him a bright smile as reward.

"This drawing is for Josephine . . ." she began, studying her prey. Seated in an upholstered wingback instead of the invalid chair, he looked remarkably healthy. He was attired in a becoming shade of dark brown pantaloons strapped over shiny half boots, cinnamon morning robe, patterned saffron waistcoat, and his shirt was left open to show the smooth skin of his neck. A belcher handkerchief of the most startling persimmon was carelessly knotted about his throat. With no conscious mental direction, she began to sketch his polite face in revealing strokes, taking time to jot quick notes in the margins as to colors.

"Ah, yes, the one who cooks," he muttered.

"Yes, the one who *cooks*. And quite beautifully, too!" replied Marke tartly. She would not stand for criticism of her sister, as well as her drawing. "Also the one who is promised to a schoolmaster for a spring wedding, which will be attended by all the *numerous* Penwells. You see, I am the ninth of nine Penwell children.''

''It must have been marvelous growing up in a large family,'' Claymore mused, unaware of the note of wistfulness that crept into his voice.

Bringing her eyes up to study his face, Marke started to delve into the unexpected wistfulness, but remembered in time that she would be broaching a very painful subject. And to do so would undoubtedly have incited the man's despotic temper.

She flipped the page and captured the sad, wistful little boy in quick strokes as she answered him. ''I would agree, for the most part, with the description of 'marvelous,' although I would liken my childhood to a large litter of puppies. One does tend to get lost in the pack unless one is very demanding of a fair share.''

Claymore snorted. He could well imagine this one, so forthright and gregarious, as most demanding of her fair share. ''And were you lost in the pack, Miss Penwell?''

Marke stopped to ponder that question a moment, then decided to answer truthfully. ''Well, not lost as much as never quite fitting in. Standing on the outside, so to speak. You see, I am quite different from the rest, in coloring as well as in attitude.''

Her candid answer piqued his interest in earnest. He withdrew his finger from his book and absently smoothed a hand over the embossed leather of the cover while studying her. Although not for the past year, he was known to move widely in the circles of the ton, and he could not place any Penwells among his acquaintance. There was something, possibly only diversion, that led him to prompt her to expound on the subject. ''And pray tell, just who is Miss Margaret Penwell? And what makes her different from the rest of the puppies?''

Marke laughed gently. Funny he would pick up on her euphemism of puppies. She turned to a new page and began to sketch this new, more pleasant, expression as she told her story. ''Mrs. P's ninth child is called Margaret

Catherine Penwell, and nicknamed Marke for an obscure reason only her mother fathoms, for none of the others have nicknames at all. She was the only Penwell offspring lucky enough to be born at St. Catherine's Court, and as she grew up, she continuously fabricated the tale that the house was named for her—'' she flashed him a brilliant smile ''—and not the other way around. The day she was born was the eleventh birthday of Thomas Horace Penwell, Mrs. P's first child, and only son. It has been said that more attention was lavished upon the birthday celebration than on the newest addition of the Penwell family. And, being a well-mannered, undemanding infant, an easily self-amused youngster, and an amazingly intuitive young woman, it never got any better. Perhaps she always knew she would one day suddenly strain against that stereotype.''

She paused to raise her eyes to the view of the bay stretching out far below her with a slightly pensive expression. ''One day when the winter wind has blown for weeks at a time, when people are forced to walk along at a slant, struggling against a storm, when the rain has beaten down even the most resilient head...'' She turned her eyes to his, lost for a moment in the rapt expression he was showing her. The man was really too startlingly beautiful, she thought. Flashing her brilliant smile again, Marke finished gaily, ''She will rebel in such a way that they will all stare at her with mouths agape, and perhaps see her clearly for the first time.''

Claymore, intent on the rapidly changing expressions on her funny, little face, pondered the girl. There was something about her that, well, he wasn't sure what, but he felt the knot of tension in his neck and shoulders ease somewhat. There was something strikingly calm about her. Something guileless and genuine. He even smiled a bit as he suggested at last, ''That makes you, from a large family, sound as lonely as I, the only child of very self-absorbed parents.''

Marke wanted to ply him with questions about his parents, but instead she laughed gently and returned to her sketches. She was pleased with her quick lines, deciding she had captured him very well. The three sketches showed a diverse, complex man operating under a great emotion. She flipped the sheets back to the charcoal-and-ink drawing of her still life. "Perhaps a bit, but there are too many exciting sectors of life to dwell much on one small missing piece of it. I am not unhappy. I would rather my mother was not failing as she is, but..." She shrugged complacently.

"Yes, God does have his way of exacting revenge upon the soul in the most devastating fashion," Claymore complained bitterly, dropping the book onto the floor beside the chair with a loud thud.

Marke pursed her lips. She had no wish to begin a spiritual discussion with him. Her views were not the most popular and, once the discussion commenced, it could only end in argument. She was not one for blaming every terrible catastrophe in life on a nonvisual, nonverbal entity. She believed more in acceptance. Accepting what could not be changed, and accepting responsibility for what could. Realizing the marquis was waiting for an answer, she hedged, "Revenge? Oh, I can not condone bestowing life with the capacity to take aim against me in any way, vengeful or rewarding. It's just that, well..."

"It's just what? Finish your thought." Claymore prompted, leaning forward, watching her lively face closely, desperate to glean an answer from her if she might have one. There was something about her that prompted the unconscious feeling that perhaps she had a lifeline to throw to draw him from his drowning pool of misery. Again he was unaware that the misery he felt was mirrored clearly in his eyes.

Marke's heart reached out to him, and she smiled gently to lessen what she feared he might take as harsh insight on her part. "Sometimes life throws dirt in great black clods upon our windowpanes, and isn't always possible to *not* think it was thrown there on purpose. You know, scraped from cold hearths, dredged from stagnant bogs, with only *our* windows in mind. It's simply that things happen. Birth happens—" she softened her voice "—death happens. Love and... and cursing—"

"Cursing?" he interjected, jerking upright to stare at her.

"Of course, cursing," she avowed, tilting eyebrows upward with innocent conviction. "You cannot *possibly* think that those terrible words that fly from your lips are carefully thought out!"

The statement was so wonderfully absurd that Claymore threw back his head and laughed heartily. It was a clear, wonderful sound, starting at the belly and rumbling upward. It was a healing sound, Marke thought, greatly pleased with herself. But then his laughter brought about a fit of coughing, deep and racking, that seemed never to stop and when it did finally pass, left him slumped, pale and exhausted, in his chair. Marke rushed to the sideboard to fetch a glass of water. Returning, she set it next to him and placed a cool hand on his brow. While he did not feel feverish, perhaps he was more ill than she had thought. Oh, why had she pushed so far, she reproached herself, although how was she to know that laughing could be so detrimental.

Irritated by her open show of concern, Claymore brusquely waved her away. "It's nothing! Only slight smoke damage to the lungs. John Barrows assures me it will get better, but—" he made a rude gesture toward his body as if it were an enemy to be abhorred "—it has been a twelvemonth already."

"More time—" Marke began, only to have him jerk violently away from her with a dark, scathing glare.

"Bah, *time!* As if that is all it will take to right the wrongs of the world!" he scoffed, turning his attention away from her. "If you would please ring for someone, Miss Penwell, I am ready to retire."

His manner was so suddenly withdrawn that Marke held her tongue and simply did as he asked. When Henry arrived, she politely turned her back and busied herself with her tablets and pencils as he took his seat in the invalid chair Dr. Barrows swore he no longer needed. He was wheeled from the library with no word to her. But even with his coughing, and withdrawal behind a wall of self-pity, she would count this morning's work as successful. She felt she had made an improvement in his day. She had drawn his thoughts away from the dead and back among the living for a small portion of it at least.

Dropping into the leather cushions of the window seat, she stared out the window instead of retrieving her drawing pad. Empathy filled her chest for the marquis's grief. So much sadness and anger locked tightly inside one man was not good. Dr. Barrows was right to think he might easily self-destruct. Suddenly she wanted more than anything to be the one to ease his suffering. To be the one to bring merriment and laughter back into his life. She felt helpless before it all, and yet hadn't she made him smile last night and laugh outright this morning?

"That cannot be considered too helpless, Margaret Catherine," she admonished herself with a shameless grin, suddenly very pleased with herself and eager to seek out Sitter with a full accounting.

Chapter Seven

On the third day following the incident in the library, after which the marquis had unequivocally refused to leave his chambers, Heaven broke every oath of service he diligently upheld and confided to Marke that for two of those three days, the marquis had refused to leave his bed or take nourishment.

Marke was at a loss for a suitable manner in which to correct any blunder she might have committed, a blunder so terrible as to send the marquis to bed to starve. She sought Sitter for a long stroll. Confined indoors by ill weather, they toured the expansive portrait gallery in the long hallways. Bundled against the chill of the stone walls and floors in the unheated corridors, she tucked her hand in the crook of the older woman's arm and drew her close.

"Oh, Sitter, I am most distressed. I can think of nothing I might have said to bring about this terrible withdrawal on Lord Perfect's part."

"Oh now, Marke, you must not blame yourself. Of course, you did nothing wrong. It's with no small degree of depression that I admit this is just the way it is. Each time Claymore approaches life with any interest, he immediately follows it with a desperate sinking, then he withdraws from everyone and everything. It's been a sad pattern, I'm afraid to say." She shook her head and sighed deeply.

Marke worried her lower lip with uncertainty. She was still unclear on the place Sitter occupied in the family and, while she was desperate to find a way to draw the marquis

forward, she felt some attempt must be made to remain
sensitive to any painful subject for Sitter's sake. But how
was she to help if she didn't know certain things? Well, as
her father said, turn before the wind and let it run, so with
a deep breath, she launched her ship in uncertain waters.

"Sitter, perhaps you should tell me more of the family,
his parents...the tragedy," she suggested tentatively,
glancing at the woman's face to gauge her reaction. "I
don't wish to pry where I shouldn't. And I wouldn't for the
world wish to cause you undue pain. Can't have you retir-
ing to your bed as well to escape my blundering about, can
we? I just wish to be aware of any storm on the horizon, so
to speak."

Sitter smiled down at her young cohort, patting her hand
appreciatively. "Marke, you mustn't be overly concerned
about my own feelings. I do so appreciate your sensitivity,
but I have completed my grieving in the healthiest of manners possible, by kicking, wailing and shaking my fists at
God—" she demonstrated such with a laugh "—and have
since come to grips with my loss of dear Edward."

Marke glanced down quickly to hide her expression. Edward? Claymore's *father!* So Sitter's attachment had been
to the elder Marquis of Boothe-Ashmore! A virtual flood
of inexplicable joy surged through her. Then, before she
had time to wonder at the strange feelings, they were
quickly replaced with sadness for the older woman and the
loss of her loved one. She grasped Sitter's hands to squeeze
them affectionately. "Oh, Sitter! I am so sorry for your
loss. I have no wish to pry into private things, but I do so
long to help. And I applaud your strength and straightforwardness with me. It makes things so much easier in the
long run, don't you think?"

Sitter smiled into Marke's eyes, seeing past the youth and
inexperience of a girlish prankster, into a very tender soul
weeping for another's pain. She pulled her gently to a padded deacon's bench along the wall. "Marke, being gently
reared as you undoubtedly were, I can only imagine your
thoughts of me, but you are mistaken to deem there was

anything, well, truly seedy about the alliance between Edward and myself."

"Oh, Sitter, I could never think too terribly of you," Marke rushed to assure the woman.

Sitter placed her fingertips against Marke's lips to still her protest. "Edward and I were great friends, as well as lovers, and I have no doubt that given different circumstances, we would have wed. It all began a long time ago, and Edward provided for me very handsomely over many years. And because of this, I have an excellent house with adequate income and servants to make me comfortable during my old age, so I am not unhappy."

"And Claymore, er, Lord Perfect, always knew of your existence?" Marke asked. It seemed such a strange thing to her, that he should embrace his father's mistress, rather than show disdain of his father's infidelity to his mother.

"Yes, Edward generously included Claymore in his small secondary family, at quite an early age. I fear Elizabeth Perfect was, unfortunately, of an obsessive personality. From Claymore's first year on, she experienced one miscarriage or stillbirth after another. The poor woman dwelled so heavily on the babies she lost, or failed to carry to birth, that she allowed no time whatsoever to attend or love the one son she did have. When Libby was finally born, Elizabeth doted on her as if protecting a miracle from the cruelties of a harsh world. And I suppose it was only natural for the child to be the darling of her parents. You see, Libby was only five to Claymore's nine and twenty when she perished in the fire."

"Oh, how terrible," Marke whispered, without understanding clearly herself, whether it was to the poor Libby or the grieving Claymore that she referred.

"Yes, it is, and in my heart, I credit Claymore's depression to feelings of guilt. I fear he feels he failed his mother by his inability to rescue his sister from the fire. He truly believes she was the one thing on earth that Elizabeth loved above all else. Perhaps he thought he could win his mother's love by... well..."

"Oh my," murmured Marke.

"I do not care what has been written to the contrary, I steadfastly hold that, adult though they may be, a person never stops yearning for the love of their parent if deprived of it in childhood," Sitter said.

Marke glanced up, startled at such an astute statement from a normally flighty lady. She thought of her own father, absent so much of her life. "I suppose so, but do you think such feelings are something one can overcome? Such a frantic desire for something that is, now more than ever, unobtainable."

"I can well understand your thoughts. But, my dear, you have known Claymore such a short time, and therefore can have no measurable idea of the marvelous man he truly is. Before the fire, his life was pretty much as he would wish it in every way. He was crème de la crème of the ton. Much sought after by the gents, as well as the ladies. Strongly placed in his contacts, delving into parliament and having his views well received, and a favorite of both the king and the queen. He was truly blessed with a brilliant future."

"And is there no one in his life...?" Marke began, then halted. Suddenly she did not want to know if he was enamored of someone. Somehow, perhaps beyond her own comprehension, it was very important that she not be presented with a picture of the handsome marquis with affections engaged. She shook her head to clear it of such stupid concerns and chided herself. She must not allow sympathy for the man to shadow her opinion of his basic nature. It made no difference to her if he had a string of west end comets a mile long, which he undoubtedly did, she told herself sternly. She gained her feet and smoothed the perfectly agreeable, tarlatan plaid jumper, in all the wrong shades of blue and burgundy for a red-haired girl, and gave Sitter a conspirator's grin. "*That* does not signify in the least, now does it? What is important at this moment, is to rout his lordship from his bed, and from the mental mire he has fallen into."

Sitter took note of the hesitation, and Marke's gently flushed face. She rose to take the girl's hands in her own. "Marke, you are truly a sweet young thing, and have become quite dear to me. But I would caution you against engaging your tender emotions and possibly entertaining hopes and dreams where Claymore is concerned. He is very unpredictable at present, and may be for a long time yet, and if fully recovered has prior obligations.'' She paused, then burst out, "Oh, Marke, I truly have no desire for you to be hurt!''

"I shall take your advice to heart, Sitter, but rest assured that there is no possibility of that occurring,'' Marke reassured. Being too forthright to dissimulate, especially when Sitter had favored her with such personal confidences, she quickly changed the subject. She refused even to acknowledge that weird sense of release she'd felt to discover Sitter's involvement with the elder marquis, and not Claymore. But that aside, at present, she had actions to take and she'd best get to it. "Sitter, if I pen a note to Mrs. Lithgow at St. Catherine's Court, would it be possible for someone to carry it to her? I would like reassurances of my mother's continued state of comfort, as well as request the packing of paints and supplies to be sent to me here.''

"Of course," Sitter said. "You do not even have to make such a request. You must consider Innisfree your home as well now. And Heaven will gladly see to everything. Just run and pen your note.''

"I shall do that just as soon as I have extracted his lordship's cowardly head from beneath his bed covers." Marke spun on her heel and determinedly stalked off, footsteps ringing on the black stones.

Sitter watched the retreating back of the resolute girl with no small amount of trepidation. Although she could not help but wonder, she made no move to inquire as to the exact method for routing that Marke intended to employ upon the unsuspecting Claymore. He was not a pleasant man to confront head-on, and she did not envy Marke the task. In fact, a safe haven might be prescribed for just such an event. Shivering, she drew her pelisse closer about her and hurried off in the direction of her sitting room and its welcoming fire. She would send a note to John, inviting him for tea. They had much to discuss. She fretted that she and the good doctor might be taking unfair advantage of Marke's generous nature. Using her, as it were, to further their own desires with little thought to any damage they might be inflicting upon her young head and tender heart. She sighed a deep sigh. Worry though she might, her first loyalty and regard must be given to Claymore. Edward would have wished it of her and, in fact, would have demanded it.

Conscripting Heaven into her conspiracy, Marke marched upon the marquis's bedchamber. As soon as the majordomo, with a hasty peek around the door, had ascertained an acceptable degree of modesty prevailed—if there was such a thing to be had for the young Miss Penwell's presence in the master's bedchamber—he disloyally stepped aside to allow Marke's abrupt push into the room.

Claymore was propped upon innumerable pillows in a great canopied bed, with a host of books surrounding him. He was miserably staring out the windows at the relentless mist that seemed to enclose Innisfree in its tight embrace. Although the weighty titles might have been tempting at any other time, now the volumes were strewn about the counterpane of purple-covered goose down, clearly abandoned for the dismal view outside the expanse of leadpaned windows on the far wall. He did not deign to lend attention to whoever might have entered his door. There was no curiosity for anything, nor concern for anyone, in his heart. It was on days like these that he was depressed to the point of complete and utter despair.

Marke stood for a moment pondering the marquis. When he did not turn to acknowledge her presence, she stalked straight around the canopied bed to place herself squarely before his eyes.

Claymore's eyes slowly focused upon her, blinked thrice, widened in total disbelief that she would exhibit such gall as to invade the privacy of his bedchamber. "What the bloody hell?" he said through gritted teeth. His mouth turned down petulantly that she should thus disturb him without mercy for his condition.

"What ails you today, my lord?" Marke asked, not unkindly but sternly prepared to repel any self-pity mewling for imagined ailments.

"I'm ill."

"Ill? How ill?"

"Just sort of ill all over. There's no particular pain anywhere, it just hurts everywhere ...." He began to explain, then barked, *"Just ill!"*

Marke stepped to the bed to place a hand on his cool forehead. The marquis took great exception to that and jerked his head away. She quickly decided the man displayed no more symptoms than he normally did, and was therefore merely hiding out to wallow in self-flagellation. Her mouth pursed in a fair imitation of her mother's when examining a sick puppy. Mothers, she reassured herself, as well as future mothers, must be good judges of human nature in their dealings with little boys—and men who acted like little boys.

The situation was so absurd to her, the marquis scowling from his bed and Heaven posted before the door—his purpose, whether to dash back through it if the going become rough or to prevent his lordship's escape, wasn't clear—that a sudden rush of prank overcame her. She fought the twitch of laughter on her lips and totally ignored the scowl on his face as he glared first at her, then at the old man in the doorway. Looking him over frankly in a diagnostic manner, her brown eyes sparking with mischief, she decided at last. "What you need, my good man, is a good cleaning out. I'll just run down to the kitchen, and tell Cook to heat up a pitcher of water. I'm sure she has a liberal amount of salts to throw into it. Then, I'll be right back."

"You shall do no such thing!" Claymore roared with unbelievable strength.

If Marke had not been raised in a family of quarreling, complaining, shrilling female voices that were only silenced by the thunder of a man's resounding shout, she might have cringed in the same intimidated manner that Heaven was exhibiting at that moment, but instead, she merely fussed with the blankets, removing the books and fluffing the indentions from the goose down. "Oh, it is no bother, I promise you. It's a simple enough project. Heaven shall pinch your nose, while I pour the forepart down your bow and your valet can haul the afterpart out though your stern. It's bound to do you a world of good."

"Good Lord! Heaven, has this entire household lost its grip on sanity? Miss Penwell, leave this room immediately!" Claymore ordered in a voice that quite possibly rattled the windowpanes and was clearly meant to brook no disobedience. When Marke did not immediately scurry from the room, and actually exhibited the impertinence of planting both her hands on hips and scowling right back at him, he swore sharply and unwittingly rewarded her with the action she was seeking most of all.

Marke was delighted when he threw the covers back and shakily gained his feet, displaying in the process a pair of well-turned, well-shaped limbs, at least it would seem so to her, having limited experience in such matters.

"Heaven, drag her out!" Claymore bellowed, grasping the bedpost for support. His head felt light from his self-enforced retirement, but anger strengthened his resolve to gain his feet and take charge of this unruly houseguest. "Now, by damn!"

Marke could no longer hide the smile teasing at the corners of her mouth and allowed it free rein. True to her promise to Sitter, she had indeed routed the marquis from his bed, and now considered the battle called for a hasty retreat. She sped around the bed, slipping past Heaven and through the doorway, with the marquis's resonant bellow following her down the hall.

"This is too much, by damn! Is there nowhere in this blasted house that I am safe from infernal female interference?"

Marke laughed aloud, then slapped a muffling hand over her mouth. She had done quite enough disturbing for today. No need to rile him further. More than satisfied with herself, she merrily skipped down the hall toward her room to pen her note to Mrs. Lithgow at St. Catherine's Court.

Chapter Eight

Ensconced in a small drawing room on the third floor, Marke might have been accused of hiding out herself, unless one understood an artist's relentless thirst for the perfect lighting in which to paint with oils. And she was no exception, as she mixed and remixed paint with murmured words of dissatisfaction in a seemingly futile attempt to acquire the exact color of Claymore's walnut curls. Having transferred the most flattering of her sketches to the easeled canvas, she was dedicated to finishing a satisfactory portrait before the holiday season. Confident of her skills, she was determined to make the marquis eat his unkind remarks about her drawing in large chunks, and with his Yuletide feast. Besides, painting, requiring concentration and focus, relaxed her and calmed the restlessness the wet weather and inactivity generated.

Heaven, the only one besides Sitter to know of her sanctuary here, paused in the doorway and cleared his throat gently, intent upon drawing her attention without startling her.

Marke glanced up with a smile for the gentle old man. "Yes, Heaven?"

"I am sorry to disturb you, Miss Penwell, but his lordship has requested you join him in the library, if you are not otherwise engaged."

Marke's eyes grew large in her face and her lower lip disappeared between her teeth. "He asked for me?" she squeaked. "Specifically?"

"Yes, miss. Specifically."

"And did he happen to say in what reference?"

"Not to me, miss."

Marke replaced her lip with the wooden tip of her paint-brush and bit down sharply. She supposed, at best, she should expect a severe reprimand for her outrageous be-havior the day before, and at worst, an abrupt ejection from the house, although nothing had been mentioned of the incident the previous night at dinner. True enough, the marquis had been withdrawn and surly, eating little of his pallid fare but not otherwise giving the appearance of be-ing inordinately put out with her. Well, whatever the con-sequences, she decided, it would have been worth it to witness Sitter's blatant relief at having him out of bed, smartly attired and below stairs again.

"Please inform Lord Perfect that I shall be with him momentarily," she instructed, then reluctantly began to put away her paints and clean her brushes. Whatever it was, it might as well be faced in an expedient manner. Best to eat one's spinach first than to stare at it on one's plate throughout the whole of the meal, she reasoned. Stepping back to squint at the portrait taking shape beneath her brush, she was pleased with what she had accomplished thus far. The shape of the face was strong, the nose noble, the eyes just the right shade of warm brown with golden glints, and the mouth curved in a smile that brought forth his dimple—if memory served her—for she could count the number of times that she had witnessed his good humor on one finger, she thought sourly. With a childish itch, she thought to dash a fine pair of horns and black, pointed chin whiskers on the portrait. It would serve the marquis right to be presented with a truly accurate picture of himself on Christmas morn, she thought. Then, before the tempta-tion became too strong to resist, she dashed down the cor-ridor to freshen herself before bearding the lion in his den.

Tapping lightly on the library door, Marke slipped in-side without waiting for the marquis's bid to enter. Paus-ing beside the door, she consciously forced her shoulders to relax, as they wanted to climb stiffly toward her ears in nervousness. This all felt remarkably familiar, similar to being summoned into Thomas's library to have her deplorable habits listed in great detail.

Claymore glanced up from his book to see her standing uncertainly by the door. "Come in. Come in," he prompted with a wave of his hand. "Surely one as stouthearted as you could not be faltering before my presence...out of bed, that is?"

Marke blushed and hated herself for it, for being so transparent. "Of course not! Do not be absurd!" she denied emphatically, jerking away from the door. She swallowed the retort that if he didn't growl like a lion and grate like a bear most of the time, perhaps others might seek his company more readily. She stalked across the room and plopped unceremoniously into the chair opposite the marquis, only resisting the urge to glare openly at him by dropping her eyes to her hands, neatly folded and falsely contrite, in her lap.

Claymore smiled at her obvious discomfort. True enough, he'd been sufficiently angry yesterday to throttle the chit for her audacity to invade his bedchamber, but then the very thought of her tenacity had begun to tickle him. It pleased him now to increase her discomfort as she had his the day before. "Do you wish to share something with me, Miss Penwell?" he asked in a stern voice. "Judging by the flaming color in your cheeks, I am justified in thinking you are operating under strong emotions of some sort." When she did not raise her head, he lifted his frosty glass from the table at his elbow to touch it lightly against her flushed cheek.

It was cool on her skin, and Marke looked up, startled. "No! I mean, th-there's nothing," she stammered. Quite taken aback by his soft teasing, she swiped away the damp from her cheek with hasty fingers.

Claymore watched her startled eyes loom large in her face with amusement. "Do you know, Miss Penwell, you look just like a startled fawn. A fawn with limpid brown eyes," he said, swirling the liquid about his glass before taking a sip.

Muddled that his eyes should glimmer so warmly with
amusement, Marke leaned back in her chair, wishing to put
as much distance between them as possible. Her cheeks
flushed even more brightly beneath his teasing. A surge of
irritation welled up inside her, much of which was directed
at herself. How could she stammer and stutter like a
schoolgirl the very moment he spoke sweetly to her? Her
embarrassment altered to suspicion at this sudden change
in him. It just went to show, Marke decided quickly, what
a practiced charmer he was. Being of the greatly advanced
age of thirty, there was no doubt he'd stalked many women.
Of course, she thought with sudden dawning, he was one
of the men Thomas had droned on and on about. Men who
excelled in the ways of seduction and in melting the de-
fenses of unaware misses. Her eyes narrowed specula-
tively. Well, Lord Perfect, I will acknowledge that you are
a dangerous man, but I have no intention of joining your
crew of conquests! You shall never boast at Whites that you
shanghaied Miss Margaret Catherine Penwell even before
she bent her knee to the queen.

Claymore tilted an eyebrow upward. Whatever could
have set the girl to such frowns, he thought. He watched her
teeth worry her full bottom lip. She looked quite pretty today, less of a child, in a morning gown of russet merino.
The color was a nice match for her eyes and brought out the
creaminess of her complexion. With her unruly red curls
somewhat tamed, he thought, she would be quite pretty
indeed—for a bothersome chit, that is. "Why are you
frowning in such a way, Miss Penwell," he drawled. "Have
I trod upon your feelings in some forward manner?"

Marke blushed again at her apparent transparency, and
rose so hastily that she almost tripped on the hem of her
gown. Straightening, she sought to recover her dignity with
stiff hauteur. "You must forgive me, Lord Perfect. I was
given the impression by Heaven that you wished to see me
concerning some important matter. I can see he was obviously mistaken."

Now it was Claymore's turn to frown. "Of course, I
asked Heaven to seek you out. Now, be seated, for God's

sake! It's nothing to go flying about the boughs. It's simply a letter forwarded from St. Catherine's Court. From your mother, I suppose."

"My mother!" Marke exclaimed. She knew that was not possible. Could it be from Mrs. Lithgow? Was something wrong? She dropped back into the chair, whereupon Claymore tossed the missive into her lap. Snatching it up, she breathed a great sigh of relief to see Thomas's haphazard script sprawled across the cover. "Oh, it's just from Thomas. Probably with instructions on deportment, admonishments to remain frugal, and reprimands on my deplorable character, called up to the mast to answer charges of misconduct, so to speak."

"Ah, well that is the role an older brother plays in a sister's life, is it not? Although I do not see how he could possibly be privy to your most current rampaging actions so quickly," he drawled sarcastically. His energy suddenly drained, he wished he had merely sent the letter to the girl with Heaven, rather than calling her down to the library. Retrieving a book from the table, he flipped open the cover in as good a dismissing gesture as he could affect.

Marke, perceiving he was blatantly no longer interested in her letter, nor her continued presence for that matter, stood up and tucked it into her pocket. She was fully prepared to grant him with great pleasure the expedience of her departure. The man displayed moods like quicksilver, she thought. One never knew what to expect from him, and it was becoming tiresome, to say the least. "Thank you for the letter, Lord Perfect. I shall just have time to read it, and perhaps draft an answer before luncheon."

"Bah, luncheon," he snorted, flipping pages rapidly. "A dubious pleasure I shall forgo, thank you."

"Oh, but you must eat to regain your strength," she began to protest, only to have him present the flat of his palm in her face to silence her.

"Do not presume to lecture me, Miss Penwell," he advised. "I fear I shall not take kindly to your highhandedness this morning."

"Oh, but I must insist—"

"No, by damn! No!" he bellowed, slamming his hand down on the book.

Marke clamped her mouth shut and drew herself erect. "Then I'm sure you will excuse me, my lord." With her head in the air, she spun on her heel and exited the room without granting him time to reply. Muttering furiously to herself, she bounded up the stairs toward her room. But the thought of being confined within four walls with so much anger was not palatable to her. Nor did she dare return to her painting, for to do so would most definitely result in unflattering alterations. Hurrying to her room, she flung off the morning gown in favor of a woolen skirt, shawl-necked sweater and sturdy walking boots. There was only one thing to do and that was take to the cliffs and head-lands, where she could vent her feelings for the odious, unpredictable, imperious tyrant without fearing recriminations from anyone.

Kicking at loose stones in her path, heedless of the drizzle that seeped through the cap thrust down over her eyes, she felt the tension slipping from her body. Lifting her face to the wet, she breathed the moisture deep into her lungs and exhaled joyously. Calmer, she was able to assess the situation in a more rational light, although an acceptable excuse for feeling so extremely put out by the marquis was totally beyond her. All she could do was admit to feeling quite disturbed, when in fact she should be feeling nothing. Water off a duck's back, that's what it should be. She pondered the short yet innocuous exchange of this morning. Her feelings of irritation changed to chagrin, then to indignation that he would so easily tease her, then rail at her head when she took offense at being treated like a child. But still, ever truthful with herself, she knew she had not handled their encounter with any degree of sophistication, and that annoyed her, as well. It was becoming obvious that the marquis considered her a naughty and unruly child. But just why that should perturb her so very much was beyond her powers to explain.

Granting him his due, she could admit to the rightness of his frustrations with the injustices he felt life had dealt him.

It must be terrible to be so confined, a thing she could only imagine as she leapt agilely from one wet rock to another along the path descending down the cliff to the bay. Put in his place, even she might be surly and unpleasant, as well. That thought jarred her to a standstill. Look at me, she thought. Stalking off anger. Dispelling emotion with arduous physical activity. What would I have done this morning, if I had been denied this release, as the marquis is every day? I'd probably be impossibly tense, ready to leap from my skin at the slightest irritation, until everything and everyone became one ceaseless irritation. Perhaps that could explain his rampant mood swings and displays of temper. Obviously an athletic gentleman, and now to be denied that familiar outlet, it was scant wonder that he was foul tempered. He must be at a loss for a suitable replacement to vent his emotions.

How would she herself respond in a similar situation? Looking far over the gray of the water melding into the mist-laden sky, she pondered carefully. She would have painted, lost herself in her still life drawings, busied her hands and her mind with countless activities. None of which could she imagine Claymore readily engaged with.

"Of course, right from the beginning, I would have accepted the physician's diagnosis of hope in a more positive light than he has. I have no doubt at all, that I would have been on my feet by now and making daily progress toward reclaiming my life," she declared to the cliffs. "No one and nothing could have kept me down."

Carefully seating herself on a flat rock somewhat sheltered from the wet, she pulled Thomas's letter from her pocket and spread it on her knee. His handwriting scrawled across the page, taking up most of the sheet with very few sentences.

Dear Margaret,
In answer to your earlier letters, I must inform you that there is nothing I can readily do from distant London to ease your situation with our mother. Having accepted the responsibility of her care in exchange

for a lion's share of our birthright, I am distressed to
find I must remind you to do your duty. I fully expect
that I shall not have to repeat this letter, nor shall I be
forced to endure your childish complaints on this subject again.

Thomas

Marke folded the letter slowly and carefully. "Well, one
cannot be clearer than that," she muttered. Feeling somewhat slapped in the face, she unfolded the letter again and
reread the hateful, uncaring words a second time. They did
not improve with repeating. Her brother was an ass, and
there was nothing she could ever do to change that. But,
from this day forward, she would take his abrupt advice to
heart. "I will never again ask him for anything," she declared. Methodically ripping the paper into tiny pieces in
her lap, she stood up and shook out her wet skirt, letting the
wind take the fragments across the bay like snowflakes,
sending her hurt feelings flying with them.

Tilting her face to the sky, watching the wheeling, quarreling sea gulls overhead, she breathed deeply. There was
nothing she could do to change the inevitability of her
mother's condition. Mrs. P was as happy and comfortable
as she could be at the present. She would now turn her attention to the things she could change. Besides, wasn't she
the resourceful one? The grand old girl? A huckleberry
above most people's persimmon? Capable of conquering
even one as reclusive as the Marquis of Boothe-Ashmore?
She allowed a slight grin to cross her face. He was a puzzle
for sure, but she had her direction. She must find a release
for his tension. He must be given something to look forward to each and every day. She must replace something in
his life that he felt had been taken from him as thoroughly
as the fire had taken his family. Something that would give
him some feeling of control over his life. But what? What
would give him pleasure at this very moment? Something
feasible and easily obtainable? Suddenly the grin turned

into a full smile, then burst into an outright laugh. Clapping her hands, she executed a jaunty little jig on the rocks before spinning to dash back up the cliff, her mind awhirl with plans.

Chapter Nine

Sitter poked her head into the makeshift studio to find Marke, head bent over her work, muttering what could only have been described as a fair imitation of Claymore's cursing. "Marke!" she admonished. "I am ashamed of you! Your mother will have my head for allowing Claymore to corrupt an innocent."

Marke started guiltily, then giggled when she saw it was only Sitter witnessing her fall from grace. "I have found them to be the most comforting of words, Sitter. You should try one. Go on, do!"

"I shall do no such thing! And you, Margaret Penwell, shall not do so, either. Now, behave yourself, or I shall be forced to..."

"To do what, may I ask?" Marke saucily teased, wiping her brush on a cloth. "I would place a wager that I could outrun you should you attempt violence upon my person, besides as my brother has so kindly informed me just yesterday by post, I am a grown-up person now, and answerable only to myself in all things. What do you think of that, my dear Mrs. Sittlemeyer?"

"Rubbish and nonsense!" Sitter declared, then remembering her purpose, drew a hand faintly across her forehead in a fair imitation of one taken suddenly ill.

"Sitter, are you unwell?" Marke exclaimed, rushing to assist her to a seat.

"Merely a headache, dear," she murmured with convincing despondency. "And just when Claymore has asked

me to spend the morning with him in the library. I fear time
lies heavily upon him today."

"I'm so sorry your head aches. Shall I have Cook fix you
a restorative?"

"Oh, I shall just lie quietly in my darkened room until
luncheon. A bit of peppermint oil at my temples and a cool
lavender compress on my forehead will set me to rights by
then. I have come to ask you to take my place with Claymore. That is, if you can leave your painting for a spell?"

Marke's brow furrowed. Spending time alone with that
thunderstorm was the last thing she wished this morning,
but Sitter was obviously unwell and she did care deeply for
the woman. "Of course, I shall do my best to take your
place, if you think the marquis will settle for it. I fear, we
do not always rub well together."

"Oh, surely you exaggerate, dear. He will be most
pleased with your presence, you'll see," Sitter assured her
with a pleased expression on her face, which quickly
changed to one of pain as she recollected herself.

Marke raised her eyebrows in disbelief. She did not think
the marquis would ever be pleased by her presence, but she
would do her best. "I shall go down then, just as soon as I
clear my things here," Marke said with feigned good cheer.

The marquis was, as before, seated in the wing chair beside the library fire when Marke entered. He looked up with
no particular expression on his face, then frowned un-
pleasantly as he was obviously expecting Sitter. When she
hesitated in the doorway, he waved her brusquely forward.

"Sitter has asked to be excused this morning, my lord. I
fear she is feeling unwell, and she has retired to rest until
luncheon. If it pleases you, she has sent me along as a poor
substitute," she said, hesitating to seat herself until he gave
an indication of his wishes, half praying he would release
her to return to her painting, and then half fearing he
would. It seemed she was forever in a muddle around him
of late.

"I merely thought Sitter might distract me for an hour or
so," Claymore admitted. "But if she is feeling unwell—"
he paused to sigh deeply and rub fingers across his fur-

rowed forehead "—it's just the morning that wears inordinately long with the dismal weather outside the windows."

"If it pleases you, I should do my best to act as stand-in," Marke said, moving quickly to his side. "Shall I read to you? Or perhaps you would favor a game of whist? I am reported to be a fair enough player."

"Oh, read if you want, or simply relate a tale of interest," he said, and sighed, displaying apathy and a lack of regard for anything she might suggest. He leaned his head wearily back against the chair. "I would lull this cursed, disagreeable head pain of mine away, if possible."

She moved quickly to tug at the bellpull. "Oh, head pains seem to be the affliction of the day, as it is Sitter's complaint, also. My brother, Thomas, suffers terribly with head pains," she sympathized, turning to Heaven as he appeared in the doorway. "Heaven, would you please ask Cook to brew a lime-flower tea sweetened with honey for his lordship. I would suggest allowing it to steep for three minutes."

"Of course, miss," Heaven said, then bowed from the library before the frowning marquis could counter the sensible request.

"I really do not think a cup of tea—" Claymore began only to have Marke interrupt his refusal with a dismissing wave of her hand.

"It's an excellent remedy for a head pain. Perfectly harmless and quite soothing to the senses." Marke seated herself across from him, spreading her tarlatan skirts about her in an unconsciously graceful gesture. She paused to watch his tense face, noting the strain around the eyes as if he had slept poorly the night before and needed soothing. The only peaceful tale she could readily bring to mind was of the sea. "Do you like the sea, my lord?"

"Oh, I like the sea well enough, I suppose," Claymore muttered, laying his head back and closing his eyes.

She cast about for a way to begin a tale that might prove as distraction. "If I had been so fortunate as to be born a son, I would have lived my life for the sea. Like my father.

My father was, without a doubt, one of the truly great shipmasters." She paused, but there was no comment from him. "He was born to a shipmaster and his lady wife, and practically on the docks of Liverpool, I was told, as it would seem my grandmama was forever insistent upon sailing with her husband. It should have been no surprise to his parents that my father was destined to have a large amount of seawater in his veins."

"Your grandmother sailed with her husband?" Claymore prompted, wishing her to continue speaking. Her voice was soft, feminine and soothing, and possessing a lilting quality he noted that was seemingly unaffected on her part. But then everything about her seemed unaffected and natural. Even her rowdiness.

"Yes, it's been said that she did not trust him around the corner from her sight, much less absent for months on end. But I choose to think she was devastatingly enamored of him, and he equally so of her," she said, laughing slightly.

Claymore opened his eyes and looked at her thoughtfully, aware that she always flushed sweetly under his gaze. "You mock that? Does that mean you do not believe it possible to be so deeply in love with another as to wish never to leave their side?"

Marke blinked, startled that he would pose such an intimate question to her. Instead of her characteristically candid answer, she merely grinned and countered, "Of course I do. I am female, am I not? Surely you must know such romantic fantasies are instilled in the womb... along with gender."

He watched her face a moment. She seemed quite young to have such a biased outlook on love. That interested him. "And did your mother sail with your father, also?"

"No, she did not," Marke stated rather bluntly, leaving no opening for that subject to continue. She was relieved when he lay his head back again and closed his eyes, rather than delve further, and quickly returned to the tale before he changed his mind. "Grandfather Penwell was a respectable shipmaster himself, sailing in small brigs mostly for a variety of shipping lines. In the summers, my father would

sail with him, oh say, from his fifth year on, and at the
tender age of twelve, he went to sea as seaman.''

"Mmm..." Claymore murmured as encouragement for
her to pursue her discourse. The throb of his head furrowed his brow, and he gripped the arms of the chair
firmly, attempting to concentrate on her voice, the texture
of the leather beneath his palms...anything but the ripping ache in his head.

Aware of his acute discomfort, Marke rose to move to his
chair. Hesitantly she touched her fingers lightly to his forehead as she'd seen Jessell do for Thomas when he complained of head pain. The marquis startled for a moment,
opening his eyes to stare up at her in puzzlement, but she
passed a palm over his face, closing the questioning eyes
again. As he offered no resistance to her touch, she began
stroking his forehead from middle to temple with her cool
fingers. The satin of his finely pored skin was a marvel to
her. If asked to hazard a guess, she would have said a gentleman's skin would be coarse, and perhaps thicker than her
own. She lowered her voice to a soothing murmur as she
stroked first one direction, then the other.

"Father learned his business in the China tea trade. The
ships who would grant such a young lad full seaman's berth
were usually old and leaky. They sailed with woefully small
crews, who knew no privileges. Captain's son or no captain's son, a boy on such ships learns the sea the hard way.''

Marke lengthened her stroke to slide her fingers into the
silken, walnut curls at his temples. Devoid of Macassar oil,
it was silky soft and his scalp smooth to her fingertips. She
probed his scalp, pressing gently at pressure points. His
pleasant scent filled her nostrils and she was startled to find
herself beginning to tremble slightly. Such a response could
only mean that she must be coming down with the same
ailment as the marquis and Sitter, for surely the mere touch
of this man, one she knew to be arrogant and top-lofty with
a foul temper, could not be affecting her so oddly.

"Please," Claymore murmured, his breath whispering
against her wrist, "go on with your story.''

"Oh, s-sorry. Ah, well—" she quickly smoothed a palm over his eyes, lest he open them and see her confusion "—Father sought his master's license with a diligence, sailing on bad ships with lazy or drunkard captains who would leave the helm, and the decisions to his discretion. And it was because of this that he took with him a great deal of experience to the first deep sea ship that he served upon."

Reaching down, and with a single finger, she traced along the arch of his eyebrows, gently over his eyelids, moving to his ears and nose, around his mouth, cupped his cheek to feel the rasp of new whiskers just beneath the skin. She was amazed to find that touching him was the most pleasing thing she had ever done. Whatever was wrong with her? Was she demented? To find such excitement from a simple touch? She closed her eyes and drew in a shaky breath, exhaling into her story.

"But mere seaman was not enough for my father. With every cent he could beg, borrow or steal, he acquired a ship that should have been mercifully sent to the depth of the ocean as scrap. But, stripping her of all luxuries and weight, almost to the bare bone, and sailing with as small a crew as possible, he set about breaking all records for voyage time. He took chances that most captains gained reputations for avoiding. And, contrary to what you would have thought, seamen flocked to sail with him, as he paid well and he fed well, even though he drove them hard."

Claymore felt the tension leaving his body, and his mouth relaxed as the pain eased in his head. The soothing fingers stroked his ears, massaging the lobe between forefinger and thumb, then slipped to stroke behind his ears. Barely restraining a groan of pure enjoyment, he allowed his head to loll sideways, pressing comfortably against her breasts. It had been a long time since he had felt such release.

Marke's breath quickened, and she fought to still the racing of her heartbeat for fear he would hear and misunderstand...what? She did not know herself why she was feeling this way. She began to speak more quickly to distract herself, at once kneading the tight muscles in his neck in a more determined, impersonal manner. "He never rested his ship in port, never waited for a cargo to become available, to come down, or to ripen or be harvested. He diligently, feverishly, sought freight. He would run small passages throughout the area instead of resting his ship. And when others were lying idle for months on end, he was always working, as agents knew they would trust Captain Penwell when others might falter."

Without conscious thought, Marke's touch softened again to a caress. She stroked his chin, his throat and over his collarbone, boldly slipping fingers past the open neck of his boiled shirt to smooth over his chest, teasing the silken hairs there, reveling in the sensual intimacy so cleverly disguised as a healing massage.

Claymore unconsciously burrowed his face into her full breasts, enjoying the sensual comfort from their pliant softness without realizing he was provoking sensations of such force that they were snatching Marke's breath away, making it difficult for her to speak normally. "Um, go on please," he prompted again.

Marke swallowed carefully. Her voice had again become low and breathy and very unreliable. "In truth, I believe they revered him because he dared things that others could not dare. I have heard it said that he never sailed with the favorable wind, but battled his way, in the direction he wanted to go whenever and wherever he wanted. He bent the Trade Winds to his authority with the utmost confidence that he was irrevocably right—in everything."

"You make that seem a bad thing," Claymore murmured, smoothing his cheek across her breasts, allowing the light floral scent, heated by the warmth of her body, to work its long forgotten magic upon his body.

The vibration of his voice ran through Marke's body. She drew in a deep, shaky breath and exhaled slowly to calm herself, trying hard to focus on the tale she was weaving. "No, not...not bad." She ran her fingers down his cheeks, cupping his jaw and passing her thumb slowly across his lips, wandering what it would feel like to bend forward and press her own there as she'd also seen Jessell do with

Thomas. "But let's just say that I did not gain my insights into the acceptance of life from my father. Captain Penwell could be quite insufferable at times."

"And *you* cannot, of course," Claymore mumbled with a chuckle.

Stung back to awareness by the very normalcy of his chuckle, Marke breathed deeply and gave herself a mental shake. With her palm, she pressed his face flat, pinching the nose, cutting off his breath until he jerked open his eyes. "You're a terrible heckler, my lord," she teased, shaking her hand and therefore his face. "But a very pretty boy nevertheless."

"Nonsense! I am no such thing," he grunted. Raising his head from her breasts, he dislodged her fingers. He felt such irrational irritation at having the pleasure of her touch and scent dissipated by a childish prank on her part.

With impeccable timing, Heaven appeared in the doorway with a small tray and the lime-flower tea. Marke quickly stepped away, flustered at the depth of the raging sensations coursing through her body. She hesitated to accept the teacup in her unreliable hands, and finally motioned Heaven toward the marquis instead. Moving to the far wall, she pretended to contemplate a portrait of a matron with the most astonishing number of chins one woman should ever wish to display, as distraction until her emotions had quieted somewhat.

"Ahem, luncheon, my lord. Miss Penwell," Heaven informed them. He bowed and backed from the room with a wink and conspirator's grin for Marke.

"Thank you, Heaven," she said, returning the smile, spinning to make sure Claymore had not observed the wink, for that would surely have spoiled the surprise. "Is your head better, Lord Perfect?"

"Yes, actually it is greatly improved," Claymore admitted, rubbing his forehead tentatively in test. "Thank you, Miss Penwell."

"You are very welcome! And now you shall feel up to enjoying luncheon, shan't you? Sip your tea, as it will aid digestion, also," Marke instructed, moving to retrieve the invalid chair.

"I no longer acquaint luncheon, nor dinner for that matter, with the word *enjoy*," he snorted. Stubbornly leaving the cooling tea on the tray, he threw the lap robe from his lap and motioned her forward with the chair.

Marke did not obey but leaned on the back of the chair with a significant glance at the teacup. Claymore looked as if he would rail at her head, but then, with surprisingly easy compliance, drained the cup in one swift swallow. "Thank you, my lord," she answered, shoving the chair forward, exhibiting a willingness to cooperate with him, if he would with her.

Using the chair's arm as lever, Claymore easily gained his feet, and Marke was thrilled to see that he made no show of requesting aid. Though unsteady, he was standing quite straight, giving her a pleasant surprise to see how he towered over her own height. Immobilizing the invalid chair as he settled himself, she chastised herself harshly. She must not be foolish enough to believe the man was other than her first impression of him, which was for the most part arrogant and disagreeable and someone she would otherwise have cut to the quick and duly ignored. As she had no ready explanation for the emotions that had flooded her senses so strongly but a few moments before, she would simply lay them aside to be studied later. And for now, regardless of her low opinion of Lord Perfect's character, she would do her best to be pleasant and advance his recovery, from regard for dear Sitter and her promise to Dr. Barrows. And if that included touching him in such a way, then so be it. But she must also heed Sitter's warning to guard her emotions.

Marke wheeled the marquis into the small dining room to find Sitter standing behind her chair, practically dancing in high spirits and barely restraining the laughter that threatened to burst from her throat. Claymore looked warily at her as the footman seated her to his right. "I swear I am becoming as jumpy as a mouse in a cathouse—" he began, only to have Sitter interrupt him with a slap on his knuckles for his disgraceful choice of words.

"Claymore, really!"

"But it would appear that Sitter has either swallowed the canary, or found a cache of hidden Christmas presents," he continued, with a glance over his shoulder. "Which one of you will let me in on the prank? Miss Penwell?"

Marke laughed and shook her head. She stationed the chair at the table and hurriedly took her own seat. "Not I, my lord."

"Sitter, then?"

"Claymore, behave yourself and attend your elbow or you shall have your lunch in your lap," Sitter admonished gaily, waving toward Heaven, waiting to serve him.

Heaven placed the soup bowl in front of the marquis and stood back to watch his face with eager anticipation that matched, and may even have outstrided, Sitter's. The marquis looked down at the sumptuous fare that filled his nostrils with temptation, then back up at those surrounding him. It would seem all eyes were upon him, even to the smallest footman against the wall, each eagerly awaiting his reaction.

"I say, can this possibly be for me to consume? My stomach fears I am the brunt of a callous prank," he said, dipping his spoon into the thick, hearty chowder and gently sampling the fare. "Oh, this is marvelous, indeed."

Marke laughed at his obvious enjoyment. "Sitter and I decided it was time you had something less to complain of," she explained.

Sitter adamantly shook her head. "Oh, no! I can take no credit. Marke gave Cook instructions for it, and I have been to the kitchen twice to steal a taste. Aren't you pleased, Claymore?" demanded Sitter, then at his exaggerated nod, clapped her hands in glee. "Oh, that's wonderful. You must thank Marke, for it was she who braved the autumn chill yesterday to ride down to John for permission to extend your diet."

Claymore studied Marke with a puzzled frown, then cleared his throat uncomfortably and returned his glance to his soup bowl. "You rode all the way to Bantry for permission from John?" he asked. "I was under the impression it rained the whole of yesterday."

"Oh, it did, but the ride was exhilarating," Marke said, then attempted to change the subject. "Your lordship possesses a marvelous stable. It has been a very long time since I have had the pleasure of such splendid mounts."

Sitter smiled fondly at Marke and teased enthusiastically. "My, my, a learned artist. An experienced equestrian, and now, we find you are a chef, as well?"

Marke blushed uncomfortably at all the attention and shrugged her shoulders. "It's nothing really—just a chowder—poached salmon, carrots, potatoes, peppers—" she grinned slightly at Claymore "—and *mushrooms.*"

"Pray be done with the modesty, Marke," Sitter charged. "Everything you do is most admirable, and—and wonderfully proficient. Isn't that so, Claymore?"

Claymore raised his head and studied Marke closely again. He was taken aback by her endless generosity. It was as if she gave without concern for return, simply because it might bring another person pleasure, or relief in his case. She was an enigma to him. Quite out of the realm of his experience. Finally he lent his agreement to Sitter's. "Truly, Miss Penwell, thank you. This is most admirable."

Marke, flustered by the agreeable attention, and embarrassed by the effusive praise, sought to turn the attention away from herself with a prank. "The simple truth of the matter is, my lord, the entire household was desperate for relief from your foul moods. It's toward that end that there is also a mountain of chestnut cream, with a crisp meringue center, for dessert."

Claymore straightened and showed his mock offense by glaring at both the ladies. "I anticipate the dessert with great relish, Miss Penwell, but I do *not* have foul moods!"

Sitter made a face behind her napkin and Marke giggled. Then to soothe ruffled feathers, she eagerly leaned forward. "And this is not the best part. For dinner, you shall have your palate tempted with forcemeat—I believe

Cook is stuffing pheasant—and there's to be baked butternut squash topped with maple-hazelnut crumbs, and dried cherries to stir memories of summer orchards, and Dutch apple tart drizzled with cinnamon-vanilla custard. A virtual feast! Truly the glory of a bountiful summer garden, preserved as the best a winter pantry has to offer.''

Claymore shook his head in amazement before turning to signal the replenishment of his bowl. "Marke, you have the most lyrical way of stating the obvious."

Marke's breath caught in her throat at his casual use of her Christian name. She loved the way it rolled from his lips and sent gooseflesh up her arms. Feeling Sitter's eyes on her pink face in speculation, she sidestepped into laughter to disguise her emotions. These strange feelings were too new to her, too private to share with others, even by the shine in her eyes. "It would seem I'm discovered. And to justify your praise, just you watch, one rainy day I shall invade Cook's domain and put up a nice selection of flavored vinegar from nature's best. What say you to blended berry, lemon dill, gingered orange, opal basil, cinnamon apple cider, and of course, a red pepper vinegar—which I shall name after you, Lord Perfect."

"My, what a low opinion you seem to have of me, Miss Penwell," Claymore muttered. He shook his head in bafflement of such an unfair thing, then smiled at her.

Beneath the full benefit of his smile and dimple, Marke blushed and laughed again in confusion and utter happiness.

Claymore watched her radiant face betray her excitement with pleasure. Her eyes positively danced with merriment. Her voice was jubilant, her laughter ringing out with delicious abandon. He could no more resist the impulse to laugh with her than one could refrain from smiling at the glee of a winsome child. For some unexplained reason, the revelation disgruntled him and he returned his attention to his plate with singular focus.

Sitter's sharp eyes noticed the pretty blushes on Marke's cheeks and recognized the girl's confusion. While she doubted Marke herself was wholly conscious of the true meaning of her emotions, Claymore was of an age and experience to understand his own growing interest was nothing more than a response to the womanhood inside the child that was beginning to assert itself. And, though she reveled in Claymore's renewed interest in anything, she set about once more worrying for the hearts of those dearest to her.

Chapter Ten

Dinner, a virtual feast as promised, had passed as a congenial affair for the small company, with wine and good humor in abundance. The mood had been casual, and more familial than formal. Afterward, having arrived at the drawing room ahead of both Sitter and the marquis, Marke wandered about the room, strangely puzzled by her restlessness and her pensive mood. She paused before the mirror to pull off a pearl drop earring. She rubbed her numb earlobe with a grimace. The things a woman did for vanity, she sighed, replacing the offending earring. Clasped around her neck was the matching rope of creamy pearls that had been Mrs. P's wedding set—presented to her by the captain following the exchange of their marriage vows.

At the same time Thomas had sent their mother to St. Catherine's Court to live out her life, he had generously divided the contents of Mrs. P's jewel case among her daughters—with the lion's share going to his own wife, Jessell. The pearl wedding set had been the least valuable piece in her case, and therefore the piece least valued by her daughters. It had been for that reason alone that Marke had stubbornly insisted upon having it, not that her sisters had complained overly much. Affectionately she smoothed the fall of the necklace over her bosom. There had always been a sentimental thought in her head that deep feelings were attached to the pearls. Perhaps feelings of love the captain might have expressed to his bride at that intimate moment, and shy emotions returned by her mother for her new hus-

band. With childish imagination, Marke had always
planned to wear the set at her wedding, and then pass them
to her daughter upon her own wedding day, along with
stories of love and faithfulness. But now she must recon-
cile herself to the sad possibility that there might never be
a wedding for her, nor a daughter to pass the pearls to.

Marke stared deeply into her own eyes reflected back at
her in such seriousness. Did she truly need a husband to
gaze at her with admiration and desire? She studied herself with a critical eye. She did look rather fetching and fine
tonight. Her gown was one of the few she owned that had
been designed especially for herself, and the fall of the
draped robe of chocolate cherub-lace over the slip of almond satin was perfection. The brown lace flattered her
coloring and made her brown eyes loom much larger than
she was sure they were in actuality. Would John have
thought so, if he had seen her tonight? Given the right circumstances, could she pine after the fine doctor with a
rapidly beating heart and a rush of heat to her face, such as
she had felt touching Claymore? No, she harbored no such
feelings for John, dear friend though he was. While she
liked the doctor well enough, and he had made it very clear
he'd be at her beck and call with only the slightest encouragement . . .

Suddenly she pulled her face down into a comical mask
and chastised herself. "What are you thinking, Margaret
Catherine? That you can't be happy unless the man you
have vehemently stated to dislike sweeps you off your feet?
Takes you to wife and gives you a daughter to wear your
mother's pearls? Now that *would* be believing in sorcery."
The sound of the invalid chair's squeaking wheel sped her
away from the mirror lest someone catch sight of her talking to her reflection. "Wouldn't that be something, silly
girl?" she muttered. "Caught talking to yourself as if ad-
dled, on top of admiring yourself before the mirror as if
there were no other who wished to do so!"

But then, having admonished herself, her eager face was
most becomingly flushed and her breathing irregular when

Henry wheeled the marquis sharply around the divan to place the chair near the fire.

"Sitter has asked to be excused," Claymore declared.

"Oh no, I trust she is not ill again? Perhaps I should go to her," Marke said, leaping to her feet with concern.

"No, no. It's nothing more than gluttony over that fantastic dinner, or so she says," he reported, waving her back. "She declares that a tonic water and a long sleep will set her to rights. We are not to concern ourselves."

"As she wishes then," Marke capitulated uncertainly. Lord Perfect had been so congenial over dinner, dare she hope he would concede to remain with her instead of seeking solitude in which to brood the night away? She cast about for a temptation that would assure such a thing didn't happen. "So... that leaves just the two of us then. Do you have a preference as to entertainment this evening, my lord?"

"Do I take my life in my hands if I suggest the challenge of whist?"

"Most certainly not!" Marke replied, with a mockhorrified expression at his insult to her honesty. She eagerly moved to the green leather-topped card table placed beside the window, suddenly elated that he would remain with her and determined to be good company. "And to prove *my* trust of *you,* I will take no offense, should you suggest a wager of shillings and pence to spice the game."

"Now, I really should heed the warning bells sounding in my head, for I feel I am in danger of being fleeced," Claymore teased. Expertly spinning the invalid chair within reach of the card table, he transferred himself to a chair more suited to its height.

"Yes, perhaps you should," Marke readily agreed. She shuffled the cards efficiently and slapped them onto the table with all the marks of a challenge. "We Penwell women are a hearty lot, to say the least. Quite given to demands of equal treatment, you know."

Claymore deftly cut the stack, slapping them sharply in answer to her challenge. "I would imagine that to be so," he quipped, watching her deal the cards quickly.

"Yes, my grandmother quite distinguished herself by feats of absolute heroism."

"This is the grandmother who sailed with her philandering husband?"

"The same, although I do not recall actually stating that he was a philanderer," she remarked, playing quickly and expertly, easily taking the first hand.

"My mistake. And just how did this grandmother distinguish herself?" Claymore conceded the hand and watched her shuffle again.

"She was aboard the *Pristine Poop* and bound round the Horn when smallpox struck the crew. Grandpapa, his officers and most of the crew went down with it, but Grandmama was not taken ill, you see."

"Of course she wasn't."

Marke leveled a mocking, stern look in his direction. "Ahem—as I was saying, your lordship, there were barely enough men left fit to work the ship. In this extremity, Grandmama took command of the *Pristine Poop*. Oh, don't think that there wasn't a bit of murmuring among the men. A deputation of two came aft and demanded that she put into the first port that could be safely gained. But Grandmama, knowing full well they would not be accepted into any port with sickness on board, faced them down. I can quite imagine her drawing up straight and tall, looking them right in the eye and saying—" she stared into Claymore's amused eyes as if it was she, instead of her ancestor, who challenged the sailors "—'Relinquish the ship? Not while my husband draws breath! Now, back for'ard with you or suffer the lash!'"

"And they went?"

"And they went! Grandmama nursed her husband and the mates, and looked after the men. She had a small baby, which also took the smallpox, and she nursed it too, *and* saved its life. That would be my father's youngest sister, I believe."

Claymore chuckled, shaking his head at her rendition of history. "I do believe you should have been on the stage, so great is your imagination."

"Oh, fiddle! It takes no imagination to act out someone else's words. The imagination comes in placing your words in other mouths and on other tongues. But you wound me—" she glanced up through her lashes to pout with pretended hurt "—for you sound as if you do not believe me."

Claymore slid his eyes over the pouting mouth and thought to mention the fact that it looked most invitingly succulent, but instead countered, "And just how could she possibly know navigation?"

"Aha! So you would doubt me?" Marke exclaimed in high spirits, then declared, "Married to my grandpapa at sixteen and sailing with him from day one of their marriage, she had ample time to read everything written on navigation."

"Possible, I suppose," he conceded.

"More than possible. And that was only the *first* time she took the helm. The second time, though I am uncertain of the exact location of the ship during this dilemma, was when my grandpapa was taken ill with a brain fever. The mate had been hauled away to his cabin in irons, for alleged insubordination, which I suspect may have had some connection with Grandpapa's breakdown. The Penwell men do not take easily to the questioning of their orders. My grandmama took command that time, also. Sailed the ship to her destination port and made a good passage, too."

"Most admirable, Miss Penwell," he said. "And I do not doubt that you, as a dauntless Penwell woman, could do the same."

"Thank you for those kind words, good sir," she said, and executed a shallow bow from her seat, "although I shall never have that opportunity, now shall I?"

"Perhaps not. Life is unfair, isn't it?"

"Of course! If life was fair, I would have been a son. Or at least firstborn. You have no idea what it's like to have ninth pick of everything, whether it's at the dinner table, or in childhood games. Even in the selection of gowns!"

"Such indignities!" He chuckled again. "And do you see your mother as dauntless? Well, perhaps not. You did say she never sailed with your father."

"No, my mother was a country girl most of her life," Marke said. She could not stop the slight tightening of her voice that caused the marquis to look up in wonder. Marke answered his questioning look with a smile. "Captain Horace Penwell did not believe in women on board ship. Just as he did not believe in women living in London or Liverpool. And no one ever—*ever*—crossed Captain Horace Penwell."

"You make him sound very hard, and very unforgiving."

"My father was hard—and soft, horrid—and wonderful, like..."

"Like most fathers," Claymore finished for her, with such a sad look that it reminded Marke painfully of the recent demise of his own father. But, as Sitter insisted he must confront and accept the fact, she did not divert the subject from fathers.

"I suppose, as a little girl smitten with her bigger-than-life father, I was vexed by his long absences—" she slapped the cards down rapidly before looking up at him "—and that he should retain a residence in Liverpool large enough for our whole family, and yet insist that Mrs. P and his children remain at King's Gate outside Sussex. He would be absent from April through January, only coming home after the winter storms for one short—deliriously happy—month. And then he would ship his family to St. Catherine's Court for the spring and summer, again sending a ship to transport us back to the English countryside for the fall and winter. He moved his family about as one moves cargo." She pulled a wry face with that statement.

"Hmm, but very orderly and organized, just as one would expect of a ship's master," Claymore said, defending the man for want of anything else to say in this instance. He watched the fleeting expressions pass over her face, seeing flashes of the mischievous little girl she must have been.

"Yes, the captain was, above all else, a master of schedules." Marke leaned forward to grin impishly at him. "Perhaps that is why all nine of Mrs. P's children were born in October—nine months, almost to the day of his return each year.''

"Surely not all?" Claymore protested, staring at her in dismay, suspecting a prank once he was suckered into her tale.

"Yes, all." She raised her hands and ticked them off. "Two on the twenty-third of October, three on the twenty-fifth of October, and one on the twenty-sixth of October, and two on the twenty-eighth, and one on the twenty-ninth. Apparently old Doc would come around like clockwork the last week of October, and not once did he make the trip in vain. A regular schedule keeper also—our Mrs. P.''

"That is the most fantastic thing I have ever heard," Claymore declared, leaning back in his chair with cards forgotten.

"I was the only one to defy the captain's schedule."

"Now, *that* does not surprise me in the least."

Marke frowned at him in mock displeasure. "Let's just say he had a run of misguided stars. In 1815, the storms were fierce, and more than one Penwell ship was lost. There was no trip home for the captain that winter and therefore, no Penwell born the following October. But the year after, the ninth and last Penwell, arrived. Me!''

"And how was it that you were born in Ireland?"

"Oh, the tail end of his misguided stars, I suppose. He did not send a ship to St. Catherine's Court at all that year, thus I was born in Ireland, but still in October." She smiled slightly and riffled the cards several times, although both had been distracted from the game. "As a little girl dreaming of suitors and husbands, I carried a mental picture of my father standing on deck of a great ship in the foaming autumn seas, thinking anxiously of his darling wife as all expectant fathers are supposed to, cursing the sea for its claim on his heart and life. But somehow, I doubt that was true."

"You sound very bitter."

"Oh, it's nothing," she answered, but could not quite bring about the laugh she felt should accompany the lie to make it convincing.

"Are you sure, Marke?" he asked gently.

There it was again. That easy use of her name that reached her ear somehow as a caress, and made her shiver with delight, which the marquis mistook as a chill.

"You are chilled. Come, let's move closer by the fire. If you will just steady the chair for me, I shall lever—" he twisted toward the invalid chair behind him "—or call Henry, perhaps."

She rose to stand beside him. "There's no need for the chair. I will pull you to your feet and you can lean on me if need be. I'm really quite strong. Surely, taking it slow and working together, we can make just the short distance to the divan."

"I suppose it's possible," he said, embarrassed at his helplessness, irritated at his embarrassment, and then suddenly furious with life in general. Reaching out for her hands, he was surprised when she leaned quite close and slipped her arms about his waist. His senses were assailed with the scent of roses, and felt warmed by her soft body. The immediate and profound force of his body's reaction to her scent unsettled him, and he wished to do nothing more than gather her onto his lap. He wanted to kiss that pouty lower lip until she was breathless. He wanted to test the generosity of her nature with his mouth and his hands upon her body. He jerked back from her abruptly.

"Lord Perfect?"

As a man of no little experience, Claymore was not above recognizing intense sexual excitement, and though he had not felt such in a very long time, it discomforted him greatly to feel it now, for carnal cravings were not something he wished to muddle his life with. He dismissed Marke with a wave of his hand, refusing to look at her. "Actually, I would rather you retire, Miss Penwell," he ordered brusquely. "Sitter will have my head if I allow you to take a chill for my own selfish gain."

Thoroughly confused by the swift change of mood, and discontented at being sent to bed like a misbehaving child, Marke nodded a curt good-night. Spinning on her heel, she marched forcefully from the drawing room and through the hall, only slowing on the stairs. She could not quite make out what there was to be disappointed about, but she did feel decidedly low in spirits. Perhaps the time had come for her to return to St. Catherine's Court. The fortnight would be cut short, but the marquis was greatly improved in his spirits, and there really was no reason for her continued presence.

Without calling for Kittie, she slipped into her flannel night rail and climbed beneath the comforter without braiding her hair. It was just as well that she turned her back upon Innisfree and its disturbing master. She was finding the marquis positively *too pleasant* at times. Turning to her side, she tucked her hand beneath her cheek. How Sarah would laugh with malicious glee to see her baby sister mooning in the dark over a man so far above her grasp. Sitter was right, she must not allow her head to be turned to flights of fancy by Lord Perfect's congenial mood that came and went with the unpredictability of a spring thunderstorm.

Sometime later, lying awake in the dark with a busy mind, Marke heard the marquis's resonating voice on the stairs. He was roughly raking Henry over the coals for some imagined infraction, and sounded intoxicated beyond belief. Heaven could be heard admonishing him to be quiet before he disturbed the entire household, to which Claymore rudely told him to go to hell in a handbasket. Marke turned over to her back and sighed deeply. Only a terrible person would drink to such excesses and then speak so meanly to Heaven, who was truly a dear old thing. So much for mooning over that man, she decided suddenly. Her first instincts had been correct. He was insufferably arrogant, unbelievably overbearing, and—and not at all kind. He deserved to be treated just as stingily as he treated others. Invalid, indeed! He was not deserving of her compassion, and would receive none from her in the future. She rolled over with irritation and determinedly pulled the pillow over her head.

Heaven, assisting Henry in disrobing the foxed marquis, sighed with patient resignation as he pulled the nightshirt over the dark curls. Claymore grabbed the majordomo's lapels and pulled him down to stare straight into his eyes.

"Heaven, what do you think of Miss Penwell?"

"In my estimation, she is a most remarkable young lady, my lord."

"In my estimation, as well. Most remarkable, indeed."

"If my lord will just assist me here, I shall attempt to close your nightshirt."

"Of course, Heaven. Pray manhandle those buttons into submission. Can't go to bed with an unbuttoned nightshirt, now can I?"

"Of course not, my lord."

"Did you know Miss Penwell was born in October, Heaven?"

"No, my lord, I was unaware of that fact."

"All the Penwells in the world are born in October. It's a requirement of being a Penwell, you know."

"Most assuredly, my lord."

"Tomorrow, would you find out which October day—the twenty-first, twenty-fifth, twenty-sixth, twenty-eighth, or the twenty-ninth—is the inestimably remarkable Miss Penwell's birthday. I wish to present her with a gift, you see."

"Of course, my lord."

"What do you think she would like for her birthday, Heaven? A mushroom, perhaps?" He chortled merrily.

"I expect a mushroom would be a most admirable birthday gift, my lord. Now if you will just assist me a bit, I shall swing your legs under the coverlet."

"Heaven, I will most definitely need you to attend me on the morrow. I cannot be overly sure at this moment, but I think I shall require your verification that my head has retained its rightful place upon my shoulders come morning."

"I quite expect you will, my lord."

"Good! Glad that is settled." Claymore sighed, then he rolled over and pulled the pillow over his head.

Chapter Eleven

Morning came with a vengeance for the Marquis of Boothe-Ashmore. Though he fought to remain blissfully unconscious, wakefulness was relentless, knocking insistently from inside his head. Finally he rolled onto his back with a groan of regret.

"Good morning, my lord." Heaven moved to turn the coverlet back from his face. "I see we are awake at last. Having anticipated the inevitability of the unwelcome event from your moans, I have sent for coffee as a substitute for tea. Hot and black."

A light knock on the door announced the anticipated coffee, with Marke briskly following the tray into the room. Claymore eased himself into a sitting position and groaned at the sight of her. "Go away!" He meant it to sound as a command, but it came out as a hoarse whisper, and even that caused his head to pound most painfully.

"No, I will not go away!" Marke retorted, stalking to the side of the bed. With her low opinion of the marquis firmly in place, and her resolve to resist any leniency for him stiffened, she planted fists on her hips and clicked her tongue at his sorry state. "I contend, your lordship, that if you can keep the household awake half the night with your drunken behavior, I feel you should rise at a decent hour like the rest of us."

"Go away, I said," Claymore whispered again. "Please have mercy on me and go away. Can't you see I look sick?"

"You look fine to me. As for mercy? I have none. Surely you have discovered that of me, if nothing else," Marke declared, making no effort to soften her voice in deference to his throbbing head. "Besides, I have come to tell you that we are to drive to Bantry this morning. A snootful of fresh air will do you a world of good. I shall expect you properly attired and at the front door in one hour, no more."

"No."

"Yes."

"No!"

"Yes!"

"Impossible wench!"

"Hopeless wretch!"

"Out!" he shouted in spite of his head.

"Not without your promise to be downstairs in one hour."

"This constant flouting of common courtesy in my own home will cease! Do you hear me?" he roared. Angrily flinging the covers back, Claymore swung his legs over the side of the bed and shakily gained his feet.

"Have a care!" Marke cautioned, quickly stepping to him when he would sway alarmingly, unsure if it was the weakness in his legs or his head that made him wobbly.

Leaning heavily against her soft, rounded figure, the floral scent of her hair wafted up to Claymore's nose, enlivening his senses. The cushion of her soft breasts against his chest was a delight, as well as a torment to him. His misbehaving body reacted instantly to her overwhelming, thoroughly desirable femininity. He shoved her roughly away and roared even louder. "All right! I shall be on the damn front stoop in one hour! *Now get out of my bed-chamber!*"

Having gotten what she came for, Marke gaily skipped out the door and closed it tightly behind her before he could change his mind. Heaven stood there, almost but not quite suppressing a grin that threatened to burst forth at having witnessed such a scene. The marquis rubbed a hand over his face and shifted his frown upon the majordomo, irked by the man's poorly disguised amusement at the unquestionable muddle his once orderly and serene life had become.

"Well, Heaven. How do I look to you this morning?" he asked sarcastically.

Heaven's eyes flickered down, then quickly came up, and with a measured, proper tone, he replied, "I would have to say, my lord—highly aroused."

"Out! Get out of my bloody sight!"

Heaven fled just a second before the bed pillow hit the door with a plop. The old man's laughter could be heard echoing down the hallway, doing nothing to better the marquis's rapidly deteriorating mood.

Pacing the width of the driveway, Marke swished at her black skirts with her coachman hat, wondering if Claymore would indeed show up as promised. Her face brightened as the most beautiful pony cart she'd ever seen swung into view. The square body was painted a deep, rich blue, with the shafts, springs and wheels a sunny yellow. Even the leather seats had been artfully dyed a bright yellow. The pony was a dappled gray Welsh, with yellow ribbons gaily plaited in his black mane and tail. Marke ran a hand over the soft muzzle and crooned softly to him. He was so perfect—smooth in conformation, standing with such dignity with pretty manners—fully equal to any blooded hunter... and she coveted him greatly.

The scowl on the marquis's face as he was wheeled into the crisp air forestalled any expression of enthusiasm she might have made over the beautiful equipage and pony. Instead she silently climbed into the cart and waited for the marquis to slide in beside her. The invalid chair, also fitted in by Henry, made for close quarters, but it was still with a great deal of satisfaction that she gave the pony leave to proceed down the driveway at a brisk clip.

As the marquis gave no indication that he was ever going to speak to her again, Marke wisely held her tongue. And at first it was enough to be out in the open, to drive over the leathery red and gold autumn leaves, to sniff the hint of winter in the air and ponder the upcoming holidays. But so great was her pleasure that she found it harder and harder to contain her enjoyment, wishing ever so much to share it with him. She slipped glances at his stony face from time to time, but he did not acknowledge her, seemingly far away in thought. He was classically dressed this morning, in immaculately tailored black pantaloons, and a frock coat of charcoal Bath, and a dove gray waistcoat beneath his driving coat. Henry had tied his ivory neckcloth in such intricate fashion that it quite defied her comprehension. Always startlingly handsome, and only as perfect as his name declared him to be, she felt a wash of yearning rush through her. Suddenly she thought she would simply die if he were to stay angry with her much longer.

She chewed on her lip, then tentatively ventured, "How is your head, my lord? Has the air cleared away the cobwebs?"

"Yes, quite nicely, thank you," he commented, leaving her no opening to continue the conversation.

She squirmed on the seat but managed to hold her tongue until the marvelous pony swept into Bantry at a smart pace. Miserable at his snub but unable to allow him his silence, she made yet another attempt to draw him out. "Shall we stop for refreshments? I do not wish you to become overly tired."

"No, I am quite well enough to continue," he replied with such awful politeness.

Grinding her teeth with frustration, she tried yet again. "Or we might stop at St. Patrick's Cathedral," she said, indicating a tiny, quaint church with ivy-covered walls and quite possibly more than one hole in its roof. "I remember it well from my childhood. Even then, it was empty of people, but quite full of little marble figures to commemorate the congregation lying beneath its cold stone floor, you know the ones memorialized by tarnished brass plates?" He would only nod his head. Marke grimaced, but she was like a terrier at a rat hole, she would not give up easily. "I always wished to fill its aisles with long-stemmed thistles, perhaps a few clover leaves, and some thornless blossoms, jasmine perhaps or honeysuckle—that would seem the right thing to dispel the odor of neglect."

"Such places always smell of mold, as in every church where no incense is being burned," Claymore explained, then resolutely turned his head away.

Marke's frustration gave way to anger. This soft autumn day was entirely too beautiful to waste on childish games. Either he would act as a man full grown, and drop the selfish petulance, or she would just take him back to Innisfree and he could rot in Hades for all she cared. "Lord Perfect, is it your intention to withhold your company for the entire outing?" she demanded. "For if it is, I shall begin to regret my invitation for you to accompany me."

Claymore turned a disbelieving face toward her. *"Invitation?"* he quipped sarcastically. "Is that what you call barging into the privacy of my bedchamber—to manhandle me from my very bed, Miss Penwell?"

Marke opened her mouth to deliver a stinging retort, then closed it again as she could think of nothing to say. He was right. Her behavior had been deplorable, and just because she had been sicced on him by his physician and Sitter, just because she deemed it for his own good, did not give her permission to behave like an unmannered, unrestrained delinquent. Suddenly she wasn't sure just who was acting the more childish. She should be thanking her lucky stars he hadn't tossed her out of Innisfree, *and* taken away her license ever to call again. Perhaps it was she who should be doing the apologizing.

"You are quite right and I am truly sorry," she whispered, sincerely contrite.

"And well you should be," he gritted. "Enough is enough, by damn."

His disagreeable tone of voice, instead of the polite forgiveness she had fully expected, wiped out all of her guilt and brought her chin up again. How dare he be so sanctimonious when she was, in truth, neglecting her own business to spend time and energy dragging him, practically by the heels, out of the doldrums! She pulled the pony off the street and brought him to a standstill. Facing the marquis squarely, she sarcastically begged his forgiveness for caring whether he lived or died.

"I sincerely wish to apologize, Lord Perfect. My interference in your business has been deplorable. I admit it," she said, with a growing strength in her voice. "I should never have pushed myself upon you in the first place. You are a man of adult years and have every right to throw away your life, if you so desire. Just say the word and I shall drop you at Teddy O'Flannigan's Bar. There you can lock yourself away in a drinking booth like a horse in a stall, to wallow alone with whiskey and pain, to lower yourself into the pit of passivity, for as long as your coin should last."

"Good Lord!" Claymore expelled, tilting his eyes heavenward seeking patience before such a tirade.

"Actually, I doubt the good Lord frequents such places," Marke pronounced firmly. "Although perhaps he should, as there is more misery and hopelessness to be found there than in one of his many churches."

Claymore's withdrawn veneer cracked. He'd had all he could take of her pushing and prodding and meddling in his affairs. "And what could you possibly know of such things? Of misery? I doubt you have had one moment in your limited, little life when you have felt hopelessness and despair as black as what now consumes my entire future," he argued.

"I am certain you're quite right, my lord. My life is wonderful. My life is marvelous. My life is exactly as I wish it, for I will have it no other way. For I alone dictate my fate, and no other. But I applaud your decision to float away from the surface of your miserable life. I salute your refusal to take part in any way in the weary treading of everyday water. Perhaps you are right to ignore the meaningless, repetitive things that make up living. Shall I drop you at O'Flannigan's now?"

"Good Lord! Is it no small wonder women are not allowed in these pubs," he muttered, flinging his hands in the air in defeat. "God knows, it's the only place a man has to escape the nagging of harpies."

"*Harpies!*" she squealed, then visibly calmed herself. "Oh, of course, my lord, you are right—*they* are right—to disallow women to frequent such places. A man should be alone with his whiskey, far removed from all the activities in which he has been forced by female *nagging* to participate. Such activities known as society, family, occupation and . . . and honor."

"A man shouldn't be forced to participate if he doesn't want to!" Claymore muttered, growing weary of the argument as there was no winning against the relentless little chit. He looked down the street with a stony face.

But Marke was not ready to give it up yet. She flipped sideways, leaning forward to peer into his averted face. "Ah, but surely you see the fallacy there? Even there he is a participant nonetheless. He is making the barkeep's day, for he is making the barkeep's wife immeasurably happy with every coin he passes under the drinking booth door into the barkeep's pockets. Don't you see? Life continues in an endless cycle. And even refusing to participate is participation nonetheless."

The marquis turned to glare at her with astonishment written on his face. She could not tell if he was amused or furious, because the one trait she had firmly grasped about him was a quality of self-control that seemed almost impregnable. When he did speak, it was with a definite strain in his voice.

"Miss Penwell, you are absolutely merciless."

"Yes, disagreeable of me, isn't it?"

"Most."

They lapsed into stony silence, side by side, both staring unseeingly down the street lost in their separate thoughts.

Claymore wondered whether he would ever understand this complicated woman-child beside him, and if he even had the strength to try. She was absolutely exhausting, filled with the exuberance and innocence of life one would expect of someone so young. But he knew from experience, once life slapped her down a few times, she would become more realistic in her outlook.

Marke felt a strange dissatisfaction from the altercation. There just had to be some way to make him understand that life, to be fully enjoyed, required active commitment. Life was being involved with the people around one, sharing in joys and griefs. Surely if one didn't care about those people, then one had a pretty shallow life. But she was beginning to suspect that the Marquis of Boothe-Ashmore, so big and brave, was truly terrified to care for anyone again. For to love someone deeply was to suffer greatly if they are suddenly, and brutally, taken away from you. But, oh, how lonely to deprive oneself of such love.

Blissfully unaware of the temptress ahead of him, an Irish constable cheerfully ambled down the street toward them. Claymore watched the man raise his cap with friendly ease to each passerby. Good Lord, he groaned inwardly, just how much cheerfulness was a man expected to withstand in one unfortunate day?

Without turning to face him, Marke sensed the marquis was watching the man as she was. Grasping the neutral subject as a way to defuse the tense, uncomfortable silence, she commented on the constable. "He is probably the descendant of a king or the grandson of a poet or the great-nephew of a saint?"

Claymore snorted, then countered, "Descendant of a king? I hardly think so, Miss Penwell. I quite imagine the function of peacekeeper in this sleepy little hamlet was the theme of one of the countless songs his mother used to sing to him in his cradle. Nod to the ladies, chuck the babies under the chin, and keep one eye on the clock and the other on the Paddys in the pub at closing time."

"What a foolish, humiliating occupation for the descendant of a king, the grandson of a poet, the great-nephew of a saint," she answered, pleased that he would engage in conversation with her, stilted and pessimistic though it might be. She was beginning to despair that the man would ever see the joys and pleasures around him.

The constable's amble had brought him to the side of the cart, and he dutifully touched his forefinger to his cap. The constable smiled, Claymore nodded curtly once, then glanced away, hoping to discourage him from lingering. But contrary to the marquis's obvious wishes, Marke beamed

brilliantly at the man and, to Claymore's chagrin, the unwanted official greeting for the day began.

"And how would the day be finding ye?" queried the
constable.

"Oh, not so bad, how's yerself?" Marke answered,
mimicking his lilting tone.

Claymore snorted his irritation at being trapped in such
ritualistic repartee. Must she be friends with everyone?
Such a child! A wayward, undisciplined child—one who
should be taught consideration and respect for her elders,
he thought sourly. He emitted a long, very audible sigh of
intolerance, thinking it would prompt her to end the conversation before it could gain momentum.

"Could be better, but 'tis a nice day, wouldn't ye say?"
the constable answered, cheerfully unaware of the marquis's wish to be elsewhere.

"Beautiful—or do you think it's going to rain?" Marke
retorted.

The constable obligingly looked to the east, to the north,
west and south, and the sensuous solemnity with which he
turned his head, sniffing the air, conveyed the regret that
there are only four points of the compass, then he returned
meditatively toward them. "It might still rain. Ye know, the
day me oldest daughter had her youngest child—a dear little boy with a fine pair of blue eyes—it was three years ago,
about this time of year. We also thought 'twas a lovely day,
but in the afternoon the heavens parted, and it fair
poured."

"Yes," said Marke, happily falling into the parody. Her
smile was genuine and her eyes filled with sparkle. "When
my sister-in-law, the wife of my only brother, had her first
baby—a sweet, fair-haired little girl, a delightful child, believe me!—the weather was pretty much like today."

"'Twas a terrible day too when Tom Duffy took the big
sorrel roan gelding from the mayor's stable. That day was
a day of sunshine—beautiful the whole of the day—and
'twas on me way to the coast with me oldest daughter's
oldest girl, but instead 'twas called back to be picking up
old Tom. 'Twas at home in bed, he was, sound asleep, and

d'ye know what the fellow would be saying when I shook the sleep from him? Did ye ever hear?''

"I do believe I was in England at that time."

"Well, I would be telling ye then. 'Damn it all,' he yelled to me, ''Tis a stupid, foolish world, when all the right things belong to all the wrong people.' Yes, 'twas a wonderful day and there I was, bringing in silly old Tom.'' He shook his head in docile resignation.

"Oh, my," sympathized Marke with a clicking of her tongue. '''Twas the same on the day my fourth oldest sister—Sarah that would be—proclaimed her intent to be off to London to appear before Lord Chamberlain as candidate for lady-in-waiting to the queen. That day was also a glorious day...for the morning at least. Then the skies opened and it simply flooded!''

In utter and profound disbelief, Claymore glanced from Marke to the constable, and back again. He was indeed losing his sanity here! His life had entered the realm of nightmares and he seemed helpless to regain control. And somehow it all centered around this red-haired, relentless, remarkable woman-child beside him. Never would he have guessed one person could generate such disruption. He resolved at just that moment to see the back of her through the door of Innisfree, the very moment they returned from this journey through hell.

The constable clicked his tongue against his teeth in sympathy of such misfortune. "Aye, I be hearing ye. Just like the day me old mam had all her teeth out—rain in the morning, sunshine at noon, then came a terrible storm in the afternoon—'twas the day Katie O'Malley stabbed the priest from St. Mary's...should have been home with me mam, yet there 'twas prowling about in the pouring rain, looking for Katie.''

Marke canted a merry, shining glance sideways at Claymore, before prompting the constable, "And did you find her? Katie, I mean?''

"Ahem, Miss Penwell?'' Claymore interjected, thinking to prompt an end to this senseless conversation, but Marke seemed to have become deaf to his rather broad hints, and the constable was well into his rhythm now.

"Nay, sitting for two hours or more at the police station, she was, just waiting for us, but 'twas nobody there as we were all out looking for her. *She* finally came out to find *us*, down by the church wall!" He slapped his thigh in glee.

"Kind of her to do that," Marke chortled. "Did they ever find out why she did it?"

"Aye, refused her absolution, he did. She kept on defending herself in court by saying, 'There I was dying, and he would deny me—d'you expect me to die covered in all my sins?'"

"Marke," attempted Claymore again, even going so far as to touch her hand. Marke duly ignored him. He reached for the leathers, but without giving him so much as a stare, she refused to release her grip on them. With no other way to gain them than by an out-and-out tug-of-war, he sat back with an exasperated sigh, glancing heavenward as if seeking some answer to dealing with this stubborn, irritating personage who had invaded his life, other than physical violence, that is.

Marke, pleased at thwarting the marquis's desire to depart, focused on the story. It was just too delicious to bear. With a giggle, she prompted the constable. "Did she show any remorse?"

"Nary a bit. Stood right out in the storm and declared to all, 'Why ye be wailing? He's on his way straight to heaven. What more could he be wanting?'"

"Ah well," Marke empathized with a sad shake of her head.

"Aye, 'twas a day of terrible weather that day." The constable rocked back on his heels in delight. "Rain lashing our faces, snatching at the nuns' garb, for nothing would do but they all traipsed out to hear a confession. Walked beside us, all strung out in a row, when we took her in—praying for her poor soul, they were. The wind was so fierce it lifted those heavy wet robes, and 'twas the damnedest thing." The constable gloated to be passing the

time of day with the quality, and took his time continuing
in hopes the whole of Bantry would chance to see how
friendly they be to him. "For 'twas then I saw what I saw.
Ye'd never guess it, but among all the dark brown underpants, there was one the most shocking red."

Claymore swiveled his gaze to stare at the man. Surely he
was pulling a yarn and would be having a good laugh at
their expense later, over his tank of ale. He then stared at
Marke. Unbelievable, but she apparently was hanging on
the man's every word. He thought to protest this discussion of nuns' underpants in front of an unmarried miss
such as Miss Penwell, I mean, there must be a limit to this
lunacy, but she leapt in ahead of him.

"Red! They weren't!" Marke exclaimed, with a wide-
eyed stare.

"I kein what ye be thinking? 'Twas nobody else to believe me, either. I told them, 'twas the nun which would
keep crying out for the poor dead priest, declaring, 'He be
an angel now.'" The constable's eyes began to shine, and
his face, somewhat bloated from whiskey, battled for a
solemn expression, and suddenly he looked very young.

"Funny thing." Marke glanced up through her lashes to
Claymore and wiggled her eyebrows in a comical manner.
"You know, Lord Perfect, I've never heard of this nun with
the red underpants. I cannot believe something like this
would have escaped the ears of Mrs. P. Although I will
confess that lately there is a great deal that does."

Her aside was so blatantly part of the ridiculous play,
fully expected by the constable and clearly meant to be
overheard by him, that Claymore could not stop the grin
that flashed his dimple. The little witch! She was gam-
moning with him, leading the constable on to make him
laugh. How like her to find pleasure in everything that surrounded her, he thought, and insist on dragging everyone
else along with her. Just look at the sparkle in her eyes now.
They fairly danced with gaiety. He could see she was fighting hard to control her laughter. Her lips twitched in the
most delicious manner.

The constable rambled on. "'Twas the most remarkable thing, for the nun seemed to disappear before any questioning could be done. And when 'twas discovered, they put out a search for her, thinking of more foul play, ye kein. Well, 'twas a terrible row, of course, with the nuns saying 'twas an angel sent by God to escort the poor murdered priest to heaven, and us wanting to inspect the underpants of all the nuns in Ireland."

At that, Claymore capitulated. He threw back his head and laughed heartily.

"And did you ever get to see them—the underpants, I mean?" Marke asked, giggling at the constable and thrilled at Claymore's surrender. It had taken him long enough.

"Nay." The constable affected a sad expression. "Never did. But ye kein what I really wondered about? If 'twas truly an angel, does it mean they actually wear red underpants in heaven?"

"My good man, that's a question to pose to the archbishop himself," countered Claymore, shaking his head and chuckling at a tale well told.

"You know, I just might do that," the constable agreed. "The next I see him." Suddenly he seemed reminded of his real, his tiresome, his earthly life. His face suddenly grew old again, and gloomy. "Well, best be on me rounds. Top of the morn to ye both. Watch yerself that the rain don't catch ye too far from home."

Claymore slipped the reins from Marke's now-willing fingers and whipped up the pony. He was amazed to find that he felt enormously lighter in mood. He could feel Marke trying to control her mirth, and yet the laughter that she would not allow to voice showed on her face, shining brightly in her merry brown eyes each time she glanced up through her lashes. Finally, grinning a wide grin, he addressed her, "I would say probably not the descendant of a king, and most possibly the great-nephew of a saint might be stretching the imagination, but most definitely the grandson of a poet—if not the poet himself."

Marke giggled and immediately found joy in the day once again, never questioning just why the marquis's rapid change of attitudes should affect her own moods so considerably.

Chapter Twelve

The rousing storm, accurately predicted by the constable, relentlessly battered the windows with rain and brought out the darkness in Claymore's soul. He stared moodily into the library fire, watching the flames dance about, licking, teasing, searing and finally greedily devouring the peat blocks thrown into its midst as sacrifice for human comfort. Repulsed by it, yet drawn to imagine the horror of death in its heat, he shuddered. Though it was something he would rather not contemplate, his thoughts relentlessly turned morose, and were filled with death.

"How did your father die, Marke?" he asked, without raising his gaze from the flames.

Marke, snuggled into the deep cushions of the window seat with her nose buried in a book of seafaring adventure, glanced up at the sound of her name. "Pardon?"

"I asked how your father died?" Claymore repeated, shuddering again as the peat block fell apart with a shower of sparks. "Was it peaceful, in bed with clean sheets and his loving family gathered around him?"

"Not at all," Marke said, closing her book on her forefinger and regarding his dispirited face closely. Was this the opening she had been waiting for? His need, at last, to speak of his family's tragedy with someone? "My father was lost at sea, during a violent storm that took his ship and crew."

"That must have been hard, not knowing for certain the nature of his passing. I mean, did he just not return home from the voyage?"

"No, we were fortunate enough to have the story from the one seaman who survived the wreck."

"Do you ever wonder if it was violent? If he was in pain, in terror?" he persisted with his morbid probing.

She laid her book aside and moved to drop into the burgundy leather chair opposite the marquis. "No, I do not wonder. Because he died doing the one thing in his life that had more meaning to him than anything else. He would have been standing on the deck, shouting orders and raising his fist to the storm in defiance. I think he would have been happier at that moment than at any other time of his life."

Claymore jerked his eyes to hers. "Why do you say that? How could any man feel happy, faced with the certainty of his own death?"

"Because my father would have considered it honorable to be taken by a more powerful opponent. Captain Horace P. Penwell would have hated succumbing to old age, disease and frailty."

"Yes, that I can well understand." Claymore struck his leg with the flat of his hand in disgust at its weakness.

Marke, sensing his mood, set out to distract him from his fatalistic ramblings before he sank into a depression as deep as the well hole and then retired to his bed to drown in it. "Shall I tell you of my father's last voyage, or what we know of it, I mean, as told us by the sole surviving seaman?"

Claymore shifted his tortured eyes back to the fire, and when he didn't immediately answer her, she leaned forward to place her hand on his to regain his attention. He looked down at her soft, white hand on his much larger one, then raised his eyes to met hers. There was so much compassion and warmth in her eyes. And such invitation to the gentle curve of her mouth. Her whole being suggested passion—passion for living, for exploring, for sucking the very last drop of pleasure from her existence—he suddenly wondered if her intensity for everything that was considered part of living would extend to love. His eyes slipped down the smooth column of her white throat and came to rest on the swell of her full breasts beneath the trim green velvet bodice. They were of a size to nicely fill a man's hands. Would her nipples be lightly tinted pink, he wondered? His neglected loins tightened with the thought of carnal pleasures such as flicking those pink nipples to attention with his thumb and tasting that sweet mouth beneath his own. He unconsciously leaned toward her.

Marke's eyes softened and she tilted her face upward, fully prepared to accept his kiss as the most natural thing on earth at that moment.

Sitter bustled into the room, snapping Marke up straight in her chair and jerking the marquis's eyes toward her with an expression that could only be described as guilty as hell. Although Sitter lifted a questioning eyebrow, she did not make reference to the fact that she had obviously, and quite fortunately, intruded on an intensely intimate moment between the two. "There you both are!" she called brightly. "I have napped away most of the afternoon, and now I am tediously bored."

Claymore was nonplussed as to whether he welcomed this intrusion, or did he really wish he had locked the damn library door. That thought, of being locked in the library with Marke, again brought a quickening to his manhood. Glancing at Marke's pink face, he cleared his throat slightly, drawing the shawl higher over his knees in an unconsciously defensive move. Waving Sitter toward a seat, he sought distraction immediately!

"Please join us," he invited, in what he hoped was a casual enough request. "Miss Penwell was just embarking upon a long tale of Captain Horace Penwell's final, and I'm sorry to add, fatal, voyage."

"Oh, marvelous!" exclaimed Sitter, obviously not realizing they spoke of Marke's father. "I shall just ring for tea and settle in. Such a delightful idea. I do so love storytelling, even if it stems from the unromantic bowels of real life."

Marke laughed and winked broadly at Claymore. He startled for a moment at the familiar gesture, then smiled slightly at her. She was such a child, yet a joy and a comfort to be around—well, perhaps not always a comfort—but had she always been so deliciously desirable, he wondered? Or had he merely been blind to the ripeness of her form? Good Lord, whatever was the matter with him? Lusting after his houseguest! Yes, Miss Penwell, perhaps you should embark upon a long tale of the captain's adventures, he decided. The distraction would be most welcome to his body and mind, as both were strangely unmanageable this afternoon.

Marke rose to move Sitter's chair closer to the fire, and waited until instructions for tea and sweets had been given to Heaven. Once that was done, and Sitter settled into her chair, she began her story. "Let's see. Well, the captain's last voyage was against the family's strongest wish, my brother's especially, as the captain was six and sixty at the time. *The Agate* was a new addition to the Penwell line, and she was the worst of the lot, full of strife and mutiny. And, of course, he was determined to straighten out the problem or to cane the captain and throw him overboard. His aptitude was still sharp, and he discerned right away that the officers were a poor lot." Marke felt her cheeks flushing with the intensity of the marquis's gaze and dropped her eyes to the fire, lest she begin to stammer. "The mate was something of a bucko—a bully, if you will—and the captain, though a good man and an excellent seaman, had a fatal weakness. He was too easygoing and lacked the essential qualities of leadership. It was immediately clear that he had not put his bucko in his place, as he should have done in the very beginning. Instead, he suffered his behavior."

"Ah, and one should know that is not the manner to deal with a bully," Claymore interrupted the tale with his caustic remark directed toward Sitter, but tilted an eyebrow at Marke when she glanced at him in surprise.

"Sometimes a person requires a bit of bullying," Marke countered, raising both her eyebrows at him to stress her meaning.

"But bullying breeds rebellion if it goes on and on for months," he said, as a pointed remark.

"Shall I continue the story, Lord Perfect?" she asked, in a prim governess's schoolroom tone. "Or do you wish a debate?"

"By all means continue, Miss Penwell," he conceded with a wry grin for having stirred her temper. "I am properly chastised, and shall not interrupt again."

"Thank you," Marke said, pleased to see him distracted from his brooding and intent upon deviling her. "My father would have been alive today if he had replaced the captain, but instead he went to sea to teach him how to be a leader. That was his first mistake. His second, and one I cannot believe he would make, was to foolishly sail on a Friday. This may seem a small thing, but it was flying directly in the face of all maritime tradition, and strictly taboo to all sailors, as they are a superstitious lot. To begin a voyage by deliberately flouting such a taboo was to ask for disloyalty—and Father got it in spades!"

"So why do you think he did it, Marke? Sail on a Friday that way?" Sitter interrupted, leaning forward with a look of concern on her face.

Claymore smiled at her rapt attention to the tale. Sitter was dear to him and he had been negligent in her care lately. And Marke, she did have a way about her, an amazing talent for drawing people to her. Dangerous woman, our Marke, he thought, for he was feeling strongly drawn himself. Marke smiled impishly at Sitter, then at Claymore, drawing out the suspense before shrugging her shoulders. Claymore's eyes darted to her breasts so well defined beneath the green velvet. Damn it all, he thought. He leaned his head back against the chair and closed his traitorous eyes. Was blindfolded the only way he could be in her presence and still behave with any decency?

"I am not sure why he would sail on a Friday," Marke answered, pleased to see the marquis relaxing back into his chair. "Perhaps as instruction for the captain—to gain domination over the crew. But for whatever the reason, *The Agate* at first raced along, well on her way to a splendid passage. The bucko mate had the crew working well, although one hand named Mason, a great barrel of a man, remained completely useless. He was not liked by the crew for the obvious reason that they all suffered when his share of the work was thrown upon their backs. The bucko mate went out of his way to haze the man, and my father allowed this, supposedly waiting for the captain to take hold and right the situation."

The tale was again interrupted by the arrival of Heaven and tea, closely followed by Dr. Barrows, apparently in high spirits. He stepped through the doorway, then paused to press his hand to his chest. "Ah, such a cozy family gathering, and here I am blundering in. But in the manner of all good physicians—a point, I should tell you, that is stressed rather stridently in medical school—I have arrived just in time for tea."

Sitter looked up with a great smile of delight on her face. "John! What a pleasure. You have indeed timed your arrival with that of the tea service—" she patted the seat next to her invitingly "—and in time to hear Marke's tale of Captain Penwell."

"Oh, I had not realized Miss Penwell's talents lent themselves to storytelling, although I would cry liar to anyone who dared tell me she could not admirably accomplish her end, once she had placed her mind upon it. Miss Penwell, your servant as always," he teased, bowing low to place a lingering kiss on Marke's hand. He beamed into her eyes. "Remarkable lady, our Miss Penwell."

Marke laughed and inclined her head in acknowledgment of such ridiculous compliments. "Enough, or you shall have my head swelled beyond my neck's capabilities and then I shall become known throughout Bantry as that poor misshapen Miss Penwell. And I should hate to be the object of pity more than anything."

Sitter nodded sympathetically, pretending to be unaware of any prank, but Claymore snorted at the doctor's encouragement of the chit's outrageousness. "But just consider, Miss Penwell, the good that could come of such a thing. John could write a medical paper on the phenomenon and become quite famous, and once again, you should be lauded as a remarkable young woman for having aided in the advancement of such a worthy man as our good Dr. Barrows."

Marke stubbornly shook her head. "You must forgive me, Dr. Barrows, for any stunting of your career advancement, but I shall not retire to my bed with a swollen head just to appease your misguided desire for accolades in the field of medicine."

John, thrilled to see the comic byplay of the marquis, affected a pained expression and turned moony eyes on her. "Pray do not lay the sin of vanity and desire for praise at my door. The suggestion was not mine, but yon blackguard's there. I would rather perish than have you think poorly of me, Miss Penwell."

Marke giggled and held up her hand. "Enough of this. Far too much like the inane social prattle I remember from London drawing rooms between people who could not speak a straight phrase if their very lives depended upon it. What brings you out on such an inclement day, Dr. Barrows?"

"Purely good works, I assure you. I called upon your mother this morning, and found her hale and hearty, the proud recipient of yet another canine wonder. A sheepdog of some sort. Amazing-looking animal—quite as large and as woolly as a bear."

"Oh, lud!" groaned Marke. "Where does she acquire those things?"

"And having had my heart broken at finding you absent from St. Catherine's Court, I thought to pass on the news of your mother, at the same time I fetched Sitter, as I promised to do, the very next time I was invited by the Earl of Bantry to view his orchid greenhouse." He turned to beam at Sitter. "As the weather seems to be clearing..."

"Oh, John!" Sitter exclaimed. "Wonderful! I shall pop upstairs and fetch my new hat. Oh, this is so exciting, you know. A trip to Bantry."

Marke laughed as Sitter dashed out the door. It was good to see her friend excited about a social outing, even such a rare treat as a trip to quiet Bantry, which she only did every third day anyway. "So, Mrs. P dwells well during my absence?" she asked, wishing to probe for further details, but hesitant about discussing her mother's infirmity in front of the marquis.

John seemed to sense this and followed her lead. "Quite well, actually. The bitch Cleo had presented her with an astonishing litter of twelve just last evening and it was of great concern that such a brood might be too taxing on her good temperament."

Marke grinned and shook her head. Then turning to see Claymore's puzzled expression, she thought to explain about Mrs. P and her dogs, but Sitter returned at that moment, and the need to satisfy his curiosity was lost in the excited flurry and tangle of their departure. Only when the library was quiet again, and they were alone, did she turn to him with shrugged shoulders and tilted eyebrows.

"Well, I suppose that puts an end to our storytelling. Having given our solemn oath to Sitter, and on the pain of death to boot, that we must not continue until she returns rather stymies it, doesn't it?"

"That it does," Claymore agreed. "But I'm rather distracted anyway. How about a stroll—" he grimaced slightly and amended his remark "—of sorts, through Innisfree's own conservatory?"

"Wonderful idea. Amazingly enough, I've yet to venture there," she agreed, stepping to roll the invalid chair closer. "Shall I call for Henry, or do you think we can accomplish this voyage on our own?"

"Perhaps, although it might bruise my spirits irreparably to fail in your eyes," he teased, nevertheless flipping the shawl from his knees and pushing himself quite competently to his feet.

"Ah, yes, failure is sad, indeed, but not to try at all is sadder still." She shoved the chair close to him and steadied him with a hand on his arm.

Settled in the chair, they rolled down the long hall toward the conservatory. For some reason, her statement bothered Claymore unduly. Surely she could not think he did not try. Perhaps her continual pushing and prodding indicated her belief that he was reconciled to his helplessness, or worse, playing upon sympathies in an unmasculine way. The thought of Marke holding only pity for him was surprisingly disturbing, and ruffled his male ego no small amount. Being confined, for the most part to an invalid chair, did not lesson his feelings as a man, and he took offense that she might think it did. Never one to fear facing squarely certain truths, he confronted her with his suspicions. "Sometimes, Miss Penwell, I feel you must pity me greatly."

Marke frowned behind his back. She felt he deserved an honest answer, but first she had better be honest with herself. Did she pity him? Did she see him as crippled? No, actually she did not. "Pity? No, I do not think so. I have great compassion—"

"Compassion and pity are one and the same!" he snorted. That was not the answer he wished to hear from her.

"Not so, Lord Perfect," Marke countered. "Compassion and pity are very different. Compassion is the spontaneous response of caring..." *And loving,* she almost said. "While pity is the involuntary reflex of fear."

"I do not understand your reference to fear."

"Fear that the malady could be transferable..." Marke swung the double doors to the conservatory wide and interrupted herself with a wide-eyed gasp. "My gracious! It's an English garden in the middle of Ireland!" she exclaimed, spinning down the path in a flurry of green velvet skirts, displaying a goodly amount of neat ankles amid lace-trimmed petticoats. "Oh, this is so—so..."

Claymore smiled at her excitement, wheeling himself through the doors in her wake. "What's this? Miss Marke Penwell rendered speechless?"

"This would render anyone speechless. It's like a fairy-land!" she enthused, staring about her, taking in the fully leafed vines clambering up the walls, and the baskets hung from the lofty ceiling, spilled with greenery. An immense glass hall attached to the southeast side of the castle, the conservatory created an everlasting garden even in winter. No matter the weather outside, plant beds here were lined with blossoms and greens. No matter what the season, guests could stroll the pathways edged with neatly trimmed hedges of laurel and holly. "I've never seen anything like this before. It's a marvel!" Running toward a large three-tiered fountain with water cascading over the shoulders of naked nymphs and bubbling from the urns of chubby, loincloth-draped cherubs, Marke plopped herself on the rim to dip brave fingers into the water to tempt the rushing, ever-hungry carp.

Claymore's breath caught painfully in his throat, as her posture—the very act of teasing the carp—was something his sister was fond of doing. His mother's voice rang out in his head, delivering the so often repeated warnings of be careful—be safe—don't get hurt. He wheeled himself forward slowly, watching the curve of Marke's cheek as her lips spread into a delighted smile. Was that the tug of emotions he was feeling for this young woman? Merely missing the presence and innocence of his little sister? The thought displeased him greatly. It made him feel disloyal to the memory of Libby, and dishonest in his reactions to Marke. No! He would deny that thought most vehemently. His feelings for Marke were nothing more than the normal, reawakening desire a healthy man feels for a beautiful, sensual woman, and he would prove it to himself in the most rational manner possible.

"Marke, come here."

Marke turned with a startled expression. This was a tone of voice she'd never before heard from him—soft but definitely commanding. Could he be ill? She immediately moved to him, kneeling at his side. "Are you feeling unwell, Lord Perfect? Shall I ring for someone?"

Staring down into her upturned face, Claymore felt again the filling of his manhood, stretching and straining. She was truly a beautiful thing—fresh and fragrant—with the light dusting of freckles over her perfect nose and her earthy eyes filled with green and gold lights. He cupped the back of her head in his palm and drew her up to him, momentarily surprised that she came so willingly, so filled with trust. Leaning forward, he placed his lips upon hers, kissing her lightly, tenderly. Lifting his head, he stared down into her wide, questioning eyes. She seemed to be holding her breath and looking at him with confusion, but she did not struggle against his hold. At first, he thought to explain his actions to her, then he decided to order her brusquely from the room. In the end, he did neither. Grasping her beneath the arms, he drew her quickly to his lap to capture her lips to his own again. He kissed her ardently, tasting her inexperience on his tongue and pleased at her willingness to allow his impassioned kisses even when she must surely be frightened at their fierceness. She tasted so sweet beneath his lips, and felt wonderful, so round and soft, in his arms.

Marke thought her heart had stopped. Never having been kissed before, she was amazed to find it so entrancing. Claymore's grip on her waist was clasping, and his lips firm, moving over hers as if he meant to devour her. She let him kiss her, his tongue sliding across her full lower lip so insistently that she allowed him the access he demanded, granting control of her rioting emotions to him because she wished it so very feverishly.

Claymore, warmed by the tenderness of her surrender, groaned as his arousal flamed, pressing against her buttocks. Breaking the kiss, he slid his hand slowly over her throat to her breast, down her waist and over her hip to her long thighs. The very feel of her was as intoxicating as heady wine. She moaned softly, deep in her throat, and closed her eyes as he pressed his lips to her neck, the hollow of her throat, the valley between her breasts, his hot

breath searing her through the velvet. He buried his face in
her neck, taking in the heady scent of her body mixed with
roses. The sound of her breath, first held then let out in soft
gasps, fired him. He groaned deep in his throat with need,
with desire, and with pain as his body came back to life,
demanded he feel and respond as a man, leaving behind his
resolve to bury such feelings beneath grief and withdrawal.

Marke, nearly senseless with new and wonderful emotions running unchecked through her body, thrilled at the
feel of his hot breath against her neck. Drunk with sensations and ragged breath, her head was thrown back, curls
tumbling from their knot to fall over his arm. She could
stand no more. She must touch him, too. Feel him beneath
her hands, taste his flesh on her tongue. But when she
would raise her hand to stroke his cheek, he snatched it
sharply, as if he expected her to strike him, and levered her
abruptly from his lap to her feet.

"Do not expect me to suffer missish offense now, when
you have been such a willing participant, Miss Penwell," he
growled. He was badly shaken by the force of his arousal
and sought to turn the incident to his advantage by glow-
ering up at her. She stood before him, her hair mussed, her
mouth red and trembling, eyes unfocused and dreamy. She
was wanton and utterly desirable, and she made him ache
to know her. "But I warn you," he said, laughing uneasily. "Take to your heels now or suffer the consequences for
I am a man in every way, despite this chair, and I would
delight in teaching you the ways of intimacy between a man
and woman."

Marke drew a shuddering breath of disappointment. Yes,
it was better this way, she told herself. To tease away the
rampant feelings that raced with such heat through her
veins, at least, until she had opportunity to examine them
closely, a thing that must be done far away from the disturbing presence of Claymore, Lord Perfect. Pressing her
hands into the folds of her skirt, she fought to still their
trembling, and smiled a wavery smile. "As I obviously
didn't have the common sense to think of striking you for

impertinence, perhaps you're right. I shall prove what a fast learner I can be, and finally display my good sense by fleeing your presence as if the very rats of hell were nipping at my petticoats,'' she vowed. Running lightly to the door, she called over her shoulder in a light, teasing tone, "Until dinner, my lecherous lord."

Claymore sat for a long time beside the fountain. His thoughts were as scattered as his emotions. Were all his efforts to deny and slay the emotions of his life to be completely undone by the lace on the petticoats of one saucy miss? Suddenly he felt alive again. He felt desire. He felt merriment. He felt gladness, but his rational side warned him that to feel all those good things would mean he must also feel pain again, for sorrow followed happiness as surely as night followed day. Wasn't life equal parts good and bad? No, the bad far outweighed the good. And pain and grief negated any limited happiness life granted. He ran a hand over his eyes in dread. There was absolutely no doubt in his mind that he would never be strong enough to endure such agony a second time. But neither was he strong enough to withdraw from Marke, for she was the only lifeline he could grasp for survival. It was only in her presence that the nightmare seemed far away. It was only in her presence that his soul felt whole once more. It was truly a quandary. Be with her and feel . . . or be without her . . . no, it was too late for that. He wasn't sure quite how it had happened, but suddenly the idea of life without Marke wasn't very appealing at all.

Chapter Thirteen

October twenty-eighth dawned gray. The air was heavy with mists that curled and swirled about the nooks and crannies of the mountains high over Innisfree. Marke, having spent a restless night, torn by wavering emotions and startling revelations of her true feelings for Claymore, had watched what light the approaching dawn could offer from her window seat. Having first denounced such revelations as foolish and dangerous, toward dawn she finally accepted the capture of her heart by a man as fractious as Lord Perfect. Margaret Catherine Penwell was in love. Today was her nineteenth birthday, and she was in love. Suddenly the very thought of being in love with Claymore excited her to no end. Disentangling herself from the coverlet, she rushed to the mirror to see if she was physically altered in any way.

"Today I am nineteen, and I am in love," she announced to her reflection. The very act of making the statement aloud brought laughter bubbling forth. "I am in love with Claymore! Claymore, my love!" She laughed again and spun away into the room, heady with the thought.

Kittie, posted as sentinel, poked her head around the door to gape at the sight of the young miss dancing about her room in her night rail. Shaking her head, she closed the door quietly behind her and dashed down the stairs to alert Heaven. Because it was the young miss's birthday, his lordship had firmly instructed them all that he must be awakened the instant she moved about this morning, although Kittie doubted he would be any too pleased at the earliness of this hour. He'd never been one for rising before the first cock crow, as Miss Penwell was.

Quickly braiding her hair into a single plait, Marke pulled on her woolen skirt, sweater and sturdy boots without waiting for Kittie. Regardless of the early hour, she truly could not delay her day until the young maid made her appearance. This day was entirely too special for remaining indoors, especially as the mists were calling her to wander the cliffs before breakfast.

As usual, Marke was galloping unladylike down the stairs when she realized the entry hall was filled with people. She stumbled to a sketchy halt in surprise, a dull flush of embarrassment creeping into her cheeks at being caught behaving like a hoyden by so many. It would seem the entire staff, headed by a beaming Claymore and a yawning Sitter, were gathered in the entry below the main staircase. At the sight of her, they all broke into a rousing birthday song for her. Surprised and delighted, Marke rushed down to hug Sitter, and as many of the others as she could lay hands upon.

"Oh, you've really surprised me! How did you know?" she demanded of Claymore, shyly pecking him on the cheek.

Claymore laughed at her, gratefully accepting his kiss after all the others, although he would have preferred his to be first. "Why, it's October! The birthday of all the Penwells in the world. Now come get your birthday present, then we'll have a breakfast celebration, if we can keep Sitter awake."

Everyone laughed and parted a path to the front door. Claymore wheeled his chair ahead of her, and Sitter dragged her forward by the hand. As everyone crowded on the front steps, a groom led forth a dancing, fire red filly, festooned with a yellow ribbon about her middle and a giant bow upon her withers. Marke's eyes grew large, rapidly filling with tears so that she had to blink to clear her vision.

"Oh my! Oh my!" she gasped, looking first at Sitter, then at Claymore. She wanted to throw her arms about someone in the worst way, but being unsure who the gift was actually from, she finally raced down the steps to throw her arms about the filly's neck in an exuberant hug. The startled filly danced backward in protest, but not quickly enough to escape Marke. She refused to turn loose of the prancing filly, partly because she was absolutely thrilled with the gift, but mostly because to do so would be to display a tear-streaked face and eyes that would not stop their embarrassing overflow. It was just the best gift she had ever received in her whole life.

After repeatedly extracting Claymore's assurance that Marke would be returned in a timely manner for her celebration dinner, Sitter gaily sent them on their way to a birthday tea with Mrs. P. It was with a great deal of pleasure that Marke waved to the St. Catherine's Court gatekeeper, strutting himself and his gaudy livery for the amused marquis, and prepared to show off her home to the man she loved with her whole heart. Tossing the reins to a groom, she rushed into the house with Claymore being wheeled behind her. Giving her black driving coat to Mr. Biddle, she paused to draw a deep breath of beeswax, candle smoke, and the fainter scent of wet dog, into her lungs.

"Ah, St. Catherine's Court! It feels as if I've been gone months instead of weeks. Mr. Biddle, is my mother receiving this afternoon?"

The butler sketched a slight bow with just the right sobriety. "I am certain she is, miss. Shall I tell her that you and the gentleman are in the library?"

"If you would, please. We'll take tea there, also," she answered, pleased that the man was a master of quickness, of sensitivity—and of deception.

Sweeping into the library behind Marke, Claymore settled himself into a comfortable upholstered chair before the fire. He surveyed the library with great interest, much as Marke had done his own. "It would seem, Miss Penwell, that you are the owner of a certain number of books yourself," he commented drolly, nodding at the shelves.

She laughed gently, pleased that he would remember that encounter. "Yes, although I am of a mind that they were included in the acquisition of the house, as neither my father nor mother were great readers."

"And have you read them all? How was it phrased? Discovered the reason the author sought to place his thoughts upon paper for others to read?" he quoted, watching her face flush slightly as she came toward him in the purposeful stride that nevertheless displayed an unconscious grace of movement. There was an unaffected femininity about Marke that he was beginning to appreciate greatly. She placed no airs upon herself. She seemed to have no expectations of those around her, other than to enjoy to the fullest what each day presented her. And, while she was terribly exasperating at times, there was a calmness, a relaxing quality about her that soothed him. He glanced about the library again, taking note of the elegance tamed into homey repose, then back at Marke seating herself in the chair opposite him. What was it about her that made him want to cling to her in the most infantile manner?

Marke smiled at him now, and waved at the laden bookshelves. "As I have always had limited time at St. Catherine's Court, I must admit to dividing my time unequally between indoors and out of doors, with the stables and woods demanding most of my attention."

"So, reading was not a priority for your summer afternoons?"

"I have always enjoyed reading, but confess to having only read up to the second shelf, as my enlightenment was restricted by childish height."

Claymore chuckled deep in his throat at the picture of a little girl stretched on tiptoe to reach a book. "And what were your literary interests as a child of such restricted height?"

"Oh my, I suppose that would depend upon the year. It would most probably have began with anything written on horses, then turned to the sea before my heart was broken by the knowledge that girls weren't allowed to be shipmasters, and then advancing to little girl romances and weddings, and on to—" she tilted eyebrows upward as she made her shocking confession "—ah, medical journals."

"Medical journals? Strange reading for a young girl. Did you find those on the lower two shelves?"

"Oh no, I fear those required a ladder to reach, followed closely by a secreted trip to the attic for private perusal. And, before you inquire, I believe I was greatly intrigued as to the whispered differences between the genders of our species."

Claymore laughed at her candid confession, enjoying the way her eyes sparkled and danced with barely contained laughter even if her rosy lips were somewhat under control.

They were interrupted by Mr. Biddle discreetly clearing his throat in the doorway as his way of begging permission to interrupt them with tea, served in an array of little ceramic pots hidden beneath knitted cozies of muted greens and purples, arranged on a diminutive round tray table with a mottled green marble top. Much more cozy, more intimate, than the heavy sterling service at Innisfree, and somehow, perfectly suited to this setting and this hostess.

"Mrs. Lithgow has asked me to inform you, miss, that Mrs. P will join you shortly," Mr. Biddle said.

"Thank you, Mr. Biddle."

"Also I wish to point out, miss, that Cook has made Pansy specifically for your enjoyment on this birthday afternoon."

"Pansy!" Marke exclaimed, lifting the cover from the pastry dish. "Oh, she has! I must remember to thank her. Lord Perfect, you are indeed in for a treat."

Claymore smiled at her childish enthusiasm, and yet watched with anticipation as she carefully placed a puffed tart on a plate for him. "And, pray Miss Penwell, what exactly is a Pansy, besides a small flower with a face, that is?"

"A Pansy, my lord, is a pastry, the ultimate in sensory pleasure. Not only is it filled with what can readily be described as essence of chocolate, in the very center is a candied pansy. I assure you, the exquisite texture of the chocolate alone would have been sufficient to assure one's undying gratitude, but to include a candied pansy—well, you will just have to tell me once you have tasted it for yourself."

"I shall most assuredly do so, but shouldn't we await your mother?"

Marke glanced quickly at Claymore, with her bottom lip tucked between her teeth. "Oh, Lord Perfect, I should explain about my mother..." she began, but she had left it too late. Mrs. P, elegantly turned out in ruby silk, rounded the corner on Mrs. Moran's sturdy arm, followed closely by a springer spaniel bitch and three tumbling, barking puppies that immediately ran to leap upon Claymore.

"Oh, dear," Marke exclaimed, dragging one away and signaling for Mrs. Moran to gather the animals. "I am so sorry, my lord."

Claymore laughed and pulled a lolling puppy upon his lap to rub its head. "Do not distress yourself, Miss Penwell. I have a great fondness for dogs."

Marke watched in startled awe as Claymore scratched the spotted head and seemed pleased beyond belief with the experience. It was only then that she fully realized that there were no dogs—or cats—roaming the halls and spilling about the rooms of Innisfree. "Then you may indulge your fondness to saturation in this house, my lord, for Mrs. P also has a great fondness for dogs," she said, rising to place a kiss on her mother's cheek. "Isn't that so, Mrs. P?"

Mrs. P ignored her daughter, and frowned down upon the man seated before the fire. Drawing herself up regally, she expressed that frown in no uncertain terms. "Young man, is it considered polite to remain seated when a lady enters the room?"

Marke's stomach flipped over with dread. Oh, no! Why, oh, why hadn't she explained Mrs. P to Claymore sooner? She hurried to interrupt her mother before the marquis could be further humiliated. "Mrs. P, I wish to present Lord Perfect, the Marquis of Boothe-Ashmore."

Mrs. P turned a stern expression upon her daughter. "And you, young woman, should not have brought a man into this house. It is not the place of a governess to entertain gentlemen in the library. Shame on you, Marke!"

Claymore, quickly assessing the situation, placed the puppy on the floor and used the chair arms to lever himself to his feet. "Mrs. Penwell."

"Yes, I am Mrs. Penwell," she answered, redirecting her gaze to him,

"I do apologize for my lapse of manners, and you are quite right to scold me. If you will please say you forgive me, and allow me to resume my seat, I shall be your servant forever," he said, flashing a charming smile at her.

Mrs. P looked confused, as if she had forgotten why he was here. "Oh, how stupid. Of course you may sit down. Marke, pour the tea. I am very thirsty." She plopped down upon the sofa and patted the seat beside her, encouraging all three of the rowdy puppies up beside her. The spaniel bitch sat at her feet with lolling tongue, shifting equally adoring glances from her mistress to the tea tray.

"Miss Penwell, if you will seat yourself, I believe we may resume our tea," Claymore said, easing back into the chair. "And erase that frown of worry from your face. Smiles are more in your nature."

Marke wondered for a second at his easy acceptance of the situation. John Barrows, of course! The town crier! With a sigh of relief, she plopped down herself. "Thank you, Lord Perfect. I am so sorry for not preparing you—"

"It is of no importance, now, is it?"

Mrs. P accepted the pastry and bit into it greedily, then addressed the marquis with a full mouth. "I do not need another servant, you know. And especially not one so attached to the governess."

"You are very right to feel that way, Mrs. Penwell," Claymore politely agreed with her. "A governess's position is one of great importance, and her attention should never be allowed to be misdirected."

Mrs. P became distracted by the wiggly pups attempting to invade her teacup. "Stop that, you silly, greedy puppies. Oh dear! Oh dear!'' The unconcerned Mrs. Moran deftly removed the puppies without ruffling a feather, and unceremoniously dropped them onto the floor behind the sofa.

Marke suddenly felt very tired. She sipped her tea, thankful for the hearty Irish brew that Mr. Biddle knew strengthened her.

Claymore watched her closely, sensing her withdrawal, her weariness. It was a heavy burden for a young girl to shoulder, and yet she seemed to be managing splendidly. He set about to distract her and bring back her sparkle. ''Miss Penwell, I have just discovered the candied pansy, and you are right, it is an overload for the taste buds.''

Marke laughed gently in appreciation of his kindness. Mrs. P glanced about for the puppies. ''Oh, dear, I seemed to have misplaced the puppies. Oh, how dreadful of me! Here puppies. Here puppies.''

Mrs. Moran calmly stepped forward and complacently relieved Mrs. P of her teacup and saucer. Drawing her charge to her feet, she escorted her to the door with murmured words of encouragement. The spaniel bitch dutifully followed, but apparently the puppies had fallen asleep in mid-tumble, as babies are known to do, for they were piled in a tangle of wet noses and puppy paws behind the sofa.

Drawing a deep breath of relief at the silence, Marke wondered whether to explain or not. Uncertain how to go about it, but feeling that it must be done, she began, ''Lord Perfect, I—I—''

''Miss Penwell, I admit we are not of long acquaintance, but this is hardly polite society, now is it?'' he interrupted, leaning toward her with a smile. ''Do you think I could persuade you to feel comfortable calling me by my Christian name—Claymore? And, perhaps grant me license to use yours, as well?''

Happiness surged through her being. She wanted to shout yes! Yes, call me ''Marke''! Call me ''dearest''! Call me ''darling''! But please call me ''yours forever.'' Instead she inclined her head politely. "I would like that very much, Claymore."

"Thank you, Marke," he countered. "Or would you rather be called by your full name. Margaret, isn't it?"

"Yes, Margaret Catherine. The name Margaret has been in my mother's family for at least seven generations—that is, seven that I know of—and was my grandmother's name. The Catherine, of course, is after this house. But I much prefer the shortened version of Marke."

"Then Marke it shall be."

"Wonderful. Claymore, would you prefer a libation with more, shall we say, *spirit* to it? The drive over was a little chilling."

"Yes, as a matter of fact, I should appreciate that most definitely, Miss—" he grinned at her and amended "—Marke."

Marke rang for Mr. Biddle to remove the remnants of tea and the tray table, but served Claymore a bumper of whiskey herself. Sitting across from each other before the fire, they reposed for a time in companionable silence with Claymore studying the fire and Marke studying the marquis. Mr. Biddle's discreet knock interrupted their quiet, and he began to gather the tea things.

"I'm sorry to disturb you, Miss Penwell, but Mrs. Lithgow is wondering if you were aware of the turn in the weather, and if she should see to changes in dinner and, perhaps ready the blue guest room—third floor, north wing?"

Marke glanced quickly out the window. "Oh, my, it truly is raging outside, isn't it? Lord Perfect, I think perhaps we are quite stranded at St. Catherine's Court."

Claymore, too, was startled to see wind-driven rain lashing the windowpanes. The diversion, the comfort and the ease of being with Marke had kept his thoughts quite occupied. "So it would seem the clouds were right in their predictions, after all. Yes, I feel it may be best to linger here. Even in a closed coach, it would make for a wet, chilling ride."

Marke nodded at Mr. Biddle. "The blue room will be perfect, Mr. Biddle, and perhaps you might find some of my father's necessities in his rooms?"

"Of course, miss," the butler said, bowing himself out.

Marke crossed to the window to stare out at the deluge, watching the gold and scarlet leaves race across the lawns as if fleeing before the threat of winter.

"Marke, how long has your mother been slipping?" Claymore asked.

Marke sighed and tilted her head in thought. "It seems to me my whole life. Oh, not as bad as she is now, but she was always scattered. My father's death is hard for her to remember. He was absent so many months of each year that it's easy for her to think he will be coming back. Perhaps it's because of this that she dwells in the past more than in the present."

"It seems a strange thing for her to be here, rather than in London with her children, if you do not mind my saying so."

"No, I do not mind." She moved to seat herself before the fire. "But I suppose she became a burden for Jessell, my brother's wife, as that one keeps herself in such a whirl of social advancement for most of the year. And, my sisters—mainly Sarah, Kathleen and Charity, all of whom are flogging the petticoat line this season—felt she was a detriment to their prospects on the marriage market. So Thomas sent her to St. Catherine's Court and—" she paused to bestow a radiant yet somehow false smile upon him "—I followed."

Claymore returned her smile and deftly changed the subject to draw her away from personal conflicts. "And are you sorry for that? A young girl like yourself, wouldn't you rather be whirling about the social scene yourself?"

Marke tilted her head. "Truthfully? No, I found such people, with what little time I spent around them, to be exceedingly false, and forever distancing themselves from everything and everyone around them with cattiness and unkindness. I much prefer being housebound here, with Mrs. P and—" *You,* she desperately wanted to add "—the dogs. How does Mrs. P phrase it? Muddy boots, sheep and wool, and dung, and good dogs. That's St. Catherine's Court.''

"Well, I can admit to you, were I to be housebound, I can think of no finer place than St. Catherine's Court, and with present company.''

Marke's cheeks grew pink with pleasure, but she managed an incline of her head nevertheless. "I thank you, my lord, for the compliments to my house, as well as to myself.'' There it was again, she thought. He was being nice to her and she was flustered as a debutante talking to the king. Whatever was she to think of herself? Best to make a radical change of subject. "Just as I thank you for the wonderful red filly. I can hardly wait until she is broken to saddle. You have quite touched my heart by giving her to me, you know. I shall be forever in your debt.''

"That is good," Claymore said. "For I fear I may be forced to call upon that debt in the very near future when I plead protection from Sitter. My head will carry quite a premium as I shall never be forgiven for keeping you from your birthday celebration at Innisfree tonight. Weather or not.''

Marke laughed, but inside she was wondering just what the premium would be should she bar the doors and never allow him to leave at all.

Chapter Fourteen

Marke shifted once more among the pillows piled against the headboard of her bed. Sleep was elusive tonight, as it was most nights. And the book she had carried up from the library, once she'd cracked its pages, held no interest whatsoever. She was just pondering returning to select another, or blowing out the candles and demanding sleep from her active mind, when a light scratching on the sitting room door drew her attention. With an exasperated snort, she threw back the covers and flung a tattered shawl over her old flannel night rail. If one of the dogs was scratching at her door, she'd raise hell with someone. She'd taken great pains to dispatch the bulk of them to the out of doors, leaving only those her mother could not seem to do without in the house. And those few were to be confined to Mrs. P's bedchamber or to the back drawing room at night. Rushing across her bedchamber and through the sitting room on chilly toes, she threw open the door, only to be confronted by the marquis, robe clad and seated in his invalid chair.

"Cl-Claymore," she sputtered, gathering the old shawl about her body and curling her bare toes. "What is it? Is there something wrong?"

"No, no, nothing wrong," he reassured her, then shrugged his shoulders. "I am often unable to sleep, and well, I saw your light—would you mind—I mean, I was wondering—hell's bells!" he finally exploded. "I am unable to navigate the stairs on my own, and I was wishing a book or something from the library!''

"Oh, of course," Marke reassured him. "How thoughtless of me. I should have made provisions—I can't sleep, either. Never can—never could. Ah..." She glanced over her shoulder at the inviting sitting room and its dim fire. "There's a fire, er, would you like to join me? I can fetch us a spot of hot toddy, or brandy maybe?"

Claymore hesitated for a moment, looking into the room with ill-disguised yearning. "I would like nothing more, but do take a moment to consider your reputation. I do not wish to compromise you, although the company would be most desirous."

"Do you plan to seduce me, my lord?" Marke asked with a twinkle in her eye, half wishing he would say yes.

"Of course not!"

For just a second, Marke was taken aback at his immediate and forceful denial. Was she so undesirable that the thought was unthinkable to him? Probably so in her tattered night rail and bare toes sticking out beneath its too-short tail. Then she recovered herself enough to step from the doorway. "Then come in so that I may stir up the fire and fetch my slippers. This floor is terribly cold. My feet are freezing."

Dashing to the dressing room, Marke quickly dug through the wardrobe. Flinging off her tattered robe and old nightdress, she hastily donned a new pin-tucked batiste nightgown, then dropped to her knees to fish beneath the bed for a pair of velvet slippers embroidered with alpine flowers. Once more digging through the wardrobe in search of a flattering robe, she pulled forth a summer coverall of a deep shade of burgundy with a grimace of distaste. It would offer no warmth and warred violently with her red hair, but it would have to do as it was the best she owned at present. Not overly satisfied with her outfit, but deciding it was serviceable, she rushed to the mirror to tidy her hair. Applying a comb ruthlessly, she did not take the time to question why her color was so high or why her eyes shone so brightly, as the familiar protests of the invalid chair wheel moving about the sitting room beckoned. Slightly flustered by the intimacy of a midnight tryst with Claymore, she drew three deep, calming breaths before returning to find him looking intently at her watercolor of serene Irish greens, roses and golds hanging over the fireplace.

"Besides the library, this is where I spend a great deal of my time," she said, shoving an overstuffed chair in a muted floral print closer to the fire. "Make yourself comfortable. I will dash downstairs to raid the pantry for a midnight feast."

Claymore merely nodded, retaining his seat until she had left the room. Considering the state of her dress, or undress as it may be, he thought it best to keep a fair distance from her. Settling himself, he scrutinized the large room with curiosity. This was definitely Marke's private place, and a direct reflection of her personality. Obviously the rooms she loved best, he decided, all had an amber glow of warmth, like firelight. Toasty shades of cocoa, slate and old gold encouraged by splashes of pumpkin and red. Places of warm wood, leather-bound books and deep chairs speaking of solid comfort, just as Marke herself was comfort. The room boasted elaborately carved moldings one usually found in these old houses, and time-softened paintings of Irish landscapes, in muted greens, blues, lavenders and contrasting vibrant reds and golds. He closed his eyes and drew in a deep breath, exhaling the bad dreams, letting the serenity of the room quiet his tormented thoughts.

Marke returned carrying a tray, weighty with slices of coarse bread, goat cheese, and two uncorked bottles—one of whiskey and one of a light local wine bearing the label The Sign of the Sorrel Horse emblazoned on its barrel. She grinned at Claymore as she set up their midnight picnic before the fire. "Doesn't this bring out the child in you? Mercy and I used to have midnight picnics whenever we could get away with it. It depended on the diligence of the governess we had at the time."

"Mercy? I do not believe you have spoken of her. Which one is she?"

She quickly counted down in her head "Ah, Mercy is seventh in the Penwell line. Mercy's a sad little muffin, and seems very satisfied playing maiden aunt to Sybil's brood. Besides she has her poetry, which is quite good enough to publish if one could only convince her of it."

"Ah, yes, I recall now, the poet," he said, gratefully accepting the glass of watered whiskey. "These are nice rooms, Marke. Distinctly feminine, and yet do not overwhelm a man with fussiness. St. Catherine's Court is a fine home."

"Yes, it is. I have great feeling for it. Partly, it's for the romantic history. You see, it was purchased, sight unseen, by Grandfather Penwell as a wedding gift for his bride simply because of its name. My grandmother's name was Catherine, like mine." Marke moved to the mantel and ran her hand along the smooth wood, unconscious of the fact that the firelight outlined her figure nicely and bounced gold and red highlights in her unbound curls in a most alluring fashion.

"Aha!" he exclaimed in triumph. "You have told me on several occasions that you were named for the house! Now, here surfaces a grandmother named Catherine. 'Fess up, Marke. Which is it?" Leaning back in the chair, he extended his long legs to the fire, crossing his ankles in preparation of another of her entertaining tales. Sipping the warming spirits, he reveled in the shared intimacy of this moment. It must be like this between married couples who still remained in good humor with each other.

Marke blushed beneath his gaze and sipped her wine self-consciously. "Oh, we children have spent a great deal of time debating our names. Thomas is my father's middle name and the name of our grandfather. Mary is Mrs. P's first name. Sybil is Mrs. P's mother, and Josephine is father's eldest sister. Sarah Grace is father's youngest sister, Grace, and Sarah's Mrs. P's middle name. Kathleen is father's middle sister. And there the namesakes end. We figured Mrs. P was begging for God's ear when Mercy was born. And Charity Hope, as eighth, speaks for itself. And as the story goes, when I was pronounced as yet another daughter, Mrs. P looked resignedly at the ceiling and said quite plainly, 'Oh hell, just name her after the house.' My father tacked on Margaret, an ancestral name of Mrs. P's side."

Claymore shook his head in disbelief. "I confess to being greatly confused about your family, and greatly entertained, also. But is that reason enough to have such strong feelings for this house?"

"Yes. That and childhood memories, I suppose. I loved the summers spent here as a child. It has been a pleasure to begin the restoration toward its former splendor. Though there are many rooms unused at this time, I have made conscious effort to refurbish the family rooms and the servants have finally stopped saying—" she grinned shamelessly at him and mimicked "—'but miss, that rug, chair, commode,' or whatever piece I am rearranging, 'doesn't belong there.'"

Claymore grinned at her playacting. "My mother was one for moving the furniture about, also. To the great chagrin of my father, as he was one for stability and sameness." His face was saddened and his voice had tapered off.

Marke squelched the urge to soothe him. Speaking of them was a giant step toward openly grieving their loss, and it was only right to remember them with love and happiness, for in that way they continued to live. "Mrs. P has never cared one way or another about such things. Although I quite imagine Lady Perfect entertained a great deal more than my mother. Her life, with my father absent so often, was fairly overwhelmed by her many children and her dogs. Then, of course, when the captain was in residence, the entire family was devoted to him."

"Yes, I imagine so," Claymore noted. He felt his good mood shifting. He truly did not wish to speak of mothers or fathers or sisters. The mere thought of his family brought a deep pain in his chest. "Let's speak of something else."

"You should speak of them, Claymore. Dr. Barrows says—"

"Please, Marke, no lectures," he interrupted her, turning his face to stare into the fire again. Marke shook her head at his stubbornness. "But Claymore..."

"No! Stop!" he ordered, as if knowing she were going to be encouraging, to voice useless platitudes, both of which would only set his teeth on edge. "Do not tell me it takes time! Do not tell me that I will cease to care!" Affecting a comical grimace that he hoped would forestall the lectures and yet not destroy the closeness he craved, Claymore grabbed the cord from the mantel cloth, made a noose and slipped his head through it.

"Do not play that way," implored Marke, shivering. She moved to the tray to refill her delicate wineglass.

Claymore pulled the cord away from his neck, but sat with it twisted in his hands. "Sometimes I feel just that way. It would settle everything, you know. The thought that I must wheel my way through life, enduring pity where once I commanded great respect, is almost more than I can bear."

"Pray, stop feeling sorry for yourself," Marke admonished rather sternly. "It could be worse. Why you could be a hunchback, you know."

Claymore looked up at her, startled. "A hunchback! You would jest? I assure you, being confined to this blasted chair is not something to joke of."

"I meant it as no joke. It's just that your perception is focused most constantly upon the darkest side of life," she said, then sought to change the subject. "It's chilly in here. Shall we move closer to the fire?"

"As you wish. Perhaps if you will just hold the chair steady, I will..."

Marke moved to hold out her hands to him. "Grasp my hands and pull yourself up. I am strong enough to hold you."

"No! Push the damn invalid chair closer."

"Claymore, you cannot depend upon that chair for the rest of your life," she implored him. "Dr. Barrow says your back and limbs are healed. You only need strengthen the muscles again. And that will never happen if you refuse to use them.''

"To bloody hell with John Barrows!" he flung at her. "Now, bring the chair closer, or ring for someone who will!"

Marke, in a fit of pique at his stubbornness, turned and shoved the invalid chair viciously. It careened wildly across the room and crashed into the far wall. "There's your damned *invalid* chair! Go and get it if you want to remain an *invalid* the rest of your life," she challenged.

"You are the most obstinate woman I have ever had the misfortune to run afoul of, Marke Penwell!" he bellowed. "Can you not understand that I injured my back? My limbs do not always operate properly."

She moved to kneel before him, grasping his hand in hers. "I understand that your limbs can be made stronger through exercise. Claymore, I do understand."

He shoved her aside. "You understand nothing. I am a cripple! A hopelessly dependent cripple!"

"You are no such thing! You *can* regain your strength and walk as strongly as before. I just know you can. Given time—"

"Time!" he thundered. "I have given it time! Must I prove it to you?" Shoving away from the chair, he hastily gained his feet to take two steps before his right leg buckled. Marke leapt to his side, but his weight bore them both to the hearth rug, with her soft body cushioning his fall. Embarrassed at his infirmity, and angry at his embarrassment, Claymore grasped her chin with cruel fingers and forced her to face him. "Now do you understand?" he demanded. "Did you not see?"

"Yes, I see," Marke whispered, staring defiantly into his eyes. "I see that you took two full steps. That is more than you took yesterday. Tomorrow it could be four."

"Oh, Marke, Marke! Why are you such an optimist?" He shook her chin roughly, then lay his forehead against hers with a sigh. "If only I had your faith."

"You can, Claymore. It's not that difficult," she whispered. She felt his hot tear strike her cheek and slip down into her ear. She eased her fingers into the curls at his neck to caress him softly, her heart overflowing with unexpressed love. "Just look toward the future and what can be, rather than at the past and what was."

Claymore drew a ragged breath and tightened his arms about Marke, drawing her closer. "Perhaps not difficult for you, with your rosy outlook on life, but for me it is most difficult. The nights are so long. My mind will not let go of the images of horror. The nightmares . . ."

"Shh, don't think of it now," she murmured into his neck.

Her body, her warmth, felt most comforting to him. He slid his cheek over her softer one, feeling the damp of his babyish tears. Her arms cradling him were soothing. Her gentle fingers stroking through his hair were caressing. It was the most solace he had felt in a long, long time. Seemingly without thought, he gathered her tighter and pressed his lips to her cheek. She felt like satin to him. His mouth moved along her cheek until his lips rested lightly against hers.

His scent filled Marke's nostrils. She shivered with a longing that she had no experience to identify as passion. With her hands in his hair, she pulled his head closer, deepening the feel of his warm mouth on hers, yielding to him in love, telling herself that it was to comfort him and nothing more.

Claymore felt her shiver and it moved his senses, excited him, filled him with sweet longing. Raising his head, he stared into her soft, unfocused eyes. When he'd knocked on her door, his intention hadn't been to seduce her. Not after the stern lecture he'd given himself the last time he'd forced himself upon her, and *forced* was not too strong a word when one considered her innocence. Nor had he meant to kiss her, and now that he had he wasn't exactly sure what he had meant to do next. But the feel of her soft, pliant body in his arms was too good to give up. Suddenly kissing Marke seemed to be a very good idea. He slanted his head and captured her mouth once again, teasing, nipping, tasting her inexperience, overwhelmed by her eagerness.

Pulling him tightly to her with her strong, young arms, Marke freely gave of herself. Love for him surged throughout her body. A love she had only recently recognized, blooming into overwhelming acknowledgment, now became a welcome feeling of caring, surrender and yearning. His tongue began to trace the delicate curves of her ear. His warm, moist breath sent a shiver of sensation darting down her limbs. Then his mouth was back on hers, his kiss deepening still more this time, becoming domineering and determined. She accepted it. Encouraged it willingly.

Claymore felt desire, intense and demanding, flood through him. It was like a friend of intimate acquaintance returning home after a long absence. His passion became all-consuming, pushing distressful memories and troublesome thoughts from his mind, releasing him from his perpetual nightmare. He pushed for more, for prolonged relief from the torment that dogged him night and day. Sliding his hand into the flap of her coverall, he caressed the rise of her full breast beneath the thin night rail, teasing the nipple into a sensitive peak. She lay on her back, pliant beneath him, accepting of the exploration of her body, her breath shallow.

Dragging his lips over her cheek, then her mouth, down her throat, Claymore shoved the coverall aside to press his mouth just above her breast where the buttons began. Flipping the tiny pearl buttons from their thread loops, slowly, meticulously, he pressed his lips to her satin flesh as she became exposed to him. The quickening of her breath inflamed him.

Marke jerked spastically beneath him. How delicious it was to feel the night rail come open, to feel her flesh cooled by the air, then warmed again with his mouth against her. Her breath caught in her throat and she pushed at him slightly, although she truly had little desire for him to stop. Titillating sparks of yearning surged through her, and it was only through her moralistic upbringing that she sought to shove him away. "Claymore, we mustn't!"

"Shh, Marke," he whispered against the corner of her mouth. "I'll not hurt you, I promise." He reclaimed her mouth, teasing at her lips with his tongue.

Marke's mind reeled. Oh, you're shameless, Margaret Catherine, she scolded herself. Why must he stop when the touch of his lips makes you ache to surrender to him? Dragging common sense back through sheer will, she again shoved at him. "No, I c-can't. Please let me up. Please." When he only held her closer and teased her nipple to mind-stealing stimulation, a sense of panic swept through her. *"Claymore!"*

Stung by her panicked cry, Claymore instantly released her and rolled away. Shifting to settle his back against the sofa, he raked a hand through his curls. "Oh, God, I am so sorry, Marke. I didn't mean—you must know I would not have you hurt for the world."

Marke sat up and smoothed her hair, gathering the coverall tightly about her. "No, please. It's my fault—I shouldn't have..."

"No! No, Marke, I shall not allow you to take blame for my despicable behavior," he brooded. He raised tormented eyes to her face and Marke felt she was looking straight into his tortured soul. "It was me, all me. It's just for a moment, everything felt right again. I felt whole, I suppose."

Marke watched him rake restless hands through his hair and rub vigorously at his face. She felt his pain, alive and throbbing, inside her heart, as well. She glanced away in confusion. How could she profess love and compassion in one breath, then deny him escape from his torment in the next? She felt selfish and hateful, and dizzy with want for him to touch her again. Looking back at his beloved face, love surged through her being. There truly was no decision to ponder. She slowly gained her feet and turned her back to him. Refusing to think of the right or the wrong of it, she let the coverall fall to pool at her feet on the hearth rug.

Claymore glanced up as Marke turned to him. He could only stare at such a vision of loveliness. She stood between him and the fire, her body clearly defined through the thin batiste of her night rail. She was long of limb, and round in all the right places. He never would have imagined such perfection of form was hidden beneath her bulky woolens and heavy shanty knits. Her face pinked delightfully with maiden modesty, as if she were uncertain what she should do next.

Claymore's gaze upon her body was so intense, so hot, that Marke had to consciously still the urge to cover herself with her hands. Instead, she smiled self-consciously and shrugged her shoulders slightly. "I never imagined, my lord, that I would be standing before a gentleman in such a manner, or I would have adorned myself in satin and lace, rather than cotton and plain hemming."

"You are so very beautiful, Marke," he breathed with a tightening in his throat. She knelt down beside him on the hearth rug and he reached out to run fingertips over her cheek. She shivered deliciously at his touch, tilting her face toward his hand to press her lips into his palm. "Marke, do you know what you are doing?"

"At this moment, Claymore, I know nothing except that I care deeply for you. As to the other..." She raised questioning eyes to his, looking deep, seeking some sort of reassurance from him that she was doing the right thing.

"Your eyes are full of questions that I have no answers for, Marke. All I can say to you is that, for some inexplicable reason, I need you. Beyond that, I can make no promises," he whispered, stroking fingertips down her throat.

"Then I shall ask for nothing more than that," she whispered breathlessly. Leaning forward, she offered her lips to him.

With a groan, he drew her astride his lap to bury his face in her breasts. "Oh, Marke. Sweet Marke. Don't you see, it's because you ask for nothing but give everything, that I must hold myself in check and send you away."

"Oh, Claymore," Marke whispered. She knew he was right, but that did nothing to ease the ache inside her. Slipping her arms tightly about him, she hugged him to her, conscious that this might be the only moment she was allowed to do so with such openness.

Claymore raised his head to plant one last lingering kiss upon her tempting mouth before gently removing her from his lap. Now was not the time, he chastised himself, to begin a love affair, no matter how tempting and sweet she was. Not when his emotions were unsettled and he feared it was only need that drove him. Besides, fidelity was not his to give. He was not a free man, and Marke deserved his honesty. She would have to be treated more fairly than to be taken upon the hearth rug in a midnight tryst. She was special and giving, but she was not for him. He must assign himself the position of an older brother and hold himself firmly in restraint whenever he was around her. While he might tease and flirt, the thing foremost must be to protect her generosity and innocence . . . even from himself.

Although such rational thoughts filled his head, it was with no small sense of regret that he watched Marke reluctantly move away from him to shrug into her burgundy coverall.

Chapter Fifteen

"I hate rain."

Marke turned from her sketch pad to contemplate Claymore's lengthy figure stretched full measure upon her sitting room sofa. The morning had not brought a lessening in the autumn weather, and the dark skies and relentless storm seemed to be affecting the marquis's mood greatly.

"Rain is good, Claymore."

"I prefer scorching sunshine. I hate bad weather. I hate *Irish* rain!"

Marke pondered him for a moment, then returned to her sketch. "There's a restlessness about Ireland's weather, its rains, its mists, that appeals to me. I much prefer Irish rain to English rain," she countered, flashing a brief smile at him, intent upon her drawing. "Irish rain is absolute, restless and magnificent. To call this rain bad weather is as inappropriate as to call scorching sunshine fine weather. Besides, it's all simply weather—rough weather. It reminds us forcibly that its element is water—falling water."

"This storm blew in from the south and damn well should have stayed out to sea!" Claymore frowned at the rain-drenched windows as if such a dark look would intimidate the supreme being of weather into bringing forth the sun.

"Don't be silly. Of course, it must come ashore," she murmured absently.

"Oh? And just why must it?" he demanded, pushing for confrontation.

"Because it must," she insisted. "Amazing though, when you think how much water a storm can collect over three thousand miles of ocean. Imagine how a storm must rejoice when at last it reaches land...people and houses...after having fallen only into water, only into itself. How much enjoyment do you imagine rain can have, always falling into itself."

"Miss Penwell, I suspect you are poking fun of me!" Claymore accused, frowning at the top of her head as she seemed determined to remain engrossed in her drawing. "One would think you enjoy being housebound by foul weather."

"Housebound? Oh, I suppose I don't mind, though it's always a good thing to have candles, some tobacco, a pack of cards, perhaps a little whiskey in the house, like sailors preparing for a storm." She glanced out the window for a moment, then returned to her work. "Also knitting needles and wool for the women, a well-stocked library—shall I fetch you a book? This storm seems to have a lot of breath, and might go on for days."

"I am suffering terribly, you know," Claymore lamented.

"Oh, people for the most part are not interesting unless they have suffered a small amount, you know," she drawled, glancing up to grin at his misery. He was simply bored and seeking to draw her attention away from her drawing. He looked very rumpled and homey in her father's navy morning robe and black lounging trousers. His feet, being larger than her father's discarded slippers, were bare and peeking from beneath a woolly lap robe thrown over his legs. The very sight of him, here in her home, assuming the pose of a disgruntled husband, filled her heart to bursting. The memories of the intimacy they had shared the night before, consummated or not, brought a blush to her cheeks.

Claymore took note of the blush and her quickly lowered head, correctly surmising her thoughts. The same thoughts brought a quickening to his body. But that was something he must not dwell upon, he reminded himself.

Still he wished more of her attention than he was getting at present. He shifted higher on the sofa and pondered a means in which to tempt her away from her pad and pencils. "I think I might have a fever, you know," he ventured.

"Oh, well, that will undoubtedly keep you warm on such an inclement day," she countered. Darting a glance at his little-boy expression, she smiled a slight smile but dutifully returned her merry eyes to her work.

Claymore frowned and made yet another attempt. "I think the fire is getting too low, needs more peat," he suggested petulantly. "These peat fires do not burn as warmly as English wood fires. Not near as cheery."

Marke glanced at the brightly burning blaze performing its task quite efficiently, then returned to the minute detailing of the leaf she was effecting on her tablet as a Christmas gift for Sitter. "Peat produces a very nice fire. Just look at it. What could be more cheerful than a red flame licking at the dark lumps? It leaves a pale ash, light, odorless, almost like cigar ash. Perhaps you would like a smoke, Claymore. Shall I fetch your pipe from the library?"

"No, I do not wish to smoke my pipe," he said through gritted teeth, as again he was outmaneuvered.

"My father smoked cigars when he was at home. I could always tell his mood by the time he spent with his cigar. Like time chopped into butt ends discarded in the ashtray. Practiced a little mysticism, so to speak—there they would be, the half-smoked butt ends of a man who was rushed and distracted, and might not have time for a little girl." She glanced up again, throwing him an impish grin with sparkling eyes. "But oh, the joy of a butt end leisurely smoked all the way down to the very tip. I would most definitely seek him out at those times."

Claymore's mouth turned down, his brows knitting in a scowl. "That damn complacency of yours. And that damn drawing pad. Do I rate so little attention?"

Marke looked up at his dear face and conceded to lay her drawing aside with a small sigh. At this rate, she might not have the drawing completed by Christmas, and Sitter would receive something far less personal. Turning to face him, she finally gave him her full regard. "What would you have me do, Claymore? Rant and rail at things that cannot be changed? No, I believe that to accept is the only way to live one's life."

Claymore shifted higher on the sofa, eager for a debate to while away the time. "You would grant control of your life to the whimsy of others?"

"Not to others necessarily. She tapped her pursed lips with the tip of her pencil. "But think of it as a stone wall that's barring the path of your life. What good can come of running headlong into a stone wall? While you may be able to eventually topple it by repeatedly doing so, is it worth the bloodied head in the process? How much simpler to accept that the wall is a solid fact, and then, redirect your energy into discovering the fastest route around it, whereupon you can then proceed to explore the delights on the other side."

"Very simplistic," Claymore snarled.

"Exactly." She beamed at him.

"I meant, *too* simplistic," he corrected with an exasperated expression.

"Not so." She moved to seat herself on the floor before the hearth and leaned back against the sofa. "If you apply it to each situation, you will find it is more than plausible. The rule to live by is elemental. Don't worry!"

"Now that is impossible, and does not even deserve the dignity of a rebuttal." Claymore snorted in derision of her silly rule. He flicked fingers through the wisps of curls escaping the haphazardly placed hairpins to skim the nape of her neck. He knew he should not be so casual in his touch, but it seemed an impossibility not to indulge his senses. Just because he had made the decision to deny himself her body didn't mean he must forsake all pleasures, did it?

Marke shivered as gooseflesh raced over her arms. Oh, please let him go on touching me forever, she thought, reveling in the closeness, the naturalness of the physical attention. She forced her attention back to the topic under discussion. "Ah, you display such little insight today, my lord. It *is* possible. It only means that if you can do something about your dilemma, then do it and stop worrying. If you can't do anything, as with weather, then forget it, but for goodness' sake—*stop worrying!*"

Claymore laughed and leaned forward to drop a kiss on the top of her head for it was the most natural thing to do with someone as impossibly sweet as Marke. He was vastly amused by her impractical outlook on life, and immensely fond of her generous nature. "Impossible wench!"

"Hopeless wretch!"

"All right, my impractical Miss Penwell. Let's apply your principles to real life. How would you accept your life if you were faced with the loss of your limbs."

Marke smiled to herself in satisfaction. This was exactly the opening she had been hoping for. "By expanding, in every way imaginable, upon the remedies given to me by the physicians."

Claymore frowned at her. That answer came far too readily. "In what way?"

"Well, Dr. Barrows has made the diagnosis that your back is sufficiently healed to support your weight without pain, and your limbs have only become weakened through lack of use. He prescribes light exercise."

"Yes, and I have allowed Henry to massage and exercise my limbs daily for the past twelve months. You have seen the results. I still totter about like an infant leaving his mother's arms for his first steps."

Marke rose to her knees and leaned toward him with a rapt expression. "Claymore, I spoke to Ditty, my stable master. He's a wonder with lame animals and—"

"Marke, are you changing the subject on me again? I swear I must engage a secretary to stand behind me at all times, diligently taking notes on our conversations, just so I might keep up with your rapid flights."

"I merely consulted him as to his recommendation for a lame horse."

"So now you would liken me to a lame horse? Really, Marke, hardly flattering. What has happened to your tenderness?'' he queried in prank. He planted his hand over his face as if in despair of her unjust treatment of him.

Swiping his hand from his face, Marke chose to ignore his barbs and insist he pay attention. "Ditty is very progressive with his theories. And though he is scoffed at by most in the area, they cannot deny that he is a wizard for placing a lame horse back under saddle in remarkable time. I place great credence in his words."

Claymore frowned and thought this over. He was perplexed at her direction and suddenly irritated at her insistence in pursuing the subject. "That is a marvelous thing, I'm sure, but what does that have to do with me?"

"Everything. I required of him a schedule for the course of treatment he might employ with an animal that had suffered an injury that required a lay-up of some duration, say a twelve-month?"

"You are beaming at me in the most delightful manner, Marke," he declared. "But I refuse to believe that you expect me to subject myself to some regime your stable master has laid out for a lame horse."

"But why not, Claymore?" she argued, sitting back on her heels. "If you would just listen, it seems most sensible to me."

Claymore studied Marke's intent face. It was obvious to him that she was not pulling a prank on him, but deadly serious in her research and her belief in this stable man's theory. "You know, Marke. You are the most outrageous, most demanding, most seductive creature in my world. I am quite at a loss to say why, but I believe you are in touch with mystic forces that others have yet to discover."

"Oh, definitely discovered, my lord, but perhaps not acknowledged. But there is no magic. It's nothing more than looking beyond the surface and using common sense." She grinned impishly at him and wiggled her eyebrows. "And listening to the wee people's whispers in the night."

"Now *that* I would believe most readily. Therefore I shall not doubt you for I should hate it above all else to add a curse to my already limiting afflictions," he conceded. "I shall listen to your recovery plan and we shall see."

"Oh, thank you, Claymore!" she exclaimed, throwing herself across his chest to smother his face in kisses.

When released, he laughed heartily. "You really must inform me at which times I might expect such favorable rewards as this, for then I can be depended upon to capitulate much sooner."

"Lecherous man!" she retorted, attempting to draw back.

"Luscious woman," he murmured, foiling her attempts to leave his arms, burying his face in her hair and nipping lightly at her earlobe.

"Lord Perfect, my reputation! If you do not release me this instant, I shall be forced to cry foul and bring the brawn of my footmen down upon your head," she threatened, all the while wishing him to capture her in his arms forever.

"I sadly fear, Miss Penwell, that my having spent the night on your sofa and the entire morning in your private sitting room with the door firmly closed, your reputation is already a gossip morsel among the servants this morning," he said. His face became serious at the possible harm he had brought to her. "Marke, I am so sorry about that. I would not have had that happen, although it wasn't as if I could quietly creep back to my own bed in the middle of the night!" He slapped his legs angrily.

"I am not a child, Claymore, that needs such protection," Marke declared. "But you sidestep the topic of your recovery totally, and that I shall not stand for."

"You are an overbearing chit, you know," he insisted, sighing deeply and folding his arms across his chest in resignation. "All right, I shall listen and pay proper heed to your stable master's plan for putting me under saddle again as quickly as possible."

"Beast!" Marke said, socking him playfully on the shoulder. "First, he suggests tincture of aconite or chloroform liniment be rubbed into the sore joints, as he is sorry to say that he feels you can expect stiffness and aching in the injured parts as you grow older, then steadily increasing strengthening exercises, including long swims." She shrugged as if apologizing for bad news.

"Swims!"

"Yes, he feels vigorous water exercise strengthens the muscles while lessening the chance of further injury by keeping the weight from the weakened limbs. He says that is the secret of his success with the horses. He swims them on a lead in the catch-pond twice daily!"

"Well, damned if I shall consent to swim about the catch-pond on a lead, I can tell you," Claymore proclaimed with indignation.

Marke rose from her knees and moved to the mantel. "I suppose it was rather a ridiculous idea on my part. Probably catch your death and lay in bed railing at my head for being the cause of your demise."

Claymore laughed at her. "Ah, minx, I fear you shall be the death of me whether I swim or not. But surely you must see that your idea is most inappropriate," he reasoned, waving at the wind-driven November rain lashing at the windowpane. "Perhaps if it were summer."

She immediately seized the possibility of compromise he offered. "Ah well ... if it were summer, would you consent to the prescription?"

"Yes, I believe I would," he conceded. "The idea is radical but sound."

Marke giggled with glee. "And that's as it shall be, my lord. For Ditty has laid out a plan for the building of an indoor exercise tank ... a boiler of sorts with heated water."

Claymore stared at this leggy, red-haired beauty. "You are a puzzle to me, Marke Penwell. Nothing baffles you. Nothing daunts you. Nothing deters you once you have set your mind upon something. And as tiresome as that may be, I shall surrender my health and recovery to you. Lord help me, I'm sure, but what would you have me do to begin?"

"Just a moment," she exclaimed in excitement, and dashed from the room.

Claymore could only wonder at this new plot of hers. Was he forever to feel like the mouse behind the dresser with her kittenish plotting and planning? He could only smile indulgently though, when she hurried proudly back into the sitting room to hand him a beautifully carved walking stick of knurled wood.

"And what have we here? I say, this is excellent work. Weighty but finely carved," Claymore said, admitting to the exceptional craftsmanship.

"It actually belongs to Ditty, but I purloined it," she said, and waved aside his shocked expression. "Oh, with his permission, of course, and I have requested one similar to this made for you. And to answer your question as to how you begin your recovery—you rise from the sofa, leaning heavily on this stick, and on me—and walk with me."

"I am really uncertain that I can do that, Marke," Claymore said, hesitating somewhat.

"Ditty does not say it will be easy, or painless, Claymore," she promised. "But he does say it will come. With dedication and diligence on your part, it will come."

"We shall see," he murmured. "And just where are we headed on this miserable morning stroll, my dear Miss Physician?"

"No farther than the bedchamber door, my dear Lord Perfect—and back again." She grinned mischievously at him. "For I have no doubt you will be petulantly demanding the sofa by the time we get that far."

"To the bedchamber? Ah, my sweet thing. You think to offer just a glimpse of heaven, then withhold the treat? What marvelous incentive to offer a struggling man. And here I thought to label you an innocent in the way of tormenting men."

Marke flushed brightly, but wisely held her reply. What was she to think of him? Hadn't she offered her heart and body to him last night, only to have him refuse her? Now he would tease and tempt as if it were she playing the reluctant? She supposed she should feel shameless for her willingness, but she knew he had only to crook his little finger and she would walk into his arms forever.

Chapter Sixteen

Claymore sank deeper into the heated water and flexed his legs. The improvised swim tank, having been installed in St. Catherine's Court's conservatory, with its stone floor and numerous drains, was an ingenious contraption. Although cumbersome and probably the ugliest piece of equipage in industrial history, with its pipes and unfinished surfaces, it was proving most effective. Immediately christened the "stew pot" by the marquis, it nevertheless served its purpose admirably as the strength was returning to his legs far more rapidly than even the optimistic Marke would have predicted. The full month of November had flown with Marke and Henry, overseen by Ditty, imposing an exercise regime determined to place the marquis not only upon his feet by Christmas, but fully recovered and dancing. And although Claymore complained bitterly at times, he threw himself into the program with a zeal that surprised everyone.

"Marke, are you out there?" Claymore called. His voice was heavy with irritation this morning.

"Yes, I'm here," Marke answered. "I've brought a book from the library."

"Well, come around the damn screen, will you? I feel abandoned."

With a sigh, Marke rose from the comfortable chair she'd placed by the sweet-smelling fuchsia, and moved around the privacy screen. Some days his mood was very agitated. And while she attributed this to the change in diet, the exercise and possibly the renewed hope of returning to an active life, it could also be most trying at times. He was driven to impatience, and sometimes pushed too hard and suffered setbacks that inflamed his already volatile temper even more.

But in her own way, Marke was just as fractious, as he would continue to treat her as a wayward child to be indulged in good humor, rather than as she wished to be viewed. And that was as a desirable woman in the full bloom of her youth, desperately in love with him. She strained against the desire for them to be closer than congenial friends. She was puzzled by the affectionate pats on the head and light kisses on the forehead. Otherwise he had sternly and regrettably kept his distance from her. The love she gave to Claymore was the love a woman gives to the one man she has chosen above all others to be her man for all time to come, to father her children ... their children, and to grow old and gray at her side. It was the love of a woman, not a child, and there would come a day soon when she would tire of being patted on the head and kissed on the forehead. Then she would take matters into her own hands to settle their future together. And she had no doubt in her heart that theirs was a future intertwined for many years to come and bright with promise.

"Here I am, in plain sight. Is this better?" Marke asked. Forced by propriety and the presence of Henry to maintain a missish distance, she sat down in the wheeled invalid chair and, with a shove of her feet, sent the chair rolling back toward the glass wall, until it was a fair stretch from the tub and the delectably nude body of the marquis. Given a choice, she would rather have leaned over the edge of the stew pot and kissed his temper away.

"Quite, thank you," Claymore said, resuming his exercises with seemingly more contentment. "I hate yelling around that damn screen. Now, what was it you said? You have brought something from the library?"

"Yes, and it's called *The Wild Irish Girl* by a Lady Morgan, and appears to be written in the form of letters. I thought it most appropriate as it's concerning the adventures of the son of an English nobleman in Ireland," she explained, affecting a wide-eyed look of innocence at his snort of derision.

"Judging by the description and the title, I say it sounds most *inappropriate,* especially for your ears."

"Well, it *was* on one of the upper shelves," she admitted with a sassy grin. "But be that it may, I do not subscribe to the popular belief that the indiscriminate reading of novels and romances is, for young females, a most dangerous tendency that agitates their fancy of pleasure to unattainable heights, which will only lead them to wretchedness and inconsolable sorrow."

Claymore snorted again. "Oh, and is that the popular belief? I never would have suspected as much. Pray, I would never have that happen to you, Miss Penwell. Not for the world. Perhaps we should forgo the reading of such literary works as *The Wild Irish Girl* just in case there is some truth to their findings."

"Oh, according to the latest findings of the horrified professors at Oxford, that is the lesser worry for mamas of innocent maids. They also report that a strong imagination inflamed with the rhapsodies of such corrupting novels shall mark them as fair game for even the least profligate villain bent on the odious purpose of seduction. Is that a fate that you would wish me to avoid as well, Lord Perfect?"

Claymore gave her a pointed glare at this improper remark. Not that he himself considered it so improper, and given different circumstances, he would wish for her to be anything but proper in his presence, but one must be faithful to society's strictures and to one's obligations. Besides, there were appearances that must be maintained in view of servants.

But Marke would only grin mischievously at him, and continue her inflaming observations. "Fortunate that such perils do not prey on the stronger gender, as well, for that would not leave anyone to protect the weaker."

"Marke!" Claymore warned, shaking his head at her. Henry ducked his head to hide his broad grin. The trials the marquis suffered, brought about by the pluck of this young girl, were of great amusement to them. It heartened those fond of him to see his spirit returning and an end put to the grieving.

Marke continued in her tease, knowing that she was driving Claymore to exasperation, but in the end he would laugh, and laughter was a potent healer. "I will confess, if I were a person given to envy, I should envy men. They are so wise and strong. And so confident in their wisdom and strength. They form such great plans, and are able to talk about them in a large, disinterested way—" she tossed her head and flipped a hand in the air "—that their opinions pass for what they are worth. But woman is such a creature of feeling she can hardly give her views free of personalities, and hence her judgment is received doubtfully. She may feel as deeply, know as intelligently, and understand as thoroughly, the premises in a certain case as her lord and master, but being a woman is evidence against her." Sho shrugged eloquently. "She must meekly bow to fate, and retire from the field of argument to attend babies and bake bread."

Claymore glared at her for a moment, then realized there was no way he could win against her. He might as well throw in the towel early in the game, thus saving her the effort of piling on the agony. There was nothing hen hearted about Marke when it came to pleading her case. He threw back his head and laughed. "You win! You win! I shall bow before your maidenly judgment. Read at will, although I would rather you finish your tale of the daring Captain Penwell's final voyage."

Marke lay the book aside, satisfied that she had tempted him from his bad mood, as well as elicited the desired laugh. "Now, Claymore," she admonished, "you know perfectly well we have given our oath not to complete that story without Sitter's presence. And at this moment, she has retired upstairs to her rooms to secret herself behind closed doors. She was muttering harsh words about Christmas and the deplorable state of Bantry shops when I last saw her."

"Well, just talk to me then. Have you received word from your family? Shall any of them be joining you for the holidays?"

"No," Marke admitted. "Jessell wrote that they will gather at King's Gate for the month of December. Weather is poor and travel difficult and she is increasing again, so perhaps it is all for the best." She really did not wish to delve into the fact that she'd rather face a hurricane at sea than have her bevy of sisters descend upon St. Catherine's Court. They were entirely too beautiful, too accomplished, too everything she was not, and she would simply die if Claymore fell in love with one of them and not her.

"Ah, well, I think we shall manage to make a merry time of it on our own then. But on with your story! What shall it be this time? Tell me of Thomas. Why is it that he was allowed to avoid the sea and the life of a shipmaster?"

Marke laughed and shook her head. "*Allowed* is correct. You have gathered a fair impression of my father, but Thomas is dry subject for entertainment."

"Hell's teeth, Henry! Leave off with the wood! Would you have me boiled alive?" Claymore snapped at the valet.

"Claymore, stop harassing Henry. You know the water must be hot to relax the muscles. Now behave yourself or I shall seek out Sitter and proceed to gossip about your deplorable temper over tea and crumpets."

"All right. All right. Henry, I apologize for harsh words. This is all quite tedious today," he complained, settling back again as steam rose around him.

"Bear up with goodwill and stop being such a grouch," she admonished.

"Well then, distract me," he ordered, his frown deepening into a scowl of returning foul mood. "Even as a dry subject, I would know of your brother."

"My brother, I am sorry to admit, is not a nice man. Perhaps his failings stem from having a larger-than-life father, but for whatever reason, I feel Thomas is a man who finds himself extremely hard to live with. He seems to forever be trying to make up for his appalling shortcomings by false piety, or tremulous shouting and petty faultfinding of those he should hold dearest. My father found early on that subjecting him to the sea would not improve him much."

"And how do you know this to be true? You must have been a small child at the time," Claymore challenged disagreeably.

"Yes, I was a small child," she admitted, then laughed. "But a small child who leaned upon her father's knee at every opportunity, enthralled with his stories and harboring dreams of being the first female shipmaster bound for adventures on the high seas. Also, having developed the deplorable tendency of listening at keyholes, I was an undetected third party to most of the captain's lengthy lectures to Thomas."

"Eavesdropping? Miss Penwell, I am indeed, shocked to my very toes."

"Pink wrinkled toes, Lord Perfect?"

"Continue!" he growled.

"Well, as it turned out, Thomas, although an excellent navigator, was afraid of his ship. He proved totally incapable of rousing any self-confidence. The captain used to lecture him relentlessly on landfalls. It would seem whenever he approached land, he became quite unnerved, and often hove her to rather than trust himself and let her stand on to pick up the land. He dreaded coming into port."

"Perhaps it was facing your father that put him off coming ashore."

"Too true," Marke laughed. "But it was his lapse into drink that finally brought his career back to land. The sailors swore the ship hated him and would take him to his death, even if it meant she must dive to the depths herself. The captain must have believed so himself, because he brought him home and had him instructed in the business side of the company."

"Probably a smart move. Thomas could not have been happy, and a man unhappy in his life usually makes for an unhappy family."

"What of your father, Claymore? We speak endlessly of my family, yet I know nothing of yours," Marke asked, as if it were the most natural question in the world. She smiled encouragingly at him, and attempted to appear as if her breath weren't caught in her throat, only exhaling when he answered her query with seemingly no thought or pain of memories.

"My father was a saint. And I say that with no reference to his tragic death. To me, as a small boy growing up, and on into manhood, he was patience and kindness itself. There was a love inside him that he never thought twice about sharing with those closest to him, and his friends were boundless. Active and well received in parliament, he was from strong, sturdy stock, and maintained a true sense of pride in his ancestry, much as your father."

Marke laughed again. Partly with delirious happiness at the ease with which Claymore spoke of his father, and partly for his assessment of the captain's pride in ancestry. "We British have a decided gift for investing the less savory characters in our history with a glamour which they probably did not, in reality, possess. Or is it simply that distance lends enchantment, and even respectability, if the elapse of time has been great enough? I strongly suspect the Penwells descend from a long line of pirates and smugglers."

Claymore merely grunted and sought to gain his feet. "Perhaps. Shut your eyes, Marke, for I must get out of this damn stew pot or turn into a prune."

Marke obediently closed her eyes—well, perhaps not so tightly as to shut out the sight of Claymore's magnificent body, all gleaming from wet, emerging from the tank—and waited for his call that he was decent. Clad in a robe of floor-length burgundy velvet and scuff slippers, he shuffled toward her with only the courtesy of Henry's arm. Marke started to rise from the invalid chair, but he waved her down and traded Henry's arm for the back of the chair.

"I shall use you as ballast, and the chair as my cane today at least as far as to the stairs," he advised, easily wheeling Marke before him. "And what shall we do to while away this afternoon? If it's possible to extract Sitter from her solitude? I've hardly seen her since her arrival from Innisfree."

"Oh, I suspect she will emerge soon enough. John is to stop by for tea, which will make for a merry time."

"Mmm, at least Sitter will appreciate the company," Claymore murmured.

Marke tilted her head back to look at him. "You, my lord, are indeed in a foul mood. You know John is excellent company."

"Mmm, I suppose," he conceded. Then, as if the most natural thing on earth, he bent to brush his lips lingeringly over hers.

Marke startled, then dropped her head in confusion. *That* was not a sisterly kiss on the forehead! What did he mean by it? Was it something to build a hope upon, or merely a gesture without thought.

Claymore grimaced and chastised himself for his actions. Damn it to hell anyway! Why did she have to be the sweetest thing to ever come into his life? He'd taken such pains to treat her as he would have treated Libby. Was he to regress to his deplorable behavior and accost her innocence and betray her trust with lechery as easily as that? As punishment for being unable to keep his hands from her, he should be forced to remove himself—Sitter, Henry and all—back to Innisfree immediately. Serve him right to rot in seclusion for being such a thoughtless cad. He meant no harm to Marke, yet it seemed he cluttered her life each time he came near her. But, although the thought was sound, it seemed an impossibility to leave her, even if that would be the best for her. No, he must strengthen his resolve to keep his distance from her in thought and deed. He cleared his throat uncomfortably at her continued silence.

"I'm sorry, Marke."

Marke roused from deep thought. "For what, Claymore?"

Halting the invalid chair, Claymore eased down into a wicker chair and pulled the invalid chair around to face him. "Marke, I seem to forever be compromising you, and after I have repeatedly promised to keep my distance and remember the gentlemanly manners taught to me by my mother. For that I apologize."

"Oh that," Marke murmured, glancing down at her hands rather than let him see the disappointment that surely must be mirrored in her eyes.

Her uncharacteristic quiet irritated him. It made him feel guilty and he did not want to feel guilty. It only served to illustrate clearly that he was doing damage to her sunny personality. The one thing he must never do was make Marke unhappy, but blast, neither could he leave her...not yet. "What? No quick retort? No adverse remarks on my waywardness?" he demanded. The force of his irritation brought strength to his voice.

Marke looked up with narrowed eyes and asked solemnly, "Why are you so angry, Claymore? Why are you so filled with rage?"

Claymore snorted and shoved both hands through his hair. "Damn that, and damn your lectures!" he said through gritted teeth, giving proof to his anger. When he began to rise, Marke leaned forward to place staying hands on his knees.

"No! Tell me, Claymore. What makes you so angry. Surely it wasn't always in your personality to be this way. Did it begin when you thought not to recover the use of your limbs?"

"Perhaps."

"But that should ease now. As you can see, you will be dancing by Christmas so there's no need for such rage."

Claymore looked at the slim hands resting so comfortingly on his knees, and even though he knew he shouldn't, he caressed his own over hers. "You are right, you know...about the rage. I don't know why but sometimes I am just consumed."

"Or did it perhaps begin with...the fire," she pressed.

He looked over Marke's head as if pondering the onslaught of the black emotion, then brought his eyes back to hers. "It's just that...when the beam fell and I couldn't move to help them...I lay there, listening to their screams, their calls for help—" he closed his eyes and passed a hand over his forehead "—until long after they'd ceased. When rescue finally came and they lifted the beam, I could see blood, but I felt no pain...only rage. I was filled with rage...and I still am.''

"And when the doctors said you'd never walk again..."

"That was nothing compared to the agony that was consuming my heart. It was so devastating that I simply refused to feel anything...no love, no sadness."

"Only rage?" Marke prompted gently.

Claymore returned his gaze to her face. Such sweetness. Such goodness. Such desirability, he thought. And so wise for one so young. With a wistful smile, he said, "Some man is going to be the luckiest sot on this earth, Marke. When he earns your love. If only I were free..."

Marke drew back abruptly. Some man? Some other man, but not you, my perfect lord? "Oh, tar and fiddle!" she exclaimed with a wrinkle of her nose. "Me with my deplorable hair and freckles? Me with my argumentative nature? Surely you jest."

Claymore, gratefully grasping upon her change of subject, pushed himself from the chair and resumed his place behind the invalid chair. "Perhaps you are right, now that I think of it. No sane man would wish to take on such a liability."

Marke dropped her head back to pull a face at him. "Cad!"

"Desirable witch!" he countered, then dropped a kiss on her lips, which was a return to the exact place they were but moments before.

John, having been given their direction by Mr. Biddle, bore witness to the kiss. He paused, not wishing to intrude upon a private moment, as well as desiring time to ease the ache in his heart. Perhaps he'd always known that Marke could never be his, but to see such evidence of it was still painful. Taking a deep breath, he strode forward. Lifting his eyebrows at the sight of Marke in the invalid chair and the invalid pushing from behind, he called, "What's this? Has the ailment proven contagious?"

"Oh, John," Marke called, scrambling to her feet in embarrassment. She could feel her face flushing a bright pink. Had he witnessed the kiss? What must he think of her? Although the fact that she was in love with Claymore was most probably common knowledge among her own staff, she certainly did not wish rumors of it broadcast from one end of Bantry to the other by the town crier. Latching onto the handiest subject, she waved her hand toward Claymore. "As you can see, my good Dr. Barrows, the Marquis of Boothe-Ashmore is ever so much better today."

John, not amused at her embarrassment, shifted questioning eyes to his patient. Could the marquis be taking unfair advantage where he shouldn't? Claymore shrugged and moved around to seat himself in the chair on remarkably steady legs. "Our Miss Penwell is physic, you see," he retorted with a grin. "And I've decided to find it charming."

Marke blushed to her curly fringe, and yearned to give Claymore a stern kick upon the shins, but thought better of it in light of his physician's presence. John might take a dim view of an attack on the very limbs he was endeavoring to repair. "You may make fun of me all you wish. But you are upon your feet most of every day, and you are much improved!" she confronted Claymore. Then turning to John, she shook her head at him. "My advice to you, John, is to take this disagreeable patient of yours upstairs to complete your exam in an expedient manner, then join Sitter in the drawing room, for the marquis is deplorable company at best. As for myself, I shall attend to the running of my household?"

Claymore frowned as Marke, without a backward glance, swept from the hall. Now just what had put a burr under her saddle, he thought. Gripping the wheel, he sent the chair heading for the stairs. "Perhaps we should do as she says, John. She can be most intimidating when aroused," he advised. Intent on navigating the hallway, the marquis did not see the soft look on John's face as he looked after Marke. It was a look of such open yearning, mixed with the sadness of unrequited love, when the realization occurs that one's desires might never come to fruition.

Instead of harassing perfectly efficient servants, Marke detoured back through the music room and entered the makeshift kennel in the crimson and gold drawing room, where she was certain to find Mrs. P amid her dogs.

"Mrs. P?" she called.

"Yes, Marke," her mother answered from the floor in front of the divan. "I am here. Do come and see?"

Concerned to see Mrs. Moran hovering over the divan cushions, Marke quickly approached them, fearing something was amiss with Mrs. P. Rounding the divan, she gasped to see them both intent upon the delivery of a litter of spaniel puppies. "Oh, must you do that in the middle of upholstery? Really, Mrs. P, this is unforgivable."

"Oh, Marke, just look at their tiny faces. How can you hate such a sweet face?" Mrs. P wailed, holding up a puppy to her. Great tears gathered in her blue eyes and spilled over onto her cheeks.

"Oh, Mrs. P." She sighed, dropping to her knees to enfold her upset mother in her arms. "I don't hate them. It's just..." She lay her head on her mother's shoulder and stroked the tiny spotted head with a forefinger. "Never mind, Mrs. P. The sofa will just have to be reupholstered, that's all, and yes, it really is the sweetest, squished-up little face in the world."

Mrs. P beamed a smile and dropped a light kiss on her cheek. "That's very good of you, Marke. And really, what does it matter? I do love them so."

"I know you do. And you only love them half as much as I love you, Mama," whispered Marke, returning the kiss on her mother's soft cheek. "And you are quite right, you know. What does it matter?"

Marke eased away from the makeshift surgery and plopped into the chair beside the fire to watch as her mother became the proud grandparent to yet another spotted litter of remarkable size. It pleased her to see her mother happy, and in truth, it was a simple matter to insure that happiness remained. She rocked gently, smiling at her mother's concentration as she placed her approval upon each and every one with kisses and soft murmurs. Mrs. Moran, ever silent and efficient, bustled from the room, bearing soiled towels and papers at arm's length.

"I am most gratified to see you happy, Mrs. P."

"Thank you, Marke," Mrs. P answered. She carried a tiny grunting puppy to deposit gently in Marke's lap. "See how lovely they are?"

Marke accepted the puppy with an absent smile, cupping the tiny, blind creature in her hands for warmth. "If only my own happiness was as easily obtained. Oh, Mama, how could I have been so stupid to think my heart would not be broken? I fear I gave it too freely, and without the realization that love only deepens over time, and in fact, increases with each little pleasure that's shared between the two of us. Never would I have thought it could become so—so engrossing, until I can't seem to get enough of his glances or his words or his touches?"

Mrs. P came to retrieve the puppy and placed another one in her lap for inspection. "I should expect you will have to make some decisions, won't you?"

Marke's head jerked up in surprise at such a reasonable and sane suggestion from her mother. "What did you say, Mrs. P?"

"I said, you will have to come to grips inside yourself as to what you want from this man?" Mrs. P paused to peer intently at Marke. "What is it you want?"

"I w-want..." Marke stammered, cupping the squirming puppy in confusion. "I suppose I want the same thing every woman wants from the man she loves. I want marriage, children, fidelity." Mrs. P came to exchange puppies yet again, a ritual that Marke assumed would continue until she had inspected each and every member of the sizable litter. "Mrs. P? Do you know, I mean, are we truly discussing this?"

Again the exchange took place with Mrs. P crooning softly to the tiny baby in the process. "Of course we are, and I was simply making the point that you should first determine what you want from him. Then make a critical assessment of the circumstances as they stand this very moment, after which you simply plot a course to take you where you want to go. Haven't you learned anything at all from the Captain?''

Marke studied her dear face, still unable to tell if she was focused in the present, or simply lecturing the silly, lovesick governess. "Yes, Mrs. P, I learned a great deal from the Captain. I learned that I want a husband who is at home with me at night. I want a husband who is present when my babies are born. And I want a husband who remembers the names of his various daughters without prompting."

Mrs. P cocked her head sideways as if assessing the validity of such a list of wants. Then she sank down upon the divan and looked sternly at Marke. "And are those things truly possible with this man, Margaret Catherine?"

"I don't know—yes, well—there are times when he is all consideration and kindness, and then there are times that he distances himself from me. But I feel he is a good person inside and would bring me great happiness."

"It's just as I told Mary when she decided she wanted that stuffy Alfred. First, I suggest you make the determination that your feelings are justified, that he is a good person—if that is ever possible with a man—strange creatures, men. Once you know for sure that he is, then pursue him, haunt him, be indispensable to him. That is what I did with your father, you know. But then, I mean . . ." She faltered in her efficient reasoning and her blue eyes seemed to fade. Her voice became uncertain, only to come back strongly as a reprimand. "But you must realize that I shall expect a full month's notice if you are going to run away with that man. I cannot allow my girls to be without a governess, you know."

Marke smiled through her disappointment and said gently, "Thank you, Mrs. P, for such admirable advice. I shall follow it exactly as you say."

"You are most welcome, I am sure, Marke," Mrs. P said, then turned her attention to the spaniel bitch surrounded by her new babies. "We must always try our best for our children, mustn't we, mama dog?"

Chapter Seventeen

Morning found the sun brilliant over the orange and gold hills, beckoning the stouthearted from the warmth of their fires to explore the last soft day of the autumn. Marke bundled into her woolens and made a fainthearted attempt to lure Sitter from the house. Accepting the first refusal from that lady in apparent good graces, she sought Claymore to prod him mercilessly into joining her in just such an excursion. If Mrs. P's advice was to be taken to heart, this seemed the perfect time for offensive action.

"Please, Claymore. Christmas snows will be here soon. Such a glorious, sunny day should not be wasted. A picnic is in order!" she begged.

"A picnic!" Claymore snorted, with a wry glance outside.

"Absolutely," Marke demanded. "I have asked Cook to scare up a luncheon basket, and fill it with goodies. We'll take the pony cart to the top of the ridge. There's a lovely waterfall, and if we leave right now, the sun will provide all the warmth anyone should need."

Her enthusiasm was too infectious to ignore. He ruffled her hair as one would a child, for in truth she did have the buoyant personality of a grown-up child, and conceded, "All right! I shall be ready in thrice, before the sun decides to disappear altogether."

True to her word, Marke guided the gray pony through overgrown lanes and paths until they were high over the valley where St. Catherine's Court nestled. It was a glorious picnic spot over a narrow but assertive waterfall that plunged in two great leaps, with a good deal of froth and foam, into an indent below. There it disappeared, with mist and bubbles, into a nest of ferns. Racing to the edge, Marke gathered about her a swirling plaid woolen skirt, worn with a cropped jacket of brown velvet, and breathed deeply of the crisp air.

"Isn't it marvelous?" she asked Claymore as he came to join her. She smiled at him, pleased to see him maneuvering quite steadily on strong legs and a stout cane. He looked so fine in the bright sunlight—his walnut hair shining and the brown houndstooth jacket immaculate over a caramel suede waistcoat—that she wished to throw herself into his arms and beg him to love her as much as she loved him. She looked away lest the temptation prove too much, and her love be written too clearly in her eyes. "There, on that rocky ledge, is just the place to unpack one's watercolors. What could be more perfect than the hills wearing their cinnamon and burnt sugar shades?"

"Ah, my beautiful poetess," he teased.

Marke's heart sang. Surely he wouldn't keep calling her beautiful if he didn't care deeply for her, would he? "Beautiful? Surely you gammon me, Lord Perfect. With freckles on my nose and hair the color of rusty water?" she countered, fishing shamelessly for the compliments to continue.

"Good Lord! Hardly rusty water! Your hair is a wonderful color—autumn leaves, more likely—rich red with golden highlights," he countered, pulling a leaf from overhead to tuck into her curls. "Lo the leaves. Upon the new autumn grass. Look at them well."

"And now you could be a poet, Claymore," she teased. "I had no idea you kept such talent so well hidden."

"Alas, not my words. I am afraid I have stolen most shamelessly from the writings of some long-ago lover of the ladies. Those were lines he designated 'to be closely written on a small piece of paper which, folded into a tight lozenge, will fit any girl's locket,' and I quote."

Marke moved away from the tempting closeness of his body to shake out a coach robe of weighty wool. "I see. You would quote from the writings of a man who wrote words merely for the seduction of innocent young girls? Bad form!"

Claymore slid down to sit on a rock and stretch his legs out. He watched with pleasure as Marke spread out an adventurer's lunch of cold duck, stuffed acorn squash, and hearty breads with goat cheese. How appropriate a setting for her, he thought. As a wood nymph herself, she should be in the hills where all around played the subtle patterns and textures of autumn. She was a creature of nature, and she made him feel closer to God than he'd ever imagined possible. Turning his head, he gazed over the waterfall and down the long valley, where the stream wended mistily toward the bay. In the distance, the yellow walls of St. Catherine's Court glowed against the deeper hues of the hills.

"St. Catherine's Court truly looks mystical from here," he called, then muttered too low for Marke's ears, "if only this were real life."

Marke carried a mug of cider to him and followed his gaze. "I have always thought so. It's as if a painter has captured it on his easel—all those window squares against the golden angles of the walls and the ever-changing colors of the hills. He would only need to include a girl with the red of her skirts billowing as if she is spinning with her arms out... like so." She spun off, her plaid skirts flying about her slender legs, giving him a delightful view of trim ankles and neat, narrow feet shod in walking boots.

"You are indeed a painting, Marke," he said with a shake of his head. "Inside and out. I would wish to capture your soul in a green medicine bottle and dispense it throughout the land. Such a prescription as your sunny disposition could cure the ills of the world."

"My goodness, you do wax eloquent today." She laughed, her cheeks tinted a delicate pink at the extravagance of his compliments. "Bring yourself over here before the forest creatures steal your lunch away, and I am forced to carry your limp, weakened body back to face Sitter's wrath."

Claymore laughed and did as she ordered. "Has anyone ever told you, my dear, that you are a virtual tyrant?"

"Of course," she freely admitted, filling a plate with delectables to tempt his palate. She placed it within easy reach of his reclining form with a wrinkling of her nose. "And that is the nicest thing they have said of me."

"Why do you not take offense at such slander?"

"Oh, one should never allow herself to take offense at the truth."

"Ah, there it is again, that acceptance of whatever life has dealt you. I am amazed, to say the least, and envious at best."

He gave such a deep sigh that bordered on untold sadness that Marke shifted closer and ran stroking fingers over his smooth forehead. "It is so easy, Claymore," she murmured. "We English should set aside our feeling of superiority, and learn our lessons from the Irish, instead of calling them quaint and scoffing at them."

"Such as . . ."

"Well, when something happens to the English, when they break a leg, forfeit a horse race, lose a fortune, we wail and lament that it could not possibly have been any worse. With an Englishman, whatever happens is always the worst. With the Irish, it is exactly the opposite. Everything can be worse. If you break a leg, it could have been your neck. Instead of a race, you might have bet the horse that ran the race, and instead of losing your money, you might have lost your mind. What happens is never the worst. On the contrary, what's worse never happens."

Claymore sat up and studied her face with an unreadable expression that bordered on mirth and was edged with disbelief. Marke paused, half expecting him to laugh at her, but when he didn't, she went on. "It's so simple really. If your revered and beloved grandmother dies, your revered and beloved grandfather might have died, too. If the farm burns down but the chickens are saved, the chickens might have been burned, too, and if they do burn up—well, what's worse is that you might have died yourself, and that didn't happen. And if you should die, well, you are rid of all your troubles, for to every penitent sinner the way is open to heaven, the goal of our laborious earthly pilgrimage—after breaking legs, missing coaches, surviving all manner of poverty, of course. With us—it seems to me— well, when something happens to the English, our sense of humor and imagination desert us. In Ireland, that is just when they come into play.''

"You are absolutely astounding."

"Oh, it's not me. I did not invent these ideals. It's the Irish people who are astounding. Wonderfully resilient.'' She giggled delightfully, "Just think of the mastermind who can persuade someone with a broken leg, lying about in pain or hobbling around on crutches, that it might have been worse? It's an occupation requiring poetic talents.''

"Not to mention a touch of sadism," Claymore amended with a grin. "Imagine painting such a graphic picture of the agonies of a dislocated shoulder—"

"Or a crushed skull," Marke interrupted, with another giggle.

"—to a man with a broken leg so that he hobbles off much comforted, counting himself lucky to have suffered such a minor misfortune.''

Marke nodded her head in satisfaction. He was comprehending at last. "Thus fate has unlimited credit, and the interest is submissively paid by the Irish. If the children are in bed, racked and miserable with whooping cough, in need of devoted care, you must count yourself fortunate to be on your feet and able to care for them. Here imagination knows no bounds. The phrase 'it could be worse' is one of the most common turns of speech. One hears it often.''

"Probably because in Ireland, all too often, things are rarely good, and playing 'what's worse' offers the only consolation available.''

"The twin sister of what's worse is an equally common phrase, and one I believe I've men-mentioned to you be-before—'' Marke rolled over to her side on the robe, laughing so hard she could barely speak. "D-don't w-worry!"

"Aha!" he crowed, falling over her, anchoring her firmly against the rough wool. "I should have known it was all a trap, and here I am, being led by the nose straight into it."

Marke allowed him to capture her face easily between his hands. With her heart in her eyes, she gazed with longing into his beloved face, allowing all her love free rein to him, would he but notice.

Claymore's smile, and its accompanying dimple, faded away as he looked down at her soft, flushed face. Suddenly all words seemed superfluous between them. He gathered her tightly into his arms and kissed her with a warmth and passion to snatch her breath away. Then he paused again, to trace his fingertips tenderly over the delicate line of her lips, swollen and trembling and needing to be kissed again. He could no longer deny himself the need, the desire, the inevitability of loving Marke. "Damn it all to hell," he swore softly. "Some things are just meant to be."

Marke's brow furrowed in confusion. Then, as if coming to a decision with himself, he kissed her with a savage, demanding intensity that kindled a raging fire within her. She clung to him, almost faint with happiness, eager to endorse his decision with her whole heart. "Oh, dearest..." she began, then sighed in protest as he levered himself away from her. Her breath caught as a sob in her throat. Oh, please don't let him reject me again, she thought. I'll just die if he cries nay now. But then his hands were on the brown velvet jacket, knowing, sure and efficient in their task. Heat flushed her face as he tugged the jacket open to bare her breasts to his eager hands and avid mouth. His touch was so lingering, so penetrating, it was as if he wanted to leave his mark upon her skin. Brand her as his and his alone. He pelted her with kisses and tiny bites, his head of uncontrollable curls adding to the sensation with their tickle as she helplessly arched against him. She could only tremble, offering no complaint as he bundled her skirt to her waist and bore down upon her with his weight. The smooth satin of his arousal seared across her belly. Then finally he was between her legs. The feelings were overwhelming for her. Claymore was...hands, lips, heated ardor...at last a part of her. There was no moment of indecision on her part, only her love and the desire to belong to him. And then his mouth was on her own again, heeding her pleading, muffled cries that quickly he must come fully inside her. But the pulsing had already started. She cried out and arched hard against him, her entreaties inciting him to join her at the dizzying height of pleasure.

Chapter Eighteen

"**D**inner was a masterpiece, as always," John complimented Marke. He leaned back in his chair and patted his stomach appreciatively.

Marke looked over the remains of the sweet potato and squash soup, the mashed potatoes with roasted garlic cloves, and the forcemeat of quail stuffed with orange, cranberry and rhubarb that imparted a wonderful chutneylike flavor. "Yes, Cook outdid herself just for your honor, John. But, please, you must not tell me that you've no room for her pies. Pumpkin and mince?"

"Oh, my," he exclaimed, waving her away. "I could not possibly partake of one more bite."

Claymore laughed at the man's discomfort although he was feeling a bit strained about his own waistcoat at present. "I have a feeling that to refuse will only incite her to persevere, John, and you have it on my best advice, Miss Penwell persevering is a formidable sight indeed."

Marke flipped her curls and snubbed him affectionately in favor of tempting the good doctor. "Nonsense, Lord Perfect, I fully understand if Dr. Barrows is sated, but I could not have him regret passing up the delights of Cook's pumpkin pie, duly brandied and beautifully presented in a pool of praline sauce for want of knowing of it." She giggled as John's eyes grew larger.

Sitter laughed and tucked her napkin more securely in her lap. "I, for one, shall not pass such as that."

Marke giggled again. Her eyes danced with happiness and love, as she turned to Claymore with her teasing reprimand. "For shame! What kind of hostess would you have me seem? I would be negligent in my role to not describe the plumped raisins, pecans, brandy and cherries of Cook's mince."

Claymore smiled at her expression of secret delight, his eyes slipping over the sweet curve of her lips, readily recalling the taste and feel of them beneath his own. Sweet Marke. Wanton Marke. His Marke.

John groaned and threw his hands heavenward in surrender. "Oh, my! I do have a passion for mince. Cease, Marke, for I surrender. My life and my expanding waistline be on your head!"

The company all laughed at his capitulation. Claymore leaned back to allow the footman to place the pumpkin pie in front of him. "As I warned you, John, she can be merciless."

"Ah, perhaps so," John agreed. "But you are progressing remarkably well under her wielded whip. I must admit, the idea of the swim tank is ingenious. Quite along the lines of the hot springs at Bath, and most effective. You shall be dancing at some ball in London before the new year is aged."

Marke's heart stood still. Had Claymore confided to the physician that he was returning to England? She glanced at Sitter, but that lady showed no signs of anything amiss. In fact, she made an announcement that settled Marke's dread of the marquis's departure, and opened a whole other can of worms.

"Oh, Claymore, you shall not have to return for the little season to have London company. I received a missive from Lady Alma. It seems she and Lord Pressley intend to surprise you for the Christmas holidays. I realize it's terribly naughty of me to tell you beforehand." She canted a sarcastic eyebrow at the marquis. "Quite spoils the surprise, I suppose, but I thought advance notice might be in order."

For a moment, Claymore looked as if someone had dashed the cold water of reality in his face. Then his expression seemed to settle into an unreadable mask as he glanced from Sitter to Marke before commenting casually, "Alma? Coming to Innisfree? Amazing, she's usually toes-to-the-fire at the first sign of brave weather, and remains so until spring. Can't imagine why she would endure inclement weather to descend upon Innisfree, of all places."

Marke felt a dreadful foreboding creep up her spine. She tried to keep her voice light and natural as she entered the conversation. "Company for Christmas? An introduction of new faces into our small group might be diverting."

Sitter made a face, then turned to Claymore. "I should think it obvious, Claymore, that Lady Alma has decided it time you rejoined society. And, having been acquainted with Lord Pressley under vastly different circumstances than you, I must tell you, a greater scoundrel I've never met. Insofar as his daughters—"

Marke's hand jerked, clattering sterling against china. Daughters? She had assumed, or perhaps prayed, the Lady Alma was a wife, not a daughter. This might explain the sense of disaster she felt.

"—are concerned, the eldest girl's husband took up gaming in an attempt to satisfy his wife's impossible demands. And, then Lord Pressley *would* express such poor taste as to verbally criticize his son-in-law to any ready ear, even though he himself never spent over two weeks a year with his own wife." She lifted eyebrows and nodded meaningfully to everyone at the table. "It is rumored that it was this uncaring treatment that drove Lady Pressley to an early grave."

"I would consider all that a bit harsh, and perhaps exaggerated, Sitter. But, be that as it may, they are coming and that, I suppose, is that," Claymore declared, his tone rather flat and strained.

Marke watched the muscles tense beneath the smooth skin of his jaw. He appeared unduly overset by Sitter's comments, she thought, allowing her teeth to worry her lower lip. Was it the fact that the lady and her father were descending upon Innisfree that affected him? Or was it Sitter's criticisms of them?

Sitter was not to heed the thunderstorm gathering on the marquis's face without slipping in one additional comment. "I merely wished to point out that one should monitor their pocketbook in the presence of either of them."

"Enough, Sitter! It does you no credit to defame Alma, or her father, in the presence of people who do not have their acquaintance," Claymore stormed, shoving away from the table and marching from the room without Henry's arm as support.

Marke looked down at her plate. He had not demonstrated such anger in a long time. Irritation yes, but not this stormy anger that smacked of the same helplessness he used to feel. She was unable to discern if he was pleased at the arrival of the Lady Alma or not. There was an awful sinking in the pit of her stomach, for as surely as it would rain in Ireland, the arrival of the Lady Alma was to be bad news for her and her hopes and dreams.

"Well, I see he still has his ups and downs," John said, sliding his chair back and blotting his mouth on his napkin. "But at least he walked out of the room instead of rolled. My hat is off to both of you ladies. His recovery is remarkable. And, upon that note, I should be off. Babies to welcome, sniffles to stifle, don't you know. Ladies, it has been a pleasure as always."

After waving the physician down the driveway, Sitter and Marke strolled into the drawing room. Plopping down onto the sofa, Sitter extended her feet toward the fire. "Ah, I shall have to fight this urge to nap the afternoon away. That pumpkin pie may just be the end of me. You shall have me round as the pumpkin itself, with many meals such as that."

"Come, then," Marke urged, too agitated for sedentary pursuits. "Let us bundle to the teeth and brave the wind for a brisk walk in the gardens. The sun is peeking out, and there is no more rain. We shall stride away the gluttony with stimulating exercise."

Arm in arm, they set off over the leaf-strewn lawn. "This was a wonderful idea, Marke. Most refreshing," Sitter said.

Marke squeezed her arm tightly in affection. "I shall miss you ever so much, Sitter, when you return to Innisfree. I am afraid St. Catherine's Court will seem very empty after so much activity."

"Oh, but you must still join us for the holidays. I cannot think of you changing your plans, for there are sure to be festivities at Innisfree. I have no doubt Alma will insist on some sort of entertainment—a country ball or such."

Marke glanced out over the lawns to the rapidly thinning trees. For once the reds and golds failed to quiet her racing thoughts. She did not wish to appear eager, nor would she allow herself to be drawn into an open admission of her newly expanded relationship with Claymore, but she must know what to expect with the new arrivals. She kept her tone light when she queried Sitter. "Tell me more of the Pressleys, Sitter. New additions will make the holidays much more entertaining, don't you agree?"

Sitter shuddered in answer. "George Pressley is a disagreeable blowhard. But Alma can be pleasant enough if she puts her mind to it. Marke..." Sitter paused to draw a deep breath, exhaling her words in a rush as if wishing to speak before thinking better of it. "I do feel it imperative to warn you, although it really should be Claymore's place to do so, but... well, an announcement of a marriage between Alma and Claymore was fully expected before the tragedy. I very much think Alma still expects as much."

Marke's heart plummeted to her very toes. Not a friendship, not a flirtation, but an announcement of marriage! Fighting for control of her expression, she sought to keep the older woman from sensing her hurt and fear. She sighed and squeezed Sitter's arm. "Ah, well, I suppose it was to be expected of such a dashing and handsome man to have amours. As you said, he was crème de la crème."

Sitter continued to prattle on, either unaware of Marke's gloom or perhaps respecting her desire to keep it private. "Well, I for one wish he would turn his attention elsewhere, but you know how men are with a pretty face. Besides, it has practically been settled from the cradle. Edward and George were great friends, you see. And what more can Claymore do but follow through with his father's wishes?''

"What more, indeed,'' Marke's voice was uncharacteristically harsh, causing Sitter to glance at her. Though Marke, if she truly wished her feelings to remain hidden, should have been more circumspect. But she could not stop her questions. Best she hear it all now than be stabbed through the heart at the sight of them together. "I suppose he loves her very much.''

"Love?'' Sitter pondered, then shook her head. "Oh, I don't think so. While Claymore is kind and generous and thoughtful, I have always reckoned him incapable of developing a great passion. And if he ever did, it would not be with the likes of Lady Alma. No, I have always thought he grew infatuated with her years ago—she can be rather spectacular at times—and then she simply grew into a habit. Which, I am sorry to say, is a common motive for society marriages. It was much the case with his father. Everyone, from family to society, simply expected Edward to wed Elizabeth. So he did. And I imagine Claymore will end up buckled to Alma for no other reason than it is simply expected of him.''

"Perhaps so,'' Marke agreed miserably. Somewhere within her, under the numbness that held her still for the lashing, she felt a small point of pain, hot like the pain of scalding. She wished she had not invited the confidences. Such knowledge made it impossible for her to ponder the wonderful possibilities their morning of intimacy had promised. She had never thought of Claymore to be one to accede to other than his own wishes in any matter, but now to learn that he was more accepting of rules, strictures and expectations saddened her. Were his kisses and caresses nothing more than...what? Release? Was there no genuine affection for her in his heart? How could he not realize the depth of her feelings, of her willingness to give herself, body and soul, to him? Would that not mean something to him?

As if reading Marke's thoughts, Sitter drew her to a standstill, forcing her to face her. "One never intends to pursue a life as fashionably impure, Marke. It just happens to some of us... perhaps because we love too much. Love can be so blinding.''

''Oh, Sitter! Is it so apparent as that?''

''Well, I have not noticed a great deal of discretion on your part. Since this morning, even to the inexperienced eye, you two speak with the easy glances and words of lovers who hold nothing in reserve. I realize that you both feel isolated from censure here,'' she said, and waved her hands out over the vast emptiness of the lawns. ''But the *haute-ton,* and the rules they set forth governing proper conduct, are never so far away. Claymore is a marquis, and will be expected to return to his rightful place in society at some time...''

''And marry someone more suitable to his station,'' Marke finished for her. She felt as if she'd been slapped. ''Well, you may rest assured, Sitter, I have no intention of being set up on Chelsea Street as the marquis's kept woman,'' Marke declared, then realized the stinging insult she had unintentionally dealt Sitter. ''Oh, Sitter, I did not mean—I should not have spoken so harshly.''

''No offense taken, my dear,'' Sitter soothed, then tugged her down the gravel path. ''I became what I am entirely by accident. Having Edward come into my life when my father died was a godsend and, though I would have wished my life to be different, I am not unhappy. But you...''

''Oh Sitter, you are a dear, dear person,'' Marke exclaimed, throwing her arms about the woman. ''And you are welcome at St. Catherine's Court for all time. In fact, should you ever decide to close your house in London, please consider living out your years with me and Mrs. P. My home is your home. You can even have your own dog.''

Sitter laughed and returned the hug. ''I shall remember that, my dear. And *you* remember to guard your heart. It is very tender and very inexperienced. While a little indiscretion in Ireland would not mar a married woman's acceptance in society, it would be devastating for a young girl who has yet to bend her knee to the queen. I would caution you to end whatever alliance there is between you and Claymore before the gossipy Lord Pressley arrives.'' She quickly held up her hand to still Marke's protest. "I do not require details of what is occurring between the two of you. I am merely stating that George would like nothing better than to carry tales back to London with which to barter for popularity among the matrons.''

"Do you think Lady Alma and her father will remain at Innisfree past the holiday season?" Marke asked, praying for the right answer.

Sitter snorted. "I would imagine Alma will stay for as long as it takes to extract Claymore's promise to return to London with her.''

Wrong answer! Marke gave a soft sigh. "Blast!''

"And frankly, my dear, she will be bloody bored within three days, but wild horses will not drag her away from Claymore. Her father set her sights on the title and fortune of Boothe-Ashmore from infancy, and you mark my words, she means to have them! And, if I were you, I would never underestimate the scope of Alma's cunning if she views you as a rival for Claymore's attentions.''

Marke turned back toward the mansion. Unsure of her feelings at this moment, she could only admit to being definitely low in spirits. Ever practical, and though she did not wish to think it of him, she must consider the possibility that her hold on Claymore might have been based solely upon his need of diversion and comfort. There had been no murmured words of love from him this morning and, as he was greatly advanced in his recovery and his need was diminishing, the timing of Alma's arrival just might signal his return to London and the new season in the spring. She desperately did not want to think she had been merely a plaything to him. Her face became quite set at the thought. But if that were true, the beautiful Lady Alma—and she had no doubt that she was—must be considered soft in the head for setting her sights for one as low in the brow as Claymore, Lord Perfect.

Marke led Sitter around the garden at a brisk stride no less than three times before heeding the woman's wail of complaint and allowing herself to be dragged indoors to a warming library fire, and a liberally filled glass of sherry.

Chapter Nineteen

The night passed long and sleepless for Marke. When she lay in her bed craving the oblivion of sleep, her busy mind would not allow thoughts other than those of Claymore and Alma. She wished to do nothing more than crawl into his arms for reassurances that he cared for her even a little, but those would be reassurances he had warned her long ago that he could not give. She spent the long dark hours, alternately pacing her sitting room and staring at the changing patterns of light on the ceiling above her bed. She would heed her mother's amazing advice and assess the circumstances as they truly were. She knew he enjoyed her company, her conversation, and even desired her body. As for herself, she freely admitted that it had been more than just her body, she had offered Claymore that night in front of the fire. She had given him her heart and soul without his even asking. And though she might have said otherwise, she had, and still did, harbor dreams concerning the Marquis of Boothe-Ashmore. Dreams that had nothing to do with titles or fortunes or an exalted place in society. It had to do with loving him, wanting to spend the rest of her life with him, carrying his babies inside her body and building a family for all time. And she would not give up those dreams easily. What had her mother said? Pursue him? Could she pursue him? Play the coquette, tease and flirt until he was manipulated into submission? No, she could not. It was not in her to beg, and that was what pursuit would feel like. No, either he wanted her in the same way she wanted him, or it was just not meant to be. Her way was frankness and honesty. She would simply ask for what she needed. He would not deny her, she just knew he would not.

Decision made, Marke leapt from her bed and dashed down the hallway on bare feet. Tapping twice on Claymore's bedchamber door before receiving his bid to enter, she stepped inside. The sight of him propped against his pillow, an open book in his hands, brought to mind the picture of him in his own library, frowning at her audacity for disturbing him. She suddenly felt very unsure of her mission here.

"Claymore, I must speak to you—about Alma. Sitter—"

Claymore abruptly sat up and thrust the book across the counterpane. "Sitter should learn to refrain from gossip," he declared without warmth.

Marke, suddenly discomforted by his withdrawn attitude, gathered the full skirt of her night rail about her self-consciously. "She wasn't gossiping...exactly."

Claymore closed his eyes and gave a long sigh. This was a confrontation he was not relishing, and in fact, saw no reason to pursue at this particular moment. A moment when he was feeling guilty as hell for compromising someone dear to him, and a moment when he was totally unsure how to proceed with his life other than as originally planned. Throwing back the covers, he gained his feet and slipped on his robe. "Come, it's too chilly to be roaming the halls in bare feet. I'll walk you back." He held out his hand to her.

Shying away from his outstretched hand and its intent, Marke moved to the fire and stared into the flames. "So you propose that we simply do not have this discussion?"

"That is exactly what I propose," he said tensely, coming close behind her.

Marke spun to face him. "Claymore, I must insist—"

"No, Marke! No insisting!"

A variety of emotions played over her fresh young face. Claymore could see that she was confused, hurt, angry and determined in the space of a few seconds. He wished to reach out to her, to stroke her cheek and tell her that he wanted her, loved her and wished to share the rest of his life with her. But that was not something he was free to do. He was bound by promises made to a father newly in his grave. Something dark and dreadful inside him, that he could only identify as self-hatred, dug at him. Despite all his promises to himself, he had taken Marke's innocence when he had no right to do so, for he had nothing to give her in return but heartache. He could see that heartache brimming in her eyes with the tears that threatened.

The silence grew long and Marke was the first to drop her eyes from the tussle of wills. "As you wish then," she conceded.

"Ah, the famous acceptance," Claymore snorted, finding solace in anger. "How I envy you your easy acceptance of the facts of your life."

Marke glanced at his set face in amazement. Facts of her life? Did he truly think she was simply accepting as fact that she had been a passing convenience, a necessary part of his convalescence? And now that Lady Alma was arriving, was she simply to accept it as a signal for the end of everything she wished for in her life? What was it they had shared on the mountainside? Had he felt nothing that she had felt? "Acceptance?" she replied bitterly. "One should not be envious of something that is free for the taking."

He gave a slight galling laugh and turned his back on her pain. "How naive you are. Haven't you learned yet that nothing is free? Life always exacts a price."

Marke watched his straight back with a suddenly leaden heart. Yes, she had been naive. To believe that he would love her just because she loved him so much. Stupid, actually, to presume there would be a life—love, home, a family—with him. He was right, everything had a price, but his price was proving too high. She could not invest more of herself in a dream that was only to cause her pain beyond what she could bear.

Marke drew herself up tensely and schooled her face. "Claymore, I do, at some time, anticipate returning to London and moving about in society. I would not wish to have my name bandied about the smoke-filled rooms of White's before I could establish myself. I would ask . . ."

Claymore spun to stare at her. His first reaction was to grip her shoulders and cry out in indignity at the implication that he might brag of this, that he only viewed his time with her as conquest. But then he saw how hard she was fighting for control of her emotions. Guilt washed over him. He had not been fair to Marke. He had taken her for his own selfish needs, neglecting to consider fully the consequences of his actions. But now he must accept responsibility for those actions and attempt some repair of the damage he had done in the only way left open to him.

"It is already as if it never happened," he stated flatly. Dropping into the chair, he stared morosely into the flames, and to Marke's irritation, with a great deal of uncharacteristic acceptance, he muttered "I suppose it's safe to say that the world has encroached upon our little paradise with all its cruel realities. Harsh though it may seem, perhaps we were both naive to think this happiness would endure beneath the glare of society's scrutiny."

"Yes, perhaps so," she snapped, then moved brusquely to the door, for after all, what more was there to say? It was not possible to force someone to love you, was it?

Claymore halted her with even more cruel words. "I do believe it prudent for my household to relieve yours of its burden with all possible expedience. While I would not have you think me ungrateful for—well, everything—I shall take my leave of you and St. Catherine's Court at first light."

Marke felt pain like a hot, sharp knife rip through her chest. She drew a deep, shaky breath. So he was leaving her. She could only nod as words were impossible for her at present. When he made no move to launch more poison darts into her bleeding heart, she opened the door and stepped through. The pause she gave just before latching the door was not filled with his call for her to come back, to forgive him for playing such a cruel joke on her, to let him love her for all time, but only the stony silence of finality. She raced down the hall to fling herself headlong upon her bed, there to allow her misery full voice in wails and tears until she was at last exhausted.

Claymore sat immobile with sorrow before the fire, listening to Marke's fading footsteps in the hallway. He had no way of describing to her—so young, so eager, so blinded by the possibilities of her life—the high price one must pay for loving another too much. The pain was enormous, too enormous to be borne, when love was cruelly snatched away at the whim of fate. He had been wrong, terribly wrong, to make love to her, and had there been any way to take back his actions he would have done so gladly, although the feel and taste of her was sweetness beyond belief. But perhaps it was in this way that she was to learn it was far better to hold one's emotions in reserve, than to die a little every day with hurt. He slammed a fist into the padded arm of the chair for the pain he was again experiencing. He didn't want to love her. He didn't want to care this deeply about anyone ever again. And he *would* not!

Roused later by a light tapping on her bedchamber door, Marke was surprised to see the sky outside her window was still quite dark although she must have slept for a time. Would this night of horror never end?

Sitter slipped into the room before Marke could call for whoever it was to go to hell. One look at Marke's tear-streaked face, and she shook her head sadly. Moving to gather the girl into her arms, she stroked her back. "Oh, dear," she murmured. "I gather you and Claymore have had a falling-out?"

It was an understatement of such magnitude that Marke giggled through her tears, but the laugh changed quickly to snubs of exhausted emotions, which gave way to a great, inexplicable sense of wretchedness that sat like a stone in her heart. "Something of that sort," she murmured. Her voice was woefully unsteady, and she clamped her teeth on her lower lip to stop its quivering.

"Oh, my poor, dear girl." Sitter sighed. "I can scarcely bear the notion that I might have participated in this lamentable development. I repeatedly tried to warn you, but

I fancy any advice, coming from me, would be decidedly hypocritical.''

"Hypocritical?" Marke echoed weakly, sitting up to blow her nose.

"I should have seemed a flaming hypocrite indeed, my dear," Sitter confided. "I mean, after all, I had made you well aware of the depth of my feelings for Edward. How could I place myself as judge and jury over your similar actions? Demand you deny a *tendre* for Claymore when it was very apparent, unfortunate though it might be, that it was all-consuming for you. I was, as I stated, tempted to warn you off most strictly, but why should you have listened to one such as I? Who was I to point out the awful repercussions you were opening yourself to?"

"Unfortunate?" Marke's head fairly spun. "Repercussions?"

Sitter frowned and touched the back of her hand to Marke's brow as though she suspected the existence of a mind-fogging fever. Then shaking her head, she clasped Marke's hands. "My dear, I am referring to the gravest mistake women such as ourselves can make—that of falling first in bed with a man, then expecting the ring that makes it acceptable, to follow."

It all came to light at last. Sitter was telling her in her own delicate way that she had been dreadfully silly about the marquis and it was time to creep into the closet and lick her wounds. Another giggle welled up in her chest and tickled the corners of her mouth, but Sitter looked so sincere that she carefully straightened her face. "Sitter, you are a dear but do not fret yourself—"

"I have not yet told you the worst," Sitter interposed grimly. "The worst is that I was rather inclined to encourage the relationship. I mean, I could have told Claymore, as a man of experience and years, to mind his manners where you were concerned. But there was never any doubt in my mind that it would be the best thing for him. I mean, he did respond so favorably to you right from the beginning, and I wished him well so desperately that I convinced myself that it might be the best for you, as well. So there you have it. I admit with shame to ignoring every untoward warning in my heart, pretended to myself that they were quite meaningless."

"Dear Sitter," Marke comforted her. But the woman would have none of it. She would insist on every ounce of punishment for her crime of negligence.

"Oh, I knew better, of course, for I saw it coming early on, saw it coming even at Innisfree." Sitter bit her own lip and looked contrite.

"Innisfree?"

"Why, yes," Sitter insisted. "All the signals were there. The way you glowed when he looked at you. The avid interest that began to surface, as it does with men, when Claymore began to see you as an attractive young woman, instead of a bloody nuisance. But I did nothing to stop it, and I am so sorry for your pain now. But you are young, and while you do not believe it now, time will heal the ache of a broken heart."

"Yes, time heals all, doesn't it?" Marke murmured wryly. Claymore was right. The words were meaningless pulp and did nothing to help.

Sitter rose to pace toward the brightly burning fire. "I shall say my goodbyes now as Claymore has decreed that we must depart within the hour. I cannot imagine you wish to be on the front stoop gaily waving goodbye as he progresses down the driveway."

Marke felt tears well up in her eyes again, and her nose started to run. Sitter opened her arms, and Marke was lost. She truly loved this dear woman and readily forgave her any meddling on her part. Flinging herself from the bed, she fairly collapsed into the proffered embrace and buried her face in the bombazine collar.

"Do not cry, dear," Sitter whispered. "Everything will be all right, I promise you, if you will only permit it."

It was the empty comfort a mother might extend a fretful child with a skinned knee, but Marke was determined not to humiliate herself further. She emitted a single great sniff and drew away. "I shall do my best, Sitter, and as you know, my best far exceeds the expectations of most."

Sitter smoothed the red hair and nodded at the sally. "That's better. And I shall hear nothing from you about declining any holiday invitations coming from Innisfree. I shall expect you there with a smile on your face, and St. Nick bells on the toes of your dancing slippers. Besides I am most positive I shall be requiring rescue from deplorable company in no less than three days' time. Promise?"

"Yes, I give you my promise. And you are always welcome to batter the doors of St. Catherine's Court should it all become too much for you at Innisfree."

Sitter laughed heartily. "Do not be surprised to see me there, driven into the snow by the wails of the hounds of proper society and cruel innuendo. Now I shall bid you goodbye. Be safe, my dear."

Marke closed the door quietly behind her, then returned to sink to her knees before the fire. "I shall probably live to regret making that promise to you, dear Sitter. But then, to be honest with myself, wild horses could not keep me from Innisfree." Staring deeply into the flames, she smiled a sad little smile. "Oh, Claymore, why didn't anyone tell me how badly a person could hurt? That an emotion can ache like a physical pain. I am sorely wounded, perhaps even mortally, by all this."

Chapter Twenty

Brushing the petal softness of new snow from her head and patting her cheeks made rosy with the winter wind, Marke drew a deep breath of crisp air and exhaled it in a wide grin of happiness. The smell of greens, pine, fir and evergreen, carried in from the woods to decorate Innisfree's vast hallways, wafted through the open front door and into her face. Everything around her shouted Christmas. And like all children, and childish grown-ups, Marke loved Christmas. She turned with a radiant face to Heaven as he rushed through the door and all but threw his arms about her.

"Miss Penwell! Welcome!"

"Merry Christmas, Heaven! I trust you have been well?"

"Yes, most well. Thank you, miss," the old man answered with a face brought grim with his next statement. "I truly cannot express sincerely enough the, er, excitement and, er, well, to say it straight out, miss, the *gratitude* of the entire household staff, that you are visiting for the holidays."

"What's this? Surely not strife in the household on such a beautiful holiday?" she teased him with tilted eyebrows and a jolly good mood. It pleased her, in a most shameful way, that all was not happy and harmonious at Innisfree.

Heaven would only gesture toward the family room on the second level and groan. Marke was left to make her own assessment of that, for Sitter was tramping down the stairs at as fast a pace as could be considered both dignified and safe.

"Oh, Marke! Marke! It is ever so good to see you," she exclaimed, rushing to gather the girl in a giant hug. "I have been beside myself with excitement ever since I received your note of acceptance. Brrrr! Do come out of this drafty hallway before you catch your death and must be stuffed away from company in a gruesome sickbed somewhere. Heaven, send up tea, and mind you, Marke likes it hearty and full-bodied."

"Of course, Mrs. Sittlemeyer." He bowed, then winked at Marke. "We, at Innisfree, are all well aware of Miss Penwell's preferences, and have taken the greatest pains to make her feel most welcome."

Marke could only laugh as Sitter dragged her in the direction of the garland-draped staircase. With a wave of her hand at Heaven, she allowed herself to be drawn up and away, to the same room she had occupied during her last stay at Innisfree. The room folded itself about her in familiar welcome. The furnishings glowed warmly in gold, ruby and pink rose upholstery, with all the red-hued wood well rubbed with scented beeswax. Someone had placed a fragrant evergreen wreath on the wall above a fresh rose topiary tree and draped a delicate garland of holiday juniper and holly—spiked with rosemary and bay, dried hydrangeas and dried roses—from the posts of the bed, tying off the four corners with gold ribbon and silvery herbs, like fuzzy lamb's ears and feathery artemisia.

"Oh, this is beautiful. Someone has gone to a great deal of trouble for me." She flipped about and regarded Sitter with a stern expression. "So give over with the news, Sitter. Heaven seems beside himself, and I strongly suspect that I'm being viewed as the liberating army, or some such."

"Oh, and so you had better be! We are indeed besieged!" Sitter announced with a disgusted snort. "It can all be summed up in one word—Pressley!"

"As bad as that?"

"I cannot even describe to you how odious that man is! And Alma has done nothing but complain since her foot first crossed the threshold. I have been hiding out in my room for days and days. *Reading...* " She gave a shudder as if the very idea were too awful to express.

Marke laughed and rushed to hug her, although she could not resist the urge to tease, "Oh, and here I am disturbing you. Well, perhaps I should just take off myself, and let you return to your book then."

Sitter would only frown at her. "In point of fact, I wasn't reading at all. I was brooding, and I fancy I shall not be the only one once you have made the acquaintance of Alma and her father."

"Oh, it can't be as awful as that. Surely you exaggerate, Sitter."

Sitter's answer was delayed by the arrival of Marke's trunk and a laden tea tray to be placed before the fire. Little Kittie burst through the door before it could close behind the two grinning, bowing, blushing footmen.

"Miss Penwell, ye be here at last!" she shrieked, and if circumstances had been only slightly different, Marke was positive she would have found the little maid flinging herself into her arms.

"Yes, I have arrived, Kittie. Safe and sound, and pleased as punch to do so." She laughed and squeezed the girl's shoulder affectionately.

Catching sight of Sitter, seated before the fireplace, the maid dropped her head in embarrassment and dipped a small curtsy. "Oh, excuse me, mum. I dinna mean to interrupt ye. Shall I come back later to unpack Miss Penwell's things?"

"If you would, Kittie," Sitter answered, eager to resume confidences.

"Oh, Kittie, if you will just press this one thing for tonight, everything else can wait until later," Marke said, rushing to unstrap the trunk lid. Pulling forth a lovely creation of gold-sparkled, ivory tissue silk, designed and stitched just for the marquis's country ball, she handed it lovingly to the maid with a wink that brought back the smiles and giggles. "Have a care of it, for it's the very best that I have to my name."

"Oh, miss," the maid said, and sighed with wide eyes. "'Tis the loveliest thing. All shimmery with gold sparkles, it is. Ye will look a princess tonight fer sure."

"One would hope so, Kittie. Off with you now, as my tea grows tepid," she said, shoving her out the door and turning to Sitter. "At last, Sitter, we are alone. You must tell me what to think of all this. I have never felt so overwhelmed with welcome in all my life."

"Oh, come now, Marke, surely you jest? Do not pretend you are not aware just how well loved you are." Handing Marke a cup of strong brew, Sitter studied her with dawning astonishment. "My Lord, you are surprised, aren't you? Utterly remarkable! I was of the opinion that you were more intuitive than that. Have you truly never noticed the way people respond to you?"

Marke could only stare at the woman. Well loved? The outcast of the Penwell family? She squirmed uncomfortably.

Sitter looked kindly upon her embarrassment and gently changed the subject. "I trust Mrs. P is well?"

Marke sighed with relief. "Wonderfully well, and feeling quite pleased with herself at having sent the new governess off to her family for the holidays. It must never be said that Mrs. P is inconsiderate of her servants, you know. But that is not what I want to speak of! Tell me everything, Sitter. Company fares poorly at Innisfree?"

Easily distracted by such a pressing subject, Sitter leaned forward and began in earnest. "More poorly than can be described. As you were aware, I had not met Alma prior, as I do move in quite different circles, you know. And, I assure you, I was fully prepared to give her every benefit of doubt regardless of what I'd heard. Mainly out of gratitude to Claymore, as he would insist I be introduced as a distant family member, thus diverting the probability of a situation that could be rather uncomfortable for me. Indeed, I prayed—*fervently* prayed, I can tell you—she would prove herself altogether removed from the blight under which the rest of that dreadful family operates. She looks different, I will grant her that kindness, but insofar as character is concerned, I judge her to be far worse. Oh, my poor Claymore!'' she finished in a wail.

Marke, normally not one to take pleasure in hearing bad news of another, could not stop the singing in her heart. She thought to control her tongue and allow Sitter all the crime of gossip, for surely it could not be considered gossip in the true sense if one only listened, but Sitter's blue eyes were probing hers and she realized that some sort of response was required. ''And Claymore? Does he share your opinion?'' she asked, with her breath caught in her throat. Oh, please, please say he is absolutely appalled at her and wishes her removed from Innisfree, and from his life, forever.

''Alas, I do not quite know what Claymore thinks. I have seen little of him since they arrived, and then never alone. Alma is relentless in her pursuit of amusements, and of Claymore, as well. I fear the setting of a wedding date is imminent. Certainly George is adamant of it, and I do not see Claymore acting as if he will cross them.''

Marke's heart thudded to her toes. So it was to be that way. ''Is he happy?'' she murmured, shifting her rapidly blinking eyes to the teapot and busying her hands with the replenishment of her cup.

''Happy?'' Sitter shook her head. ''No, he is not happy. Although I daresay Claymore has never imagined that marriage would render him happy. His own parents were quite miserable, you know.''

Marke had gathered as much from the previous description of the Lady Elizabeth Perfect, plus, a man happy in his union did not settle a second household with a mistress. Why, oh, why did she feel so dead inside? Had she truly thought it would be magically different once she got to Innisfree? Had the long silence from Claymore over the past weeks told her nothing? Her happiness, and the feelings of having come home generated by her arrival at Innisfree, quickly evaporated into cold mist.

Sitter's eyes shifted to the window. "I have often wondered what would have transpired if Edward had survived the fire and the year of proper mourning. Would he have truly married me? Perhaps it is just as well that I never knew. Ah, fate."

Sitter sighed deeply and Marke felt a swelling lump in her throat. Gazing sympathetically at her friend, she declared quite strongly, "Having never made the man's acquaintance, I can only say, he would have been an utter fool *not* to take you to wife. You are the most wonderful person, Sitter."

Sitter's eyes jerked back to Marke and she beamed that warm, delightful smile. "Thank you, dear. But I digress, don't I? We were discussing that bothersome Claymore William Perfect and the deplorable Lady Alma, and much as I regret it, perhaps we shall simply have to relinquish this to fate, as well."

"Relinquish it to fate?" Marke exclaimed. She reared back in her chair and threw out a sharp laugh. "Absolutely not! I do not believe in fate. Life is an investment. It returns tenfold what you put into it. I do not intend to fill my investment with sorrow and resignation."

"This from the lady who preaches acceptance?" Sitter laughed with her.

"There is a great deal of difference in accepting the things that cannot be changed in one's life, and ignoring the opportunities presented to one as challenges."

"Oh, Marke, it is just the best thing in the world to have you here. Why, all of a sudden, do I feel that you will make everything right?"

"I cannot promise that things shall be made right merely by my presence, dear Sitter," Marke said, wiggling her eyebrows at her. "But they will at least be livelier, to say the very least."

Sitter rose to hug the girl to her, then shook out her skirts. "That they will and I shall anticipate the fireworks with great relish. Now, I shall retire to..."

"Read?" Marke prompted, pleased to see Sitter respond with good humor.

"Hardly, my dear. I shall rest before County Bantry descends upon us," she said, then turned once more before slipping through the door. "I suggest you do the same. Tonight could be a long evening."

Left alone, Marke strolled to the window to stare down upon the courtyard with a pensive face. Yes, it would be a long evening, indeed, if she was expected to witness Claymore fawning upon his intended bride. But, she reasoned, busying her mind seeking reassurances for her broken heart, when had Claymore ever given any indication that he was head over heels in love with the Lady Alma Pressley? Even Sitter said it was mere acceptance. She chuckled to herself. So he was following her advice on acceptance, was he? Most disagreeable of the blighter!

Movement below her window drew her attention. Claymore, mounted upon a splendid warmblood, its hide so black it was patched with blue, cantered into the courtyard. It thrilled her to see him astride a blooded mount, instead of trapped in an invalid chair. He was closely followed by a slight gray mare that could have been a child's mount by its size, but it was the lady aboard the gray that drew her rapt attention. Marke pressed her face to the cold windowpane, straining to see better. Claymore's companion could be none other than Alma Pressley, and it was readily apparent to Marke that the lady was not a confident horsewoman, for she sat unsteadily and clutched the leathers to stay aboard. "Mark one for Margaret Catherine," she muttered with some satisfaction. "Oh, drat!" Her breath had fogged the glass and obscured her vision, forcing her to rub vigorously at it with the sleeve of her spencer before she could see again.

From her lofty perch, Marke could tell the woman's face was quite pale against the scarlet hue of her elegant riding costume, which could be expressing fear—or more probably indicated piles of gorgeous blond hair hidden beneath the smartly plumed coachman hat. Marke took due note of the precise width of creamy lace that frothed at her neck and wrists. No doubt the height of fashion in everything she wore or said—damn her hide.

Holding her breath to keep the glass clear, she watched Claymore stroll elegantly to the gray mare's flank and place his hands upon that small waist to swing the woman to the ground. Oh, the hussy, she seethed! Just look at the way she leans against his chest, gazing up into his face. And, though the marquis did step away, it was not with the eagerness to end the adoring embrace that Marke so desperately wished to see. Although, it was to her gratitude, he did not seem ready to accompany the woman into the mansion, but strode abruptly in the opposite direction, disappearing into the stables in the wake of the groom and the horses. It was quite obvious to Marke's delight that Alma was not pleased, for she stamped her foot not once but twice on the wet ground and flipped her skirts violently in foul, childish temper before marching to the side door.

When Claymore did not reappear, Marke spun away from the window and danced across the room, singing out, "All is not well at Innisfree, and I am glad, glad, glad." She flopped into the chair before the fire to hug herself tightly. "And I shall encourage mutiny in the ranks as never before. Alma can go over the side to visit Neptune, for all I care! Claymore William Perfect is mine, mine, mine!"

Marke was still seated before the fire, plotting, when the bedchamber door slammed violently back against the frame. Startled, she leapt to her feet to confront an obviously distressed Kittie braced in the doorway. The maid's eyes were huge, and tears streamed unchecked down her cheeks. The ivory ball gown lay limp across both her arms like a mortally wounded soldier.

"Oh, miss, 'twasn't my fault, I swear. I tried and tried, but I canna get the stains out. Then Cook tried, we all tried, and Heaven was going storming to his lordship with complaint, but . . ." she wailed, dissolving into incoherent blubbers.

Marke rushed to draw the girl into the room, closing the door firmly behind her. For whatever the reason Kittie had Heaven so irate as to approach Claymore with domestic problems, she resolved to set it right, for anyone could see there was no real meanness in the girl. Fearing the tears might never cease, she removed the ivory tissue silk from the maid's arms, and away from the copious tears that would be damaging to the fragile silk. Spreading the gown on the bed, she gasped to see several large mud stains on the front skirt panel, and upon closer inspection, discovered numerous rents in the fragile fabric. "Oh, no! Kittie, whatever happened?" she gasped, suddenly very close to tears herself.

"Oh, miss, 'twas done on purpose, 'twas! Sh-she..."

Again her words became blubbers. Marke set her lips in a grim line. Her beautiful gown, the very finest she had ever owned, was totally ruined. After begging and pleading with Ressell to have it sent in time for this Christmas ball. Now what would she wear to dazzle Claymore with her magnificence? Sybil's old gold hand-me-down that he'd seen so many times?

Spinning, she gripped Kittie tightly by the shoulders, resisting the urge to shake her until she ceased her wailing. "Kittie, hush now. Calm yourself and tell me exactly what happened."

"'Twasn't my fault..."

"No one is saying it was your fault, Kittie. It's all right, really it is. What's done is done and can't be helped by casting blame, but I want you to quiet yourself and tell me exactly what happened. Right from the beginning. Can you do that for me?"

Kittie nodded her head and sniffled mightily. Marke drew forth a handkerchief from her pocket and encouraged the girl to blow her nose. Agonizingly slow to Marke, the little maid quieted enough to speak clearly. Drawing several deep breaths, she began her story, pausing to dab at her eyes whenever tears threatened.

"I pressed the gown real careful-like, and was bringing it back to ye, miss, when it happened. 'Twas on the stairs, was carrying it just so, like I was taught, so 'twould not wrinkle. Then sh-she stops m-m-me..."

"Please don't cry, Kittie. I must know. Who was it that stopped you?"

"'Twas her that stopped me—Lady Alma!" She fairl
spat out the name. "Asks me what 'twas that needed suc
careful carrying." Kittie paused to fight for control over he
quivering, tear-filled voice.

"And what answer did you give Lady Alma?" Mark
prompted. A sense of terrible prediction settled deep in
side her stomach.

"I told her 'twas yer gown, miss—a special gown, th
best one ye had—that I'd just pressed fer ye." The maid'
voice began to tremble and rise in tone. "And sh-she say
to me, 'if 'tis such a special gown, then I must see i
mustn't I,' and she sweeps it from me arms and drops it o
the st-st-stairs...oh, miss!"

"Now, don't go off again, Kittie. Just tell me what hap
pened then."

"She swears 'twas an accident, but 'twasn't. She says sh
dropped it and then stumbled, but she dinna!" Kittie'
voice grew louder and, balling her hands into fists, sh
shouted angrily, "She *threw* it on the stairs—she did
miss—threw it on the stairs and wiped her muddy boots o
it with a vengeance!"

Marke could only stare at the girl. It was even worse tha
she had imagined. How could someone be so horrid as t
destroy another's ball gown in such a ruthless, purposefu
manner. Turning, she looked at the mud-stained ski
again, picturing as she did, the pale woman stomping he
foot in the mud below her window. "So that's the way it'
to be, is it?"

"Begging yer pardon, miss?"

"Oh, Kittie, it's all right, truly it is," Marke said, an
sighed.

"But, miss, she ripped and tore at it with her mudd
boots, she did!"

"Well, it must have been very important to her that I no
wear it this evening, wouldn't you say? And just think ho
pleased she must be feeling over this piece of work, an
how filled with confidence she is, that she will be the fair
est of the fair at the ball tonight. But we shall show her
Kittie, for you and I will come up with a simply marvelou

reation from my trunk. Even with an old gown and a smile
n my face, I shall still outshine her. And you, my girl,
ust put it all behind you. There was absolutely nothing
ou could have done differently, and I shall see that there
s no blame attached to you for it. And you must tell
Ieaven he's not to go to Lord Perfect over such a trifling
natter."

"Oh, miss, ye are truly a saint, ye are."

"Hardly a saint, but I thank you all the same, Kittie.
Now, take yourself off, as I will rest a bit. Please tell Cook,
f it's not too much trouble, I might request a light supper
n my room before I begin to dress? Otherwise, I am sure
o be drowning out the musicians with the rumble of my
tomach, way before midnight supper bell rings."

"Oh, miss, Cook says all the time, that there's nothing
oo much trouble fer the likes of ye. You just nap away
ow, and I'll be sure to wake ye with plenty of time to bathe
nd dress, I will." Pausing just before pulling the door
losed behind her, the maid grinned and added, "And don't
e fret, Miss Penwell, for ye will take them all by the eye-
alls, ye will, even without a ball gown."

Left alone, Marke gathered the ball gown into her hands
nd stared down at it. It had been the most beautiful thing
he had ever owned, and she had looked so well in it. "'Tis
good thing you can take them by the eyeballs without a
all gown, Margaret Catherine, for you definitely do *not*
ave a ball gown now." A sob of helpless fury broke from
er, and she flung the ruined gown into the corner with as
nuch force as the tissue silk would allow. As it floated
ently through the air and drifted airily into the corner,
Marke could not help but laugh at her foolishness. "And
ow you feel so much better, right?" she admonished her-
elf. Retrieving the gown, she carefully spread it over a
hair. Perhaps a good seamstress could salvage enough of
he lovely stuff to redeem some of the cost. As for the im-
nediate problem, she had best see how one went about
ailing into a storm with a ship that had lost its sails.

Chapter Twenty-One

Marke stood at the top of the staircase and let the nois
of excited voices, mingling with the lilting strings of vio
lins, wash over her. She nervously wished she could hav
greeted Claymore for the first time in so many lonely weeks
without such a huge audience, but that did not look to b
possible. Although this was technically a country ball an
no receiving line had been established, all the local gentr
had apparently rushed to pay their respects to the marqui
the moment they were relieved of their outdoor things b
the attentive footmen, for he was surrounded by them now
and was attentively doing his duty as host. She watched hi
walnut curls gleam in the candlelight as he inclined his hea
to the Earl of Bantry's mother. The way that lady wa
blushing and batting her fan at him, Marke knew he wa
setting himself out to flatter. Probably flashing his dimpl
and lifting his eyebrow in that captivating way he had, sh
brooded. There was no denying he could be devastatingl
charming when he applied himself. Well, the time had com
to demonstrate her own wit and charm.

Drawing a deep breath and leveling her shoulders, sh
began her descent. Considering the crush in the hallway an
the people spilling from the adjoining rooms, she migh
possibly be the last of his guests to arrive. Heads turned a
she took each step slowly, trailing fingertips along the bal
uster. Ladies ogled her attire with interest and shock
whispering speculation and scandal frantically behind thei
fans. Gentlemen lifted eyebrows and grinned widely with

pen admiration. More than one hapless husband, standing too near his lady wife, received jabs from censuring elbows in rib cages. Marke sent mental whispers to Claymore, villing him to glance up, to witness her triumphant enrance.

Marke cared nothing for the shocked matrons, nor the ealous misses, but was grateful for the admiring glances on masculine faces, for she had outdone herself in inventiveness. Having topped a sweeping, cascading skirt of rich, deep plum velvet with a short jacket of moss green taffeta, she had basted a finely pointed lace collar to stand rigidly upright as a frame for her face. Kittie had swept her hair away from her neck and ears in a creation of sensually disordered curls that was almost sinfully implicating for a young, unmarried miss. In a pique of rebellion, and the very reason she was late in attending the gathering, Marke had stitched additional darts into the back of the jacket, so that it lay open to reveal a rather flimsy, finely tatted cream lace camisole that dipped daringly low over the full rise of her young breasts. The effect was one of suggestive disarray and implicative indulgence, as if she had just been deliciously mussed by an eager lover behind one of the palms.

She had almost reached the bottom of the stairs before Claymore, his attention diverted by the sudden widening of the Earl of Bantry's eyes, finally glanced up. His eyes met hers, then slipped down her body in a leisurely appraisal that was as stirring to Marke as his physical touch. Heat glimmered in his eyes, which only confirmed her high opinion of her appearance. Marke could feel the color rising in her cheeks but did not lower her lashes to hide her open desire for him. He started to move toward the stairs, then belatedly remembered polite company manners and turned back to excuse himself from the Earl of Bantry's mother. Taking his distraction as blatant license, John Barrows stepped forward and, with a deep bow, offered his arm. Marke accepted gladly. Let Lord Perfect wait, as she had waited long enough.

"Miss Penwell, you shall be declared the master of all entrances," John announced with a wicked grin. "And awarded all the medals."

"Thank you, kind sir," she smiled, nodding right and left as the company parted for them. "I accept the award and shall revere it for exactly what it is worth."

"Ah, you should not dismiss the value of the honor," he teased, easing her through the crowd and into the ball room. "I had thought to award it to the Lady Alma earlier in the evening, for she did cause quite a stir. But you! My, my. Never have I seen it done with more flare, nor with such response. Was it calculated?"

"To the gnat's ass, my dear doctor," Marke bluntly declared.

John threw back his head and roared with laughter. "Ah, Marke, if only I were worthy of you. Dash it all, but I would sweep you from your feet and battle to the death before I would allow any other man within one hundred feet of you. The marquis is either blind or a fool, or quite possibly both. If this choice he is apparently making is of his own free will, I can only say, he fully deserves what he courts."

"Ah, kind sir, do not down-face yourself. You are worthy of much more than a simple shipmaster's daughter," she avowed in earnest. "So am I to understand that you have made the acquaintance of the future marquise?"

"Do not rush your fences. No announcement has yet been made, and Lord Perfect is decidedly closemouthed about it. And yes, I have spent some time in the lady's company. Knowing where your heart lies, I will freely admit to a puzzle. It's very possible the pending nuptials she continues to spout are in her own mind only—and well, most certainly that of her father."

"So Sitter was perfectly correct in her surmise that Lady Alma is in full sail after Claymore? Well, she has my blessing. I hope with all my heart that he does marry her. If Sitter's judgment of her is fair, she will make him desperately unhappy, and it will serve him right for his high-handed attitudes."

"Good girl! Don't let them see they are getting the best of you," he declared, then quickly amended. "Not that they are, you understand. Didn't mean to imply..."

"Enough, John," Marke laughed. "We are friends, remember?" Sweeping her eyes over the dancers, she sought Jitter, praying she was enjoying herself in such mixed company, for there were nobles to country squires in attendance, and the musicians were proving quite good. Her feet itched to take the dance floor.

"Miss Penwell, we are gratified that you have finally chosen to grace us with your presence," Claymore commented at her elbow.

Marke turned to look up at him with what she hoped was an acceptable level of social goodwill in her eyes, and not the entire contents of her poor bleeding heart. "Good evening, Lord Perfect. And were you watching for me?"

"Ah, there you are, Perfect. Thought you might have gotten lost in the crush. Whoever would have thought there would be so many to invite to a ball in this provincial backwoods of a foreign place," blared a resounding voice over them.

Claymore was forced to forestall the ringing set-down he had planned for Marke. The very idea of her showing up in that scandalous outfit. How dare she look so utterly desirable that he was forced to count beneath his breath—and repeatedly, from one hundred down—to keep his mind from delectable memories and his unruly body from tenting his pantaloons in public. He turned to confront the booming voice of Lord Pressley, swallowing a grimace when he saw Alma clinging to his arm.

Marke turned about, preparing to excuse herself and head in the opposite direction with all good speed, but John's hand on her arm stayed her step until it was too late to escape with good graces.

"Might as well get it over with. Chin up now," John muttered into her ear.

Alma had positioned herself upon her father's arm for the stroll across the ballroom, but upon reaching Claymore's side, she immediately slipped her free hand into the

crook of his elbow in a possessive grip. Lord Pressley ap
praised Marke's neat figure up and down in a decidedly
forward manner, until his daughter sharply jerked his arm
with a scowl. The blond then looked pointedly at Clay
more for an introduction.

Claymore cleared his throat and proceeded to do just
that. "Lady Alma, Lord Pressley. May I introduce Miss
Margaret Penwell of St. Catherine's Court. Miss Penwell,
may I present my guests from London? Lord George
Pressley and his daughter, the Lady Alma."

The introductions were followed by a thick silence as the
two women clearly assessed the threat of the other. With
another uncomfortable clearing of his throat, Claymore
sought to introduce a conversation into the tension. Marke
was sure she uttered appropriate responses, but she could
not say what they might have been for she was staring with
perverse fascination at Lady Alma. She had been right—
she did possess a mop of white blond hair, and her complexion was almost unhealthily pale. She was a strikingly
tall woman, but in contrast to her height, her face was quite
round. While not classically beautiful, she was pretty, and
everything about her bespoke quality, nobility, titles,
money, London, society, *haute-ton*—everything Marke was
not. It was unfortunate, mused Marke, that her entire
bearing was so marred by her overproud expression. She
was distant, unapproachable, cold, and her eyes hard, as
hard as the ropes of glittering diamonds and emeralds
strung around her long throat. Well, one could only hope
she would trip and hang herself with them!

Claymore cleared his throat again and motioned to John.
"And of course, you are well acquainted with our learned
physician, John Barrows."

"Of course, we are most familiar with your physician
and hold him in great regard for your remarkable recovery," cooed Lady Alma. She dripped into a graceful curtsy,
tipping her shoulders forward to bare a meager chest nearly
to the nipples.

John gave a curt nod and shallow bow, then turned to beam upon Marke. "Alas, I can take no credit for the marquis's recovery. It was entirely Miss Penwell..."

Marke startled. *This* was too much for her to allow. She had no desire to stand here being lauded for something she did out of love and caring, not for public acclaim. Flashing a grin of apology at John for the abrupt interruption, she tilted innocent eyes to Claymore. "My goodness, Lord Perfect! What need have we for lighting the chandeliers tonight? Lady Alma, you quite outshine them all."

John choked down laughter, but Claymore frowned at her. He obviously did not wish a scene in front of company and he knew Alma was capable of a rousing display when provoked to anger.

Lady Alma fingered her emeralds and regarded her rival beneath her long lashes. "Penwell? Penwell? I do believe I am acquainted with some of your family. Weren't there a number of Penwells floating about London this last season?"

"Yes, my sisters, Sarah, Kathleen and Charity, are in London at present. And perhaps you are acquainted with Lady Mary Bixby—Lord Alfred Bixby's wife? Merely another Penwell in disguise, I'm afraid."

Lady Alma allowed a forbidding little frown to mar the perfection of her brow, but before she could decide if the chit was daring to mock her, and before she could come up with a suitably scalding remark, her father stepped forward.

"I say, Perfect, damn fine music for such a backward place as Bantry. No doubt you're anxious for the *dancing* to commence." As he emphasized the word *dancing*, he cast a meaningful glance at his daughter.

Lady Alma simpered coyly and batted Claymore's arm with her fan, as if he had just issued the invitation. "I really should decline you, after the way you've neglected me this past year. Shame on you, *my* Lord Perfect."

Although it all could have been harmless enough—social prattle and a cute touch of coquetry, if a bit heavy-handed—the words were delivered with dark and sinister glances at Marke. The thought to mention the destroyed ball gown came to her, but Marke had no wish for Claymore to know that she had improvised her costume tonight. No, she would not play these games with the vixen. She would ignore her as utterly unimportant in the grand scheme of things, and concentrate on her goal for this evening—discomforting Claymore William Perfect.

Claymore answered Alma in a smooth tone that could have been politeness or boredom. "I daresay, Lady Alma, if you apply yourself, you will concede there was no real intent of neglect on my part."

"Well, you would not have been deprived of my companionship had you not felt it necessary to rush off to this dreary place," Alma said coolly. "I should punish you for that, should I not?" Claymore's eyes narrowed so fractionally that Marke thought she might have imagined it. But apparently she had not, for Lady Alma flashed a gay smile, as if to say she was only jesting after all, and quickly amended. "Well, perhaps I shall not punish you. You shall have this dance and—" she leaned shamefully close into him "—as many afterward that you wish, my Lord Perfect." Giving him no opportunity to decline, Alma grasped his arm and led the way to the floor.

Lord Pressley bowed before Marke, greedily ogling her breasts in the process, and even going so far as to give her a roguish wink. "And I should be delighted to offer my attendance upon Miss Penwell."

Marke involuntarily stepped back in disgust. She could not help but recall Sitter's remark on this man's appearance, and choked back a laugh. The man did indeed resemble an overblown frog in more ways than one, and there was no way she would allow him to touch her. "I am so sorry, Lord Pressley, but I have promised this dance, and most of the others, to the good doctor, and shall not go back on my word. Dr. Barrows, shall we?"

Without giving the doctor a chance to act surprised, she took his arm and led him into the fray. Fortunately, he was a smooth if not very adventurous dancer and she was not forced to waste concentration on the steps. She repeatedly glimpsed Claymore, holding Alma lightly in his arms, whirling past. She sighed. What heaven it must be, to lie in his arms, spinning to the music. What a fine figure of a man he was. What a splendid husband he would make for someone. Why not for her? She came from good family, she reasoned. She would bring a respectable dowry in St. Catherine's Court. And she was far from ugly! She would make him an admirable wife, she decided, and a good mother to his children. But whatever advantage she might have was here in Bantry, where memories of shared trials, triumphs, and hours of loving reigned over society. Once he returned to London, all would change between them. There he would instantly become caught up in his own pursuits, and entangled in his own social circle of friends. He would most surely be lost to her then. And, it had to be admitted, there were in London a score of beautiful, accomplished women such as Lady Alma and Sarah, just waiting to throw their caps at the handsome, eligible, perfect Lord Perfect. He would have no time for an untutored hoyden of a red-haired, freckle-faced miss left behind in Ireland then.

"Your heart is in your eyes, Marke," John's soft murmur came in her ear.

Marke quickly shuttered her eyes and smiled a brilliant smile for the kind physician. "Sorry I am so inattentive, John. Do forgive me. Perhaps it is best that I have been sequestered in Ireland, for I would surely disgrace myself, and my sisters, in London society with such countrified manners."

"Ah, if the truth be known, you are sequestered in Bantry by the jealousy of those sisters. They can only be too aware that the full force of your personality and beauty would place them in the chill of the shade."

"My goodness, John Barrows. I do not know what to think of you this evening. You shall have my head quite turned with all these compliments."

"If your head could only be turned in my direction, then I would have accomplished my aims."

"Oh, John," Marke murmured, squeezing his hand in sympathy. "Pray don't engage your heart over the likes of me. I am not worth heartache, I promise you. As you have witnessed, I am too forward. Why, I was not even considered ready to enter society, so numerous are my faults."

John threw back his head and laughed, then swung her in a wide circle. "I rather think it should be stated the other way round, dear Marke. I would venture to guess society would not be ready for you. But as you are so obviously insistent upon pursuing the scoundrel, so be it. I shall cease and desist."

"And please count yourself lucky enough to have escaped a turbulent future by doing so," she assured him with great relief. "But not so lucky as to not be counted as one of my dearest friends."

"And that is not such a bad thing, my dear Miss P. Just know that I shall be present to dance at your wedding, and attend the birth of each of your children. And that is my way of saying, I shall always be here for you. You need only call," John promised, swinging her through the doors into the conservatory.

Marke could only stare about her in amazement. The autumn chrysanthemums had been whisked away and the bed replanted with cyclamens, tulips, deliciously fragrant paper-whites, and poinsettias of pink, white and vibrant red. Wreaths and swags festooned the panes of glass and immense chandelier-like blossoms swung lavishly overhead. The tiered fountains splashed merrily, while minstrels played behind potted palms and guests in their finery wandered the pathways. At the very center of it all towered a twenty-foot fir, laden with tussie-mussies, prisms and roses from the rose house. An evergreen garland framing the doorway was laced with green velvet ribbons with ivy leaf clips to hold clusters of mistletoe amid holiday greeting cards from faraway friends, amid antique cherub lace. It was a fairyland come alive.

John swung her to a standstill beneath the mistletoe, and gathered her lightly in his arms to plant a sturdy kiss upon her laughing lips to the enthusiastic applause of all present. The only unhappy face was that of the Marquis of Boothe-Ashmore, and his frown was apparent, for anyone wishing to notice, for the entire length of the ballroom.

Chapter Twenty-Two

Chapter Twenty-Two

After a delightfully entertaining supper in John's company, Marke stood up for a set of country dances with him. He seemed to have swallowed his hopes for their amorous future with characteristically good humor, though it soon became clear he would be taking his assigned role of friendship quite seriously. So seriously that, once the music drew to a halt, he escorted her from the floor—and straight to a scowling Claymore. He even went so far as to place her hand directly into the marquis's.

Claymore nodded to John, but turned his gaze full upon Marke to ask with sarcasm, "Miss Penwell, as I apparently have your escort's permission, may I lead you back to the dance floor?"

Although it was posed as a question, Marke was spun and led abruptly away without given the opportunity to answer. Across the room, Alma glared furiously after them, her ice blue eyes searing into Claymore's retreating back as he led Marke toward the first set of dancers.

Marke caught the glare and shivered. My, poor Alma looks ready to throw a tantrum, she thought. Why, her anger was so apparent that high color even had the audacity to creep into her white face. She turned her attention back to Claymore. He was looking so fit, well built and muscular, holding himself superbly. He moved with such ease now, with fluid grace and control, with no apparent weakness left in his limbs, although at the moment he was walking a little fast for her liking. This was a ballroom, for goodness' sake! Not a tramp in the woods.

During the progress down the long ballroom, he had addressed not one word to her. Marke decided the time to remedy that had come. "Lord Perfect, please," she muttered breathlessly, for he had a firm grip on her arm and she was almost forced to run to keep up with him. "Won't one of these sets do? I shall be tuckered before you—" She glanced over her shoulder as they passed the last grouping of dancers without slowing their pace "Claymore, where the devil are you taking me?"

Without an answer, Claymore strode on, his face set in grim, purposeful lines. He had words to say to her, but he desired privacy to say them.

Beyond the last set of dancers, he steered a course through the conservatory. Marke glanced at the mistletoe with regret as they breezed by without a pause. She would have liked very much to be kissed right now. On the far wall, and apparently the marquis's destination, she noticed a small door almost hidden behind a long damask curtain. Pulling back, she frowned. This really was too much. But he paid her protest no heed. Flinging open the door, he hustled her through it to a broad courtyard, graced by squat stone urns filled with flowering shrubs all of which were as frozen beneath their heavy blanket of snow as she would soon be. "Claymore!" Marke protested as he firmly closed the door behind them. "Have you taken leave of your senses? I can't go off with you this way? Oh, look, you're ruining my slippers!"

Roughly Claymore pulled Marke across the courtyard, to the point where the stone wall was illuminated by a coaching lamp hanging from an iron hook. Swinging her around so her back was to the wall, he tilted her face up to him, with the lamplight shining down on her flushed cheeks. "Now," he said menacingly, "I believe you have some explaining to do, Margaret Catherine Penwell."

She stared up at the man towering over her. "Of all the stuff and nonsense!" she flared. "If anyone owes the other an explanation, it is you! How dare you pretend you wish to dance, then drag me out here into this—this cold place. Why, we are quite alone! Would you have my reputation smeared beyond repair on my very first ball?"

Claymore laughed. "Oh, Marke, you have a rare spirit. *We are quite alone!*" he mimicked her mercilessly. "That is rich, indeed, coming from one who has been quite alone with me on more than one occasion."

"Yes, and look what that got me," Marke muttered. Glancing down at his hands, which were pinning her shoulders against the icy wall, she declared. "Claymore, are you aware you are holding me here against my will? I truly do not understand."

His tone was steely as he said, "Understand this, my beautiful, autumn-haired twit. You are staying right where you are until you give me a satisfactory explanation of your conduct tonight."

"Beautiful!" Marke exclaimed in delight. "Do you truly think I am beautiful?"

He shook her roughly, and growled, "An explanation, if you please."

"Whatever do you mean, my lord?" cooed Marke, fluttering her eyelashes at him in fair imitation of a coy miss.

His hot gaze raked her nearly exposed nipples. "I am referring first of all, to the way you are flaunting yourself before every male in the place."

"Oh, that! Well, you see—"

"Don't you dare interrupt me!" he thundered, shaking her again. "This is not appropriate behavior for a young unmarried miss! What of society?"

"Why, whatever could you mean? What society?"

"The society you were so worried about when you threw me out of St. Catherine's Court!"

"Threw you out! I never! You left of your own free will!" Marke exclaimed. Her humor began to slip and she replied scornfully, "And I assume by society, you mean your London *guests*."

"Have a care, Marke," he warned. "I am not the kind of man who will tolerate such high-handed behavior. Is that clear?"

Marke's eyes blazed with indignation. The audacity of the man! "You, of all people, would presume to accuse me of loftiness?" she demanded. The irony of the situation might have been utterly amusing, if only it involved a less infuriating man than the Marquis of Boothe-Ashmore. Frantically she tried to wiggle free from his grasp. The incomprehensibly overbearing, utter *gall* of the man! His strong hands held her firmly against the wall.

"Stop wrestling with me, Marke!" Claymore demanded.

His tone brought her to an abrupt standstill. Unable to escape his hands, she glared up at him and declared with a defiant toss of her curls, "Lord Perfect, had you just approached me with a quiet, reasonable manner this evening, I might have responded differently, but instead you would drag me out into the snow, then speak to me as one would reprimand a wayward child. I do not feel I owe you anything, much less any explanation. But if you insist, which you seem to be doing in your own refined way," she said, and glared down at his hands on her arms with meaning, "I shall be only too happy to comply. And if you wish to call upon me one afternoon at St. Catherine's Court in the weeks coming, I shall be more than happy to spare you five minutes of conversation on the matter."

A gleam of admiration and humor touched his brown eyes. "You are a proud minx, no mistaking that," he said with an exasperated shake of his head. Then, leaning into her, he went on softly, "You owe me more than an explanation, Marke Penwell, for you have made my life completely and utterly miserable."

Marke grew still, watching the light in his warm, brown eyes before retorting. "I was of the impression that gentlemen suffered their miseries in stodgy silence."

He smiled, flashing his dimple, and whispered softly, "I would have thought I had demonstrated my manner of suffering miseries to you more than adequately in the past, Marke."

Marke took a deep breath and willed herself to look him straight in the eyes. She found it a curiously disturbing experience. She must not give into the seductiveness of his voice. She must hold firmly onto any advantage she might have at the moment. "It appears to me that you have quite recovered from your injuries, Lord Perfect. You are very strong," she said unsteadily.

Claymore cleared his throat and leaned even closer into her warmth. He gazed down at her, and a slight smile played over his lips as he watched the changing expressions race over her lovely face. Lord, but he had missed her. "I fear you misunderstand the nature of my suffering."

Marke blushed. She knew then of what he spoke. It was clearly his intention—judging by the nearness of his body, the caress of his fingers on her cheek, and the draw of his lips—to reduce her to a quiver of desire. Oh, and he knew he could do it, too, she thought. How he would enjoy her surrender, how he would greedily partake of her love, her body. And, blast it, that was what she wanted, too, with every fiber of her being, but not without a declaration of love and commitment. It was just not to be, she reminded herself sternly. *You may be more experienced than I, Lord Perfect, but I will teach you to disregard my feelings. This is no simple country lass from Ireland that is fair game for a rogue like you. You are undoubtedly blissfully ignorant of the fact, my love, but if there is one thing that I am celebrated for, it's knowing when and how to seize the leverage.*

Marke ran the tip of her tongue slowly over her lower lip, then said boldly, "I gather, Lord Perfect, that you require solace from me for your misery?" Before he could reply or make a move, she reached up to cup his face in her palms. Placing her lips softly against his, she moved them sweetly, teasing with the tip of her tongue. Surprised, he dropped his hands from her shoulders, leaving her free. Marke remained perfectly still, scorning the opportunity to flee to the ballroom. She would not run away, she declared, regardless of the protection she needed from her own raging emotions. Not only must she battle with the marquis, but against her own yearning to surrender as well. "Does that

)ring you satisfaction and comfort?'' she whispered against 1is mouth before leaning back again.

"Frankly no," he drawled, with a strange look of resig- 1ation on his face. "I doubt I could ever be satisfied where /ou are concerned. You have muddled my life, Marke, and :here are times I wish to hell I'd never laid eyes upon you.''

With a sharp intake of breath, Marke raised her hand and struck him with all her might across the cheek, but even :hat did not still the pain that ripped through her heart. Claymore did not flinch, though the resounding slap of the)low echoed around the courtyard. Marke stood her ;round, though she was suddenly terrified he would retal- ate by knocking her to the stones. She was appalled at 1erself for allowing him to drive her beyond control. Never 1ad she resorted to physical violence in her life. Her im- nediate reaction was to beg his forgiveness and kiss away :he red stain that appeared on his cheek.

Instead of reacting in anger, however, Claymore took a)ace back and stood with a face turned to stone. When he at last spoke, his voice was grave and low... and so awful vith politeness. "I beg your pardon, Miss Penwell. I have)ehaved unforgivably.''

Marke too schooled her face, and bit down on her lip to still the quiver of tears that threatened.

Claymore turned his head toward the mansion, listening for a moment. "Shall we return to the ballroom. I believe the set is over. I say, for propriety's sake, we agree to for- ;et our differences, and take our places for the next?''

"Very well," agreed Marke. As she took his proffered arm, she was not surprised to find that she was trembling. Not an inappropriate reaction for having one's very life ripped apart, she thought.

Slipping through the conservatory, into the thronged)allroom, they took their places in the nearest set. Marke :ast an anxious glance around, hoping their absence had ;one unnoticed. To her relief, the others seemed too en- ;rossed with their dancing partners, conversations and merriment to have noticed much past their own pleasures.)r so she thought.

Alma had been acutely aware of their prolonged absence. Just as she was now taking note of the high color in Marke's cheeks and the set face of the marquis. Oh, how she wished to storm across the room and tear them apart! But instead, she was forced to smile and make nice-nice with the most boring people in the world while her fiancé dallied with another in his arms.

Marke was mercilessly unaware of Alma's searing scrutiny as she focused on the steps of the dance. Gradually, lulled by the ritual of the steps, the lilting rhythm of the music, the furious pounding of her heart receded. She looked around as if more than a little dazed. She had been at the ball for less than one hour, she thought, yet she had already been embroiled in a scandalous row and struck the man she loved. And, though she would admit to holding her own in the fray, she could not see where either of them had come out of the encounter as a winner. Glancing up at him as they glided down the floor, she sighed deeply. "Forgive me, Claymore, but I did not mean—"

His face darkened and his brow drew down in a scowl. "What now, Marke? Do you wish for blood? Leave it alone. Haven't I already apologized?"

"Yes, but I must insist—"

"No, Marke. No insisting. The subject is closed, and that is my final declaration on the matter."

Marke opened her mouth to protest, but he quelled her with a frightening glance. And in glacial silence, they completed the final steps of the dance. Afterward, since she was bereft of a female relative as chaperon, he led her across the floor to Sitter. Marke, already disgruntled and close to tears, was discouraged to see Alma and her disagreeable father making up a part of that group. After her confrontation with Claymore, she felt in no mood for further verbal tussles with the frosty Alma. Although, if her heart hadn't been so numb, she might have delighted in that the lady was looking remarkably put out when they joined them. The petulant expression marring her pretty face, it would appear, had been brought on by some abrasive remarks from her father.

"Ah, there you are, Perfect!" boomed Lord Pressley. "Come and lend me your support. I was just telling Alma that she ought to take some riding instruction. She's apt to ruin that pretty, gray mare's mouth if she goes about tugging at the leathers the way she did this morning."

Sitter nodded in a moment of rare agreement with the offensive lord, although she might have sided with the devil himself if he had been heaping negative words upon the complaining woman. "All young ladies should learn to feel at home on horseback. It is considered a first-rate accomplishment," she announced.

Alma tossed her blond head and sniffed. "With respect, Father, I must beg to differ. A lady should not be required to leave the comfort of the carriage to perch upon the back of some beast to be deemed accomplished." She stared pointedly at Marke, then raked her attire from head to toe. "Nor should she be expected to parade about in muddied boots."

Marke lifted her eyebrows. The comment was obviously meant to bring her ruined ball gown firmly to mind, and Alma's glare was an open dare for her to bring the subject to light. Marke merely countered sweetly, "Horses are not necessarily all beasts, Lady Alma, although it is unfortunate that one must endure mud upon one's boots, isn't it?"

The ice blue eyes held the warm brown ones in challenge. "Well, of course, someone like *you* would be unaware, Miss Penwell, but special attention is given to the paths in Hyde Park, where the *haute-ton* promenades. They are either cinder or grass, just so we ladies of quality do not sully our boots."

Marke, seeing no benefit to sparring with the vixen, held her tongue. Alma looked smug at her silence, as if triumphantly establishing herself as an intimate of the *haute-ton*, in this gathering of country rustics.

Lord Pressley, blissfully ignorant of the undercurrent, would not be denied his opinion. "Well, I propose we all meet at the stables tomorrow, once the ladies have decided to leave their beds, of course. They always sleep late after a ball, you know. We could all engage in a rousing dash across the countryside. This blasted weather permitting, you see. What say all?''

Enthusiastic nods came from most of the small group, much to Alma's irritation. But to decline joining in the party would be to lose time in Claymore's presence, while she was sure Miss Penwell would attend merely to make the most of her absence. ''Oh, if we must. Lord Perfect,'' she said, and leaned gracefully upon his arm, ''I am so parched. Perhaps a touch of something cool?''

''Of course,'' Claymore said. ''And for you, Miss Penwell?''

''No, thank you, Lord Perfect,'' Marke replied frostily as he bowed himself from the group. She watched his strong back disappear into the crowd.

Lord Pressley beamed his approval at the marquis's willingness to do his daughter's bidding. ''Yes, yes! And wine for me as well, Perfect. Ah, wait. Here's a tray now! Over here, my good man,'' roared Lord Pressley, flagging a passing footman. He handed Sitter a chilled champagne and retrieved a glass of the marquis's best claret for himself. As he grasped the stem, Alma idly raised her hand to fan her face. In doing so, she jogged his arm, and the claret tipped from the glass, spilling right down the front of Marke's jacket, plastering her lace camisole to her breasts and splashing over the plum velvet skirt.

''Dash me!'' exclaimed Lord Pressley, pulling forth a handkerchief, obviously prepared to mop the ruby mess from her chest. ''I am monstrously sorry, Miss Penwell. Damned clumsy of me.''

''It was not your fault, Lord Pressley,'' said Marke quickly, snatching the handkerchief from his hand and stepping out of his reach.

Alma whirled round, her face a perfect picture of regret. ''Oh, Miss Penwell, what a dreadful thing to happen. I fear your, er, gown is stained irreparably. Such a misfortune. But as you are an overnight guest, it's a simple thing to dash upstairs and change into another ball gown, isn't it?''

As Marke mopped at the stains with Lord Pressley's handkerchief, she reflected wryly that thanks to Kittie's inadvertently spilling the beans, Lady Snake in the Grass was only too aware she had no fashionable alternative hanging in the wardrobe at Innisfree, nor at St. Catherine's Court, either. She glanced at Claymore winding his way back to the group with a chilled champagne ice for Alma in his hand. Feeling suddenly overcome by fatigue, Marke wearily conceded defeat. You have won this round hands down, Alma, she thought sadly. You have not only wrecked two of my dresses today, but you have wrecked my evening, as well. Quickly excusing herself, she quit the ball before Claymore could witness the mess she was.

Chapter Twenty-Three

Marke settled restlessly into the window seat of the small, unused drawing room on the third floor. It had been her intention to complete work on the marquis's portrait this morning, but the winter scene from the window had beckoned stronger than her paints. A letter from Jessell, forwarded from St. Catherine's Court and as yet unread, lay forgotten in her lap as she watched the mists rise and swirl in the mountains beyond. It was promising to be a wonderfully clear day, with just the right amount of nip in the air to snatch at your nose and frost the breath in front of your face. A perfect day to tear about the snow-powdered hills on horseback. She was restlessly eager to be off but, as yet, it appeared she was the only one to stir from her bed.

Regardless of the lateness of the hour when she had retired, with more than just her gown trampled and stained, first light had seen her eager to be up and about. But it should not be thought that she was zealous to be thrown into the company of the Pressleys again. Her idea of a congenial time did not include listening to Lord Pressley's loud, grating bray, nor parrying Alma's snipping at her jugular. After that horrendous display of last night, she was beginning to wonder why she had accepted an invitation for the holidays at Innisfree in the first place.

"Because, widget," she scolded herself, "you planned to seduce the marquis away from his London amour. But then, when you were finally alone with him, you just had to give into hurt feelings and set about knocking the man's head from his shoulders. Remember?''

She exhaled a sigh from the very depths of her toes. Why, oh, why had she allowed her hurt over his chance remark to shake her so easily? Why hadn't she teased around it? Hadn't the man been looking at her with—what? Love? No, most probably lust. She gave a snort of disgust and flipped open the letter in her lap.

''To the devil with him,'' she muttered. She'd not spend such a wonderful holiday hashing over a regrettable action brought on by the heat of the moment. She'd apologize to him the first chance she got, and take her cue from his response. Either he had feelings for her, or he did not. One could not force another to fall in love, now could they? Satisfied with herself, she turned her attention to Jessell's letter.

My Dearest Margaret,
How pleased we were to receive your latest letter. All is fine here as well, except Thomas does complain of the sniffles due to the inclemency of the weather this time of year. Personally, I believe it is nothing more than an excuse to remain hidden in his library surrounded by his ledgers night and day, and accompanied by his brandy. Although I hold my tongue on this suspicion, as any good wife would do, and attend my duties for my husband's comfort, I have made it a point to monitor the amount of medicinal brandy being carried into the library by that valet of his.

As I am positive you have received news from Mary already, I shall only briefly touch upon Sarah's engagement to Viscount Rosemund Bradberry. Needless to say, while Sarah is all atwitter—it has been unanimously agreed to be the match of the season—Kathleen is high in the rafters over it. And I do admit, at first, the viscount did seem so obviously taken with Kathleen that it is small wonder she entertained such expectations. But then who is to understand the fickleness of new love?

Marke lowered the letter to stare outside again. Fickleness of love? Hardly! She would come closer to believing skulduggery on Sarah's part! Kathleen should have been well aware that Sarah would never allow a younger sister to snatch such a plum while she remained unattached and on the vine. She only hoped Kathleen's heart had not been engaged. How terrible to be in love with the husband of one's own sister. Such drama, and she was well out of it. A sense of dawning flashed over her face. But was she truly? Although they were not sisters, nor even friends, weren't she and Alma at odds over a man? She snorted in disgust and returned to the letter.

In closing, I wish to add Thomas's note of concern over the ivory ball gown sent to you for the holiday season. It is of his opinion, which I must say I share, you were to be attending our dear mother in a solicitous manner, not pursuing an active social life or—as I believe he phrased it most admirably—establishing yourself as social tilt-a-whirl. I can just imagine the stubborn lift of your chin as I write this, but you must not blame us for having it foremost in our minds, Margaret, that you are an unmarried girl who has not officially "come out," nor do you have a chaperon in the true sense of the word. You must have a care of your reputation, dear, as misconduct, even in that remote place, could reflect very poorly on the rest of the girls. With this in mind, Thomas and Mary are discussing the possibility of sending your sisters, with the exception of Sarah, of course, to summer with you at St. Catherine's Court. Along with a suitable chaperon for the whole lot. I am sure one of them will be corresponding with you concerning this in the very near future. It has crossed our minds that the marquis you spoke of might be just the thing to take Kathleen's mind off the viscount. Wouldn't that put a bee in Sarah's bonnet . . . Kathleen a marquise while she's only a viscountess! Please accept our best holiday wishes, and know that you are missed around the family tree this year.

Sincerely, Jessell

Marke gritted her teeth and barely resisted the urge to wad the letter into a missile for the fireplace. Just because she had moved to Ireland did not mean she had agreed to be a hermit, nor did it mean she would have no need to replenish her wardrobe occasionally. *Social tilt-a-whirl, my grandmother's bottom! So they think to put a bee in Sarah's bonnet by sending Kathleen here to snare Claymore, do they? Hardly!* This time the letter was wadded and aimed unerringly into the flames. While she had no intention of withholding St. Catherine's Court as summer residence from family, it must be clarified at once that she, and she alone, was mistress of St. Catherine's Court. And if there was to be a bee in Sarah's bonnet, it would be because she, *not* Kathleen, was wife to Claymore.

She leapt to her feet to rush off in search of pen and paper, then paused to chide herself. She was too angry to reply with good sense at present. It would do no good for her case to dash off a letter of childish pouting. Best to allow time for her temper to cool, then approach the matter with authority. Besides, wasn't there a certain truth to Jessell's words concerning her behavior. Her esteemed sister-in-law would most probably deem tumbling in the bushes with the Marquis of Boothe-Ashmore as unseemly misconduct for an unmarried miss.

Marke paced the length of the room to halt before the portrait. There was really very little to complete. Perhaps rearrange the neckcloth a little, and the hair color still was not rich enough to suit her, but would have to do. How strange it was, even before realizing the depth of her feelings for him, or having been shown the extent of it, she had captured the side of him that was soft, teasing and loving. A side she'd certainly been denied since her return to Innisfree. Again the urge to paint horns and chin whiskers on the portrait came to her, but she laughed them off. Emotions rode high and she felt ready to explode if she was forced to remain indoors. Blast these people for sleeping a day of their lives away. Didn't they realize it would not be given to them at a later date? That once it was gone, it was gone forever? Just as she could be gone in the blink of an eye. She need not wait for them! And she would not!

Once that decision was made, it was within a short quarter hour that Marke was striding to the stable, snapping her crop against her black boot in cadence with her step. Without her awareness, the mismatched riding costume was most becoming to her coloring. The rust brown skirt was Mercy's hand-me-down, and the short black jacket that fit so snugly about her trim figure had once been a part of Sarah's wardrobe. But the black and brown speckled jockey cap cocked over one eye, outfitted with a jaunty peahen feather, and her great-aunt Pearl's garnet brooch, was all Marke Penwell.

Having sent word ahead to the stable master, Marke was not surprised when a mount was quickly led out for her. What did surprise, and delight, her was the dainty filly that minced beside the young groom with such neatness of form and gentle intelligence in her large eyes. A sorrel, as red as an autumn sunset, without one white hair on her sleek hide, she was absolute perfection.

"Oh, it's my birthday filly," she exclaimed, laying her hands on the soft muzzle and pulling the delicate head down to feel the filly's warm breath on her cheek. "And she's broken to saddle already?"

"Aye, miss, 'tis her, all right. We call her Little Red, if it pleases ye. 'Twas started by his lordship hisself, 'twas," the lad answered, with a grin and a nod toward Marke's own bright hair.

Marke snorted. So he would make fun of her, would he? But did he say it in a mean way or with a gentle tease? Curiosity brimmed over, but good manners kept her from prodding the boy with unsuitable questions. She climbed aboard the dancing filly, settling herself in the sidesaddle and arranging her skirts. "Well, one thing can be said of the marquis. He certainly does know good horseflesh."

"She be a mite fresh this morning, miss. But she's jest young. T'ain't a mean bone in her body, I promise ye. She's been brought along real slow and careful, so she'd be jest right fer ye."

"I'm sure she'll behave herself," she said, grinning down at the lad, "and make you proud of her."

"Already proud of her, I am. I be Jem, miss. And 'twas me that helped his lordship find her," the lad boasted, throwing out his chest in pride. "'Twas all over the countryside I was, seeking jest the right one fer ye."

"It sounds as if the marquis—and you, Jem—spent a great deal of time and trouble on my behalf," she prompted, feeling somewhat guilty for pushing the lad into gossip, not that much pushing was required with the talkative boy.

"His lordship dinna act as if 'twas a bit of trouble, miss," Jem hinted, grinning ear to ear when she blushed a pretty pink. Encouraged by this, he rushed to add more. "Be taking time every day ta watch me work with her, too. Said she had ta be done jest right, ye kein. Then jest this morn, he says ta me, 'Jem, be sparking Little Red out extra fine fer Miss Penwell.'"

Marke grimaced to herself. After her deplorable behavior last night—actually physically attacking the man—she was sure he regretted every second he wasted on planning a surprise for such a violent person. Gathering the leathers, she sought to change the subject. "You've done marvelously with her, Jem. I thank you from the bottom of my heart, and I shall remember to thank the marquis, as well."

"He'll have me hide fer spoiling the surprise and tacking ye out b'fore he gets back, but I ain't afraid," Jem confided, then leaned over to whisper for her ears only, as if no one but himself was privy to the information. "He barks awfully loud something, but he don't bite."

Ignoring the last part, Marke latched onto the first part and before she could stop herself, she blurted out, "Gets back! Where has he gone?"

"Taken hisself to the hills, he has. Ain't no more than a breath ahead of ye. If we hurry, we can overtake him."

Marke's teeth worried her lower lip. Should she seek him out? It might not do to put him in a foul mood by invading his solitary ride. She could well imagine how she'd feel if unwanted company tracked her down when she'd set out

to be alone with her thoughts. Although it would serve him
right. While she was willing to beg forgiveness for striking
him last night, she must not forget his unkind statement. It
was abominable of him to treat her like a loose woman,
thinking to ignore her, then expecting her to welcome his
hands beneath her skirts. Then, to add insult to injury, to
say he wished he'd never met her. He might not have deserved to have his person brutally attacked, but he definitely should have been taken to task for the rest. And if
that wasn't enough justification for running him to ground
like a hunted animal, she added to herself, it just might be
the only opportunity granted her by the pressing duties of
her hosts—and by Alma—to thank him for the filly away
from prying eyes.

"Mount up, Jem. We'll make it an adventure overtak-
ing the marquis."

"Aye, miss. We'll be doing that before the other miss fer
sure," Jem hollered, swinging aboard his gelding, but
Marke had already set the red filly to a smart pace and
didn't hear him. He clamped spurs to his horse and raced
after her out of the mews and across the frosted hills.

The wild gallop over the hills, with the chilly air snatching Marke's breath, brought out the color in her cheeks and
exhilarated her with high spirits. In just under an hour,
they'd sighted the marquis, astride the blue-black warmblood she'd seen the day before, topping the rise ahead of
them. With a whoop and a yell, she leaned forward over the
filly's sleek neck to send her careering down the hill in hot
pursuit.

Her yell reached Claymore across the valley, and he
reined in to watch her mad dash with great pleasure. She sat
the filly well, and rode with the same exuberance she displayed with everything else in her life. Reaching the bottom of the hill, she set the filly to a small stream that
meandered through the valley. Ears up and neck arched in
alarm, the red filly made the leap with more air than necessary between her belly and the offensive water. Marke's
laughter soared up the hill to him as the filly snorted and
danced sideways in childish excitement. He watched as

Marke reined her in slightly and patted the sleek neck to soothe her. She was progressing at a controlled hand-gallop along a line of trees, easily outdistancing Jem on his heavy-bodied gelding, when the accident happened.

The gray mare, head thrown back and eyes rolling wildly, with Alma frantically sawing at the reins while applying spurs, burst from the trees to Marke's left. Claymore rose in his stirrups and put his hand to his mouth to yell a warning, but there was no time. The gray mare, driven by spurs and blinded by pain as Alma ripped at her mouth with the bit, leapt forward uncontrollably. Without warning, she slammed into the red filly's side with such force that the filly was knocked violently to the ground, pinning Marke beneath her.

"Marke!" yelled Claymore. He spun the stallion and put him down the hill at breakneck speed, frantic to reach Marke before the filly struggled to regain her feet. Jem, being on the level, reached her first. He leapt from his saddle to plant a restraining knee upon the thrashing filly's neck. Alma had recovered control of the panting gray mare and sat off to the side, watching with horror in her eyes, her hand clamped to her mouth, carefully concealing the glee on her lips. Claymore slid to a halt and vaulted from the saddle without notice for anyone but Marke.

"Marke," he yelled again. "Are you all right?"

"I think so. Nothing hurts overly much," Marke hurriedly reassured both Claymore and the worried Jem. "Oh, please tell me I've not hurt Little Red."

"Is your foot caught in the stirrup, Marke?" Claymore asked, bending to shove his hand as far under the filly as possible. "Wouldn't want to give her license to gain her feet if your foot is caught, now would we?" He forced himself to speak calmly so he didn't frighten her, when he truly wanted to rant and rave, and wring someone's neck.

"N-no, I don't think it is."

"All right, Jem," he told the groom. "Let her up real easy. I'll mind Miss Penwell's foot."

Stepping back, Jem soothed the filly and urged her to gain her feet, with Claymore standing ready to release

Marke's foot if it were indeed caught in the stirrup. The filly scrambled up, with no apparent injury other than trembling legs. Jem crooned to her softly, stroking the nervous sweat from her long neck. She snorted and rolled her eyes about as if fully expecting another barbarous attack from the bushes and trees around her.

"Is she hurt, Jem?" Marke demanded, worried sick that her carelessness might have lamed the sweet, game little filly.

"Nay, miss," he answered with an encouraging grin that did not ease the worry from Marke's face. "Jest shook up some from the fright."

"To hell with the horse, Marke!" Claymore said through gritted teeth, running his hands along her leg. "What of you? Where does it hurt? Can you stand?"

"Of course, I can stand. I'm fine, Claymore," assured Marke, shoving his hands from beneath her skirt. "Just give me your hand—"

Grasping his strong hands, she allowed him to pull her to her feet. And at first, she thought she was being truthful, until her right ankle buckled in a stabbing pain that raced up her leg in red-hot heat and snatched all air from her lungs. With a cry, she swooned dead away. She never heard Claymore's startled oath, nor felt his arms tighten protectively about her limp form.

Coming back to herself, she found herself cradled against Claymore's broad chest, with her nose buried in the warm wool of his coat. Drawing in a deep breath of damp wool, tobacco, winter wind—and him—she sighed in contentment. A most comfortable place to be, she thought. Then, in a flash, she remembered the accident, the filly—but nothing about being loaded upon the warmblood into Claymore's arms. How like her to forget the best part, she thought irrationally. She felt very detached from it all, but she supposed she should rouse herself to care. His arms tightened when she struggled to straighten.

"What happened?" she asked, dazed.

"We're home now, Marke," said Claymore. He eased her down into the waiting arms of a strong footman, while barking orders to anyone who would listen. "Send someone to Bantry for Dr. Barrows! Get her upstairs to her bed, and call for Sitter! Here—will someone take this damn horse!"

Marke shook her head in an attempt to clear the bees from it. She surmised that she had drifted throughout the ride, and maybe that had been for the best, as her ankle no longer hurt her at all. Pulling her skirt up over her foot, she peered optimistically down, horrified to observe that it had begun to swell and, as her boot and stocking had mysteriously disappeared, she could see the pale flesh was rapidly becoming an interesting shade of blue and purple. Glancing over the footman's shoulder as she was carried into the entry hall, she saw Claymore raising his arms to lift Alma from the gray mare's back. She gritted her teeth at the sight, then reprimanded herself for uncharitable thoughts. She should be pleased that no one but she had been injured.

"My Lord, Miss Penwell!" Heaven exclaimed, ringing his hands with worry.

"Marke!" Sitter appeared from the drawing room and rushed to her side. "Whatever has happened to you?"

Claymore stomped into the entry and flung his gloves in the general direction of a hall table. "She has injured her ankle a bit," he snapped, hoping to avoid a hysterical scene over the incident. "Although I daresay it's nothing serious, I've sent for John, just in case."

Alma strolled into the entry hall, trailing after all the commotion. She had not expected such ado about nothing when she sent that damn horse careering forward. She had merely wished to unseat the chit in the mud so that she'd look ridiculous to Claymore, not make her the heroine of the hour. She watched the circus move up the stairs with narrowed eyes. Well, at least this should confine the girl to her room for a day or two. That, in itself, was something. Turning to Claymore, she had just opened her mouth to call to him, when he slammed the door to the library shut—in a very final manner.

Chapter Twenty-Four

Marke, waking in the middle of her bed, lay back for a moment, luxuriating in the afterglow of a wonderful dream, where Claymore had cradled her most tenderly in his arms. The room was darkened by drawn draperies and a fire burned brightly in the grate. Too brightly, for she was overly warm. She kicked the goose down comforter away and was rewarded with a stabbing pain in her ankle that brought the fact of her accident rushing back.

"Miss, are ye well? Do ye need something?" Kittie rushed to the side of the bed. Her mop cap was askew and her little face etched with worry.

"No, no, I'm all right," Marke said, with a sour thought. Liar, liar, pants on fire! She was not all right. Her ankle hurt abominably, and she did not want to spend Christmas stuck here in bed, being cosseted and pampered by Kittie, while everyone else played in the snow and made merry.

Only slightly relieved, Kittie set about tucking the suffocating cover securely about her. "Well, ye jest rest easy. 'Tis a nasty turn on that ankle, but Doc's been sent fer. That woman's got the whole house in an uproar, she does."

"What woman? And what uproar?"

"Why, Lady Alma, miss. Did it on purpose, ye know. Flat run her horse into ye and meant ta kill ye, she did."

Marke pushed herself higher in the bed to stare at the maid. "Oh, no! It's just that she's not a very experienced rider. Who is spreading such rumors?"

"Jem done told us all about it," Kittie said, then had the grace to look sheepish beneath Marke's stern look "Well, 'tweren't no rumors if he was there ta see!" she insisted, a stubborn look replacing the sheepish one. "And all them below stairs knows what's what. Ye be lying up here injured, the marquis is slammed into his library with his whiskey, and that one, Lady Alma, is rushing about protesting to anyone who will listen. Jest what does that say ta ye?"

"No, I'm sure you are mistaken, Kittie. It would have been a foolish thing to do. She could have just as easily been seriously hurt herself. Besides what advantage can this be to her?" She waved toward her foot.

Kittie would only tighten her mouth and look mulish. "That she doesn't like it one bit that Lord Perfect has a marked liking fer yer company over hers. And what advantage? Jest look at ye! Ye's bound to the bed while she's prancing about in her fancy gowns, having him all to herself. That's advantage enough, if ye be asking me."

Marke would only shake her head, which she had decided was aching abominably. Leaning back and closing her eyes, she gave a deep sigh of weariness, which brought the frown of worry to the maid's face.

"Oh, miss. Here I am rattling on and ye be feeling so poor. What can I get fer ye? All ye have ta do is ask, and I'll do it, ye kein?"

The words *peace and quiet* almost slipped out of her mouth before she could amend them to accomplish the same end. "Water, Kittie," she said. "I wish for cool water from the well. Would you get that for me?"

"Of course, miss. I can do that," Kittie said, then chewed on her lip in indecision. "Mrs. Sittlemeyer's got my promise that I'd not stir from yer side."

"Do not bother about that, girl. I shall mind our invalid while you run your little errand," Alma announced from the doorway.

Kittie's merry little face settled into a frown and her lower lip thrust out in defiance. She would not be leaving Miss

Penwell with the likes of that one, not with her helpless in bed.

Marke, correctly reading the look, rushed to intervene before the girl sank her ship in murky water. "It's quite all right, Kittie. Lady Alma will sit with me only until you return. Run along now."

Alma pointedly slammed the door closed behind the maid. "Really, that girl acts as if she expects me to push your head beneath the pillow and throw my weight upon it," she drawled.

Marke lifted an eyebrow at this rather half-witted statement to make to a person already laid low by none other than herself. She looked over the red pelisse and straw bonnet decorated with silk poppies that was so becoming to the woman's coloring—too becoming, actually—causing Marke to hate it instantly, feeling very rumpled and unattractive in comparison. But she was determined to be polite even if it killed her. "Are you on your way out, my lady?"

"Yes, Claymore and I are to stroll in the garden. I merely wished to pause a moment to inquire into your health. You actually do not seem too direly injured to me. To hear the servants talk—"

"It is only my ankle, and I am placing my wager on a sprain instead of a break. Nothing life threatening, I'm sure, but painful nevertheless. I do so appreciate your concern," she said sweetly.

"Just as I thought. Unfortunate, but not life threatening," Alma said with a dismissing flip of her hand. She moved to the dressing table, fingering through the brushes, ribbons and such there. "It shall do you no good in the long run, you know, Miss Penwell."

Marke narrowed her eyes in resignation. So, politeness be hanged! It would seem we are to dive straight from the ship's bow into the deep, she thought. Hitching herself higher against the pillows, and only barely controlling a winch at the stabbing pain, she girded herself for the rout. "And just what are you speaking of, my lady."

"This flinging yourself at the marquis's head," Alma answered conversationally. She came to lean against the bedpost, crossing her arms over her chest and flicking her pale eyes over Marke. "You are totally unsuited to be a marquise, you know. While I, on the other hand, have been raised from the cradle for just that purpose."

"I see. And what makes one more suited to carry the title of marquise?" Marke asked, expressing genuine interest in the answer.

Alma smirked and moved languidly toward the door. "To begin with, I shall not expect him to be hopelessly in love with me."

Marke was slightly taken aback. Was this what Sitter meant when she spoke of a *mariage de convenance?* It seemed such a sad thing to her. "And why would you not wish your husband to love you, my lady?"

"Oh, I have no use for such romantic nonsense. Without such muddle, Claymore and I shall have an excellent marriage. Oh, do not doubt that I shall do my duty by providing heirs to secure the title and family name. But once that is done, we shall go our separate ways as is only proper in a society marriage. You see," she drawled, mistaking the paleness of Marke's face for something other than extreme pain, "I shall not even mind these little flirtations of his."

Fortunately, Marke was spared the necessity of response by Kittie bursting into the room, all flushed and out of breath as if she had run the entire way. Alma excused herself with a slight nod of her head and slipped out the door, apparently satisfied with this afternoon's work.

"Here we are, miss, nice and cool. Jest like ye wanted," Kittie huffed.

"Oh, thank you," Marke said absently, and with the response of a good patient, she forced herself to drink every last drop.

"The doc should be here soon and he'll make it all better, ye'll see."

"And that he shall," boomed John's voice from the doorway. He followed Sitter's tiptoeing figure into the room.

"Shh." Sitter rounded on him, admonishing his exuberance. "There's no need to raise your voice so, John."

"What's this?" he demanded, sweeping a hand over the darkened room.

"Really, John." Sitter smacked him on the arm with her fingers. "I told you! Marke has taken a fall. It is essential that she lie in quiet and darkness."

"Stuff and nonsense, Sitter!" he retorted, amused. "I do not hold with all this creeping about and speaking in hushed tones."

"John Barrows, must I remind you that it is I who must answer to the marquis for her welfare. And it is too vexing of you to stride into Marke's bedchamber and commence issuing orders in this uncouth manner."

John would only grin and wink at Marke. "My dear Sitter, please forgive me. There really is no need to become all sensitive. The plain fact of it is, I wager to say, Miss Penwell here has come off more horses over her years than she cares to count. And I am willing to assure you that your *invalid* will agree with me, it's only terrifying the first time. What say, Marke?"

"I say my foot hurts like the very dickens and I do wish you two would leave off with the bickering and tell me if it's broken or sprained. After which, I shall leave this infernal bed and get on with the holiday activities."

"Ah, in a good mood, are we?" John said, moving to lay a cool hand on her forehead. "Sitter, have those drapes flung back and let the light of day into this room. It's positively medieval to think this blacked-out room is healthier than the sight of snow-covered mountains. Besides, mollycoddling this patient will merely encourage her to put on self-indulgent airs."

"Really!" Sitter snorted but did as he requested, nevertheless.

"Please, you two, give it a rest," Marke begged through clenched teeth. It appeared she might well die waiting on these two for medical aid. Easing upright against the pillows, she drew the linen up to cover her chest, even though she could not say there was anything immodest about her night rail. Childish, schoolgirlish and flannel would have described it accurately enough.

"Testy! Testy!" John admonished, flipping the corner of the bed covers back to ease her foot into view. "Well, let's just take a look at this ankle." Marke gritted her teeth. John's notion of a "look" was a seemingly endless interval of agonizingly painful poking and prodding, but eventually he confirmed her own prognosis. "Nothing broken, but very badly sprained. I'll wrap it tightly and you must promise me you will not place your weight upon it for a week or so."

"Oh, what a bother," muttered Marke with a grimace.

"Your promise, Marke!"

"A great way to spend Christmas!" She pouted.

"Marke? You still have not promised. Just because your ankle is not broken doesn't mean it's something you can sneeze at, you know."

"Of course, she promises. I shall see that she is a good girl until you pronounce her fit again," Sitter interjected. She gave Marke a stern look and smoothed the covers again. "And now, John, let us leave her to rest, while I pour you a dash of something warming before you venture out again."

"Marvelous idea," he readily agreed, with little more than a parting wink for Marke.

They marched out, leaving the door ajar and Marke feeling dreadfully neglected and writhing in pain. After a murmured conversation in the hall, the door eased open again. Marke gritted her teeth, fearing the good doctor was coming back to torture her some more, but it was Claymore who peered around the door frame. She snatched the bed covers to her chin and absurdly wished for a lace and satin nightdress as temptation.

"May we come in?" Claymore called, then just when she feared Lady Alma might be accompanying him, he pulled a cat of a different sort from behind his back.

"Oh, it's a cat!" she exclaimed. "Thank you, Claymore." She hoisted herself upright, quite forgetting the schoolgirl nightdress she wished to hide, and eagerly held out her hands to the small orange tabby.

"I found her in the kitchen and thought she might be company for you," Claymore admitted, then added with a self-conscious shrug. "I know you are used to furry things about the house."

"Oh, she is so sweet," she said, and snuggled the purring cat into her arms, "and, my goodness, so obviously about to have an enormous litter."

Claymore looked somewhat nonplussed, then stammered, "G-good Lord! I am sorry."

"Oh, relax, Claymore," she teased with a laugh. "I wasn't accusing you of paternity. I do think highly enough of you to defend you against charges of philandering with the cook's cat."

With a grin, he plopped down on the edge of the bed, eliciting a loud groan from Marke as the covers bound down tightly over her bandaged ankle. He immediately leapt to his feet again. "Damn! I am sorry, Marke. Is it throbbing terribly? John did say it wasn't broken."

"No, not broken, but I can't imagine a broken bone being any more painful."

"Well, it could have been worse."

Marke's head snapped up in surprise. "Well, of all the insensitive things to say!" she exclaimed. Then belatedly realizing what he was about, she reduced herself to giggles. "Yes, I suppose it would have been worse if the bone had broken."

"Or if it had been your head," he heckled, easing himself back on the bed, taking care to fluff the covers into a tent over her feet. He idly stroked the cat's head as it settled contentedly upon such a forbidden surface as a goose down comforter. "Or you could be expecting a litter like Cook's cat here."

"I can think of nothing better to while away the winter months than preparing for the arrival of a child," Marke said, dropping her head to watch his hand stroke the cat's furry chest. "Although a litter might be a bit much."

"Yes, perhaps," Claymore said, then abruptly changed the subject. "Cook says the cat is not hers particularly, and that even if it was, you are most welcome to her. Apparently it doesn't even have a name, so that decision is yours." He fidgeted a bit, seemingly as uncertain with her as she was with him.

Marke accepted the change of subject with more regret than she could show. What had happened to the ease they used to feel in each other's company? She missed her friend, her confidant…her lover. "Well, pray inform Cook that I shall most assuredly accept her generosity," she said. "And I shall be personally responsible for naming her, and every one of her babies, as well. I am positive they shall deal well enough with Mrs. P's dogs, once we return to St. Catherine's Court."

"Good Lord, I hadn't thought of that," Claymore said, giving a deep chuckle at the imagined ruckus a cat in the midst of all those dogs would create. "But, on that subject, shall I send word to your mother concerning your accident? I had thought not, but…"

"No, she would not understand, and if she did, it would only fret her for no good reason. I shall be up in short order."

"Not according to John and, I must warn you, it would appear the entire household is determined to keep you abed and overwhelmed with care. I do not know what to make of the extremes the staff appears prepared to go for your comfort. Apparently you have been thoroughly adopted."

"They are good people." She shrugged her shoulders then grinned shamelessly at him. "With poor judgment, perhaps."

"Hardly that."

"And the red filly? She was not lamed, I hope—oh, Claymore, she is the most splendid thing!"

"I meant her to be a surprise—that she was ready to bear you about the countryside—but I'm afraid you stole the thunder from me. You sat her well coming off the hill and over the creek, until Alma pulled that stupid stunt.'' His face darkened.

"Oh, Claymore. Surely you do not think she did that on purpose."

"I do not know what to think. I am prepared to admit to her lack of horsemanship, therefore there is the possibility, as she states, she was only attempting to overtake me.'' He dragged his hand through the tossed walnut curls. "I can only speculate as to what might have occurred by what I saw,'' he concluded darkly.

Marke watched his dear face with tenderness. She hated to see him so upset, and, typical of her nature, set about easing his worry. "Well, it is all over now. Whatever the cause—''

Claymore nodded, then interrupted to say, "But I do know that Alma is quite distressed, and consumed with guilt for having been the cause of injury to you. She was in tears earlier."

Marke's tolerance, and her budding forgiveness, were quite swallowed in a flash of disbelief. How could he be so blind? She considered a dozen scalding retorts, the mildest among them telling him, word for word, her conversation with the *distressed* Alma not one hour before. But before she could select the most devastating response, she realized he would probably place anything she said against Alma as sour grapes on her part. "You may speculate to your heart's content,'' she said coldly, "for I do not intend to discuss the matter any further. What's done is done and the worst was not realized.''

"No?'' Claymore asked, tilting his eyebrow up at her abrupt change of tone. "And did we ever surmise just what the worst would have been?''

"Of course!'' Marke snapped. "It would appear the worst to *you* would have included the Lady Alma in the number of those injured by her foolhardy stunt!''

Claymore frowned down at her. "I must say, jealousy does not become you, Marke.''

"Jealousy!'' Marke gasped in disbelief. "Jealousy! You think I am jealous of a spiteful cat like Alma Pressley?''

"I should not do you such injustice, Marke, to make the statement if I did not believe I spoke the truth," Claymore noted. He paused, but apparently she had been rendered quite mute. He cleared his throat and continued while he had the floor to himself. "And to that point, I shall request you do not make performance of your injury before the company. While I realize it must be somewhat painful, there is nothing to be gained from adding insult to Alma's guilt."

Marke found her voice. "Get out!" she snapped.

Claymore rose stiffly to tower over her. Whatever had he done to fire her so? "I am sorry if I have upset you. I merely wished—"

"Get out of this room!"

"As you wish," he said, confusion replaced by cold anger. He negotiated an elaborate bow and backed away from the bed.

Marke raised her voice to follow him. "And I promise you I shall remove my disturbing presence and—and that of my cat—from your doorstep as soon as I can put both feet beneath me."

"Marke?" Sitter bounded through the door, grinding to a halt just inside. "Oh, do pardon me, Claymore. I didn't know you were still here. I shall return—"

"Do not bother yourself, Sitter," Claymore barked. "Miss Penwell has just ordered me from her presence, and I was at the point of bowing to her wishes." He strode across the room to throw open the corridor door, then whirled back around. "And the presence of—*the cat*—is not disturbing in the least." He proceeded into the hall and flung the door closed with a resounding crash that made both women jump, and sent the cat disappearing beneath the bed.

Sitter spun from the door to Marke. "Oh, good Lord! What now?"

"It was nothing, really," Marke murmured. Her voice was wretchedly unsteady and she blinked rapidly to stave off the tears that threatened.

"Yes, I can see that it was nothing at all," Sitter agreed, shaking her head at such a bald-faced lie. Gently perching upon the foot of the bed, she tucked her feet beneath her and leaned back against the corner post. "Now, tell me."

"It's just that—well, he said, implied rather..." she mumbled, then shrugged her shoulders. Hanging her head, she looked like a small child whose favorite toy had just broken. Her lip thrust out and tears welled up in her eyes.

Sitter clicked her tongue in irritation at seeing her patient upset. "And how much of it had to do with Alma?"

Marke raised her head and gave a watery grin. "Always straight to the point, aren't you, Sitter?"

"And therefore forestalling misunderstandings. Now, straight out with it, my dear."

"It's just that he seems much more concerned over her pretended guilt than over my injury. Why are men so—so dense?" she snorted, searching for words. "She's as clear as a windowpane of highly polished glass to me!"

"Oh yes, to me, also," Sitter agreed. "But you must remember, dear, she does not readily show an honest picture of herself to just anyone."

"No, I would think not. This morning she stood just there—" she pointed firmly to the offending spot on the carpet "—and explained herself in bold-faced terms. And I will tell you, the picture of the marriage she is planning for herself as Marquise of Boothe-Ashmore is not a pleasant sight. Sitter, sh-she does not even lo-love him," she finished in a wail.

"Well, I would imagine not. If she did, she'd be much more concerned with *his* happiness. I've explained to you before, among the *haute-ton*, such marriages are most common. And I shall admit, having seen successes on both sides, I truly feel it's best if a woman doesn't develop a *tendre* for her husband. They do tend to take advantage if you do."

"Sitter, what a terrible thing to say!"

Sitter only shrugged her shock aside and pondered the new invalid with a sorrowful gaze. "And what of you, Marke? Do *you* love him?"

"Oh, Sitter, I do! I love him most severely," she whispered, allowing her lower lip to tremble and tears to spill over and trace down her cheeks.

"Lord help you then."

Marke patted the bed as encouragement for the timid cat to return to her side. "Yes, Lord help me, indeed."

Sitter watched the cat settle back beside Marke with a thoughtful expression. "Have you told him?"

"Told him what? That I love him?" Marke asked, startled at such a question. "Of course, I haven't!"

"Why not?"

"Well, well..." She floundered, then stated defiantly, "If he can't tell that I love him with everything I've done and given—"

"Tell him, Marke."

"I just couldn't, Sitter. What if he laughed at me, or didn't care at all? I would just die."

"Then show him," Sitter insisted. "Let it shine in your smile and your eyes when you are with him."

"I'm afraid it would be blinding to him if I let it shine."

"Sometimes men must be blinded to see what's before their very noses."

Marke slipped down to snuggle around the sleeping cat, stroking fingertips gently through the fur on the swollen belly. "Perhaps you're right. There's certainly nothing to lose, is there?"

"And everything to gain, my dear," Sitter said gently.

Chapter Twenty-Five

⎯⎯⎯⎯◦⎯⎯⎯⎯

Marke slept fitfully through the night and well into mid-morning, and was only awakened when a hand shook her gently on the shoulder. She reluctantly opened her eyes and found Kittie peering down at her.

"Forgive me, miss," Kittie whispered. "If ye truly are going to go down fer luncheon—and I'm telling ye, I'm not alone in thinking ye shouldn't be leaving this bed—but if ye are, then ye'd best be seeing to yer hair."

Truthfully Marke did not wish to join the others for any activity, today or ever again, but she'd be damned if she'd allow Alma to get the best of her! And she did promise Sitter to try again with Claymore. She forced herself upright and shoved the unruly curls from her face. The cat stretched and yawned, too, but showed no interest is leaving the bed.

"Yes, I daresay it would show a marked amount of good sense if I'd just stay where I am," Marke muttered behind a wide yawn.

"That ye should!"

"But I have no history of such, you know, so let's be up and about."

But the task was more easily said than done, for Marke quickly found her swollen ankle resisted even the slightest bit of weight. Abandoning the desire for a bath, she washed haphazardly in a basin carried to the bed. Then, forced to balance herself precariously on one foot, she moaned while Kittie trussed her into an open robe of gold jaconet and topped it with a slightly darker spencer trimmed in bronze satin. She then managed to hobble to the dressing table, where she beheld a perfect picture of a disaster if ever there was one. Her hair, sleep tossed and matted, with a goodly amount of meadow grass tangled on one side, stood about her head in a riot. She almost faltered and crawled back between the sheets in defeat at the sight. However was she to present a desirable counterpart to the elegant Alma looking like this?

Kittie, vigorously applying the hairbrush, correctly read her expression. "Don't ye fret now. We'll do our best."

Kittie's best was astonishingly good, considering the obstinate tangle of curls presented to her, and Marke no longer resembled a dairy maid tumbled in the haystack when she hobbled to the door. Half hopping, half limping, leaning heavily on Kittie, she made her way painfully to the head of the stairs. Kittie leaned her against the wall and pondered the steep flight of stairs with a wry shake of her head. "I don't believe ye can hop down those, miss, not without killing yerself, and me, in the doing of it. But don't ye worry. Just wait here and I'll call fer Mr. Heaven. He'll know what to do."

Kittie rushed down the stairs, leaving Marke sagging against the wall, as the clock struck the noon hour. Her ankle throbbed to a jungle drum, matched beat for beat by the pounding in her head. Suddenly luncheon didn't sound very good. And what did it matter if Claymore married the witch, anyway? If he couldn't see what was directly beneath his nose, didn't he deserve every miserable day of his life? Her stomach began to churn disagreeably, and she peered down the hall, wondering if she could manage to hobble back to her bed without assistance. She had just determined to make the attempt when Kittie galloped into view, dragging Henry with her.

"Lord Perfect has arranged a surprise, miss," panted Kittie. "It's waiting at the bottom of the stairs fer ye. And here's Henry to carry ye down. Now have a care, Henry. 'Tis her right ankle."

With a wink, the brawny Henry gathered her carefully into strong arms and fairly trotted down the stairs, bouncing her ankle painfully with each step. She heroically bit her lip to keep from crying out rather than scold him, for after all, hadn't she been witness to the fact that sharp words never deterred Henry? When they reached the bottom, he deposited her unceremoniously into Claymore's abandoned invalid chair.

"This is Lord Perfect's surprise?" she asked in dismay.

"Had it carried down from the attic, he did. Early this morning, although I doubt he thought you'd use it this soon," Henry admitted.

Judging by the cobwebs still clinging to the hastily cleaned chair, Marke could well believe no one expected her up and about this early. "I suppose I appreciate his concern. And, Henry, you shall be rewarded for carrying me up and down the stairs."

He blushed mightily at her praise. "Ah, miss, don't need no reward."

She could only nod, for he was already pushing the chair industriously forward. She gritted her teeth, dreading the spectacle she would present wheeled so dramatically into the dining room. No wonder Claymore had developed such a foul temper. It was most difficult being presented as a spectacle. However, her fears were almost groundless, as there was no lull in the conversation. Sitter was conversing with Heaven beside the groaning sideboard, apparently over something dreadfully important, as her hands were flying through the air. Alma was imparting some *on-dit* into Claymore's ear, and though his head was bent in a solicitous manner toward her, he was drawing aimless designs on the tablecloth with the tines of his sterling fork. Lord Pressley was busily rearranging his utensils into a more pleasing order beside his plate, clearly in anticipation of food. Marke waited fully half a minute for someone to note her entry and then irritably cleared her throat.

"Miss Penwell!" Lord Pressley leapt to his feet, rushed to the door and seized Marke's hand. "Permit me to express my deep dismay that my own daughter should have been the cause of your suffering an injury. I told her again and again to take some riding instruction. Surely you will remember that I did, at the ball. Deuced dangerous on a horse, my Alma."

All through this tirade, he made an exaggerated production of flagging a footman to remove a chair and clear a space for the invalid chair to be drawn up to the table. Unfortunately, this was to the marquis's left, and the last place at Innisfree she wished to be seated. Henry propelled her to the table, and Claymore acknowledged her with a nod so cool, so slight, that she fancied she might well have imagined it. But the frown of irritation upon Alma's face was something no one could have imagined, and lightened Marke's mood considerably. Pleased at his work, Lord Pressley immediately resumed his own place and glanced at Sitter expectantly. She signaled Heaven to serve.

The soup was mulligatawny, and a dismal failure. Marke's stomach wrenched as an overpowering odor of curry wafted up to her nostrils. She was inclined to shove the bowl as far as possible across the table, but Claymore was regarding her rapidly whiting face with a deep frown. Not wishing to be sent back to bed, she affected a weak smile and began to swirl her spoon about the bowl with pretended enthusiasm.

Lord Pressley attacked the soup with relish, speaking around his spoon. "I must say, I had not thought to see you at the table this soon, Miss Penwell, but I will admit to a great deal of admiration for such fortitude. Can be bad, you know, taking a nasty spill from your horse. Done so more than once myself. Isn't that so, Alma?"

"Yes, Father, more than once," Alma answered dutifully. "And you were certainly bucko about it. It never kept you from the table."

The only one to miss the snippiness of her remark was the lord himself, as he was seeing only the bottom of his soup bowl. As soon as he relinquished his grip of the bowl rim, Sitter signaled for a remove. Marke closed her eyes and prayed the next course would be more tempting to her stomach. The footmen bounded forward, whisked away the

bowls and presented plates of cold ham, cold duck, cauliflower and peas. Marke picked up her fork and made a
game try at the peas, as they seemed the least offensive, and
hoped Lord Pressley would be swayed from his present
discourse. Hadn't Claymore made it a specific point of requesting she downplay her injury for Alma's sake? But
surely he could see that the boorish rambling of the woman's own father was not her fault. Lord Pressley was not to
be deterred from the subject, although he was the only one
interested in pursuing it to great length.

"It's such a shame my own physician wasn't available.
Most remarkable man!" He waved a laden fork at the
marquis. "Why he could even have had you on your feet in
time for a wedding last season, Lord Perfect." He paused
dramatically, obviously expecting some sort of positive remark from the marquis, then tapered off when Claymore
maintained his stodgy silence. "But I suppose we shall
simply have to wait and see, for Miss Penwell's recovery, I
mean."

Good gracious, can't someone shut the man up! Marke
thought. She cast Sitter a pleading glance the length of the
table, but the woman kept her eyes on her plate with a
strange little smile playing over her lips.

The silence proved too much for Lord Pressley and his
eyes flew around the table. "Yes, we shall simply wait," he
added, finishing off the last morsel on his plate and lacing
his hands over his ample waistline. "I always have sub-
scribed to the theory that these things happen for the best."

Marke shoved her peas to the right side of her plate and
the cauliflower to the left. Her foot was beginning to throb
with a vengeance, and she could not for the life of her see
how this could be the best for anybody.

"Could have been worse, you know," he finished.

Claymore made a strangled noise in his throat, and
Marke darted a glance at his face to catch the fleeting smirk
on his lips. Jerking her eyes back to her own plate, she
fought to stifle the laughter she knew would burst forth if
their eyes met.

"Enough of this," Alma bluntly interjected. "Let's speak of something else. Shall we make plans for a sleigh ride this afternoon, it will be a wonderful prelude to the Christmas Eve festivities tomorrow night? The snow has begun to fall wonderfully heavy." She pouted prettily. "Oh, my, *you* can't venture out in the cold with that ankle, now can you, Miss Penwell?"

"Oh, I daresay, I shall be quite content to remain here before the fire," she began, only to have Lord Pressley rudely interrupt in that booming voice.

"Excellent idea! Seeing as how our ride was cut short this morning. Oh, begging your pardon, Miss Penwell. Didn't mean anything."

Sitter flicked an eyebrow at Marke and smiled that catty little smile. Marke, not understanding in the least what she was about, finally decided the lady was up to no good, and that was a fact. But, as she had already proven herself wise in the manner of such things, and Marke did trust her subtleties and instincts more than anyone else, she would accept that somehow she thought it a good thing to have Lord Pressley spouting his boring nonsense undeterred, *and* to have Claymore and Alma thrown together a great deal of the time. Suddenly Marke was ravenously hungry, wolfing down two slices of peach torte, an enormous bunch of grapes, and three full glasses of dark, sweet sherry. After all, it was almost Christmas Eve.

After the group departed for their romp in the sleigh, Marke divided her restless attention between the seeds and berries spread on the table before her, and the heavy snowfall outside the window. The flakes were drifting straight down in a white winter land of wonder. How she ached to be out in it, pummeling Claymore with snowballs, and making snow angels. She envied the others having the afternoon to play out of doors. She was not a submissive patient. Try as she would, she chaffed at the inactivity.

"Ahem, miss?" Henry cleared his throat and edged into the doorway with a grin as he held up tissue and red string in his hand. "Mr. Heaven has instructed me to wrap the

portrait before the marquis returns. Wouldn't want to spoil
the surprise for his lordship, now would we?"

"Absolutely not," Marke exclaimed. Pleased at the
company, she waved him forward. She turned to gaze at the
completed portrait leaning against the drawing room wall.
Heaven had unearthed an elaborately carved frame in un-
tarnished gold leaf in which to display it to perfection. She
gathered a great deal of inner satisfaction whenever she
gazed at it, although she very much doubted her subject
would share that pleasure, and she would not be overly
surprised if he would deny the likeness entirely. Without
conscious effort, she had captured a side of Claymore that
he took great pains to hide from others. There was an intimacy in the handsome face, a softness about the smiling
mouth with its deep dimple, and a twinkling of merriment
in the warm brown eyes that made her heart ache to look at
it. But then, when she had completed the work, she had
been painting with eyes of love, and from an intimate
knowledge of the man. The face smiling gently from the
canvas had become an amazing replica of the face he
showed her when he held her tightly to him to kiss and tease
her.

"And what's this?" Sitter demanded, waltzing into the
warmth of the drawing room. "What are you two up to?"

"Sitter! Are you returned so soon?" Marke asked, and
glanced through the doorway behind her, suddenly fearful
Claymore would stroll through and see the portrait pre-
maturely.

"Oh, I didn't join the others," Sitter said, again with
that secret little smile. "As you know, I am not much for
confronting discomfort when it can be avoided. I'd much
rather sit with you. Oh, you've had the portrait framed!
Marke, the likeness is absolutely uncanny. I fully expect
him to burst into laughter whenever I look at it. You have
a truly remarkable talent, my dear."

"Thank you, Sitter, but I only hope Claymore agrees
with you. Henry is going to wrap it before he returns."

Sitter moved to the fireplace and settled on the divan with
a speculative look at Marke. "Whatever are you doing

there?'' she asked, inclining her head at the table drawn close to Marke.

"Oh, Kittie is decorating the bird's tree for me. See?'' she said, eagerly displaying thin wooden hearts and stars covered with honey, into which she was pressing seeds and berries. "Bird cookies. Kittie will set them outside to harden, then they can be hung on the tree outside the window there. I've already strung berry ropes with chunks of apple. They'll come in droves—all dressed in feathery finery, and chirping a merry tune—downy woodpeckers, chickadees and cardinals.''

"Amazing,'' Sitter said, shaking her head at Marke's childlike enthusiasm. "You find the most remarkable variety of things to keep yourself busy.''

Marke laughed at her dismay. "But Sitter, it's Christmas!''

"Yes, it is Christmas, and I demand an early present,'' she said, hoping to distract Marke throughout the afternoon. "Finish your tale of your father for me. I am most interested and it would help while the time away. I'm sure Henry would be most interested, as well, wouldn't you, Henry?''

Henry glanced up from his task and smiled. At first Marke thought to protest that Claymore should be included, then thought it made little difference now. That promise was made a whole lifetime ago, between two people who were no longer close. "Oh, as you wish. Let's see, where did we leave off?''

"Your father had sailed on a Friday, which inflamed the crew. Then to make matters worse, there was a bloke that would make things harder on them all, and the captain allowed him to get away with it,'' Sitter prompted.

Marke could only smile at Sitter's avid interest. It amazed her that she had retained their place in the story so exactly. "You are amazing, Sitter. And quite right. The sailor was named Mason, and the bucko mate would continue to haze him mercilessly.''

"Yes, and your father allowed him to do it, hoping the captain would step in as was his place to do so," Sitter prompted.

"Well, despite the hazing, Mason never ceased expounding the horrors he anticipated would befall the ship. He predicted the vessel would be demasted, or run into icebergs, or collide with an island in the fog. In short, he clearly maintained they were to be overtaken by severe calamity sooner or later. These dire predictions began to wear on the crew's nerves. With Mason croaking day and night, and the mate's unreasonable bullying, the crew was totally undone."

Henry completed the wrapping of the portrait and placed it behind the tall cedar waiting to be decorated on Christmas Eve. He then came to sit on the ottoman at Sitter's feet. Marke could only imagine Heaven's reaction if he caught the young man lounging about, but she appreciated the company too much to send him about his duties. Sitter placed a hand on the young man's shoulder with the affectionate ease of long acquaintance through trials and grief.

"It's shameful to say it, but if either Mason or the bucko had been swept overboard, *The Agate* might have kept out of trouble. But Mason became impossible."

"What happened, miss?" Henry asked, eyes round as a child's hearing a ghost story. She lowered her voice, and both he and Sitter leaned closer with wide eyes.

"Early one morning, when a course alteration made it necessary to square the yards, Mason happened to be on lookout. Now, the squaring of the yards is not a great deal of work, but it is very important that it be done properly. We cannot be certain, but it would appear that the work was never done. When the mate saw this, he yelled the order a second time, but still the work was not done. Not willing to brook such open disobedience, the bucko stormed the forward braces in a rage. Mason was lying in wait for him with a capstan bar and some crazy idea in his head that braining the mate would end the curse on the ship. But the mate seized the bar from him, turning the tables, and when all was said and done, it was Mason who lay dead. It was exactly at this moment that—'' she paused for a beat for effect ''—the calm hit. The men declared that Mason's predictions had been true, and *The Agate* was, indeed, a cursed ship.''

"Oh, miss," Henry breathed. Then turning to Sitter, he unnecessarily explained the obvious. "A calm at sea is a terrible thing. Why, food and water can run short and all hands perish for want of such if the calm lasts too long."

"Oh, no! How horrible," Sitter exclaimed, clasping a hand over her throat.

Marke smiled at her captured audience and continued her tale in a voice that hinted at dire things. "Now, Mason dead was more trouble than Mason alive. Fearing for his life, the bucko locked himself in his cabin, and the captain took to pacing the deck, going without sleep for days at a time. The calm was eerie, oppressive, foreboding. The ship lay in dead calm for over a week. The men were reduced to a state of terror, and stirred to a position of declared mutiny, convinced that one giant hand of the sea held them fast. On the eighth day of the calm, at four bells, the captain walked over the side. A boat went out, but no sign of him was found. Almost at once, a faint breath of air got up and began to grow. *The Agate* was sailing again. The crew believed whatever had held the ship in its palm had been appeased by blood sacrifice.''

"And is that what you believe, Miss Penwell?"

The trio spun to see Claymore and Alma standing in the doorway. Having no idea how long they had been standing there, Marke grew worried when Henry leapt to his feet with such a guilty look on his face. She rushed to fill the silence. "Actually, I do not harbor superstitions concerning the sea. I respect it greatly, but I do not fear it. Nor do I grant it powers beyond that of nature."

Claymore advanced to lay a staying hand on the valet's shoulder. "Best stay for the ending, Henry. I, myself, shall prompt her to continue as soon as Heaven brings hot toddies to restore the circulation in my toes. There's a storm gathering in fury out of doors. A tale will fill the rest of the afternoon as we're sure to become housebound."

"There is really not much more to the tale, I fear," Marke hedged.

"Well, whatever there is, I find myself waiting with bated breath, much like Henry and Sitter here, for the finish to come," Claymore stated, arranging himself in the chair opposite her. "Alma, I am sorry you were not privy to the beginning of this tale. Or for that matter, to all the interesting stories of Miss Penwell's flamboyant family."

Marke glanced up quickly to scan Claymore's face. Was he making fun of her in front of Alma? The thought bothered her greatly. But no, he was wearing only a pleasant look of congeniality, and there was no indication whatsoever that he might be making prank at her expense.

Alma moved with languid grace to the fire, holding out her hands to the blaze. Her face might have been expressionless, yet her thoughts raged with frustration. Why must this red-haired chit capture the marquis's attention whenever she was in attendance? Furious at the turn of events, Alma swept her scarlet skirts away from the flames and marched to the door. "As I am ignorant of the tale in its inception, I shall take this opportunity to change my gown and perhaps rest before dinner. If you will excuse me?" She paused dramatically in the doorway, waiting for Claymore to beg her to remain.

"Pray continue, Marke," Claymore prompted, gazing at her through the steam rising from his cup. He was pleased to see the pink blush come to her cheeks and her shyly lowered eyes. He'd missed her greatly. Her unaffected sweetness and saucy charm. So why was he denying himself?

Marke blushed at his appraisal and lowered her eyes to the seeds and berries. She quickly picked up the line of her story, only then remembering that she was to follow Sitter's advice. Rather than schooling her face into careful expressions, she was supposed to allow her love to shine through her eyes. But somehow that was so difficult to do for fear of appearing a fool before him.

"Well, as I was saying, the wind came up as if in answer to the blood sacrifice. The crew was appeased and it looked as if the voyage would continue without incident. But that was not to be the case. The wind rose steady throughout the night and by morning it was clear that a full-scale storm was chasing *The Agate* across the seas. The men were again terrified and it took the lash on their backs to keep them at their posts, although there was nowhere for them to run to escape the fury of the storm. Dillon, the sailor that survived to tell us of Father's demise, and the death of *The Agate*, was swept overboard during the fury of the tempest. He managed to cling to a barrel throughout the storm, always within sight of the ship, but with no way to reach her decks again. It was from this vantage point that he saw the storm take her masts down, one by one, rendering her helpless to face the giant waves, and saw her hull finally split to admit the deadly sea into her belly. The sea took her at dawn the next day. The way Dillon told it, the exact moment the last board of *The Agate* disappeared beneath the waves, the storm abated and all was calm again. The clouds parted and the sun came out strongly."

"Amazing," Claymore said.

Sitter fanned herself with her handkerchief as if faint from the thought of the sinking ship with all hands aboard. Henry, having stood behind the marquis's chair for the finish of the tale, leaned forward.

"Pardon me, miss. But how did Dillon make it back to port?"

"He rode the barrel for three days. Near crazed for water, and delirious with the sun, he was giving up hope when, as if sent by providence, a ship sailed over the horizon, and held her course directly toward him. The captain returned him to Liverpool some months later."

"Ah, I see. Wonderful tale, miss! Thank you for allowing me to hear the ending. Now I'd best be off myself," Henry said, bowing slightly. "Excuse me."

"Oh, I should be off, too," Sitter abruptly announced. With no explanation, she hurried out in Henry's wake, firmly shutting the drawing room doors behind her.

Marke glanced after her in surprise. Heavy silence settled over the room. Was it obvious only to her that the entire household was pushing them together? When Lord Pressley burst into the room before a private word could be spoken between them, she could only imagine how disappointed they would all be.

"John Barrows has blown in on the storm, Claymore. Seems he's in a pickle and looking for assistance," he called, rudely shoving a frowning John before him into the center of the room.

Claymore was on his feet instantly, holding out his hand in welcome to John. "Bad weather for trouble, John. Is it serious?"

"Nothing more disastrous than a lamed horse, and a baby that might not wait much longer. I was on my way to Doug O'Shannon's. His first is making an appearance tonight of all nights, and I wasn't anticipating trouble, but have suddenly found myself afoot. Lucky to be close enough to Innisfree to beg assistance. Marke! I didn't see you there." He stepped quickly around Claymore and stripped off his gloves to hold out his hands to Marke with great enthusiasm. "And I certainly didn't expect you to be out of bed! How's the foot?"

"Oh, it is not so bad. I am only reminded sharply to mind my manners if I attempt any movement at all," she admitted, placing her warm hand into his cold ones. "So I've become as sedentary as an old bear in the dead of winter."

John plopped down on the ottoman and continued to hold Marke's hand in both of his, beaming into her face. Marke colored prettily at his rapt attention, something that did not escape Claymore's notice, and actually brought forth a frown of displeasure at the sight. He cleared his throat to bring the conversation back to the matter at hand.

"John, you did say you've a baby to see to," he reminded sourly. "Look, the night is growing foul and the roads will be treacherous. Perhaps I shall go with you. Always safer with two on a night such as this."

John smiled and gave a slight conspirator's wink at Marke, which puzzled her, then rose to draw on the wet gloves again. "That's great. Always appreciate the company on these all-nighters, you know."

Lord Pressley braced his bulk before the fireplace and rocked back on his heels. "And I shall stay here before the fire. Too foul for me out there. Beastly weather, this place has. I'm sure Miss Penwell will be pleased to keep me entertained with her straightforward opinions until you return, Perfect."

Marke inwardly groaned. If she had to listen to more adverse remarks concerning Bantry, Ireland or the discomforts of Innisfree, Lord Pressley just might find himself with an earful of straightforward opinions all right. Most having to do with pretty manners for company!

Chapter Twenty-Six

The wind howled miserably around the corner and carried snowflakes down the library chimney, sending the flames dancing about and sizzling in futile protest. Marke pulled the merino shawl tighter about her shoulders. Most of Innisfree was slumbering away the cold winter's night, blissfully unaware of the storm that transported snow from the mountains to Dunmanus Bay. Not a comfortable night for John and Claymore to be off delivering babies, but babies did not always wait for clement weather to make their demands for life.

To take her mind off her worries, Marke had attempted to knit, but she soon threw the needles and ball of wool into the chair opposite her in irritation at her incompetence. Then she opened a book from the stack placed beside her chair by the thoughtful Heaven, once he realized she intended to sit vigil stubbornly until the marquis's return. She read a few lines, shut the book, reopened it with determination, read a few lines, then shut it again. Levering herself from the chair with the use of Claymore's knurled cane, she hobbled painfully to the sideboard. Pouring herself a small glass of sherry, she started to return to the fire, then thinking ahead, grasped the bottle to place near her hand, just in case. Seated again with as much comfort as her throbbing ankle would allow, she pensively emptied the glass in small sips, opened another book, closed that one, too. She was terribly restless, and irked beyond belief that she could not pace the restlessness away. She sighed, reached for the bellpull, then withdrew her hand. Who was there to call for company this late at night, morning actually—it was now Christmas Eve.

One of Cat's new kittens mewed plaintively in the basket placed near the fire. Marke leaned to draw the basket to her, softly raising the blanket to peer down at the tiny balls of fluff. Cat was off hunting mice in the quiet kitchen, and she'd been trusted to baby-sit the six tiny fur-balls until her return. With a gentle smile, she lifted the orange baby to nuzzle against her cheek before tucking it carefully beside its littermates. They were sweet, and well mannered and, unlike puppies, keeping their little tongues politely to themselves.

Levering herself up again, she hobbled to the desk. After drawing out a large county map, she smoothed it over the leather top of the desk. Yellow with age and creased from folding, it was covered with mysterious signs and names written in Celtic script. It looked almost like a treasure map, but nevertheless showed the district quite clearly. Though faded in spots, the dark mahogany shaded mountains, surrounded by an azure sea, stood out sharply against the lighter brown valleys. The roads and paths were outlined in black, the little cultivated patches around the tiny village were green, and everywhere the tongue of the sea thrust into the island in deep blue bays. Small crosses, churches, chapels, cemeteries, little harbors, lighthouses and cliffs were marked. Slowly her forefinger with its oval nail moved along the road by which Claymore and John had left more than eight hours ago for O'Shannons' cabin.

Away from Innisfree, over the repaired bridge, along the narrow lane where the road descended steeply into the little bay, then past the little cemetery for unbaptized children whose bones have been carried away by the sea. They would take the left fork at Dunmanus Bay, three miles of bog, a church, two miles of bog, Beckett's shop, Teddy O'Flannigan's bar, five miles of bog, a church, three miles or bog, the village Hillscroft. Here they swung away from the direction to Bantry. Slowly the finger moved across the map until it reached the bay where the thick black line of the road swung across the bridge to St. Cross Island. The trek Claymore and John would take was now marked by a spider-fine line, following the edge of the island and in places coinciding with the blue of water. The coast was dark brown there, and rugged. Someone had written in a fine hand on the blue of the sea—200 feet—380 feet—300 feet—and next to each of these figures was an arrow to show that the figures applied not to the depth of the sea but to the height of the cliffs, which at these places coincided with the road. Marke drew a shaky breath and glanced out the window. The violence of the storm was obscured by her worried reflection, staring white faced back at her. Such a treacherous trek on such a violent night. She looked down at the map again to continue her imaginary drive with Claymore and John.

Time and again the fingernail halted as Marke tried to picture every step of the way. How often had John driven over this same stretch of coast? Did he know it well? Had he only made the journey on sunny days, or had he perhaps traversed the road on a stormy night as black as the inside of Lucifer's heart? Would that be any different than a snowy night such as this, when the wind brought distant smells of imaginary dangers to spook the horses? Such a strong wind would persistently shove against the carriage, pushing it perilously close to those perpendicular cliffs over a writhing white-foam sea. Down where many a ship had foundered, and the same wind snatched away the drowning sailors' cries from the ears of those who might have yet saved their lives, had they but heard. Marke shivered, then shook her head at her own nonsense. She was allowing her imagination to rule her good sense. Gripping the cane, she hobbled back to the fire. Piling on more peat, she poked the glowing embers till the flames leapt up merrily. Retrieving her knitting bundle, she eased into her chair and placed her foot on the ottoman. Sitting only for a second, again throwing the tangled mess of knitting into the opposite chair, she struggled to her feet. Hobbling to the mirror, she stared intently into her face.

"You are really something, Margaret Catherine," she snorted. "Can you give me one good reason why you are pacing about like a caged lion? And on an injured ankle at that, fretting for the man's safe return? Working yourself up, even when his intended bride sleeps soundly, totally unconcerned!" She looked sternly at herself, as if expecting an answer, then laughed gently. "Because you love the rascal, always have and, sadly enough, probably always will."

Abandoning her reflection, she limped to the window. Cupping her face to block out the light, she stared at the flashes of blowing snow. John was certainly being treated royally to country practice tonight. With a sigh, she hobbled back to the fire, and poured her second sherry, a large one, which finally—after being gulped straight down—began to allay her worry somewhat, and even dulled the ache in her ankle. She leaned over the basket on the hearth again. Cat had returned to scratch the blanket aside and take her rightful place as any good mother would. All her babies were lined up at their mother's teats, kneading with tiny feet. Cat looked up at her with slitted eyes and a feline smile, purring so loudly with contentment that Marke had to smile. Motherhood must be marvelous. Was Mrs. O'Shannon holding her own newborn right now? Was she as deeply contented as Cat? She certainly hoped so.

Unable to settle, she hobbled to consult the map again. Tracing with a finger, she moved it forward while she calculated. An hour, no more, along the slippery road to the bay, half an hour to the island cutoff, perhaps two more up to the O'Shannons' cabin, and if the child really did come punctually perhaps two hours for the birth. Then another half hour to an hour for the cup of tea, another three and a half hours for the ride back. Ten hours altogether. Claymore had left at five, so around three she ought to be able to see the coachman's lanterns where the road came up over the hill. Marke looked at her watch. Just now half past one. Once more slowly with the finger across the map... bog, village, church. She wished she could pray for their safety. Well, perhaps it could do them no harm. Dropping her head, she whispered words that strangely brought her comfort. "Kindly Jesus, have mercy on them."

Returning to poke at the fire, she reached for the Bantry newspaper and sank down on the hearth beside the basket. On the front page were the personal announcements—births, deaths, engagements. She read each one aloud, slowly and clearly to the inattentive cat.

"'In memory of dearly beloved...'" Two columns, forty times, for the departed she murmured, "Kindly Jesus, have mercy on his soul." Then came the silver weddings, the rings lost, the purses found, the official announcements. She read each one slowly, distinctly, aloud. When she'd completed the entire page, secretly hoping that an hour had passed, she glanced at the watch-face pinned to her bodice. Half an hour. She lowered her face to her hands. The waiting was tearing at her patience. However would the unfortunate girl who would take John to husband stand this strain? How many long, stormy nights such as this would she spend wondering if she would be a widow come morning?

The wind seemed to have lessened outside. Marke thrust aside the newspaper and moved to the window to look out at the bay. The rocks were as black as ancient ink, although the coin of the moon had floated clear of the clouds and now illuminated the snow as bright as day. Marke breathed easier and whispered, "Kindly Jesus, have mercy on them."

There was certainly no harm in saying a few times "kindly Jesus, have mercy on her" for Mrs. O'Shannon, too. She tried to imagine her. Was it over? Was she resting easily, with beads of sweat on the pale, proud face that she turned to her husband? Was he beaming down at her with love and pride at what she'd accomplished? Did that, in some inexplicable way, express both the pain she had endured for him, and the happiness at the opportunity to do so?

Marke turned away from the window. She looked disagreeably at the newspaper, the knitting, the discarded books, and then at the sherry bottle. None beckoned. She slowly and neatly placed each in its rightful place using up the time. A quick glance at her watch and her spirits rose. Almost three. One more look in the mirror, hair tidied, color unnecessarily pinched into her cheeks, and she made one more uneven journey across to the map. She traced the lines from that point where she guessed Mrs. O'Shannon had become a mother to her first child, to the cliff where Innisfree sat. If all had gone well, they should soon be safely home.

Cocking her head sideways in the stillness of the sleeping mansion, she wondered at the silence now that the wind had ceased. Slowly the roar of the surf reached her. However was Alma to endure life at Innisfree when she hated the relentless sound of the surf? Innisfree, where sometimes storms blew for weeks at a time, causing the surf to roar and the rain seemingly never to cease. But then, Alma would never live at Innisfree at all, she reasoned, but would surely demand to return to London forthwith. Well, London was certainly welcome to her!

Marke glanced at her watch again. Three o'clock! As quickly as possible, she limped from the library and across the chilly entry hall, seeking the drawing room where the windows looked out on the road. There was a dark, bent figure silhouetted against the glass. "Oh, Heaven!" she exclaimed, startled to find someone about in the house other than herself. "So you stayed up to worry, as well. Do you see them yet?"

"No, not yet." He shifted aside to allow her a space at the window. "But if my calculations are accurate, I expect them soon. I have water heating in the kitchen for toddies, as I imagine they will be quite chilled."

"I do not doubt it. But at least the storm has passed," she said with a sigh.

Heaven smiled down at her with great affection. "This has been a long night for you, miss. And, no doubt your ankle has suffered, as well. His lordship will have my head for allowing it."

"His lordship will understand perfectly when you say that there was no chance you could have prevented it,"

Marke replied with a warm smile. She cupped her hands to frame her face and stared out the window. The naked coin of the moon lit the sky. Suddenly the light of the coach-man's lantern writhed across the gray clouds as the coach climbed the hill. "There they are!"

Heaven leaned to the window beside her. They both held their breath to keep from frosting the glass, and together watched eagerly as the lights shot over the top of the rise, and dipped toward the little washed-out cemetery. The clear sound of a horn, three times and then, three times again, carried to them.

Heaven chuckled to himself. "A boy. O'Shannon has a son."

"How do you know, Heaven? The horn?"

"Yes. They would have sounded it through the village, as well, so that everyone knows all is well, and Doug O'Shannon has a son. I'm sure there were others awake and pacing the floor as we were, miss."

The carriage lantern disappeared as they made the turn to the bridge, then they could hear the rattle of wheels on the wooden planks, and it swept into full view beneath the arch, into the mews.

With Heaven's hand on her elbow, Marke rushed as quickly as the cane and her irksome foot would allow to fling open the heavy door, spearing welcoming light over the wide steps and across the driveway. Never wondering if Claymore would find it strange than she had sat through the night waiting for him...as a loving wife would have waited for her husband to return safely home to her arms.

Chapter Twenty-Seven

Innisfree lent itself admirably to Christmas. Everywhere there were herbs and flowers in profusion, arranged in all sorts of imaginative ways. Garlands of holiday greens, pine, juniper, cedar and holly, tied off with red velvet and ivory lace bows, graced the staircase and the tops of every doorway. A tree, though smaller than the one in the conservatory but nevertheless full branched and wood scented, stood proudly in the drawing room. Spread out beneath it were adornments of ruby and gold glass balls, and beribboned swags of dried roses and peonies, artemisia and tallow berries, and bunches of bay, sage, thyme and rosemary. A Yule log crackled merrily in the fireplace and an array of tempting treats—petits fours, apricot brandy cake, pumpkin and pecan tea cake, and almond pound cake with royal icing—sat atop the sideboard. A punch bowl, wreathed with greens and fresh freesia, offered Christmas wassail of cider and brandy, highly spiced and sweetened, with roasted apples bobbing on the surface. Christmas Eve was underway!

Christmas was not a holiday exclusive for children as far as Marke was concerned. She was filled with the spirit of goodwill, and only hindered from joining in the decorating of the tree by her injured foot. Although the others seemed quite content to linger about the fire while footmen decorated the towering evergreen, Marke would have been swinging from the boughs if possible. As it was, she was seated quite close, engaged with handing out the ornaments and supervising their placement, making impossible demands and dissolving into giggles at the footmen's prankish dismay over her unrealistic expectations.

Claymore stood at the mantel, pointedly ignoring Lord Pressley's rambling monologue—and the pout on Alma's face—watching Marke with growing delight. The length of fabric he had given her, presented on the sly through Sitter to forestall any chance of refusal, had quickly been stitched into a simple gown with a bodice cut daringly low to display the creaminess of her shoulders and the sweet rise of her breasts to perfection. The satin, luscious in the everchanging hue of carmeled pralines, provided a flattering backdrop for her remarkable coloring. A slight smile traced over his face. Only Marke Penwell would have completed the elegant attire by artfully tying a cinnamon paisley neckcloth about her bandaged foot. He could only imagine Henry's talented hand in that deed, for there were few others in the service of valet who could effect such an elaborate wrap as she was sporting. In fact, it was his very own neckcloth that had been purloined, and it pleased him no end that she would dare to do so. She was utterly delightful and absolutely delicious, and he ached for the feel of her sweet body with a deep need that gnawed at his insides. So why was he denying himself? It was only he who stood in the way.

Sitter, seated at the piano tinkling out carols, watched the blatant yearning on his face with glee. "I can remember other Christmases, can't you, Claymore? With hearty folk strolling the neighborhood caroling," she said, then rose to join the three at the fire. "With their scarves snugly knotted and warm woolen hats pulled down to their eyebrows. Of course, they couldn't stop at every house for a cup of steaming wassail or mulled wine, but when they did, good cheer abounded."

"Yes, I remember, Sitter," he murmured, smiling down into her tear-misted eyes, sharing the private memory. "And I, too, wish Father was here with us tonight. And

Mother. Dear, dear Libby. I have missed Libby so very much, hating the fact that she will never have another Christmas. But, it's as Marke says, life is nothing more than life. Some of it good, some of it bad. And while we may hate the bad parts, it's still nothing more than life, taken one day at a time, held dear for the parts that are good.''

Alma gave an exaggerated sigh, as if tried beyond all redemption. "Marke this! Marke that! I swear that girl must have you all bewitched ..."

Marke, overhearing Claymore's remarks, hobbled to the fireplace on Henry's arm. She smiled into Claymore's dear face, wanting more than anything to shower him with kisses, as reward for feeling free enough to speak of his loss, for being the most wonderful person she had ever known, and for all the love that welled up in her heart and shone in her eyes. Claymore startled for a moment at the strength of emotion on her face, then returned her warm smile and gave her a slight bow in a private understanding between them before settling her into a chair drawn solicitously close to the fire. Alma grimaced at the show of such caring, and attempted to redirect the marquis's attention away from the blasted girl.

"This could have been a lonely Christmas for me, as well. At this time of year, Londoners retreat, either to family homes in the countryside or nearer their own hearths. Even the queen is out of town until the small season commences. Although you mustn't think I hadn't numerous invitations, for I did." She lifted limpid eyes to the marquis. "But I knew I was fortunate in having Claymore. I could think of nowhere else I'd rather be, than at his side—"

A furious noise disrupted her pretty little speech, and a flurry of black-and-white spots shot through the doorway to disappear beneath the tree, scattering ornaments and dislodging brightly wrapped presents. Not one but three disheveled footmen burst into the drawing room in hot pursuit, closely followed by a huffing, puffing Heaven. The majordomo slid to a halt and sketched a slight bow as he tried to recover his dignity at finding himself center stage before so many pairs of startled eyes.

"Oh, please forgive us, your lordship, but, er, I mean to say..." he panted.

Marke burst out laughing and clapped her hands. "Oh, Heaven, please do not fret yourself. It's perfectly all right, believe me. Claymore, I fear your Christmas present has escaped his leash, and taken it upon himself to advance the gift presentations."

Large liquid eyes and a spaniel pup face—tinsel in his mouth and floral garland drooping about his ears—peered out at them from the depths of the Christmas tree. Claymore bent to his knee and extracted him easily. He gave a hoot of laughter as he deftly avoided the puppy's tongue in its attempt to lavish kisses upon his face.

"One of Mrs. P's finest, I should think," he quipped.

"Yes, I felt your life was too orderly and quiet, so consider it a bit of St. Catherine's Court excitement—" she looked up at him with eyes brimming every feeling she harbored deep in her heart "—with love, Claymore, from Mrs. P and myself."

"He's splendid," Claymore said, dropping the squirming puppy into Henry's arms. "See if you can quieten the little beast, Henry. Marke, I thank you, and Mrs. P, from the depths of my heart." Bending from his great height, Claymore put his face close to hers, thinking to drop a kiss upon her upturned cheek, but Marke, taking matters into her own hands, quickly turned her face and met his lips with her own.

"How forward!" Alma blurted out. Lord Pressley cleared his throat loudly and shot a meaningful glare at his daughter, as if to say *do something!* Alma raised her voice to break the kiss, and to demand the marquis's attention. "Claymore? Dearest? As we are apparently handing out gifts, I would have you open mine next. *Claymore!*"

Claymore reluctantly drew his lips from Marke's. He straightened slowly, seemingly mesmerized by the soft, warm glow in Marke's eyes. It was with great unwillingness that he turned away from her to accept the small gift from Alma. "Ah, yes, thank you, Alma. Heaven, Henry, let's have gifts passed out all around, shall we?"

Claymore stood holding Alma's unwrapped gift, as brightly wrapped boxes were passed out with Heaven's direction, and wrapping paper was ripped away eagerly. Sitter exclaimed over a shawl of royal blue merino from Claymore. Alma snorted with irk to find her gift from him an exact duplicate of Sitter's. Marke, with shining eyes, tore the wrapping from hers to discover a small square jeweler's box. When she raised the lid, the most exquisite gold compact was displayed, delicately shaped into a mushroom. Trimmed with a trailing red tassel from its slender chain and watch-fob clasp, it was perfect for slipping out of its velvet pouch between waltzes at a ball.

"A mushroom! Oh, Claymore, it's exquisite!" gasped Marke. The look on her face was so tender, so openly filled with love, so vulnerable, that the ones looking on instantly felt like intruders upon an intimate moment.

"Oh, for God's sake! Open mine, Claymore. You do still hold it in your hand, you know," snapped Alma sarcastically.

Sitter, wishing to prolong the moment between Marke and Claymore, gave the prearranged signal for Heaven to draw forth the portrait and pull the wrapping paper from it for the entire company to see.

"Good Lord! That's remarkable!" Claymore exclaimed. Dropping Alma's unopened gift on the mantel, he strode over to examine the portrait more closely.

"I say, Perfect," spouted Lord Pressley, following closely. "Damn good likeness, that. Local artist, I suspect?"

Before Claymore could answer, Sitter clapped her hands in delight. "It's our Marke. She's the artist."

Claymore wasn't the only one to regard the portrait in disbelief. Alma's eyes widened, then slitted with pure, undiluted hatred. She had a terrible sinking feeling, an acid churning of realization, in the pit of her stomach. The ex-

pression Claymore displayed in the portrait was one of a
man quite obviously entranced with the artist, and it was an
expression he had never once shown in conjunction with
her.

Claymore turned from the portrait to look at Marke. She
was fending off Lord Pressley's flowery compliments,
shifting that tantalizing body, so warm and perfect, laughing gaily with those merry lips he wished to taste again.
Claymore yearned for her with such an undeniable desire
that he had to force himself to restrain it. So why was he
denying himself? The same question nagged at him again.
It was a question he had been battling within himself, since
that fateful day of their picnic when she had lain in such
sweet surrender beneath him, then again, when experiencing the all-too-familiar horror of seeing a loved one in
danger, of Marke crushed beneath the red filly. But never
more strongly than during the long tedious afternoon in the
sleigh, with Alma and her father, repeatedly parrying
Pressley's demands that a wedding date be set. Why was he
denying himself the pleasure of a life with Marke?

His glance slipped to Alma. She was seated on the divan
with her silver skirts spread over its entire width, listening
to her father drone on and on, with that bored, petulant
expression she affected whenever she felt ignored. And, of
course, being anything but the center of everyone's attention was Alma's definition of being ignored. Beautiful,
stylish, always proper, cold-as-ice Alma. He had been
promised to Alma Pressley since infancy, in the expectations of family and friends, if not formally, with every
gathering preceded and consummated by reference to it,
and his father's wishes expressed quite clearly on the subject. Because of that, he had never stirred himself to imagine a marriage other than the accepted *mariage de
convenance* of the *haute-ton*—until Marke had stormed
into his life—demanding he step up to the mark and accept a life, complete with all its responsibility, its joys and
its sorrows.

His gaze slipped back to her again. Marke, who also had disappointments and unfulfilled dreams in her life, but chose to accept what she couldn't change as inevitable and to dwell only on the pleasantries. The words to describe Marke Penwell were too numerous to contemplate. But *loving, caring,* and *devoted* topped his list, closely followed by *exasperating, provoking,* and *relentless.* All of which he suddenly realized he had no desire to live without. He had no way to express the craving that had rushed through him, seeing her standing in the doorway last night, ignoring the blast of cold air and the obvious pain in her ankle, welcoming him home. Solicitous of his health, she demanded he drink not one but two hot toddies against a certain chill, bringing a sense of merriment and prank to the gathering, even reducing staid Heaven to embarrassed giggles. Marke—beautiful, faithful, exacting Marke. He could no longer ignore the effect she had on his entire household. Hell, on everyone everywhere. Strange what confidences surfaced when two men shared adversity and danger. John had told him straight out that he intended to pursue Marke's hand deliberately, but only if the marquis was determined to be blind himself to the love Marke offered, or was stupid enough to let her pass from his life. Well, he was neither stupid, nor was he blind any longer. At that very moment, he had no wish whatsoever to live his life without her at his side. He wished her wearing his wedding ring, sharing his bed, bearing his children, facing whatever life brought them—pleasure or pain.

His immediate response to this sudden insight was to rush to her side and beg her to be his from this moment forward, but he held himself back from such an impetuous act. No, Marke deserved a proper proposal. And for that he needed a ring, and a speech, and the privacy to assemble both. Turning abruptly on his heel, he rushed for the door.

"Really, Claymore," Alma called petulantly. "Where are you running off to now? You must know all this is tedious enough without you abandoning me, as well. Besides, you *still* haven't opened my gift to you."

The marquis spun with a frown. How silly of him. He'd quite forgotten his guests and the celebration. But his priorities were set rather forcefully at present, and he would not be detained. "I shall not be overly long, Alma. Stretch yourself a bit," he flung over his shoulder. "Try to be amusing."

Alma's head snapped back and she blinked several times as if stunned to her very depths by his abrupt statement. "Well, I never!" she exclaimed, fanning herself rapidly. Turning spiteful eyes to Sitter and her father, she vowed shrilly, "He will certainly have the back of my tongue for speaking to me like that. You may be assured of that!"

Sitter would only smile her quiet little smile and turn her gaze to meet Marke's puzzled one. She had seen quite clearly the way Claymore had watched Marke. And could have guessed, almost to the moment, when Claymore decided to declare his love. She mentally patted herself on the back for her small part in this drama. How wise she had been to ascertain finally that nothing more was needed to bring Claymore to his senses than close comparison of the two girls. And no one could be in their presence for an extended period without showing a decided preference for the sweet, vivacious Marke over the cold and calculating Alma. And with that piece of self-praise realized, she unceremoniously turned her back on Lord Pressley and his disagreeable daughter to hand Marke her own token of Christmas cheer, encouraging her worried eyes away from the door and back to the party. Claymore would return in good time, and then sparks were sure to fly.

Alma scowled over Claymore's abrupt departure and the fact that Marke was again the center of attention, as always, although she couldn't say what effort the girl put forth each time to gain that spotlight. Well, she'd had enough of this delay and procrastination. It was time to put an end to this display of poor manners over a mere schoolgirl, and she was more than ready to be the one to end it.

Rising resolutely, she marched from the room to search for the marquis and instigate a confrontation. She quickly discovered him in the library, frowning over a sheet of paper and furiously scribbling with a pen.

"Claymore, I would speak with you," she announced, closing the door firmly behind her for privacy.

"Not now, Alma."

"Yes, it will be now," she insisted, moving to stance herself defiantly before the desk. "Oh my goodness!"

Claymore looked up from his writing to see Alma staring at the ring laying beside his hand, with eyes that widened to extremes. His first thought was to snatch it away before she could touch it, then snorted at his silliness. Even if she touched the ring, it did not mean he would be forced into marriage with her. He shoved the paper aside and leaned back in his chair. "All right, Alma. Perhaps you are right. The time has come for frank speech between us."

Alma stared greedily at the ring. It was splendid. And it looked just her size. "Oh, Claymore, how beautiful! And here I have blundered in to spoil your surprise! I should have known your present to me would be much more than that simple shawl..."

Claymore rushed to interrupt her. "Alma, I had never wished to be a cause of unhappiness for you, but you must know..." He cleared his throat and continued bluntly, "Alma, the ring is not for you. I shall be presenting it to Marke this Christmas Eve—when I beg for her hand in marriage."

Alma closed her eyes for a moment at this not altogether unexpected declaration, then opened them to glare at him with cold resignation. "It is a grave mistake, you know. You and I are perfectly suited in every way, while she is—well, I do not know what she is. Nor do I understand, to be forthright, just what you see in her."

Claymore studied her icy face for a moment, then answered just as candidly. "No, Alma, I do not imagine you would understand what I see in Marke. But trust me when I say that to know her is to love her. And love her I do.

Marke, and only Marke, and I shall hold true to that love forever.''

"Such a pretty sentiment," she snapped, drawing herself up straight. "You will, of course, forgive me if I do not rejoin the party tonight. I have no desire to bear witness to your proposal, not when you have kept me dangling on your string these many years past."

Not wishing to begin an argument with her, he merely nodded. She, for perhaps the first time in her life, wisely held her tongue and left the library without slamming the door back on its hinges as he had rather expected of her. Claymore drew a deep sigh of resignation, over having closed yet another door in his life. Then, returning to the problem at hand, he picked up the paper and read again his dissatisfying attempts. There seemed to be no words to express the true depth of his feelings for Marke, but perhaps no prescribed words were needed. He would simply look into her beautiful face once again and put voice to the feelings that arose so strongly from his heart each time he did.

He lifted the black velvet box to study the ring. It was of weighty gold, and sporting a tight cluster of sizable, rose-cut diamonds gathered into a fleur-de-lis. Never a favorite of his mother's, it had rested in the vault at Innisfree for too many years, awaiting a bride, the next Marquise of Boothe-Ashmore.

Heaven, concerned at the marquis's abrupt removal from the celebration, tentatively opened the library door. "Is there something you require, my lord?"

Claymore looked up at the bent old man who had been a part of his life for as long as he could remember. Turning the black velvet box toward him, he asked, "Do you think Miss Penwell will approve of it, Heaven?"

Heaven came to stand before the marquis and the ring. A delighted smile cracked the veneer of his face. "I quite think Miss Penwell would approve of a piece of twine tied around her finger, my lord, if it came straight from your heart."

Claymore grinned at the picture, and knew it to be true. It was him she wanted, not his title, not his fortune—but him. "I would hardly dare offer her less than my heart, now would I?" He looked down at the ring again. "And I shall probably stammer and stutter in the offering of that, like a lad over his first crush."

"I think that will be most appropriate, as well, my lord."

"Thank you, Heaven," he said, tucking the ring inside his waistcoat pocket. "Now, I've tarried too long as it is, and I find I can hardly stand not being near her again. Strange how she affects one, don't you think?"

"But delightfully strange, my lord."

Sitter, seated at the piano again, glanced up in question when Claymore returned without Alma clinging possessively to his arm. He had been gone a long time, but her frown of wonder turned to a smile of joy when Claymore dropped a few words in Lord Pressley's ear, a few words that brought his normally high color to florid red and sent him huffing out of the room without a word to either Marke or herself.

Marke raised her eyebrows in question, but Sitter merely shrugged her shoulders and left the piano to join her at the fireplace. She would wait for Claymore to broach the subject, but oh, how hard it was to control her unruly mouth, for it wanted to shout and laugh and sing a thousand songs.

Claymore did not keep them in suspense overly long. Moving to position himself rather stiffly before the fire, he gripped the mantel with one hand and fiddled with the gold chain of his watch fob with the other. He glanced at Heaven and Henry standing beside the Christmas tree, and then to Sitter's radiant face, realizing she had guessed his intent. Clearing his throat, he finally launched into his speech, without glancing at Marke's puzzled face.

"Lord Pressley and Alma will not be rejoining us for this evening, and I quite expect they will be returning to London as quickly as weather permits."

Marke's eyes widened, but she held her tongue. She was suddenly terrified his next words would say he would be joining them on their return voyage. And yet, if that were true, wouldn't Alma be here in full gloat? Why, oh, why would he not look at her, give her some clue as to the reason for his seriousness. She feared her heart would burst, unless he looked at her, trying to hear his words over the beating of her heart.

"When I first returned to Innisfree, I was infirm of body and mind, laying blame at everyone's door, including God's, for all the ills that had befallen me," Claymore continued. "But then I met a red-haired spitfire who would relentlessly lecture me on life—" he shifted his gaze to Marke's upturned face, again feeling the welling of emotion inside his heart "—and my deplorable ways of dealing with it. And, as my wounds began to heal, I listened to her to see, not only by her words, but by her actively living what she preached, that she was quite right about it all." He paused to smile at the recollections. Heaven jabbed an elbow into Henry's side, startling a yelp from the young man. Claymore glanced at them. Henry gave a sheepish grin and shrug of apology while rubbing at his side.

Marke couldn't draw her eyes from his face. She held her breath for it sounded to her, that he was, in one breath, telling her thank-you, and the next would be goodbye. Tears welled up in her eyes and traced over her cheeks unnoticed. Kindly Jesus, have mercy on me.

Claymore cleared his throat and glanced down at his hand on the pocket holding the ring, then at Sitter's beaming face. He forged on. "Marke would repeatedly tell me to step up to the mark and take in life. Accept the responsibilities of it, good and bad. That there were no rules, no outline, for the living of it. Just good sense, diligent perseverance and kindness to others. That life is just life, and I must deal with it. Although I still believe my fears were not altogether groundless, to enter the world and participate fully is to open oneself to pain and suffering, but that in itself, I suppose, is part of its spice. I came to realize, for all my education and exposure, I had led a very sheltered existence, filled only with good things. When confronted with a loss of such magnitude—'' he shook his head at the thought ''—as the death of my parents and the death of one so young, so innocent as dear little Libby, well, it was almost too much to bear. I resolved never again, never—do you hear?—to place another person in such a position of importance in my life.'' He looked down at Marke, as if speaking to her alone. ''But I've come to understand that to shut oneself away so completely is to pass on the future. And to ignore one's future is a death in itself. To heal, I needed to understand what I was agreeing to pass by. I needed to hear the ups and downs of other families. I needed to see the joy in simple things—wind in my face, Irish rain and peat fires.'' He grinned at her with dimples winking. ''I needed to hold a newborn babe, just minutes old, in my arms as I did last night at Doug O'Shannon's. Having done all that, I find I cannot pass on my future. I find I want more, much more of its sweet promise, even if I have to experience pain some of the time. So, with that decided,'' he said as he knelt down before Marke, slipping the ring box into her limp hand, ''here you are—Mrs. P's ninth child—and here I am, if you will have me.''

Marke looked down at the ring box, then into Claymore's eyes. Tears flooded her eyes and traced down her cheeks anew. She had no need to open the box. It could be filled with coal for all she cared. All that mattered in the whole world was the look of love on Claymore's face. ''Oh, Claymore, what should I say?''

''I love you, Margaret Catherine Penwell. Be my wife, mother my children, teach me to live in this turbulence you call life. Say yes to me.''

Sobbing openly, she flung her arms about his neck. ''Oh, yes! Yes! Yes! Forever yes!''

Heaven hastily pulled his handkerchief from his pocket to mop at streaming eyes, while Henry pounded him on the back in happiness and excitement. Sitter clapped her hands and laughed through tears of her own. The puppy, greatly excited by all the noise, began to bark rambunctiously. He ran in circles, first to Heaven and Henry, leaping at them for attention, then jumped upon Sitter's silk skirts. He then bounded over to Marke—clasped so tightly in Claymore's arms. Finally, as a last resort, the puppy ran around in a circle after his own tail, creating a great deal of commotion that most probably would extend throughout the rest of their lives together.

* * * * *

Harlequin® Historical

From the Maggie Award-Winning Author of
FOOL'S PARADISE

Tori Phillips

comes the delightful tale of an ill-fated
noblewoman, and the would-be monk
who becomes her protector

SILENT KNIGHT

Don't miss this delightful Medieval, available in
November, wherever Harlequin Historicals are sold!

BIGB96-10

Merry Christmas, Baby!

A romantic collection filled with the magic of Christmas and the joy of children.

SUSAN WIGGS, Karen Young and
Bobby Hutchinson bring you Christmas wishes,
weddings and romance, in a charming
trio of stories that will warm up your
holiday season.

MERRY CHRISTMAS, BABY! also contains
Harlequin's special gift to you—a set of
FREE GIFT TAGS included in every book.

Brighten up your holiday season with
MERRY CHRISTMAS, BABY!

Available in November at
your favorite retail store.

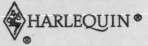

HARLEQUIN ®

Scandals

A passionate story of romance, where bold, daring characters
set out to defy their world of propriety and strict social codes.

"Scandals—a story that will make your heart race and your
pulse pound. Spectacular!"
—Suzanne Forster

"Devon is daring, dangerous and altogether delicious."
—Amanda Quick

Don't miss this wonderful full-length novel from Regency
favorite Georgina Devon.

Available in December, wherever Harlequin books are sold.

SCAN

1997
Reader's Engagement Book
A calendar of important dates
and anniversaries for readers to use!

Informative and entertaining—with notable
dates and trivia highlighted throughout the year.

Handy, convenient, pocketbook size to help you
keep track of your own personal important dates.

Added bonus—contains $5.00 worth of coupons
for upcoming Harlequin and Silhouette books.
This calendar more than pays for itself!

 Available beginning in November at
your favorite retail outlet.

HARLEQUIN ® 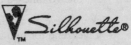Silhouette®